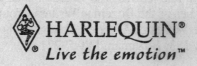

REBECCA YORK

National bestselling author Ruth Glick, who writes as Rebecca York, is the author of close to ninety books, including her popular 43 LIGHT STREET series. Her many awards include two RITA® Award nominations, two Golden Leaf Awards and three Lifetime Achievement and Career Achievement awards from *Romantic Times*. *Romantic Times* has selected *Nowhere Man* as one of their reviewers' "all-time favorite romances." Michael Dirda, of *Washington Post Book World,* calls her "a real luminary of contemporary series romance."
Ruth and her husband, Norman, travel frequently, researching locales for her novels and searching out new dishes for her cookbooks.

B.J. DANIELS

A former award-winning journalist, B.J. had thirty-six short stories published before she wrote and sold her first romantic suspense, *Odd Man Out,* which was later nominated for the *Romantic Times* Reviewer's Choice Award for Best First Book and Best Harlequin Intrigue. B.J. lives in Bozeman with her husband, Parker, two springer spaniels, Zoey and Scout, and an irascible tomcat named Jeff. She is a member of the Bozeman Writers Group and Romance Writes of America. To contact her, write P.O. Box 183, Bozeman, MT 59771.

GUARDED
SECRETS

REBECCA YORK
Ruth Glick writing as Rebecca York

B.J. DANIELS

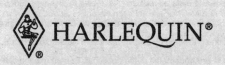

TORONTO • NEW YORK • LONDON
AMSTERDAM • PARIS • SYDNEY • HAMBURG
STOCKHOLM • ATHENS • TOKYO • MILAN • MADRID
PRAGUE • WARSAW • BUDAPEST • AUCKLAND

ISBN 0-373-83593-0

GUARDED SECRETS

Copyright © 2003 by Harlequin Books S.A.

The publisher acknowledges the copyright holders
of the individual works as follows:

NOWHERE MAN
Copyright © 1998 by Ruth Glick

HIJACKED BRIDE
Copyright © 2003 by Barbara Heinlein

Visit us at www.eHarlequin.com

Printed in U.S.A.

CONTENTS

FOREWORD
by Stella Cameron

The talented authors who write for Harlequin Intrigue have kept me entertained for years. Each of these books is unique, a little gem guaranteed to send you to your favorite reading spot, where you'll spend hours in an engrossing new world.

When Harlequin Intrigue first appeared it introduced a daring new combination of mystery and romance. There had never been books quite like these, and they continue to bring a very special blend of excitement to the genre.

If you are a first-time Harlequin Intrigue reader, get ready for a fresh addiction. If you've read the books for a long time, the ante just got "upped." Expect to hang on to your seats and turn those pages faster than ever.

Please don't forget to breathe!

Espionage, murder mysteries, police procedurals, international crimes, special forces thrillers, high tech and futuristic science at its most suspenseful, tough private investigators at work, serial killings, legal thrillers, political dramas—there is no limit to the variety of great shivery plots! And there's no limit to the fabulous heroes who will steal your heart, or the smart, gutsy heroines who show how complex women can be.

And there is the loving. If I had to mention just one aspect of the engrossing love stories that are a strong part of today's pulse-thumping Harlequin Intrigue novels, I'd tell you that the mysterious, dynamic and courageous characters who confront danger also fall in love with the same vigor and imagination they bring to fighting crime.

Conflict overlaps. A man and a woman locked together against a common danger must think clearly; romance can become a distraction if not handled well by the writer. In the Intrigue series, outstanding writers know how to balance their stories and make sure a gripping romance—already a conflict by nature—stretches the reader's' nerves while it cranks up the stakes.

My first Harlequin Intrigue novel, *All That Sparkles*, started life as a book I wrote for Harlequin Superromance. That was in 1986 when the Intrigue line was new and finding sufficient books for it was challenging. *All That Sparkles*, a story about large-scale diamond theft in Amsterdam—and a steamy love affair—was drafted!

Since romantic suspense is my natural niche, I was more than happy to write other books for the line. Eventually I moved on to write many single-title novels, both historical romantic suspense such as *About Adam* and the rest of the Mayfair Square books, and contemporary romantic suspense like *Kiss Them Goodbye*, a MIRA release in November of this year. I think the high standards set at Harlequin Intrigue helped me mature as a suspense writer.

The years since 1986 have brought changes. Since no other publisher had attempted anything quite like Harlequin Intrigue, learning what readers would really enjoy, what topics they might *not* enjoy and the balance they would prefer between intrigue and romance resulted in an evolving line of books that shifted emphasis from time to time. Dedicated to the project, the publisher watched, listened and made adjustments. Listening was their primary focus, with subtle, necessary change a close second.

What they finally decided was that the romance reader is adventurous and only too eager to experiment with a variety of stories. In response to this daring spirit, the books have kept pace with the times and have steadily grown in popularity.

I must also mention (with a bit of a grin) how the covers have undergone a number of rebirths. I hope I'll be forgiven for writing that the early art, although good, did seem to have similarities to the covers on Nancy Drew tales! However, today's covers are provocative and sophisticated, like the books inside.

As the line expands once more, I'm honored to introduce or reintroduce you to Harlequin Intrigue.

Join me as the excitement continues, and please let me know the titles you particularly enjoy. I don't want to miss anything.

All the best,

Stella Cameron

www.stellacameron.com

NOWHERE MAN

Rebecca York

RUTH GLICK WRITING AS REBECCA YORK

Prologue

Kathryn Kelley, a small figure dwarfed by the silent, eerie space beyond, hesitated in the doorway to the darkened room. Where were the lights, she wondered, her gaze probing the inky blackness. She could see almost nothing, but felt thick, chemical-tinged mist wafting toward her. It sent shivers over her skin as it collided with the cooler air of the hallway. Trying to dispel the sudden chill, she rubbed her hands along the thick sleeves of her robe.

It was Friday evening, and since the moment she'd opened her eyes last Monday, she'd sensed that something was wrong. She'd tried to ignore the oppressive sensation, but it was like a storm gathering around her. The feeling of apprehension made her glance quickly over her shoulder to confirm that the corridor behind her was empty.

Of course it was empty! She made a wry face, annoyed at the tricks her mind was playing on her.

"What's *wrong* with you?" she asked, her voice echoing in the darkness beyond the door. With a quick decisive movement, she switched on the lights and marched inside. Shrugging out of her robe, she secured her mane of red hair with a band at the nape of her neck, kicked off her shoes, and executed a perfect dive into the turquoise water of the swimming pool below her.

The cold was a momentary shock to her system as she shot downward into the pool, then came up to blink water out of her blue eyes. Straightening her limber body, she began a rapid crawl stroke. Ever since high school, when she was on the swim team, swimming had remained her exercise of choice. In fact, she'd selected her Baltimore apartment because the sixties renovation of the Cecil Arms had included a pool on the top floor.

Ten-thirty was late for a solitary swim. Actually, the pool was supposed to be closed to tenants at that hour. But she'd negotiated a lease that allowed her to use the facility after hours. Willing the tension out of her muscles, she cut rapidly through the water. Still, she couldn't outdistance the demons of the day. She'd appeared as an expert witness in a child custody trial that afternoon. Although she'd kept her cool on the stand, her testimony about the abuse of a ten-year-old boy by his father had made her stomach knot.

The mere thought of the man made her lose the rhythm of her strokes. With this child, she'd slipped over the line of professional detachment—once again. Lately it was getting harder to maintain an objective distance from other people's pain. So she swam in the Cecil Arms pool like the victim of a shipwreck flailing toward an unreachable shore, while her mind wandered to fantasies of trading in her psychology practice for a flower shop like the guy in *Bed of Roses*. Maybe the management at 43 Light Street would rent her space in the lobby.

She didn't hear the door open. But a jolt went

through her as she saw the overhead lights and the ones along the side of the pool wink out. Stopping dead, she held her breath, barely treading water, as her gaze scanned the floor-to-ceiling windows along the far wall. Below her, lights twinkled in other North Baltimore apartment buildings, yet this room at the top of the Cecil Arms was dark.

"Is somebody there?" She could hear her pulse pounding in her ears and the reverberations of her voice from the walls and ceiling of the large room.

When no one answered, goose bumps rose on her arms. She wanted to believe someone was playing a cruel practical joke on the lady who went swimming in the evening. The explanation didn't wash. In a blinding moment of panic, all the anxiety of the week coalesced into a terrible moment of certainty. On a gut level she knew who had turned off the lights, knew who had been stalking her. Now it all made sense.

"James?" she quavered.

He made her beg for the answer.

"James."

"Got ya!" a familiar, low voice echoed off the water.

She had been hoping against hope it wasn't true. Now she pictured a slender man with blond hair and blue eyes standing between her and the only door, the only escape route.

James Harrison. He had a charming smile and an easy manner, unless you looked below the surface to the rotten core carefully hidden inside.

She hadn't wanted to believe he was back. Yet deep in her subconscious she must have known. Three years ago he'd been confined to the Indiana Institution for the Criminally Insane, and he'd sworn to get even with Dr. Kelley for helping put him there.

She'd moved away, started over again in a new place with a new job and new friends. And time had dulled the memory of the curses he'd hurled at her. She'd felt safe—until this week.

A splash told her he was in the water. She dragged in a lungful of air and dove deep, praying she had a chance to escape. Surfacing at the edge of the pool near the door, she felt for the metal ladder and began to scramble up. But he must have been planning this carefully, must have studied the layout of the pool, for strong hands closed around her thighs and dragged her back down.

Kathryn had time for only a quick gasp of air before he pulled her under, pushing her below with the weight of his body. Trapped, she flailed in panic. But the watery world muted the impact of her blows. All she could do was rake her nails across his ribs. The attack didn't have any apparent effect.

Frantically, she tried to struggle upward, but cruel hands held her under. Then for a moment he let her up, long enough for her to get a blessed gasp of oxygen before he pulled her down into the dark water again.

She knew then that he was toying with her, prolonging her agony for his own sick satisfaction. With all her strength, she tried to pull free. She tried to hit him. He only shifted her in his grasp, his fingers like tentacles on her water-slick flesh. Someone had told her once that drowning wasn't such a bad death. Now she took no comfort in the snatch of memory.

Her chest was bursting, and bright dots danced before her eyes. Soon it would be impossible to hold her breath, and the water would fill her lungs. James Harrison would finally get his wish—her death.

Yet she kept fighting him. Her flailing hand brushed the edge of his swim suit. She followed the fabric downward until she encountered sensitive male flesh, then dug her nails into him with all her remaining strength. Through the muffling water, she heard him scream. As his grasp loosened she wrenched away and broke the surface, dragging in life-giving air.

He cursed and made a grab for her, his fingers grazing her shoulder. Hardly able to think, Kathryn maneuvered into open water, heading for the opposite ladder. When his hand grazed her foot, she screamed and kicked harder.

Before he could catch up again, the lights flashed on and a voice boomed over the water. "What the hell's going on in here?"

Reaching the ladder, Kathryn gave a heartfelt cry of thanks and scrambled up. But she didn't get any farther. As the air hit her body, she crumpled and lay panting on the cold cement. In the glow from the overhead lights, all her eyes could make out was an indistinct figure standing in the doorway.

"Listen up. You'd better have a good explanation, or I'm going to call the police."

Even with the echo bouncing off the walls, she recognized the voice. It was Mr. Clemson, the building superintendent. "God, yes, call the police," she croaked.

A flash of movement on the other side of the pool made her cringe toward the wall. She saw James vault out of the water, hurtle toward Clemson, and give him a mighty shove before charging through the door and disappearing.

Barely finding her legs, Kathryn wobbled toward the wall phone and dialed 911.

Chapter One

She was in a prison.

No, she had *chosen* to come to this place called Stratford Creek on a deserted stretch of road in Western Maryland, where the mountain scenery took your breath away and the security was tight as a federal penitentiary. But this wasn't a jail, and Kathryn Kelley wasn't a prisoner. She could leave any time she wanted, she reminded herself as the door to the cell-like gatehouse slammed closed behind her.

"I have an appointment with Mr. Emerson," she said, addressing a man in gray slacks and a blue shirt who stood behind a low counter. He was muscular, with a square jaw, square shoulders, and a crew cut. His unobtrusive plastic tag said his name was Mc-Court, and he kept his steely gaze fixed on her.

"Please hand me your purse and step through the metal detector." He waved toward a security entrance much like the ones that were now a fact of life to anyone who regularly used the nation's airports.

Kathryn complied, then watched him paw through the contents of her pocketbook as if he thought her lipstick was a miniaturized bomb. Satisfied, he handed back the purse and gestured toward a small wooden table. "You're on the schedule. Have a seat. May I see two forms of identification?"

"Of course," she answered, trying to match the coolness of his voice. But her hand tremored as she pulled out the chair behind the table and sat down.

He's just using standard intimidation techniques, she told herself. But she wasn't in good enough shape to keep from reacting. At least he hadn't searched her for hidden weapons.

When she thumbed her driver's license out of her wallet, he made her wait with it in her outstretched hand while he got a clipboard from the wall in back of him. As he turned, she saw the bulge of a gun riding discreetly at his waist.

Feeling like she'd caught him with his fly open, she looked quickly away and unfolded the fax she'd received yesterday evening. "This is my authorization letter from Mr. Emerson," she said, handing it across the desk.

In fact, it was one of the strangest job offers she'd ever received—and accepted. She'd be temporarily working for the Defense Department, but the orders didn't specify exactly what her duties would be, although she'd been assured during several phone interviews that her background and experience were perfect for the assignment.

As McCourt perused the fax, she tried to gather her composure. Any other time, she would have been better prepared for his subtle little power game. But she was still trying to cope with the emotional aftermath of the attack in the swimming pool two weeks ago, not to mention the police interviews and the dawning realization that Baltimore's finest couldn't guarantee her safety. Her attacker, James Harrison, was still at large, probably in the area. The Indiana authorities hadn't warned her he was coming because they'd thought he was dead. Apparently he'd set fire to the maximum-security unit at the hospital where he was being held and escaped in the confusion, making sure there was a body in his bunk burned beyond recognition.

After almost killing her in the Cecil Arms pool, Harrison had disappeared into the night, and she had gone downstairs to her apartment only long enough to pack some clothes. For the past two weeks, she'd been staying with various friends and shutting down her private practice—since the cops had no idea where to find her lunatic stalker. He'd already proved himself frighteningly resourceful, and she wasn't willing to wait around like a tethered goat for him to pounce on her again.

Finished with the fax, McCourt compared her to the blue-eyed redhead in the photograph on her driver's license and pulled a folder from a drawer behind the counter. "Your temporary clearance is in order."

"It shouldn't be temporary. I had it updated when I did some work at Randolph Electronics."

"Yes, but we have additional requirements here."

Before she could make any further objections, he handed her a form and said, "Sign here."

When she'd written her name, along with the date and time, he initialed the entry.

"I'm Chip McCourt. Glad to have you with us," he said, obviously still withholding judgment. "I'll take you to the headquarters building, Dr. Kelley."

Kathryn pushed back her chair. "I can find my way if you'll just give me directions."

"I am required to escort you," he said firmly.

Her fingers tightened on the strap of her purse as she fought the impulse to blurt out that she'd changed her mind. She was only a few hours away from Baltimore. She could turn around and drive back. But then what? She wouldn't feel safe in her apartment. Or her office. And she couldn't camp out permanently at her friends' houses. Instead of resenting the security here, she told herself, she should be grateful.

With a sigh, she stood and let him usher her outside, where he stopped and conferred briefly with another man who had arrived in a Jeep Cherokee.

"All set," he said, turning back to her.

Manufacturing a smile, she led the way to her car, thankful that McCourt slid into the passenger seat instead of demanding her keys.

Her escort wasn't much for small talk, simply giving her toneless directions. So she took stock of what had been described as the Stratford Creek campus as he copiloted her up a winding road lined with white pine trees, then past low, redbrick buildings that might have been constructed as a garden apartment complex in the fifties or sixties. Some campus. The lawns were half dirt and the wood trim on a number of the buildings was flaking. Although she'd been assured by Mr. Emerson that Stratford Creek was well funded, apparently the U.S. government wasn't putting much money into exterior maintenance.

Many of the windows had a dusty blankness that told her some of the offices were empty. Adding to the ghost-town atmosphere was the lack of traffic. She met no other cars, and as she rounded a corner, she made the mistake of turning her head to look at the remains of a flower bed in the center of a weed-choked lawn.

As she turned back to the road, she caught a blur of motion to her left. With a start, she realized that a man had materialized from behind a nearby stand of bushy pines and was on a collision course with her car.

McCourt shouted a warning as Kathryn slammed on the brakes, bringing the vehicle to a bouncing halt. But the man must have had lightning reflexes, because he'd already halted.

Time seemed to slow as she stared at him. He stood on the balls of his feet, breathing hard, his body glowing with a fine sheen of perspiration and his hands flexed at his sides as if he were ready for an attack. A myriad impressions assaulted her at once, the way they often did when she was meeting someone who sparked her interest. She let the perceptions flow, hoping she could sort them out later.

Physically, he was magnificent. His damp T-shirt was stretched across a broad, well-muscled chest, and his running shorts showcased impressive masculine details beneath the skimpy fabric. Below the shorts were the long, muscular legs of an athlete.

He moved his hand to swipe a lock of dark hair away from his forehead, drawing her gaze to his chiseled face. It was all sharp angles and acute planes that were arresting in themselves. But it was his fierce, deep-set eyes that captured her attention as they regarded her with a kind of uncensored curiosity.

They were the darkest eyes she'd ever seen as they found hers through the windshield, telegraphing a message that he needed nothing from her or anyone else. He stood alone, which should mean nothing in itself. Yet something about the look on his lean features conveyed a sense of isolation that made her breath catch painfully.

She couldn't analyze the feeling. For several heartbeats she was held by the currents she sensed flowing below the surface of the dark eyes. He broke the spell by moving his hands to his shoulders, easing a pair of straps, and she realized that he was wearing a heavy-looking backpack.

Her attention was so totally focused on the runner that she forgot all about McCourt sitting next to her. Apparently he had been as transfixed as she—until the man took a step toward the car. Then her passenger reached for the door handle.

"Who is that?" she managed.

Without answering, McCourt climbed out and stepped around the car, his face set in harsh lines. From her vantage point behind the wheel, Kathryn watched the dynamics with fascination.

"What the hell are you doing on this part of the grounds?" McCourt demanded, yet the question came out more wary than authoritative.

The runner shifted his stance. Although he kept his face carefully neutral, there was something about the angle of his firm jaw that sent a shiver up her spine. When he spoke his voice was low, controlled. "Training exercise," he answered in measured syllables, using only the precise number of words he needed to convey his meaning. "Ten-mile run. Fifty-pound pack." His voice was rough, rusty, with a kind of unused quality.

Kathryn goggled as she tried to imagine the stamina it would take to run ten miles carrying that much weight.

"You're not supposed to be here," McCourt growled.

The man drew himself up taller. "The trails are wet," he said in his gritty voice, then took a step toward McCourt who backed up the same amount of space.

"Stay away from me," he warned, a quaver in his voice as his hand inched toward the gun at his waist.

Kathryn could see he was badly rattled by the chance encounter. My God, was he capable of shooting the man for being in the wrong place at the wrong time? What kind of place was this, anyway?

She looked around. The grounds were as deserted as before. She was the only witness.

Her heart started to pound. Before she quite realized what she was doing, she stepped out of the car and joined the two men.

McCourt heard the car door open and glanced back at her. He swore under his breath. "Stay out of his reach. He'll beat the tar out of you as soon as look at you."

The runner shook his head in strong denial, then switched his attention from the lieutenant to her, apparently dismissing the other man as if he had ceased to exist. Yet she had the feeling that if McCourt made a sudden move for his gun, it would be knocked out of his hand before he could raise it into firing position.

"I will not hurt you," the runner said to her with an absolute finality that she felt as well as heard.

"I believe you," Kathryn replied, lifting her eyes to meet his.

His gaze locked with hers. "Thank you." He spoke the simple phrase with deep sincerity, giving the impression that he rarely had the opportunity to thank anyone.

"I never lie," he added.

It wasn't a boast, she decided. It was a simple statement of fact.

"Who are you?" she asked, in as steady a voice as she could manage.

It was a straightforward request for information, yet he appeared to give it deep consideration, and she had the strange feeling that perhaps nobody had ever bothered to ask the question before.

"Nobody," he finally answered with a half shrug of his shoulders.

"You must have a name."

He tugged for a moment at his left earlobe, as if the gesture helped him think. "I am called John Doe," he recited, the syllables running together into one word. From someone else, it might have been a joke or a sarcastic attempt to cut off the conversation, but the serious look on his face belied any attempt at humor or irony.

He didn't ask her name, yet she offered it anyway. "Kathryn Kelley. Kelley with an extra *e* before the *y*," the way she always said it, even as she pondered the combination of a first and last name that had very little chance of being real.

"Kathryn Kelley," he repeated in a thoughtful voice. "You are different."

"How?"

He considered the question. "Many ways. Your hair." He reached out a hand toward her red curls, his fingers making the barest contact, like a man afraid to harm something of great value. The touch was gentle, yet it sent a vibration traveling along her nerve endings.

"I—remember—" He stopped, looked perplexed.

Her breath stilled as she gazed into his eyes. He was waiting for something, and she didn't know what. Slowly, as if controlled by some outside force, she raised her hand so that her fingers were pressed to his. She could feel the blood pounding in her fingers and wondered if he felt it, too.

Neither of them moved, and she saw a look of wonder fill his dark eyes. It was replaced almost instantly by an utter bleakness that brought an answering tightness in her chest. "You are not afraid of me like the others," he said in that same gritty voice as he pulled his hand back.

"What did you do to make them afraid?" she asked.

He shrugged, his face going as blank as a window when the shades are abruptly drawn.

Kathryn had utterly dismissed McCourt from her mind during the exchange. Now he made his presence felt with a muttered expletive. "That's enough," he snapped. "How many miles are left in your run?" he asked John Doe.

The answer came back without hesitation. "Two."

"Then finish up. And do an extra two miles to make up for the interruption."

"Yes, sir." He acknowledged the order crisply, though there was an undertone of insolence that she was sure McCourt couldn't miss.

Before she could ask any more questions, the man who called himself John Doe crossed the road and started across the scraggly lawn, his long, muscular legs pumping. He picked up speed as he went, until he was moving in a blur of motion that seemed beyond the capacity of anybody but an Olympic sprinter. Yet he was settling into the fast pace for what was still a long run. In a few more seconds he was out of sight.

Kathryn stared after him, but her attention snapped back to McCourt as he swore under his breath.

"Is he being punished?" Kathryn asked.

"Like he said, he's being trained," her escort snapped. Pulling a cell phone out of his pocket, he began to punch in numbers. Then he turned his back to Kathryn, stepped to the far side of the car, and began to speak in a strained, rapid voice.

"Give me Beckton," he demanded, then glanced in her direction and lowered his voice. Yet she still caught the tone of annoyance.

Unfortunately, the rest of his conversation was muffled. When she realized she was standing in the middle of the road straining her ears to hear what he was saying, she grimaced and moved to the side of the car, resting her hips against the fender. The wind rustled her hair, and she smiled slightly as she remembered the caress of John Doe's fingers. He was strong, yet his touch had been gentle, like a man stroking a wild bird. Something she didn't understand had transpired during the few minutes they'd spent together. All she could say for sure was that she'd met a man who was so out of her realm of experience that he seemed to have dropped to earth from another planet. At the very least, she thought as she recalled his alternately clipped and formal sentence patterns, he sounded like someone who was still learning English.

Yet the two of them hadn't needed brilliant conversation to make contact on a very human level. On the other hand, he hadn't smiled the whole time they had talked, and she was hard put to imagine the harsh lines of his face softening into a smile.

Feeling suddenly sad, she swiped her hand through her hair, brushing it back from her face.

Who was he? What was he doing in this strangely controlled environment? She wanted some answers before she agreed to remain on this base.

McCourt terminated the conversation and dialed a second number. This time he spoke in a more deferential tone. As she watched him, she had ample time to start wondering if she was building fantasies around the encounter on the road. She'd hardly spent five minutes with the man who called himself John Doe. She shouldn't be jumping to so many conclusions.

McCourt shoved the phone back into his pocket and returned to the car. Silently, they both climbed inside and closed the doors.

"John Doe isn't really his name, is it?" she asked as she sat with her hands wrapped around the wheel, making no move to start the engine. "Who is he?"

"I'm not authorized to give you that information. You'll have to address your questions to Mr. Emerson," he said in a clipped voice.

"But—"

"God help you, you'll find out soon enough. And God help me if I don't have you in the office of the chief of operations in the next five minutes."

HIS POWERFUL LEGS PUMPED and his feet pounded the ground, eating up the miles between himself and the woman with the red hair and the gentle expression in her blue eyes. She had looked at him with a kind of interest that was different from Swinton and Beckton and the rest.

Kathryn Kelley. Kelley with an extra *e* before the *y*, she had told him. She was of no importance to his mission. He should wipe her from his mind.

But his pace faltered as details bombarded him. Hair of flame. Blue eyes like still water. The rounded curve of breasts and hips. The hem of her skirt where it brushed the tops of her knees. The images licked at his nerve endings like the fire of her hair.

Somewhere…somewhere he had seen her before. In a dream. It couldn't be in real life.

His hands clenched into fists as he forced the distracting visual images from his mind. Immediately they were replaced by words. His words to her. Her words to him. Every detail of the brief conversation was branded into his mind. She had talked with a soft voice, but she could hurt him—worse than the others.

She had made him feel a strange light-headedness. It came again, and he almost stumbled. With renewed concentration, he got the rhythm back and managed not to dwell on her for a full thirty seconds. When she tiptoed back into his mind, he reminded himself sternly that she was not part of his world. He would never see her again. So he could stop thinking about her.

But she stayed with him. She had stirred up something inside him, something that had been buried deep. Like the memory of a scent that would sometimes tickle the back of his throat, then drift out of reach. Or the music that rose to the surface of his mind the way mist rose from a pond in the woods and swirled in thick currents. He had never heard that music in real life. It was nothing like the classic rock Beckton played on the radio. Or the country-and-western songs some of the men liked. Yet it must come from somewhere.

His feet assaulted the blacktop as he picked up the pace in time to the music in his head. The familiar rhythm helped soothe him, and he forced his mind to more important matters. Logic. His work, Project Sandstorm.

He ran toward that goal. It was burned into him. Everything he did was focused on completing the assignment he had been given. Sandstorm was important. Essential. The reason for his existence. He must carry out the job for which he had been preparing all these months—or he would die trying.

Then it would be over. The drills on hand-to-hand combat. The survival classes. And all the other details that spelled the difference between success and failure.

His instructors, Beckton and Winslow and the rest of them, would not be there. None of the scientists or the lab technicians would travel with him to a country halfway around the world. He would be on his own. He would have to make all the decisions on weapons, logistics, deployment. And he would have to calculate the odds of success, weigh each individual detail—like the number of guards at each entrance to the general's palace.

It seemed as if he had been training for this assignment all his life. It was his destiny. And going over the details brought him a feeling that bordered on serenity. Yet complete peace eluded him.

On a deep, instinctive level he sensed that something important inside his brain had been changed. He didn't understand what had happened, exactly. And he wasn't ready to cope with it. Yet he had learned above all else to accept the world as he found it. And he knew that his feeling of inner harmony had been shaken in those few minutes when he had encountered Kathryn Kelley—when he had looked at her, talked with her.

But there was a balance to the equation. If he had lost something, he had gained something as well—an important component, he realized now, that he had lacked. It was still too unfamiliar for him to name. And he didn't know exactly what had changed or how it would affect his behavior. Yet he sensed, as he put more distance between himself and the woman, that nothing would be the same again.

Chapter Two

There was nothing besides a modest white sign with black letters to set the administrative offices apart from the rest of the buildings, Kathryn thought as McCourt directed her to a visitor's parking space near one of the drab redbrick structures. Like the gatehouse, the entrance was equipped with a metal detector—in case she'd acquired a gun on the drive from the entrance.

"William Emerson's office is the third one on the right," McCourt told her.

She couldn't stop herself from saying, "Thank you for taking such good care of me."

"Just doing my job," he returned crisply.

She immediately regretted the sarcasm. It was a bad idea to start a new job by sniping at other staff members. But the man had been rubbing her wrong at every opportunity.

He stayed in the small lobby, keeping his eye on her as she headed down the dull gray corridor. Not until she opened the door marked Chief of Operations did he abandon the guard duty.

A petite brunette secretary who looked like she could chew nails in an emergency asked her to take a seat. Kathryn sank onto one of the worn leather couches in the anteroom. As the minutes ticked by, she thought about the way she'd been approached for this job. Emerson had called her out of the blue and offered her a lot of money to accept a short-term assignment at Stratford Creek. When she'd initially turned him down, he'd upped the pay to a figure that had made her blink. At the same time, his insistence had stirred a responsive wariness, and she knew she wouldn't be here at all if James Harrison hadn't scared the spit out of her.

Emerson had been so anxious to get her to Western Maryland that she'd expected to be ushered into his office the moment she set foot in the anteroom. In fact, he kept her cooling her heels for a good twenty minutes.

She was paging through a battered copy of *Newsweek* when he finally appeared.

"Dr. Kelley. Bill Emerson," he said, holding out his hand.

She rose, working to hide her annoyance as they shook hands. "Nice to meet you."

"Sorry to keep you waiting," he apologized.

"Not at all." Her first thought was that Emerson and McCourt must have the same barber, since their crew cuts looked identical—although Emerson's was gray instead of sandy blond. He was dressed in a blazer and slacks, but he looked as if he'd be more at home in a military uniform.

He was probably in his late fifties and was only a few inches taller than Kathryn's own five foot seven, she judged. But he appeared taller because he stood with his shoulders thrown back as if expecting a surprise visit from the secretary of defense.

When he ushered her into his office, the plaques and photographs on his wall confirmed the hypothesis that he'd been in the military.

"You've recently left the army?" she asked.

He smiled. "Yes. I'm a retired colonel. But I couldn't stand playing golf and trading war stories at the Army Navy Club. When they asked me to head up this project, I jumped at the chance."

As she scanned the framed citations and plaques, she gathered that he was proud of his achievements. If she were given a chance to study the memorabilia, she could probably reconstruct a good part of his service record, she thought.

Had he been given the Stratford Creek assignment as a reward, or because the project needed a strong hand at the helm, she wondered.

"I'm glad you were able to join us," he said with a satisfied smile. "I've been perusing your record again, and it's very impressive."

"Thank you," she answered, as she sat down in a visitor's chair.

"We're a little off the beaten track. Did you have any trouble finding us?" Emerson asked, reclaiming his seat behind the desk.

"No, but the security measures here are a bit intimidating."

"They have to be. We're doing highly classified work. Once you get used to us, I'm sure you'll appreciate being a member of the team."

"Actually, I've reserved judgment on taking the assignment until we could meet in person, and you could tell me what I'd be doing," she said in an even voice.

His face registered a flash of anger that he quickly

masked. "We've gone to a great deal of trouble to expedite your hiring."

"I appreciate that."

"And I thought your personal situation was an urgent consideration," he added.

"It is," she conceded. "But coming here has raised some questions."

"About...?"

"I'd like to know more about the man McCourt and I met on the road."

"John Doe?" he asked in a tone that turned the question into a statement.

"News travels fast around here."

"I had a report from McCourt."

"Of course," she said. So that had been the deferential phone call. She should have known.

"What did you think of him?"

"McCourt?"

"John Doe."

The question took her by surprise, and she came out with the first impression she'd formed. "He was very fit."

Emerson laughed as if enjoying a private joke. "Hmm. Yes. What else did you observe?"

"Well, he appears to speak English as if he's just learned it," she answered, embarrassed to voice one of the more personal observations she'd made.

"You have well-developed powers of observation."

Another compliment. She should be pleased. Instead the man's intense scrutiny made her feel suffocated.

"He's a convict who has volunteered for a special assignment."

Kathryn blinked, completely thrown. "That's hard to believe," she murmured.

"Why?"

"I've worked with criminals. He doesn't behave like one." If she'd been asked to justify the statement, it would have been difficult to come up with supporting details based on her brief encounter with the man. It was more a feeling than a professional observation.

Luckily, Emerson didn't challenge her, but his tone was emphatic as he continued, "We've changed him a lot since he arrived. He was serving a life sentence for murder."

The unexpected words hit her like a blow to the stomach, and she gasped in a startled breath of air.

A little smile played around Emerson's lips. At first she thought he was enjoying her shock. Yet as his gaze slid away from hers, she saw something more disturbing. His eyes gave him away. For some reason, he was telling her a lie. Or he was filtering the truth.

To find out which, she'd have to encourage him to keep talking. "Is that the big secret up here? You're using behavior modification techniques the rest of us haven't discovered yet?"

"No. Our Dr. Swinton is conducting experiments which are on the cutting edge of biological research. We're doing sociobiological engineering using tools unavailable just a few years ago." Warming to the subject, he continued, "We've developed a protocol for the complete rehabilitation of criminals, if you will."

"Complete rehabilitation. That's hard to believe," Kathryn ventured, recalling the many experiments she'd read about. The success rate for preventing recidivism was abysmally low, even with the most ambitious programs—which required strong incentives for offenders to change their view of the world. John Doe didn't seem to be enjoying any special incentives.

Emerson lowered his voice and leaned across the desk as if a hidden microphone from miles down the road could pick up his words. "Dr. Swinton has used a completely new approach. John Doe won't repeat his criminal activity, because we've been able to erase the antisocial memories from his mind."

She goggled. "How?"

"Through intensive drug therapy that interrupts the flow of neurotransmitters and scrubs away previous behavior patterns and learned responses."

He was apparently unaware of the effect he was having on Kathryn as she tried to imagine someone who would want to do that to a human being.

"Are you telling me you've given him mind-altering drugs that wiped out his memory?" she managed.

"That's right. Which is why we need to have you work with him."

"Me?" she asked in a choked voice.

"Yes." He shook his head. "Sorry. I forgot you haven't been given the whole picture. During phase two of our project, he absorbed a great deal of technical information and acquired impressive physical expertise. But his social development is lagging way behind. Your assignment will be to bring him up to speed on people skills."

She was trying to come to grips with that when a loud buzzer sounded in the room, making her jump.

"What now?" he muttered in annoyance, reaching for the telephone.

She couldn't hear any of the conversation on the other end of the line, but she could tell from the rush of words and the thunderous response on Emerson's face that the news was bad.

"When?" he asked. Then, "How in the hell did that happen?"

He listened to the answer, then cursed. "Well, try not to damage him. I'll be right there." Standing, he moved around the desk. "John Doe assaulted one of his instructors and is tearing the gym apart."

"He couldn't have," Kathryn protested, wanting to be right.

Emerson gave her a dark look. "Dammit to hell. I thought this time we'd done it."

"I'm good in a crisis situation," she answered. "Let me see what I can do." Without waiting for an answer, she hurried after Emerson out the door and down the hall, moving in double time to keep up.

A government-issue brown Chevrolet was parked outside the back door.

His lips pressed grimly together, Emerson climbed behind the wheel. Kathryn slid into the passenger seat. He didn't wait for her to fasten her seat belt before shooting backwards out of the space, reversing with a screech of tires, and barreling down the hill.

She braced her hand against the dashboard, trying to keep from being flung about by the wild motion of the car and at the same time trying to understand everything she'd just heard. All her instincts screamed that Emerson's claims about John Doe's background were untrue. He couldn't be a criminal. And they couldn't have cold-bloodedly wiped out his memories. Yet she had no other information to go on. And no explanation for why he'd gone berserk.

As she struggled to keep her seat, an ambulance with siren blaring passed them in the opposite direction. She'd almost worked out a system for staying in place when they skidded to a ·stop in front of a large building with a curved roof.

Emerson jumped out of the car and took the cracked sidewalk at a run. Kathryn trotted after him.

A small crowd of men was grouped around the door. Some were cut from the same mold as McCourt. Others wore lab coats. And a sizable contingent were dressed in blue uniforms, like a private security force. Most of them eyed her curiously as she came to a halt behind the chief of operations.

"Where is he?" Emerson demanded.

"In the locker room." The answer came from a broad-shouldered black man who stepped forward. His name tag identified him as Winslow.

Emerson glanced around at the crowd. "Get back to your duties," he said in a voice that demanded compliance.

The group immediately began to disperse.

"Inside," he said to Winslow.

Deciding she was included in the terse invitation, Kathryn followed them into a small lobby.

"Let's have it," Emerson demanded after pushing the door shut.

Winslow stood with his arms stiffly at his sides. "He was late from his run. Beckton was angry because he'd been waiting for the hand-to-hand combat session. He shoved him around a little bit the way he does when he's riled up."

"And then what?" Emerson demanded.

"Doe said he was given an extra two miles by McCourt. Beckton told him to shut up and punched him on the arm. Doe got this strange look on his face and turned and socked Beckton in the gut. Beckton went down. He got up cursing and went in low, but Doe kept at him. A couple of guys dived in and tried to pull him off. He decked them and retreated into the locker room. We were able to pull Beckton out. He was unconscious when they took him away."

"What happened today that was different from past sessions?" Emerson demanded.

Winslow looked flustered. "Nothing, sir. Beckton's been rough with him before."

"Has anyone tried to get Doe out of the locker room?" Emerson asked.

"No, sir. We were waiting for your direct orders. We have Reid standing by with a tazzer. Or we can use the tranq gun. I assume you don't want to terminate the subject," Winslow added in a low voice.

Kathryn felt the blood freeze in her veins. They were discussing the man she'd met as if he were a dangerous animal that had escaped from a zoo—or a homicidal maniac.

"Certainly not!" Emerson shot back. "We've gotten further with him than any of the others."

"Let me talk to him," she said.

The men's heads snapped toward her.

"I don't think that would be such a good idea, ma'am," Winslow said.

"I'm Dr. Kathryn Kelley," she answered. "I was hired to work with Doe."

"*You're* Dr. Kelley?" he asked, and she got the impression he'd been expecting her to be ten feet tall and built like a Sherman tank.

She squared her shoulders. "I believe I'm up to the job."

Emerson nodded. "She and McCourt encountered Doe on his run. McCourt said they had quite a conversation—for Doe. She seemed to click with him."

Winslow looked from her to Emerson and back again. "What the hell did you say to him?"

"I—" She stopped, shrugged. "Not much. I asked his name. He said I was different from the other people here." She related a few more lines of the conversation, knowing she hadn't conveyed the flavor of the experience. Too much of it had been on a nonverbal level.

Was it possible she had anything to do with his aberrant behavior? Maybe. Or maybe it was simply a coincidence. Before Winslow could say anything else, or she could change her mind, she pulled open the door behind him and stepped into a large room with a wooden floor, a basketball hoop, and a track marked off around the perimeter.

"Come back, you damn little fool," he called.

Emerson said nothing. He was a pragmatist, and he was probably thinking that he didn't have anything to lose by letting his new recruit try her luck. If she got herself killed, he could hire somebody else.

She looked around at the gym, searching for signs of a madman on a rampage. The indications were minimal. A clipboard lay on the floor with the pages ruffled. A few feet away was a service revolver and ballpoint pen with a crushed barrel.

Still, as her gaze zeroed in on some red droplets spattering the floor, she knew she was viewing the evidence of the fight. Was she out of her mind to be in here?

Slowly she turned and found that Emerson had followed her into the gym. "Don't let anybody else come in unless I call for assistance," she said in a firm voice.

"Do we have a live microphone in there?" he asked Winslow through the partially opened door.

"It's shorted out."

"Damn."

She was only wasting time, she told herself as her gaze swept the room. At the far end was an exit to the outside of the building. Through the glass she could see several of the men in blue uniforms standing guard. So presumably Doe hadn't escaped.

Trying to ignore the pulse pounding in her temple, she marched to the door on her right, pulled it open, and found herself facing an ordinary dressing room, about fourteen feet square. Gray metal lockers lined two of the walls, and wooden benches were positioned in front of them. The air smelled like damp towels and male bodies, but the room was empty. The only exit was an archway at the back from which she saw steam billowing and heard the sound of running water.

It appeared that John Doe had beaten one man unconscious and decked several others—and now he was calmly taking a shower.

Before she could change her mind, she stepped into the locker room and felt the door swing shut behind her. Seconds later, she heard the water stop. God, what was she doing? she suddenly wondered, glancing from the shower room to the closed door and back again. Coming in here alone might be the most dangerous thing she'd ever done.

She wanted to bolt from the room. But she remembered the face of the man on the road. She'd seen a bleakness behind his eyes that had wrenched at her heart. No wonder, when you considered the implications of Emerson and Winslow's callous conversation.

Instead of running away, she crossed the tile floor on unsteady legs and dropped quickly onto one of the benches.

There was no noise from inside the shower room besides the steady dripping of water. And she could see nothing beyond the billowing steam.

"Hello?" she called.

No answer.

"Hello. It's Kathryn Kelley. Do you remember me? We met while you were on your run. I'm in the locker room."

She sat staring into the mist, wondering if he had heard. Or if he even remembered her, for that matter, she thought with a jolt. If they'd been feeding him mind-altering drugs, there was no telling what they'd done to him.

After several seconds she saw a form moving indistinctly in the vapor. A tall, man-shaped form. Moving closer…moving slowly on feet that were silent as a cat. Then he stepped through the doorway and into the locker room, and she couldn't hold back a gasp. Except for a towel draped across his shoulders, he was as naked as the day he was born.

She saw her own feeling of shock mirrored on his face as he came to an abrupt halt, staring at her with a mixture of recognition and astonishment. Well, he remembered her, all right. Apparently their meeting had been as unique for him as it had been for her.

The disbelief vanished as he continued to regard

her, standing comfortably with his feet several inches apart. He was tall and intimidating, towering over her where she huddled on the bench. Droplets of water clung to his skin. His dark hair was wet, making it look almost black.

"You were with McCourt," he said, his features filling with a roiling mixture of emotions before he got control of them.

She struggled to keep her posture relaxed as she looked up at him. He had been compelling in running shorts and a T-shirt. Naked he reminded her of Michelangelo's David. And he stood with the same unconscious nobility, as if nudity were the norm. His shoulders were broad, his hips lean, his stomach flat, and his sex was proportioned to inspire some very erotic fantasies.

But this was no time for fantasies or recklessness. One wrong move and she could be in serious trouble.

She swallowed hard, resisting the impulse to put more space between them. Dragging her eyes upward, she saw a narrow slash along his ribs that looked like a recent knife wound. There were other injuries to his olive-colored flesh, all of which appeared to have been inflicted within the past few months, judging from their color. He'd taken a lot of physical punishment, and the knowledge made her throat tighten.

She wasn't sure what she expected him to say. When he spoke, his words were a shock. "Why are you sad?" he asked, picking up on the emotion she had neglected to hide. She knew then, that whatever else he was, he was very good at reading people.

Her gaze moved higher still and collided with his dark, almost black eyes. They held a kind of aching vulnerability that made her fingers curl around the edge of the bench. ''I—I was thinking about how you got all those injuries.''

''Fighting. Or sometimes they hit me,'' he said, his voice even, as if his words were of no importance.

She winced. ''Like Beckton?''

He nodded gravely.

''This time he made you angry?''

The naked man didn't answer. But she could tell he was considering the question as his gaze turned inward.

Seconds ticked by. Her mind raced as she remembered what Emerson had said about him. She didn't want to accept the claim that he was a criminal. But she could believe the parts about his memories having been stolen. His present behavior was enough to convince her that he lacked a basic understanding of the social interactions of Western society. Either that, or he was a master at faking total unconcern for his state of undress.

While it might be natural for him to be conducting an extended conversation in his birthday suit, it was hardly the norm for her.

''You have to put some clothes on,'' she said, watching his face. It was as innocent as a child's.

''Why?''

''It's not polite to be naked in front of a woman.''

She watched as he moved the towel briskly across his shoulders, then down his lean but muscular body. When she realized she was still staring, she pivoted her body in the other direction.

It dawned on her that she'd just turned her back on someone who had sent a man to the hospital a short time ago. She should be afraid, but she didn't brace for an attack.

Behind her, the locker door opened. She heard the sound of the towel, then the rustling of clothing. When she turned back, he had pulled on a pair of jeans. His chest was still bare, and he was rubbing the towel vigorously across his head. Then he ran his hands through the long strands of his hair, combing them back from his face before reaching inside the locker for a dark green knit shirt and pulling it over his head.

As he sat down to pull on socks and running shoes, she framed and rejected several questions.

Again, he took the initiative from her. "The men are afraid to come in here. Yet you are small and—" he stopped and searched for the right word "—defenseless, and you found the courage."

"It didn't take so much courage."

He looked up in the act of tying his shoe. "You are not telling me the truth."

She was shocked at the bluntness of his observation.

"Okay. I was afraid at first. Then I knew you wouldn't hurt me."

"How?"

"Your eyes," she said.

He narrowed them, making his expression harder. She wasn't fooled by the feigned look of aggression.

"I'm not afraid of you. But I'm afraid of what Mr. Emerson might do to you if he doesn't hear from me soon. I'm going to open the door and tell him I'm all right. Okay?"

Seconds ticked by before he nodded.

She crossed to the door and pulled it open. Emerson and Winslow were where she'd left them—on the far side of the gym. "We're fine in here," she called out.

"Bring him out," Emerson ordered.

"Not yet."

"Bring him out, or we're coming in."

"Give me a few minutes to talk to him." She closed the door firmly and turned to find John Doe watching her intently.

"Why did you come here?" he asked.

"I want to help you."

He tipped his head to one side, examining her from a slightly different angle. "Nobody wants to help me," he said in a flat voice. "They want to train me, like an animal who can do tricks. I have many tricks."

The harsh words and the level tone sent a great wave of anguish crashing over her. Her face contorted, and unconsciously, she reached out a hand toward him. "I want to be your friend," she said, realizing that it wasn't just a ploy to get him to trust her. It was the truth. If anyone had ever needed a friend, it was this man.

He searched her eyes, slipped one hand into his pocket and said nothing more. His posture, his face told her that he wasn't prepared to believe her.

She asked herself briefly why she cared. Or why she desperately needed to prove the truth of her words. She had no answers, except that she wanted to make contact with him as one human being who takes responsibility for another. Going on blind instinct, she stood and crossed the room. Warily he watched her progress, but she didn't stop until she was standing about a foot away. Reaching out, she touched his forearm. She felt the muscles under the fabric of his shirt quiver, otherwise he stood very still, like an animal sniffing the air for danger.

She moved her hand, the barest caress and heard him draw in a deep breath.

"That feels good," he said, and she heard the wonder in his voice. It was like a little boy on Christmas morning finding the floor under the tree unexpectedly piled with presents. Yet it had taken only the touch of her hand on his arm to elicit the response.

She felt a strange fluttering around her heart. At that moment she was achingly convinced that he had no recent memory of any gentle touch. It was the strongest proof yet that Bill Emerson wasn't lying about his past history. If it was true, though, the implications were staggering. Was this really a man without memories of human interaction—good or bad?

God, what would that be like? Maybe a little like having amnesia.

If she stopped to examine the logic of the situation, she was lost. This encounter was like nothing she had ever experienced in her life. He was like no one she had ever met. They could have been two people from different galaxies making first contact. Two people trying to find common ground that would let them understand each other.

"Why do they call you John Doe?" she asked in a low voice.

It was a simple question, but more seconds ticked by while he thought about the answer. Finally he shrugged.

"If you could pick a name, what would it be?"

He considered her question. "Hunter," he finally said.

"Why Hunter?"

"That is what I am."

She didn't know him well enough to follow his reasoning, but she nodded. "I like that name."

"Then I will tell them I am Hunter."

"Yes." She liked the way he said it, his tone clear and decisive. "You chose it yourself."

He nodded, a look of pride on his face. It brought a subtle change to his features

Such a little thing, she thought with a surge of wonder. A name. Yet it made an enormous difference to him. As she gazed at him, she felt an invisible net tightening around her, pulling her toward this man who needed her more than anybody had ever needed her before. It was empowering, yet frightening. She sensed that he had let her past a barrier no other person had crossed. He was so open to her. Vulnerable. She could hurt him badly if she didn't handle things in the right way.

He watched her eyes intently as he lifted his hand and very gently ran his thumb over her cheek, down to her lips. The pad of his thumb was rough.

"Your skin is soft," he said in a barely audible voice. "I touched a yellow flower in the field once. You are soft—like the petals."

The way he said it made a shiver go through her. All she could do was nod. The emotional turmoil of the past few days had been staggering. She had come to Stratford Creek because she thought she'd be safe—that she could stop worrying about being stalked. But nothing that had happened so far had been what she expected. She hadn't met anyone here who made her feel safe. Except, oddly enough, a man who was supposed to be a criminal.

A sense of unsteadiness, of confusion, made her heart beat faster. The effort of holding herself together was suddenly too much. Without conscious thought she let her head drift to his broad shoulder. It was solid and strong. Closing her eyes, she allowed her mind to conjure a little fantasy. If she delivered herself into this man's hands, he would shield her from harm.

The notion was deeply appealing, and she sighed. So did he.

"Where did we meet before?" he asked.

"On the road."

"Before that. I do not know when it was. All I know is that it is important to remember," he continued in an urgent voice. "More important than the music. Or the other things."

"What other things?" She raised her head and stared at him.

He tugged on his left earlobe the way he had done before, thinking. "The things that come to me. A color. Or a sound. A smell. The sunset over the desert at night. They flit into my mind like a moth. Then they escape into the darkness."

"You remember things?" she asked, suddenly hoping for proof that Emerson had been lying.

"I...do not know for sure. What is the difference between memories and wishing?"

She had no answer, for she knew that it was perfectly possible, under the right circumstances, for people to remember things that hadn't happened. But the mixture of uncertainty and longing on his face tore at her, and she raised her hand to his cheek. For a long moment, neither of them moved, then he turned his head so that his lips brushed her fingers, so lightly she wondered if she imagined it.

"Another thing I remember...the touch of soft flesh against my flesh. Or perhaps I want to think it is true," he said wistfully.

His voice was husky with emotion she suspected had been bottled up inside him for a long time. She wanted to turn and gather him to her. Then she remembered that Emerson and a squad of security men were waiting outside.

Straightening, she cleared her throat. Although it wasn't easy to make herself pull back, she took a small step away from him. "I told Mr. Emerson I'd find out about what happened with Beckton," she said.

His expression hardened. "He asked why I was late. I told him. He said I was lying, and he punched me. I do not lie."

She tried to keep her voice neutral. "He hit you before, and you didn't hurt him. Why was this time different?"

"It just was."

"Why?"

His brows knit. Seconds ticked by. "You," he finally said. "Seeing you. And talking."

"I don't understand. What does it have to do with me?"

"You made me want to be different," he said, then looked startled by the revelation.

"What do you mean?" she persisted in a shaky voice.

"I—" Before he could finish the sentence, the sound of running feet echoed through the gym.

Hunter's gaze shot from her to the door through

which she'd entered. He gave her a look that was equal parts hurt and anger. Then his face went blank. Whirling, he crouched in a defensive stance, just as the door opened and a swarm of men wearing riot gear poured into the locker room.

Chapter Three

Kathryn screamed as the riot squad swarmed over Hunter like predators fighting over fresh meat. With remarkable strength, he was able to defend himself with several well-placed martial-arts moves, but there were six of them and only one of him. She saw them landing blow after blow, then, as if on an unspoken signal, a man in the back calmly lifted a gun with a needle-shaped barrel and fired into Hunter's shoulder.

Even as her mind registered that it must be a tranquilizer gun, an anguished gasp tore from her lips.

She saw consciousness slipping from him, but he fought to stay awake. Raising his head, he scanned the room for something. He was looking for her, she realized with a start as his dark gaze cleared for a moment, boring into her with the force of a drill bit gouging through solid rock. Anger blazed in the depths of his eyes like cold fire. Suddenly she was thankful that four men were restraining him.

"You...tricked...me," he flung at her, fighting to get the words out as the dart did its insidious work.

"No!"

"You came here...with soft words...so they could..."

The effort to speak sapped the last of his strength, and his body sagged.

"No," she repeated, shaking her head violently, still protesting her innocence even as he lost the effort to keep his eyes open.

The four men hanging on to him were left supporting his dead weight. Even as he slipped toward the floor, the man with the gun uttered a vile curse.

"Get him out of here, Reid," Emerson ordered.

"Where should we put him?" the man asked. "In a cell?"

"In his bedroom," Kathryn interjected.

Emerson turned in her direction, his expression indicating he'd forgotten she was on the scene.

"Are you afraid of an unconscious man?" she asked in as detached a voice as she could manage.

"He'll come around in a couple of hours," Reid said. "Then we'll have a mess on our hands."

"If you're afraid to deal with the consequences, I can be there to manage him," she answered, deliberately trying to use a word they would respect. "In fact, I was managing him very well until you came bursting into the room."

The men ignored her, waiting for orders from Emerson. "Take him to his quarters," he said.

"And don't hit him again," Kathryn added. "That's counterproductive."

"He needs to be knocked upside the head," Reid growled.

"You've already done enough of that."

"We weren't having any trouble with him until you showed up," a familiar voice said from the doorway.

She turned and saw Chip McCourt watching her with interest.

"No trouble?" she asked, her voice edged with sarcasm. "Then why did you say he'd beat me up if I got close to him?"

The man's face darkened, and she realized her jangled nerves had resulted in another tactical error.

"We haven't had an incident for a while," he mumbled. "But you obviously triggered regressive behavior."

"Maybe it was more mature behavior—in some private context of his own," she countered.

"Oh, come on!"

"I'll be better equipped to make judgments when I'm up to speed on his previous history," she said, retreating into her role as newly hired psychologist. "Perhaps we should have a strategy session before he wakes up. Those who are working with him can fill me in on what I need to know, so I won't make any mistakes."

McCourt's expression told her he thought she'd already made plenty of mistakes.

"That's an excellent idea," Emerson agreed. He turned to McCourt. "Be in my office in half an hour. You and the rest of the senior staff. Winslow, Kolb, Swinton." He paused for a moment. "And Anderson."

"Yes, sir." McCourt wheeled and left the room.

Emerson strode back into the gym.

Kathryn followed him to the car, still haunted by the mixture of anger and anguish in Hunter's eyes—and by the cryptic statement he'd made just before the security men had grabbed him.

He'd told her the two of them had met before. But he was too striking, too remarkable for her to have forgotten him. It made more sense to assume that he had dredged up a half-buried memory and inserted her into it as part of a defense mechanism to cope with a situation any sane person would find untenable. Yet even as she struggled for an explanation, she felt a kind of truth to his words deep inside herself, as sure as the pounding of her heart and the blood rushing through her veins. Perhaps they hadn't laid eyes on each other before today, but something remarkable had happened between them.

She sensed he'd told her things—private things—he had never shared with anyone else. He would have told her more, except that the cavalry had charged into the room, and he thought she'd abused his trust. Unfortunately, there was a grain of truth to his assumption. The chief of operations had been using her to make Hunter relax his defenses—so he could bring in the riot troops.

The car started, and she swung her head toward the window, feigning a deep interest in the redbrick buildings when what she really wanted to do was round on Emerson and shout out her outrage and frustration. Instead, she kept her lips pressed together. No more unavoidable errors, she warned herself. No emotional outbursts. She had to stay cool and figure out how to work within the system that had been established here if she was going to help Hunter. And she was going to help him, she silently promised herself, because in her professional career, she'd never seen anything that disturbed her as much as what they'd just done to him.

Was he really being subjected to cruel and unusual punishment as part of an official U.S. Government project? It was hard to believe, yet she had to assume from her own observations that it was true. What if

she could gather enough information to write up a
report that would close down Stratford Creek?
Though the plan had appeal, it would be risky—both
to herself and Hunter, she suspected.

She worried her lower lip between her teeth, ac-
knowledging the all too familiar symptoms in herself.
She was getting involved again—opening herself to
the depths of someone else's pain. But this time was
different, she realized. It was stronger, sharper, suf-
fused with a sense of urgency she'd never felt before.
She had never met a man quite like Hunter and never
been affected on quite such a personal level.

Bill Emerson's voice pierced her thoughts.

"You've been through quite an ordeal," he said,
and she realized that as he drove he'd been covertly
observing the play of emotions on her face.

"I'm fine," she lied, clamping down on the need
to press a hand to her temple, which had begun to
throb.

"Well, I'm impressed with the way you came in
here cold and figured out what needed to be done. I
was worried we might damage him."

The casually delivered comment made her lower
her hand so that he wouldn't see it tremble. "Damage," she repeated. "You sound like you're referring
to a piece of equipment."

"Yes. Sorry. Habits die hard." He paused for a
fraction of a second. "We've thought of John Doe as
a test subject for so long that it's difficult to shift our
attitudes."

"Perhaps it would help if you told me what he's
being trained to do," she said in as nonconfronta-
tional a voice as she could manage.

"Yes, I was about to fill you in on some pertinent

background when we were so rudely interrupted. Our subject has volunteered for a dangerous mission in a foreign country. He has to go in by himself, maybe set up a temporary base of operations, which means he's got to function in a public setting without drawing suspicion to himself. In other words, he needs a crash course in acceptable social behavior. That's where your expertise will be needed."

Several pointed observations flitted through Kathryn's mind. The first was that Hunter was backward socially because he was living with a bunch of jerks. The second was that it was a bit unfair to be undertaking a dangerous assignment when you couldn't remember having volunteered. All she said was, "What kind of mission?"

"You don't need to know any more than I've told you," Emerson answered crisply. "You just have to make sure he's ready to go."

The way he said it made her blood run cold. But she only gave him a little nod of acknowledgment.

Emerson pulled into the same parking slot in back of the administration building. However, instead of taking her to his office, he showed her into an adjoining conference room.

"Take a few minutes to relax before the meeting starts," he advised before leaving her alone.

She didn't have any problem following his advice. The moment he closed the door behind her, she slumped in one of the seats around the conference table. She'd only gotten a few moments of blessed repose when a disturbing thought drifted into her mind. Emerson had mentioned that the surveillance equipment in the locker room was broken. What if he had a recording system in here? Sitting up, she looked around, seeing nothing as obvious as a camera. Maybe it was hidden behind a picture—like in Orwell's *1984,* she thought with a grim little twinge as she inspected a landscape on the opposite wall. Well, she'd have to learn to adapt to the conditions here, she told herself, and knew she'd made the decision to stay.

Minutes later, the brunette secretary bustled into the room with a tray of sandwiches and muffins and a pot of coffee.

Kathryn tried to eat, but an image of Hunter being dragged away by the security team flashed into her mind. Dropping her sandwich on the paper plate in front of her, she rose from her seat, seized with the irrational notion that if she could make physical contact with him—grasp his hand or something—she could somehow make him understand that she hadn't tricked him. But she didn't even know where to find him, she conceded as she sank back into her chair. Even if she did, she'd only be demonstrating an unprofessional personal involvement with the Stratford Creek research subject. Not a smart move, under the circumstances.

At that moment, the door opened and Winslow strode in. After several seconds' hesitation, he gave her a curt nod and took a seat across the table—where he could keep an eye on her? Or did he want to make it clear they weren't allies?

"How is he?" she couldn't stop herself from asking.

"Sleeping. Dr. Kolb is checking him out."

At least that was something. Before she could ask any more questions, McCourt arrived. To her surprise, he turned out to be the assistant chief of security. What was he, the boy wonder?

Other men followed, each introducing himself and briefly filling her in on his job. Sam Winslow worked under Jerome Beckton, the chief of training. Doug Granger, who looked like a college wrestling champion, with bulging muscles and a ruddy complexion, was also on the training staff. As Emerson had already mentioned, Dr. Swinton was chief of research. Dr. Kolb, the facility's physician, a small man with a pale complexion and a deeply lined face, came hurrying in last.

Like Emerson, everyone was dressed in civilian clothing. But as she studied the men he'd referred to as the senior staff, she noted that they all projected a military bearing, except for the tall, balding Dr. Swinton. She pegged him as an academic type when she spotted his white socks and plastic pocket protector stuffed full of ballpoint pens. Of the men in the room, he looked the most uncomfortable in her presence. Maybe he was sensing her antipathy to his line of research.

Of the group, she found Dr. Kolb the most unsettling. His bloodshot eyes kept swinging in her direction when he thought she wasn't looking, as if he had a special interest in her, but didn't want her to know.

Emerson came in late, poured himself a cup of coffee and snagged a ham sandwich before taking the place at the head of the table. "Where's Anderson?" he asked.

"My assistant had other duties," Dr. Swinton answered, making it sound as if he didn't feel Anderson was entitled to a place at the table.

Emerson gave a curt nod, then turned abruptly to Dr. Kolb. "How is John Doe?"

The doctor jumped. "Uh…his vital signs are normal, under the circumstances, Colonel."

"Good." Emerson took in the information, then addressed the rest of the men. "I trust you've all met Dr. Kelley, our newly hired psychologist, and that you are all familiar with her excellent background in working with various types of disadvantaged individuals."

There was a chorus of murmurs around the table.

So he'd already circulated her résumé, Kathryn thought. Fast work.

"As you know, Dr. Kelley was added to the Project Sandstorm team as an outgrowth of the monthly progress evaluation being made of our subject—our prison volunteer, John Doe."

Project Sandstorm, she mused. It conjured up a stealth attack in the desert. Was that where he was going?

"When it was determined that our subject's lack of social skills was affecting the timetable of the project," Emerson continued, "various remedial solutions were suggested."

As Kathryn listened to the convoluted speech, she noted that the men around the table were judging her reaction.

Why? Everyone here surely knew they were experimenting with a prison volunteer, so what was the point of emphasizing the man's peculiar status? Unless the chief of operations was subtly reminding them of something else. She found herself conjuring an entirely different scenario. Suppose Emerson was lying about how they'd acquired the services of the man they called John Doe. Suppose their "volunteer" had met with an unfortunate accident that had wiped out his memory, and the Stratford Creek team was capitalizing on the circumstances. Suppose they were using a cover story about a prison volunteer until they thought she was inculcated with their ideas and could be trusted with the truth.

She could well be jumping to unwarranted conclusions. Yet intuition and training both told her that the colonel was twisting the truth again.

Emerson stopped talking, and she realized with a start that he was waiting for a response from her.

Straightening in her chair, she gave him an encouraging smile. "I could see you were having problems with him the moment I met him on the road."

From his place down the table, McCourt nodded, and she knew she'd given the right answer as far as the security man was concerned.

"And I think I've already begun the process of speeding up his socialization," she said, hoping she was still on the right track.

"How?" Winslow demanded.

"By making him feel more accepted. No disrespect intended, but the use of the name John Doe appears to be a deliberate attempt on the part of the staff to distance yourselves from him as an individual. However, he can hardly learn interpersonal relationships without experiencing them," she said, leaning heavily on professional jargon.

"Bingo," Dr. Kolb muttered, and earned a dirty look from the research director.

She noted the not-so-friendly byplay between the two senior staffers as she continued. "In the locker room, I suggested that he give himself a more agreeable name. He chose Hunter. After that, it was easier to communicate with him."

Mixed reactions erupted around the table—from guarded approval on the part of Dr. Kolb to undisguised hostility from Sam Winslow.

"Hunter? Where did that come from?" Dr. Swinton demanded.

She kept her reply conversational. "He says he's a hunter."

The chief of operations laughed appreciatively. "Yes. I guess it fits."

Granger managed to echo his commander's chuckle. McCourt didn't bother to mask his disapproval.

Swinton had taken out one of his ballpoint pens and was twisting it in his fingers, staining them with an occasional slash of blue ink. "I'm not sure socialization should be one of our goals," he said.

Kolb ignored him and asked, "First or last name?"

"First," she answered, hoping she'd read Hunter's intention correctly. "I think it would be beneficial if you can all start using it."

They swung their heads in unison toward Emerson like spectators at a tennis match, and he gave a little nod.

"And I have some other ideas that might help solve your problems," she added, only steps away from improvising. "Most people learn their early socialization during years of interacting in a family setting. Because Hunter doesn't remember a home life, he is seriously handicapped in his ability to interact on a meaningful level."

"He doesn't have to interact on a meaningful level," McCourt growled. "He only has to remember to zip his fly when he comes out of the men's room. And close his mouth when he chews.''

Several of the group laughed again. But Swinton pushed back his chair as if to leave. Apparently thinking better of the gesture, he sat down again. ''This is ridiculous,'' he growled. ''From the reports I've heard, it appears to me that Dr. Kelley's interactions with the subject have only set his training back.''

Kathryn tried to jump in. ''I'm sorry if—''

But he plowed on, drowning out the end of her sentence. ''I want to see a copy of Dr. Kelley's Omega clearance before she has any additional access to the subject.''

''You know that hasn't arrived yet,'' Emerson answered. ''She just got here.''

''It's procedure, and I demand that we follow procedure.''

For several seconds there was silence in the room. Then Emerson cleared his throat. ''I will make sure that Dr. Kelley's paperwork is expedited. But until the proper forms arrive, she will be restricted to alternate duties.'' Standing, he left the room.

Kathryn sat there stunned, aware that most of the men were coldly judging her reaction again. God, what a callous bunch of bastards. It was clear they didn't give a damn about Hunter's welfare. They were just doing a job. Which one of them had told Swinton so much about her interaction with Hunter? Or did he have some other spy in the training department or on the security force?

''I've been instructed to take your things to guest cottage 3,'' McCourt said, breaking into her thoughts.

She wanted to tell him she wasn't at Stratford Creek as a guest. Instead, she nodded politely.

CAMERON RANDOLPH TURNED from the window of his home office and walked back to his desk where he shuffled through the papers spread across the blotter. The CEO of a multimillion-dollar electronics firm, he would have preferred to spend his time in the lab, tinkering with inventions. Tonight he was up late, worrying about Kathryn Kelley, who had asked for his advice about taking a job at Stratford Creek.

Hearing footsteps in the hall, he automatically pushed the papers into a pile and slid them into the folder from which they'd emerged.

He looked up guiltily as his wife came in, obviously ready for bed.

"Are you coming up?" Jo asked in a hopeful voice.

"Sorry. I was just finishing."

She gave him a considering look. "If you wanted to keep things secret from your wife, you shouldn't have married a private detective," she said in a mild voice.

He grinned. "I wasn't trying to keep secrets. I was trying not to bother you until tomorrow."

"Bother me about what?" she demanded as she sat down in the comfortable leather chair across from his cluttered desk.

He sighed. "All right. I knew Kathryn was in a hurry to get out of Baltimore after that mess with James Harrison, but I advised her not to accept an assignment at Stratford Creek until I got a full report on the place."

"And now you have the scoop?" she said, gesturing toward the folder.

"Well, I know more."

Jo kept her expression neutral, but he knew she'd

been worried about her friend since the attack in the swimming pool.

"None of my Defense Department contacts will talk about the project Bill Emerson is running up there. Either they don't know how he's spending a couple of million dollars, or they won't admit they know."

"A lot of *your* research projects are secret," she pointed out. "That's not necessarily a reason to worry."

He nodded. "Secrecy is one thing. Hiring a bunch of guys I wouldn't want to meet in a dark alley is another."

"What?"

He tapped the folder. "I've gotten a list of the Stratford Creek personnel. Starting with William Emerson, U.S. Army, retired. He's a real superpatriot type, the kind of guy who can justify breaking laws if he thinks he's acting in the interests of national security. If he gets caught, he puts the evidence in the paper shredder."

"That's a bad combination," Jo murmured.

"And the rest of the staff—" He grimaced. "Either they've got Emerson's attitude, or they've gotten in trouble on other assignments."

Jo's eyes narrowed as she stared at the sheets of paper spread across his desk. "How do you know all this?"

"I called in a couple of favors." He pulled out the papers and leafed through them. "One of the worst of the bunch is the also retired Lieutenant Chip McCourt. Emerson rescued him from being court-martialed for assaulting a civilian worker on the base in Wiesbaden, Germany. He was allowed to leave the army with an honorable discharge.''

Jo's eyes widened.

Cam plowed on. "The doctor, Jules Kolb, would have been sued for medical malpractice if he hadn't been at a V. A. Hospital. The head of training, Jerome Beckton, has been jailed for several bar fights.''

"And you're saving the worst for last," Jo guessed.

"Yes. Dr. Avery Swinton. His specialty is biological research. On human subjects. He lost a research grant at Berkeley for illegally experimenting with human fetal tissue. After that he dropped out of sight. Now he's at Stratford Creek—doing God knows what under the shield Emerson has provided.''

"Just great!" Jo gave her husband a direct look. "We've got to tell Kathryn what she's dealing with.''

"I put in a call to her a couple of hours ago, but they told me she was unavailable. I could keep trying, but judging from this crowd's past, they're not going to let me get away with saying much over the phone. I need to find a way to get the information about these guys to her. And maybe arrange to pull her out of there if she wants to leave.''

"But how?" Jo asked.

"That's the sixty-four-thousand-dollar question.''

WIPING A TRICKLE of perspiration off her forehead, Kathryn climbed the steps of guest cottage 3, a stone-and-wood bungalow set about twenty yards back from one of the winding Stratford Creek roads. This was the third time in two days that she'd been out for a jog, ostensibly familiarizing herself with the grounds. But she was also working off her frustration. Since the scene in the locker room, she hadn't been allowed to see Hunter. She didn't even know how he was or what they were doing to him.

So she was reduced to the dim hope that she might run into him. But he wasn't jogging. She told herself it was for security reasons, not because he was suffering any ill effects of the tranquilizers.

A surge of helplessness welled up inside her. She'd had plenty of time to replay the staff meeting over and over in her mind—and also her two previous meetings with Hunter. She always came back to the awful moment when he'd stared at her with such fury.

More than ever, she wanted the chance to show him that somebody cared. But so far she was batting zero. Of course, she'd tried to talk to Emerson about gaining access to Hunter. But the chief of operations had been unavailable to her. And her only assignment over the past two days had been the boring task of flagging personnel with below-average performance appraisals. Talk about wasting a nice fat government salary on diddly-squat, she thought with a snort. If she could only send a message to the *Washington Post,* they'd be up here in a minute to do an exposé on government waste.

Only she wasn't going to be contacting the *Post* anytime soon. One of the disturbing things she'd found out was that new personnel were restricted to Stratford Creek grounds for the first two weeks. And only emergency phone calls were allowed. She bitterly resented the restriction to her freedom, but until she talked to Emerson, there seemed to be nothing she could do to change the situation.

Squaring her shoulders, she marched through the living room of the little house. The place was comfortable but not plush, with two bedrooms in the back, both with standard hotel-room furnishings. She'd taken the one on the right, which had a window overlooking the street and a sliding glass door that opened onto a small cement patio in the weed-choked backyard.

While she showered and dressed, she planned a sort of stealth attack on Dr. Swinton. Pulling out the copy of the Stratford Creek phone directory that had been issued with her information packet, she found the address of the research center. Swinton's office was in room 101. Perhaps if she went over there, she could act interested in the project, flatter him, and get some background information on Hunter.

Of course, she was supposed to be working on the vitally important performance appraisals, she reminded herself. But she'd bet her first month's paycheck that she wouldn't be missed.

There were few cars parked in front of the research center, she noted as she pulled into a prime space near the front door. The lobby was deserted, and she was looking for a directory board when a thin, stoop-shouldered man with wispy brown hair and horn-rimmed glasses approached. Apparently deep in thought, he was carrying a can of soda and a bag of cheese twists.

He almost ran into her, then looked up, startled.

"Sorry—" she apologized. "I was trying to find Dr. Swinton's office."

"He's out of the building at the moment."

She struggled with a surge of disappointment.

"You must be Dr. Kelley. The psychologist," he said. "Sorry I couldn't be at the strategy meeting the other day. I'm Dr. Roger Anderson, the deputy direc-

tor of research. I'd offer you my hand, but, um—''
He held up the soda can.

She nodded her understanding, then switched
smoothly to plan B. ''I'm sorry I didn't get to meet
you the other day.''

''Likewise. I had some things to take care of. Why
don't you come down the hall and we can have a
chat?''

''Thank you.'' She followed him to a small office
furnished with a government-issue metal desk and
swivel chair. The computer beside the desk, however,
was a state-of-the-art model.

He set down his food and gestured toward the guest
chair. ''Do you mind if I drink my soda? I've been
here since early in the morning.''

''That's fine,'' she assured him.

He opened the bag of cheese twists and took a bite
before asking, ''So what can we do for you?''

''I guess you know that I've been prohibited from
working with your research subject—Hunter—until
my clearance comes through.''

''Um, yes. Sorry about that.'' He lowered his
voice. ''Dr. Swinton is a stickler for procedure.''

The response was better than she had expected.
Making a helpless gesture, she said, ''I feel like I'm
marking time. I'd be very grateful if I could get some
background information on the subject, so I'll be up
to speed when we start working together.''

''Um,'' Anderson mused, around another mouthful
of junk food.

''It would help if I could see the kind of progress
he's already made.''

Taking a thoughtful swallow of soda, he leaned

back in his chair and studied her with blue eyes that held all the charm of a cat watching a goldfinch.

She tried to pretend he wasn't making her nervous.

"Yes, well," he finally said, "I'd have to ask Dr. Swinton's approval to give you written reports. However, there are some videos we've made of selected training sessions. I don't see why you couldn't look at them."

"Thank you," she answered with feeling.

He let his legs thump to the floor and stood. "Come on down to the video room."

She followed him down the hall into a comfortably furnished lounge with a couch and several easy chairs facing a thirty-inch television.

"If you'll sit down, I'll make some selections," he said.

She sat in one of the chairs, watching while he unlocked a metal cabinet crammed with hundreds of videotapes, neatly stacked and labeled. *Quite a collection,* she thought, watching him pick and choose among the offerings.

Finally he closed the door and clicked the lock on the cabinet before setting several boxes on the table in front of her. "I have to get back to work, so just leave these here when you finish."

She heaved a sigh of relief when he left the room. He'd been helpful, but he made her edgy, she thought as she put a tape into the slot.

When she hit the play button, a picture of Hunter flashed onto the screen. He looked as fit and tan as when she'd first encountered him on the road. But that didn't prove anything, she reminded herself. Undoubtedly the video had been made before she met him.

Still, it was impossible not to look carefully for clues to his state of health. Physically, that wasn't hard to determine, since he was wearing a pair of tight-fitting black swimming trunks that gave her a wonderful view of the lithe, well-muscled body she remembered.

As she stared at him, a feeling of pent-up anguish caught her in the solar plexus. "Hunter," she whispered, "I'm sorry."

There was no reply from the video image. But, strangely, the expression on his face told her he doubted her apology.

He turned from the camera, gazed into the turquoise water of a swimming pool, then executed a perfect racing dive and began to swim with a powerful crawl stroke to the other end of the pool.

As a swimmer herself, she could admire his speed and form. And she could also appreciate his stamina. But after ten minutes of watching him do laps, she fast-forwarded the tape.

The next activity was more interesting. There was still no sound, but this time, at least, Hunter was involved in a contact sport—wrestling. His opponent was the solidly built Doug Granger, whose massive body must have outweighed Hunter's by at least fifty pounds. In the first shots, the heavier man seemed to take a kind of childish delight in getting the drop on his less-skilled opponent, using superior knowledge of the sport to slam Hunter onto the mat again and again. Her hands clenched into fists as she saw how much punishment he was taking. Another man might have given up or gotten angry or seized the initiative by biting his opponent's ear. Instead, Hunter stuck to the rules and kept doggedly getting up after each defeat. And she noted with satisfaction that his form and technique were getting better as the match progressed. He was smart, resourceful and well-coordinated. By the end of the session he was claiming most of the victories, and she was cheering him on with a grin and little exclamations of approval.

She looked closely at the two men's faces. Hunter's expression was for the most part neutral, but if she paid careful attention she could tell that he was secretly gratified. Granger, on the other hand, was less successful at hiding his feelings. He was angry. When he started using obviously illegal moves to give himself an edge, she wanted to leap up and pull him off Hunter.

Thankfully, someone else must have noticed what was going on. Granger turned as if in response to a command spoken by an unseen superior. With set lips, he marched off the mat, leaving Hunter standing with his hands on his hips, breathing hard.

The scene cut off, and she eagerly looked for another revealing session. Mostly it was more routine stuff, and she began to think that she'd been had by Anderson. Probably he'd called Emerson to report that he was keeping her busy with the world's most boring home videos. Then the view on the current tape abruptly switched, and she saw Hunter standing at the bottom of a metal pit. He was dressed in slacks and a knit shirt, much like the outfit he had put on in the locker room.

Again, the video was without sound. But from Hunter's shocked reaction, she could see that he'd heard a sudden noise from above—and discovered that something bad was about to happen.

He ducked and covered his head with his hands,

and she watched in horror as an ocean of water began to rain down on him.

Her fingers curled around the edge of the chair cushion, dug in as the pit filled. At first there was so much water pouring in that she could barely see anyone. When the flood eased a little, Hunter began to pull himself up a set of rungs fastened to the side of the tank. But he couldn't climb fast enough to stay ahead of the deluge. The water rose to his chest, then higher, and she found she was gasping for breath as waves lapped at his face, then covered his head.

Logically she knew he had gotten out of the death trap. Yet that didn't stop her pulse from pounding and perspiration from drenching her body. She rose from her seat as if she could come to his rescue, then fell back, her knees like straw.

"Hunter, please," she begged. "Pull yourself up. Please."

She saw the top of his dark head. Then he gave a mighty heave and hoisted himself up, hand over hand, staying just ahead of the water. Finally, he flopped out onto a metal deck and lay on his back, panting. Turning his head, he lifted his hand, obviously appealing to someone she couldn't see, someone who might have come to aid him. When no one appeared, she felt hot tears blur her vision.

Her own breath came in ragged gasps as if she was the one who had struggled out of the death trap.

God, what kind of sadist would treat a fellow human being that way? And coldly record it on videotape. Maybe there was some justification for what had happened in the locker room. The security men had been angry and upset. But this was cold-blooded torture.

Rage overpowered her—a pure abiding rage that brought with it an almost physical pain. She wanted to smash something. Smash the television screen that had shown her the dreadful scene. But she was too rational. Instead she sat in the chair, clasping the arm-rests in a death grip and trying to get her emotions under control.

It took several minutes before she could stanch the tears running down her cheeks as she replayed the scene in her mind, saw again his shocked expression before the water hit him. Nobody had told him what was going to happen. They'd taken him by surprise—and given her a vivid insight into why he found it difficult to trust her or anybody else.

She glanced over her shoulder, almost expecting to find Anderson standing in the doorway watching her with his coldly speculative eyes.

Why had he included this revealing scene with the tapes, she wondered. Had she misread him? Was he alerting her to the kind of inhuman experiments they were doing in this hellhole with the bucolic name of Stratford Creek? Or was he warning her not to interfere? Maybe the surprise viewing had simply been an accident.

With shaky fingers, she pressed the rewind button and waited impatiently until the machine stopped whirring. Ejecting the videotape, she juggled it in her hand. She wanted to remove it as evidence, knew that wasn't an option. The tape would be missed—either by Anderson or someone else. So she ducked into a ladies' room and splashed water on her heated face, trying to make herself look normal again before she left the building.

Chapter Four

Kathryn pictured herself driving straight to the administration building, pushing past Emerson's tough little receptionist, and bursting into his office. But coming at him breathing fire was hardly the way to get what she wanted.

She'd been part of enough bureaucracies to know that it was almost impossible to get anything done unless you worked within the system. But the training center was off limits. Swinton had control over Hunter's records. And she didn't know whether Anderson was a friend or a foe. If she'd had the option, she would have driven through the front gate of Stratford Creek and back to Baltimore, where she could get some aid and comfort from her friends at 43 Light Street.

But that wasn't an option, she reminded herself.

When she reached her car, her eyes widened as she spotted a piece of paper neatly rolled into a tube and stuffed under the door handle. Probably not an advertisement for a new pizza parlor at the local shopping center, she thought as she unwound it free.

MEDICAL CENTER.
ONE-FIFTEEN. CARDIOVASCULAR UNIT.
   HUNTER WILL BE AVAILABLE TO YOU.

There was no signature and no way of knowing who wanted her to come to the medical facility. Or why. This might be the chance she'd been waiting for, she thought with suppressed excitement. What if she had an ally at Stratford Creek—someone who didn't want to announce his support for her at a staff meeting?

The euphoria faded quickly. It was equally possible that McCourt or maybe Winslow was setting her up to get caught disobeying orders. Or someone could simply be playing mind games with her.

But at least she could give herself a legitimate excuse for being in the wrong place at the wrong time. She'd been putting off surrendering the standard medical forms that she'd been given. Now was the perfect time to turn them in.

Quickly she glanced at her watch. She was going to be late if she didn't hurry.

After picking up the forms at the cottage, she drove to the medical center. As she stepped inside the front door of the building, a nurse looked up. "May I help you?"

"I'm fine," she said, then turned to locate the cardiovascular unit on the directory. First floor, right wing.

Sailing around the corner, she pushed open the door to the unit and found herself in a waiting area with a desk and three orange plastic chairs. The room was empty, and she felt a surge of disappointment as she decided someone was probably playing games after all.

But she wasn't going to give up yet. Crossing the

room, she pushed open an inner door and stepped into a dimly lit hallway. All she could hear as she tiptoed forward was the sound of her pulse pounding in her ears. One door near the end of the hall was open, and she thought she saw the shadow of a tall man standing inside. As she stared at it, she couldn't stop herself from thinking about Chip McCourt again, this time with a sardonic grin on his face.

But what if it was Hunter?

Before she could lose her nerve, she crossed the remaining distance and stepped into the little room.

With a sense of relief, she took in the dark hair, broad shoulders, and narrow hips of the man standing a few feet away. Even from the back she recognized Hunter instantly.

Her initial surge of relief gave way almost immediately to gnawing tension in the pit of her stomach. He'd left her in anger. He was supposed to be dangerous. And they were alone again.

Dressed in a gray T-shirt, sweatpants and gym shoes, he was facing the window, gazing toward men on riding mowers cutting the straggly grass. He looked as if he wanted to escape from confinement— run free across the expanse of grass and into the woods beyond.

"Hunter? It's Kathryn," she said with a little tremble in her voice. "Kathryn Kelley."

His back stiffened, but he didn't move.

Before she could stop herself, she closed the door and approached him. The room was small, and she found herself only a few feet from him, angling her gaze upward to compensate for the disparity in their height. "Are you angry?" she asked.

No answer.

"Angry at me?"

The question got more reaction than her previous tries. He turned and stared at her, his features as tight as his knotted muscles. She started to lift her hand toward him but let it fall helplessly back to her side.

"I went out jogging a couple of times, hoping I'd see you," she said, struggling to hold her voice steady.

His guarded look made her think of youngsters who had been abused. He had the same wariness in his eyes—signaling the same reluctance to trust anybody for fear of getting hurt. Well, she'd already figured that out.

"I've been wondering how you were doing, hoping everything was all right."

"Why?" He turned the question into a direct challenge.

"I didn't like what happened the other day. It wasn't what I intended when I came in to talk to you. Truly. And I've been worried that they might have hurt you."

He gave a little shrug that tugged at her insides. This time she couldn't stifle the impulse to reach out and lay a hand gently on his arm. Under her fingers, the muscles flexed. "What did the tranquilizer do to you?" she asked softly.

"My head hurt when I woke up. And my ribs. The ribs were from when they beat me."

She fought for control but found she couldn't prevent her eyes from filling with moisture. She felt a tear begin to run down her cheek.

He closed the distance between them and touched his knuckle to her face, stopping the downward flow of the droplet.

"You are crying," he said gruffly.

"Because I feel so helpless." Reaching up, she wrapped her fingers around his, feeling the warmth of his skin and the slight tremble of his hand as she clung to him. Her hand was trembling too. "I'm sorry about what happened. I didn't know that a security team was coming into the locker room."

He stiffened and pulled away. "Why should I believe that?" His voice was so low she could barely hear.

"Because it's the truth, Hunter." She saw him react to the name and added in a voice as low as his, "I'm not like everybody else around here."

He studied her face intently, his eyes darkening. She wanted to exchange confidences with him—about his life, and hers. Get him to tell her how he felt. Talk again about being friends. Clasp his large hand between her smaller ones.

But there were more important things she had to know—things he might tell her if she asked. "We may not have much time," she said.

"Time for what?"

"Will you answer some questions?"

He gave no assurances, yet she proceeded as if she had his cooperation. "When William Emerson told me about Project Sandstorm, he said you were a—a convict who volunteered for a dangerous assignment. He claimed they used an experimental technique to— to wipe out the memory of your past life. Is that true?" Her pulse raced as she waited for an answer.

His eyes narrowed. "Colonel Emerson said that to you?"

"Yes."

"I have not heard it."

She kept her gaze steady. "If you aren't a convict, who are you?"

He shrugged.

"You don't remember your family. Your mother? Your father?"

Something flickered in the depths of his dark eyes, then he shook his head. "Things drift into my mind. The memory of picking up a coin. Crumpling a piece of paper in my hand. Smelling the wind coming off the sea. And…" He reached to touch her hair. "There is no one here with hair like yours, yet I keep thinking I remember it. I think I remember you. Stronger than the rest of the things." He stopped abruptly. "But that is not possible."

He had spoken earlier of remembering her, and she wanted to believe in it. Yet her own recollection was no help. "If we know each other, where did we meet?" she tried.

He didn't answer.

"What did we do?"

He shook his head. "I cannot answer your questions. All I know is that remembering you gives me…feelings. Like when a little of the music drifts into my mind."

"What kind of music?"

"With many instruments. Complex. Blending. Trumpets. Cellos. The music swells and dies down."

"A symphony?"

"Maybe."

She watched the play of emotions on his face as he stood very still, staring into space. "Before you came here, the music was the most vivid. But with you, it is even stronger."

She tried to imagine the deprivation of being cut

off from her past—of snatching at bits of memory or making them up to fill a black void in her mind. Was he cursed with complete amnesia except for a few sensory memories? Or did he recall basic facts about history and other subjects?

"Who was president before John Kennedy?" she asked.

"Dwight Eisenhower. The first president was George Washington. The second was John Adams. The third—"

"You know all of them?"

"Yes."

Amazed, she came up with a more difficult question. "Can you name the countries on the continent of Africa?"

He began to tick them off, until she stopped him again. She didn't know many of the places he'd named.

She switched from geography to biology to math, and he answered all her questions brilliantly. Then she threw a personal one into the mix.

"Where were you born?" she asked.

He hesitated for several seconds, then shook his head.

"What's the first thing you remember about your life here?"

"Watching Swinton and Anderson in the research center." His face hardened, and he didn't elaborate.

She hated to get into deeper water, yet she wanted to trigger recollections—and emotional responses. "When was the first time Beckton hit you?"

"He slapped my face on the rifle range. He was angry because I failed a qualification test. But I missed the target because somebody had bent the gun-sight.''

''Who would do that?''

''Someone who wants to stop Project Sandstorm.''

''Who?''

He shrugged.

''How do you know?'' she demanded.

''Things happen. Colonel Emerson gets angry and announces new procedures.''

''What other things have happened?''

''A man was killed. The chief of security. His name was Fenton.''

She drew in a sharp breath. ''How was he killed?''

''I heard them talking about it. He fell off a roof. Winslow thought he was pushed. And McCourt took over.''

So that was why a guy in his thirties had such an important position, she thought, struggling to take in the implications.

''Do you know anything else about it?''

When he shook his head, she sighed. He might not have any more information about the security chief, but his own life was a different matter. ''The incident with the gun? When did it happen?''

''Time...I did not think about time at first,'' he answered slowly. ''I think it was some months ago.''

Her mind was starting to overload. She had wanted information about him, about this place. But his simple answers were providing more than she could handle.

Who was he? What was his background? How had he ended up at Stratford Creek? In her mind, she visualized him as he had looked when he first came out of the shower. He was all lean muscle and sinew, and unblemished skin, except for the recent injuries. If he'd been a criminal before coming here, it didn't show.

"Your face looks strange. What thoughts are in your mind?" he asked.

She felt herself blush. "I was remembering how your body looked after your shower."

"Why does that make your face red?"

"Social conventions," she answered. "It's not exactly polite to think about another person with no clothes on—and admit it to him."

"I think about you that way."

"Oh." She flushed again and fumbled for another topic. "Tell me about your assignment."

He didn't answer.

"What are you supposed to do?" she asked, her hand tightening on his arm.

"I cannot talk about that."

"Why?"

His gaze slid away from hers, and she sensed that he didn't want to tell her the answer.

"You must go," he said suddenly. "You should not be with me. Alone. You will get into trouble."

"How do you know that?"

"The same way I knew about Major Fenton. I hear people talk. I listen to what they say. Granger and Winslow were laughing about your assignment checking personnel records. Winslow called it shoveling chicken guano."

She nodded. Probably they talked in front of him quite a bit without realizing how much he was taking in.

"Dr. Kolb will come back."

"Where is he?"

"He was called away. I was waiting for him. You came instead."

She wondered if someone had sent the doctor a note—like the one she had received.

"Go," Hunter said.

She raised her face toward his. "Do you want me to leave?"

A shadow crossed his eyes. "I made the mistake of wanting something from you before."

The look and the words made her heart clench. In this little room, she had created the illusion of privacy, just as she'd imagined they wouldn't be disturbed in the locker room.

But the same conditions prevailed as the last time they'd talked. Someone could come in at any time. And this time Hunter wouldn't be the only target. This time she'd get a reprimand—or worse—for disobeying Emerson's orders.

In the locker room, she had told Hunter she would help him. With all her heart, she longed to assure him that none of the unspeakable things they'd done to him would ever happen again. More than that, she wanted to tell him that she would help him get his memory back. That he would be whole again. Yet she'd come to realize that she couldn't say any of that. If she gave him assurances, they would be lies. And the worst thing she could do was lie to him.

"If you are my friend, Kathryn Kelley, please go away!" His voice was harsh.

She knew he was right, at least for now. Unable to look into his eyes, she turned and hurried across the little room, feeling his gaze burning into her back all the way to the door.

By the time she had left the building, she had made

a decision. She was going to force a confrontation with Emerson. But half a block away, she pulled the car under the shade of a maple tree. It would be stupid to charge half-cocked into Emerson's office without first understanding her goals and thinking clearly about what she wanted to say. More importantly, she had to regain control of her emotions. When she reached into her pocket book for a tissue, she found the medical forms.

Stupid, she thought. Very stupid.

She returned to the medical center, and when the nurse at the front desk looked up inquiringly, she slapped the papers onto the desk. "I forgot these."

Thirty seconds later, she was out of the building again and looking up and down the sidewalk to see if anyone was watching. Luck seemed to be with her. What she wanted was to give Hunter back a normal life. However, she suspected Emerson didn't give a damn about that. He and the rest of the staff thought of Hunter as the subject of an experiment. They were training him for a dangerous assignment, and they wanted her to help make sure he completed it successfully. Somehow she had to make it seem as if her private agenda meshed with her official duties.

And maybe she had an ally, she thought, as she remembered the note. Someone who had been willing to give her the gift of a few minutes alone with Hunter. She considered the senior staff, pondering the possibilities, but could come up with no obvious candidates. Some of them seemed in favor of her working with Hunter. Some had voiced opposition. But she couldn't be absolutely sure which men were revealing their real feelings and which ones were secretly glad she'd been assigned to "shoveling chicken guano."

The only thing she knew for sure was that whoever had left the note was afraid to come out into the open.

Which only reinforced the growing realization that both she and Hunter were in a precarious position. Every contact with him made her more sure that the story about his criminal background was a convenient fiction. If she operated on that premise, the logical way to help him was to bring back his buried memories by finding touchstones to his past and using them to trigger remembered responses. And if they'd made it impossible for him to remember his past life, at least teaching him about social norms would help him cope when he finally got out of this place.

The plan had a certain elegance, and she found herself with a genuine smile on her face for the first time since she'd arrived at Stratford Creek.

She took it as a good omen when she stepped into the anteroom to Emerson's office and saw that the tough-as-nails secretary was away from her desk.

"Sir?" she called, as she knocked on his door. "Mr. Emerson, I need to speak to you. And—"

The door flew open, and she found herself facing Chip McCourt.

Their gazes locked, and she thought for a moment that he was going to bar her way. Instead he stepped aside and ushered her into Emerson's office.

"Did you get my message?" the man behind the desk asked.

She came to a jerky stop two feet inside the room. Was Emerson the one who'd left the note on her car? As soon as the idea surfaced, she dismissed it as wishful thinking. If he'd wanted to contact her secretly, he'd hardly be talking about it in front of McCourt.

Without waiting for a reply, the chief of operations

waved her toward one of the guest chairs. "I received an updated copy of your clearance this morning." He thumped a folder that sat in the middle of his desk blotter. "We've been trying to track you down so we could discuss your assignment."

"Good," she answered, striving for composure as she lowered herself into the seat. She'd come prepared to do battle. Now she needed to tone down her approach.

"You were supposed to be working on performance appraisals. Where were you?" McCourt asked.

She turned toward him, and made eye contact. "Dropping off my medical forms."

He nodded curtly, and she was sure he was going to check up on her. Thank God she'd remembered to leave the forms.

"The senior staff have been discussing how you might instill some of the social graces in...Hunter," Emerson said. "Dr. Kolb picked up on what you said at the meeting about most individuals learning to interact with other people in a home environment."

Kathryn tried to conceal her surprise. "Dr. Kolb?" she asked.

"He wondered if you'd be willing to take on that role with our subject."

"What role, exactly?" she asked cautiously.

"Providing a homelike atmosphere for him. I've been studying your professional background carefully, and I see you did an internship at an inner-city home for runaways."

"Yes."

"In many ways, Hunter is like an undisciplined teenager. At least in his emotional development. I think you could be very effective with him."

"I hope so," she responded, still trying to figure out where he was headed.

"What if we moved him into the guest cottage where you're already living? You could have access to him before and after the regular training day and when he has a break from other activities. Socialization lessons might fit naturally into that kind of arrangement."

She tried not to smile. Emerson was offering her more than she would have dared to ask for.

"That sounds highly unorthodox, but it might be a very effective arrangement," she managed in a professional tone. "I'd be able to teach social skills and reinforce them over an extended period."

"Don't minimize the risk to yourself," McCourt interjected. "We can give you a beeper to sound an alarm if you get into trouble. And we can have men stationed near the house. But we can't guarantee he won't fly off the handle."

"Hunter won't hurt me," she said with conviction. She'd just given him the perfect opportunity to assault her, and he'd acted with a lot more civility than the security forces "And if guards are looking over our shoulders, we won't make much progress." She thought for a moment, remembering the comments about the surveillance system in the locker room being disabled. "And no microphones either."

Emerson looked uncomfortable. "Okay," he agreed in a flat voice.

McCourt gave her a wry look, but said nothing.

"Of course, I want to see some quantifiable progress," Emerson interjected. "I want a report from you on my desk after the first week."

"A week isn't much time," she countered.

"I insist on results. Or we try another approach."

Beat socialization into him? Drown him until he saw things their way? She refrained from asking the sarcastic questions.

She wasn't sure if she'd won a major victory or stepped into a carefully constructed trap, but she allowed herself to be cautiously optimistic as the three of them discussed details. Still, she didn't relax. Perhaps Dr. Kolb had come up with the idea because he expected her to fail and get thrown off the project.

Afterward, when she left the building with McCourt, he asked, "So are you going to function as his mommy or his wife in this little domestic drama?"

"His sister," she shot back.

"Ah."

"You don't think it's a good plan?"

"It's not my place to make that kind of judgment."

She wanted to say she was glad of that. Instead she tried a friendly, "I'll let you know how things go."

"Your report will make interesting reading."

"I hope so."

Back at the cottage, Kathryn inventoried the kitchen supplies, then drove to the small shopping center on the grounds to buy some groceries. Apparently Kolb had even suggested that she prepare meals for Hunter. Maybe he'd expected her to back down on menial work, but she didn't mind a little cooking.

As she circled the parking lot, she mentally reviewed the meeting in Emerson's office. Really, it was stupefying that he'd allowed her such unrestricted access to Hunter. Either he had enormous confidence in her. Or...

She deliberately shut off the disturbing speculations.

Inside the store, she showed the temporary card she'd been given to the woman checking IDs. Apparently her credentials hadn't been activated in the computer because the gatekeeper wouldn't let her enter.

"I'm afraid you'll have to step into the office," the woman said.

Kathryn tried to keep the annoyance out of her voice. "I'm in a hurry. I was told I could get some groceries here."

"We can't let you through without verification."

"What's your name?" Kathryn asked.

"Miss Collins."

"Well, Miss Collins, why don't you call William Emerson's office. I was just there."

"We don't call the chief of operations about a matter like this," the woman said firmly. "We check with personnel," the woman said firmly.

"Is there somewhere else I can shop?"

"I believe you're temporarily restricted to the facilities here."

She'd pushed that out of her mind. With a sigh of resignation, she took a seat in the small office. Half an hour later, she was impatiently tapping her foot when Miss Collins reappeared, all smiles.

"Sorry to hold you up," she said sweetly. "Go on in."

By the time Kathryn was finally allowed to make her purchases, she was fighting off the paranoid feeling that the delay was deliberate, although she couldn't imagine why.

When she arrived back at the cottage, it was four in the afternoon, yet it looked much later, she thought, as she eyed the dark clouds filling the sky.

Suspecting they were in for a thunderstorm, she quickly carried the groceries into the kitchen. She had just stuck a package of steak into the freezer when she thought she detected a noise from the back of the house. She strained her ears, trying to determine if she'd really heard anything or if her overactive imagination was playing tricks.

At first there was nothing more. Then a new sound drifted toward her, a scuffling noise followed by a loud thump like a body hitting the floor.

Was someone in the house?

She hurried through the dining room and toward the back rooms. It took only seconds to gain the unlit hall, where she was forced to come to a halt as she confronted the three closed doors. She'd left her bedroom door open; now it was shut.

Her hand froze as she heard a guttural exclamation from behind the door. Pulling it open, she saw the figure of a man standing in the middle of the darkened room, swaying on his feet as he faced the open sliding glass door.

Hearing her, he whirled, and she registered that it was him—dressed in the same clothes he'd been wearing earlier—even as he closed the distance between them in a few menacing strides.

She knew, then, that she'd been a fool not to fear him. He had put Beckton in the hospital. Now there was only coldness in his eyes as he looked at *her*.

He reached her before she could run and threw his weight roughly against her shoulder.

"Don't—" she managed as he backed her against the wall. She struck it with a thud that made the breath whoosh out of her lungs.

Chapter Five

In the moments before his hands closed around her flesh, he realized who she was. Stopping the forward motion of his body, he was able to keep from slamming her into the wall with the force he'd intended. Still, he heard the breath hiss painfully out of her lungs.

It was Kathryn Kelley. The woman with the soft voice and the kind eyes that promised too much. The woman who had come into the locker room and made him vulnerable so the security force could grab him.

In the medical center she'd said she was sorry and she'd made him believe her—again. Now here she was for the second time in the same day. And he'd come very close to killing her.

Perhaps his encounters with her were part of some new test, one more dangerous than all the others Swinton's and Beckton's staffs had devised.

Only seconds had passed as his hand shifted over Kathryn Kelley's mouth while he held her in place with the weight of his body against hers. But he had to make a decision quickly, he realized, as his eyes flicked to the sliding glass door.

Two minutes ago an intruder had come through that

door. A man with a hood over his face, wearing black clothing and carrying a gun—which was now somewhere on the floor.

How did Kathryn Kelley fit into this particular scenario? Who had sent her? She said she wanted to help him. But it was dangerous to trust the words—or the look in her eyes. Or the vague memories of her from before Stratford Creek.

He could kill her easily, he knew, as he contemplated the slender column of her neck. Beckton and his team had taught him the skills he would need to kill with speed and efficiency—although they hadn't yet put him to the test. Perhaps they wanted to find out if he would do it now. Or perhaps it was part of a different plan. An unofficial plan. Like the time the trail markers had been switched in the woods, and he'd almost tumbled off a cliff.

He didn't know who had devised this scenario. He only knew the thought of killing Kathryn Kelley brought a wave of physical sickness. Was she a danger to him? Systematically he began to search along her body, feeling for the telltale bulge of a gun or the outline of a knife.

He heard her make a strangled sound as his hand paused to explore the rounded swell of a soft breast and the edge of her undergarment where she might have tucked a small weapon.

A routine search. But nothing with her had been routine. Not the things they'd talked about—or the strange surge of unexpected heat that coursed through him as his hands learned her shape. He had thought about her body, imagined it in vivid detail. He had wanted to touch her. Closing his eyes, he inhaled her scent and let it flow through him.

He blinked. What was wrong with him? Every time he encountered this woman, she reached him in strange, unexpected ways. And the images of her in his head—images from before Stratford Creek—grew more tantalizing. More real. He grimaced, torn between hopes and fears he had never known before.

With a jerky motion, he pulled his hips away from hers as his hand moved on, along her ribs, to her waist where he found a rectangle of plastic nestled against soft flesh. An alarm. With a growl, he yanked it free.

"No." She spoke the syllable against the fingers that pressed over her mouth, sending a vivid communication along his nerve endings.

Ignoring her protest and his physical reaction, he tossed the device onto the bed, where she couldn't reach it. Had Emerson issued it, or was she working for someone else?

He made an angry sound. He had told her someone wanted to stop Project Sandstorm. That had been a mistake. Would it also be a mistake to take his hand away from her mouth? Would she scream at the top of her lungs?

As his mind made rapid evaluations, his searching hand began to move again, continued down her body, lingering at the places where a weapon might be concealed and other places, too. Flare of hip, silky skin of thigh, delicate structure of knee. The touch of her flesh scalded his fingertips so that by the time he finished, his heart was pounding and he was struggling to breathe normally.

So was she. Did she feel what he did—the strange combination of weakness and strength that swirled within him when he touched her—or was she only afraid of what he might do to her?

What he or anybody else felt had never been of much concern to him. Tonight, feelings overwhelmed him. All his training urged caution. Yet there was no way of knowing where caution lay.

Kill her. Let her run to whoever had sent her. Or hold her within reach and ask his own questions—the way she had questioned him this afternoon.

He had never felt less sure. The right course of action escaped him, but he knew on some deep, instinctive level that he wanted to keep her close by his side. The scene in the locker room flashed into his mind again. Then her apology in the medical center. No one had ever made excuses to him for their behavior before.

But what did her words really mean? What would she say when he was the one in control?

Before he could change his mind, he dragged her toward the sliding glass doors. When she tried to struggle, he brought his lips close to her ear and growled, "If you do not want to get hurt, be still."

She obeyed at once, although he knew she could simply be waiting for a better opportunity to get away. Or to kill him. They had warned him women could be trained to kill. Perhaps she was only looking for the right opportunity to turn the tables.

Taking the chance, he lifted her over the threshold and carried her into the area behind the house, where tall trees had grown. Beeches, maples and wild cherries made a thick screen, hiding the two of them from view.

The branches were shivering in the wind, and dark clouds blocked out the sun, signaling the approach of a storm. If she screamed, the wind might hide the sound.

As soon as he was certain they were alone, he removed the hand from her mouth, tensing for her reaction.

Her eyes were wide and round as she focused all her attention on him. Her pale skin was as white as the chalk Beckton used on the blackboard. He watched her suck in a ragged breath and let it out slowly. Nervously, her hand went to her hair, pushing it away from her face, then patting it into place.

His breath was almost as uneven as hers as he waited, knowing he was taking the greatest risk of his life.

KATHRYN THOUGHT about running, but she forced herself to remain where she was, standing under the wind-tossed trees, facing the man who had slammed her against the wall, covered her mouth with his hand, searched her intimately. After each of their previous meetings, she'd convinced herself that she understood him—that he was a normal man forced into a diabolical experiment. As she cowered before him now, the criminal theory suddenly made a lot more sense. When she'd come into the bedroom, he had reacted with the instinctive ferocity of a cornered tiger. And she knew from the obdurate look in his eyes that if she made the wrong move, he was still poised for violence.

Yet as she faced him across three feet of dry leaves and the scraggly grass that grew under the trees, she could come up with an equally plausible theory. He had been normal and reasonable until Emerson and Swinton had wiped out his memory. Now he was simply reacting in the way he'd been trained. Unfortunately, that made the situation no less dangerous. She was still his captive, at his mercy.

"Why have you brought me out here?" she asked, trying to keep her tone even as she pressed her fingers against the rough bark of a tree trunk.

"So we can talk. There will be microphones or cameras in the house."

"Emerson promised we would have privacy."

"Do you believe everything he says?"

The only honest answer was, "No."

"He might think he's telling the truth. And someone else could be listening," Hunter suggested.

"Who?"

He answered with his own question. "Are you working with the man who tried to kill me?"

"Somebody tried to kill you? Who? When?"

"A few minutes ago. He came in through the sliding door in the bedroom. He thought I was asleep. He was wrong."

"Is that what I heard?" she managed. "You were fighting him off?"

"Yes. He dropped his gun on the floor. Are you working with him?" he repeated, watching her face carefully.

"No."

His eyes told her he wanted to believe her. They also told her he hadn't made up his mind.

"I wouldn't lie to you, Hunter," she said in as steady a voice as she could manage.

Once again, his face softened for a moment at the use of his name. Then his fierce expression was back in place, still challenging her. "Give me reasons to trust you. Why was I taken to the guest cottage and told to wait in the bedroom for further orders? What are you doing here with me?''

She couldn't hide her shock. "They didn't tell you anything else?"

When he shook his head, she hastened to explain. "Dr. Kolb thought that if you and I spent some time together, I could teach you things you need to know."

"What am I supposed to learn from you? Are you a weapons expert?"

She laughed, feeling a tiny glimmer of relief from her tension. "No. I'm a psychologist."

"Why do you keep coming to me?"

"I—" She swallowed. "I was hired to teach you socialization skills. Things you need to know to get along with other people. We would have started working together sooner, but some of the people here were against it."

He made a snorting sound. "They pretend they are all united, but they all have their own agendas."

She nodded, surprised by his perceptiveness. For a man with no memories, he was functioning on a very sophisticated level.

"You asked me to pick a name. Why do you care about that?" he suddenly asked.

"Everyone has a name. You need the same things other people need."

"Do I? What are those things?" he asked thoughtfully, as if he were considering the concept for the first time.

"People need to feel good about themselves. About their jobs. Their lives. They need to do things that make them happy. They need to love and be loved."

"I am good at my job. I do not need the rest of it," he answered, his tone blunt.

The denial—both the words and the staccato way he delivered them—tore at her. "What have they done to you?" she asked in a strangled voice.

He shrugged. She had come to hate that shrug.

But it wasn't as disturbing as his face, which looked as bleak as it had in the video—when he'd lain beside the water tank, half drowned. He'd reached out for help, and no one had come to him. Not this time. Gently, she laid her hand on his arm.

Around them, the wind roared, and she knew the storm would break any moment.

His muscles flexed, yet he didn't pull away. He'd said he never lied. Maybe not about facts. Yet despite his rough denial, she was utterly convinced that he needed the same things other people needed. She was equally sure he had long ago given up trying to ask for them.

She might have held him and rocked him the way a mother rocks a child. But he wasn't a child. He was a strong, dangerous man, trained in the craft of violence. And she needed to know more about him. Without breaking the physical contact, she went back to another topic he'd avoided earlier.

"Why won't you tell me about your assignment? About Project Sandstorm?"

"I cannot." He dragged in a deep breath and let it out in a rush as he looked at her. "There are questions you should not ask me."

"Why?"

"You said you are my friend. I want—" He stopped abruptly, and she understood that admitting he wanted anything from her was still too big a risk.

The knowledge made her throat ache. It seemed he had secrets, things that he didn't want her to know because he thought she would think less of him. But that was good, she silently added. It meant he wasn't as closed up as he pretended.

She wouldn't ask about his secrets. Not yet. Not until he trusted her enough. "It's not your fault," she whispered. "All the bad things they've done to you."

"It must be," he said in a strangled voice.

"No."

He turned his face away from her, and she sensed that he'd kept himself alive and sane in this place by hiding his doubts and fears, trusting no one. God, what an existence, she thought as she stared at the stiff, unyielding set of his shoulders.

"Don't."

"Don't what?" he asked, without looking at her.

There were no words to express all the things she wanted to tell him. Blindly she reached toward him, holding him close to her as if she could lock the horror of Stratford Creek away.

At first his body was rigid, then, as she ran her hands over the taut muscles of his back, he sighed and relaxed into the shelter of her arms.

She held him for long moments, feeling him let go of the wariness heartbeat by heartbeat. When he spoke, it was in a barely audible voice. "I saw two people like this. Outside, in the woods. A man and a woman holding each other, touching lips. It made me feel...strange to watch. I felt it again when I touched you."

He lifted his face and stared down at her, a deeply intense expression on his face. A millimeter at a time, he lowered his head and brushed his mouth softly, experimentally against hers.

She didn't move, couldn't move. She could only

stand there feeling the gentle pressure of his warm lips on hers, enjoying the contact on a level that went beyond the physical. She had told herself that he needed her. It seemed that in this place of evil, she needed him as well.

He raised his face a fraction, looking down at her as if he couldn't believe she was embracing him.

She gave him a little smile.

"He touched her hair," he said, imitating the gesture, his fingers stroking through her tresses as he made a low sound of pleasure. "Your hair looks like fire. But it does not burn. It prickles. Not just on my fingers but other places."

Pull away from him, she told herself. Yet she couldn't let go.

She had taken a job at Stratford Creek because she thought she'd be safe on a secure government installation. Every moment here had added new levels of turmoil to the chaos of her life. And it seemed the only person who had touched her on a human level was this man, whom everyone else treated like an outcast.

His fingers skimmed her face, the column of her neck, gently, so gently. "You are not afraid of me." He said it in wonder.

"Should I be?"

"Yes."

"Why?"

"I could hurt you."

"But you've shown me that you won't," she said with absolute conviction.

His lips came back to hers, the pressure harder, more insistent. There was no finesse to the kiss, only an unschooled urgency that was strangely exciting.

She kissed him back, her own lips parting to capture the taste of him more fully.

She heard him make a rough sound in his throat as his fingertips traced along the line of her neck and over her collarbone.

"Good. That feels good," he said in a thick voice. "Like the memory of you."

Yes, the memory. She still didn't understand how she and this man who had named himself Hunter were tied together. Yet as they stood here touching and kissing, it was hard to doubt there was an unexplained link between them. Perhaps destiny had brought them together.

His lips captured hers again, made a bolder foray that set up little currents along her nerve endings. When the kiss ended, she moved her head against his shoulder. She was drifting, letting things happen, letting her response build because he was right, it felt good.

But when he let his hand drift lower to softly trace the rounded swell of her breast and brush across the hardened tip, her eyes snapped open. She had been lulled into a state of self-indulgence, and she had let this go far beyond the bounds of what was right. "No." The denial came out high and shaky.

He raised his head, his eyes questioning hers.

"We can't do that," she said, still unable to bring her voice under control.

"Why not?" he asked. "It feels good." He searched her face. "You said people should do things that make them feel happy." The word came from his mouth haltingly, as though he were speaking a foreign language.

"Yes. But there are limits—conventions." She felt trapped in a tangle of words.

"You didn't like it?"

She had promised not to lie to him. She wouldn't do it now. And she wouldn't lie to herself. "I liked it," she said in a whisper.

"Yes. I can see it. Your face has a wonderful color to it now. And your eyes are softer."

She felt more blood rush to the surface of her skin.

"It feels bad to stop," he said in a harsh voice. "We should do more."

She shook her head, trying to remember that she was supposed to be in control of this situation. "The man and woman you saw were lovers."

He thought about that for several seconds.

Then a look of comprehension dawned on his face. "They were going to join their bodies? Here?" He reached down and gestured toward the rigid flesh that swelled at the front of his sweatpants.

She nodded, trying not to feel the words in her center. "How do you know about that?"

"The On-Line Encyclopedia."

She made a strangled exclamation.

"And the men talk about sex. They boast about the women they have. I would never talk about you. Never," he added with strong conviction.

"I know."

"In the locker room, you said we were friends. Can friends do it?" he asked.

She shook her head. It was growing dark around them, yet she saw his eyes close and his face contort in disappointment.

How had all this happened so quickly, she wondered, reeling from an onslaught of emotions. He might have no memories of social interaction, but she should have had more sense than to allow such intimacy.

"I must not touch you now," he said before taking a step back.

He looked as if every bone and muscle of his body ached. She might have turned away to cut off her own sense of regret, instead she stared at him, still feeling the imprint of his touch on her body. She had to think, yet thinking had become almost impossible.

She was suddenly aware that the air had grown heavy with the smell of rain. Leaves had begun to fly through the air. Before she could figure out what to say, a crack of lightning pierced the darkness.

"It is not safe here," he said. "Lightning could strike one of the trees. We must go back."

CAMERON RANDOLPH paced to the window, then turned and started back across the room. Jo watched him, sharing his frustration. For the past few days they'd been trying to figure out a way to get a message to Kathryn. So far nothing had panned out.

They had never gotten through to her on the phone. She had answered no letters. And every chatty E-mail message to her old address had been rejected.

In desperation, they'd tried putting a short, coded message inside the label of a bottle of face cream, which they'd mailed to her with a selection of cosmetics she'd supposedly asked Jo to send. The innocent-looking package had been returned—with the contents damaged.

"Did you manage to talk to William Emerson?" Jo asked.

"Bill. He insists on Bill," Cameron replied.

"Funny thing, the colonel asked me dozens of penetrating questions about Kathryn's qualifications and her background when he wanted to hire her. Today he spared me about sixty seconds."

"And?"

"He told me she's fitting right in with the research personnel."

"Glad to hear it." Jo pressed her hands against her hips. "Could you get him to tell you what she's doing?"

"No," Cam answered bluntly. He was wishing that he'd told Emerson that Kathryn's work was unsatisfactory when they'd talked the first time.

"Could we sneak into Stratford Creek with an assault team and bust her out of there?" Jo asked.

"Not a good idea. Raiding a top secret U.S. government research facility is an invitation to a hanging—or a media circus of a trial."

"I suppose you're right."

"All we can do is sit tight and wait for her to contact us."

Jo drew in a tight breath. "If she can."

TAKING KATHRYN'S HAND, Hunter tugged her across the backyard.

Although a few drops of rain had already started to fall, she stopped him when they reached the sliding glass door. He had told her the rooms might be bugged. Since she had to assume he was right, they'd better finish their conversation before they went inside.

The wind whipped at her hair, and lightning split the sky again. The storm was moving closer, judging by the almost instant crack of thunder.

Then, as if a sluice gate had opened, the rain began to fall. He looked at her questioningly.

"Wait," she said, grabbing his arm.

He turned his back to the storm, sheltering her between his body and the door. Yet his hands stayed at his sides. She wanted those arms around her, for warmth, for comfort. She was sure he wanted it, too. But she didn't ask him to hold her, because she understood that touching him now was playing with fire.

The water pelted down as she leaned toward him and brought her mouth close to his ear. "Before we go in I have to ask you a question. Can you and I keep secrets together, just the two of us?"

Lightning knifed through the sky. She had to wait through the sound of the thunder before he answered, "The staff give me orders, and I must obey. You are on the staff. If you give me an order, it is the same."

She clenched her fists. The more she heard about what they'd done to him, the more she wondered how she was going to cope with her anger. She didn't want to give him orders, but in this case it appeared to be necessary.

"All right," she said. "I order you to keep the things that have passed between us tonight confidential."

"I can do that."

Again she made herself think about what that meant—from his point of view. "I mean you should not tell anyone about the things we said tonight. Or that you and I are friends. Emerson and Swinton might not like it."

He nodded slowly. "I will keep the things between the two of us private. What we said to each other—and the kissing."

She managed a neutral nod. "Good."

"I do not want to share this with the others." His hand turned upward. "Even…even after they came with the tranquilizer gun, I wanted to believe you were my friend."

She closed her eyes for a moment, unable to speak without a hitch in her voice. Perhaps he didn't know it, but he had just given her what she wanted most— his trust. It took all her willpower not to reach for him again. Instead she took one last breath of the cold night air and stepped through the doorway.

He followed her inside, and when she turned she saw the dark hair plastered to his head and the strong lines of his body through the clinging fabric of his sweat clothes. He had kept her dry, but he was soaked.

"You should take a shower and put on dry clothes," she said.

His lips quirked. She wanted to see him smile, but she contented herself with what he could give.

"What are you thinking?" she asked.

"That I will not walk out of the bathroom naked."

"So I've already taught you something," she said, keeping her tone light.

"Yes. You should shower, too." He paused, thought for a moment. "You can go first."

"I'm all right. You protected me."

"It felt like the right thing to do." He shook his head. "I do not always know the right thing."

She brushed back a lock of wet hair that had fallen across his forehead. "You have good instincts." She wanted to tell him that he might be subconsciously remembering things from his past. Yet she was aware that what she said now might be overheard. She hadn't been hired to stir up his memories.

"What does that mean—good instincts?" he asked.

She drew her hand back. "It means you don't necessarily know in advance, but when the situation presents itself, you do the right thing."

"That sounds dangerous—not knowing in advance." He stopped short, and she wondered if he was thinking about the way he'd reacted when she first came into the room.

"Trust your instincts," she said.

To her surprise, he nodded. Then his face hardened. Pulling away from her, he knelt beside the bed. She watched as he began to search the floor. Reaching far under the bed, he pulled out an automatic pistol and held it up for her to see. The barrel was elongated, and she decided there must be a silencer attached, although she'd never seen one before except in a movie or on TV.

She'd forgotten he'd said his attacker had a gun. Now she reached out a hand to steady herself against the bureau as she wondered what they were going to do with the weapon.

He stood and reached for her free arm, holding her as he brought his lips close to her ear, the way she'd spoken outside. "My instincts tell me something...bad."

She waited, feeling the hold on her arm tighten.

"I thought the man who came into the house wanted to kill me," he whispered. "Perhaps I was mistaken about the target."

She wasn't following him. When she gave him a questioning look, he continued in a low, urgent voice. "In my training, we do scenarios."

Still mystified, she shrugged elaborately.

"Hypothetical situations," he murmured, so low she could barely catch the words and had to lean toward his mouth. "They put me into circumstances where I must respond to danger. Suppose the man who dropped the gun attacked me because he wanted to set up a scenario where he would escape and I would be on guard against attack—and kill the next person who came into the room. You."

Chapter Six

Kathryn felt an involuntary shiver go through her. He'd given her an elaborate theory—perhaps a combination of instinct, logic and recent experience, she thought, with as much detachment as she could muster. She wanted to dismiss the idea as far-fetched. Instead, she absorbed it with a kind of sick awareness. He could be right.

She saw he was watching her, watching her reaction.

"I am sorry," he said in a low voice. "I could be wrong. I should not have said it."

She shook her head. "You did the right thing. I need to understand the situation here."

He gave her a tight nod. After a little hesitation, he slipped his arm around her shoulder and held her to his side. Once again she needed his strength. When she relaxed against him, he touched her hair, and she allowed herself the luxury of closing her eyes.

"You should leave," he said. Again the words were barely audible.

"Leave the house?" she asked.

"Leave Stratford Creek, if they will let you."

Her eyes blinked open. "What?"

"The situation here is—it is not safe for you. I heard McCourt and Winslow talking about you. Using foul words. Beckton came in and told them to shut up. He was afraid someone might hear. They shut up, but they do not like having you interfering. They thought they were doing fine without you."

She brought her mouth close to his ear. "I'm not going to leave you."

He turned his head, his eyes searching hers for confirmation, and she realized at that moment she had made a commitment.

Her lips skimmed his cheek. "I mean it," she whispered.

His arms tightened on her. It was both an awkward and an intimate way to have a conversation. Holding each other close. Moving their heads so that they took turns feeling the other's warm breath against their ears.

"Why?" he asked.

As she clung to him for support, she tried to think of what to say. "We are friends. Friends help each other."

"Yes. I will protect you—if I can."

Again, he had spoken a simple truth, without censoring his words, and she realized he was making his own commitment.

"Friends," he murmured, as if savoring the idea. Yet there was a kind of sadness in his eyes, too. She was vividly aware that his lips were inches from hers, that he was staring at them with suppressed intensity. If she turned, if he turned, her breasts would be pressed against his chest and his mouth would touch hers. They both stood rigid as the moment stretched.

Once again she wondered if they were feeling the tug of a mythical past neither of them could remember.

"I wish—" he said, his voice hoarse.

"What?"

Without answering, he took a step back, breaking the contact.

She needed his warmth. More than that, she desperately needed to continue the discussion. There was so much to say. And so much to find out. But they could neither go out into the pelting rain to talk nor continue like this, because the heat building between them would reach flash point. After taking a little breath, she gave him a steady look, then raised her voice for the benefit of whoever might be listening. "Right now, we're going to get ready for supper."

"Supper? What is the difference between supper and dinner?" he asked, taking his cue from her without missing a beat.

She managed a strained laugh. "It's a subtle distinction. Supper is usually less elaborate." Turning she made a quick exit from the room, and after putting on dry clothes she went back to the kitchen. Unpacking the groceries gave her some sense of regaining control.

As she put the food away, she could hear Hunter showering. When she looked up a few minutes later, he had silently crossed the living room. He was dressed in dry jeans and another knit shirt, his hair still damp.

"Hi," she said.

"Hi." He stood very still, taking her in, and she suspected he'd been half thinking she would disappear while he was in the shower.

"I'm still here," she said, watching the color in his cheeks deepen.

He nodded, holding her eyes for several more seconds before taking in their surroundings. All at once he was like an archaeologist examining an ancient Roman city. He pondered the furniture, flipped the television off and on and studied the shelves along one wall that held books and a strange assortment of knickknacks. He picked up a small stuffed alligator, turning it one way and then the other in his hands.

"What is this for?" he asked.

"It might be a child's toy. Or a souvenir from a trip."

"But what is the use?"

"Some people like to stroke the fur. It makes them calm."

He nodded, his finger brushing the green plush. "It feels good, like—" He stopped, his gaze skimming over her hair. "It should be red."

She lowered her gaze to the box of pasta in her hand.

He moved farther into the room, testing the weight of a metal candlestick, touching the raised flower pattern on a lamp base.

Everything here was normal, ordinary. Nothing special. Yet the cottage was a novelty in his limited experience. It seemed Dr. Kolb had made a shrewd proposal. Simply taking Hunter out of his sterile environment was expanding his horizons.

She had impulsively bought a bouquet of pink and white carnations and set them on the dining-room table. Hunter studied them from several angles, touched the petals, bent closer.

"They're just to make the table look pretty." She

anticipated his question. "Make the meal more festive."

He bent to smell them again. "On television, I have seen people living in houses like this. With flowers and the other things."

"Do you watch much television?"

"No. Colonel Emerson thinks it is a bad influence."

"Why do you call him 'Colonel'?" she asked, casually.

"I think of him that way—as a soldier. A lot of the men do, too."

Maybe they'd served with him, she thought. Or maybe he wasn't as retired as he'd claimed.

"Um. Well, he's probably right about TV," she said. "Except for a few good shows, it's superficial. Silly. It plays to people with low tastes."

"Like the men on the training staff."

She laughed. "You're perceptive."

He chewed on that for a while, then asked, "Where do you live?"

"In Baltimore."

He moved on to the kitchen, opening cabinets, taking out packages of food and examining them. After sticking his finger into a jar of mustard and stealing a taste, he gave her a guilty look.

"That is not polite, is it?" he asked.

"No."

Opening a bottle of vanilla, he contented himself with a deep sniff.

After carefully putting the bottle away, he reminded her that he wasn't simply on a sightseeing trip when he pulled the gun from the waistband of his jeans. Removing the silencer from the barrel, he tucked the weapon into an upper cabinet, in back of a bag of flour.

She wanted to ask why he didn't turn it in. She supposed he thought it might come in handy. And who was going to say it was missing, she asked herself. Not the intruder, unless he'd been acting on official orders.

Careful to hide her state of mind in case somebody was listening, she cleared her throat. "What do you want to eat?"

He turned to look at her, pulling at his earlobe the way he did when he was at a loss for words. "Nobody ever asked that before. They just brought food."

She gave him a quick little smile that was meant to mask the sudden tightness in her chest. "What do you like?"

He thought for a moment, then he answered in a flow of words. "Steak. Baked potato with sour cream. Peanut butter and grape jelly. Once Beckton let me have some potato chips. They were good. We have creamed chipped beef for breakfast sometimes. I like that better than eggs." His eyes took on a dreamy look, the hard planes of his face softened. "Once I had vanilla ice cream with chocolate syrup. Another time I had cherry pie." He stopped abruptly, then added wistfully, "You probably do not have any of those."

The way he said the last part made her eyes sting. "Well, as a matter of fact, I do have some. Most men like steak so I bought it."

"Steak," he repeated with enthusiasm.

Quickly she turned toward the refrigerator, "I have apple pie and vanilla ice cream. And popcorn. I should have gotten potato chips."

"You tried to think of things I would like?" he asked, his voice full of awe.

"Yes."

"Thank you."

"Friends try to please each other," she told him.

"Friends," he echoed.

"Yes. And I brought some music," she added brightly, crossing to the machine. There hadn't been much of a selection, but she'd found the *1812 Overture*. With its stirring themes and pounding rhythms, it should get some kind of response—particularly the cannons firing at the end.

He stood and listened intently for a minute.

"Do you recognize that?" she asked.

He shook his head. "No one here plays that kind of music."

"Do you like it?"

"Yes," he answered, his voice thick and deep.

"I'm glad."

He continued to listen, his face blissful. She might have stood there watching him for a long time. Instead she busied herself with the food preparations, working quickly to keep from weeping. He mustn't see her cry. Mustn't know that she was on the edge of breaking down as she discovered how deeply he responded to a little kindness, a little color in his bleak life.

Hunter moved around the house again, poking into the backs of shelves, looking at each object critically. When he wandered into the hall she lost track of him. Several minutes later he came back to the living room and switched off the music with an expression of grim triumph on his face.

"Don't you like it?"

"I will listen later," he said, and motioned her to follow him. After moving the pan off the burner, she followed him into the hall, where he had opened an access door that she had assumed held the circuit breakers. It did, but below the electrical panel was a niche hidden by a piece of plywood. Hunter removed the wood and gestured toward the interior. "I found another toy," he said.

Inside she saw a small tape recorder.

"What do you think of it?" As he spoke, the tape reels began to move.

"It's not as much fun as the alligator."

His lips quirked, but he didn't speak, and the tape stopped moving. Then he clapped his hands several times, making it move again.

"Understand how it works?" he asked.

She nodded. Apparently it was sound activated—to conserve tape. The spools only moved in response to speech or other noises.

Hunter rewound the tape so that their words would be erased, and replaced the panel. They silently returned to the kitchen. Now she understood that he hadn't simply been curious about the contents of the house. He'd been prospecting for microphones and recording devices—and he'd struck gold.

She hadn't wanted to believe that someone was listening to their every word. Now she felt a kind of sick anger that Emerson had lied to her. Or maybe Hunter was right; maybe it was the work of somebody else.

He cupped his hand around her shoulder, gave her a little squeeze.

She closed her eyes in frustration.

"Can I help you do anything?" he asked.

Her eyes blinked open. If he could function under battlefield conditions, so could she. Giving him a tiny smile, she stood up straighter and led the way back to the dining room. "Supper's almost ready," she said as she moved the laptop computer to the sideboard. "But you could set the table."

"What does that mean?" he asked.

God, she thought, what a mass of contradictions he was. One moment he was engaged in high-tech sleuthing, the next he was totally clueless. "It means laying out the dishes and cutlery."

"Okay."

She found the necessary items in two of the drawers and handed them to him.

He stood beside the table staring at the two place mats she'd put there earlier. For several moments he juggled the cutlery in his hands before starting to arrange the items—first in a line along one side of the table, then in various configurations, each of which he studied critically before beginning to move them around again.

"Is there a way it is supposed to be?" he finally asked.

She instructed him on the finer points of table setting, and he followed her directions.

"Perfect!" she approved. "Wash your hands, and we can eat."

He complied, while she brought their plates to the table.

When he came back, he sat down at once, picked up the hunk of meat off the plate, and began to chew on it.

In the middle of an enormous bite, he stopped and looked at her, watching the way she placed her napkin on her lap and cut off a piece of meat before forking it to her mouth.

"I am doing it wrong," he said in a tight voice. He picked up his knife and fork. "They like to make fun of the way I eat, so I give them a show. I am sorry."

"That's okay," she managed.

He cut off a piece of steak, then dug into the mashed potatoes. "This is…wonderful."

"Thank you." She took another bite, struggling to swallow around the lump in her throat. Everything that she learned about this man set off an emotional reaction.

"Will you tell me about your family?" he asked.

"Yes," she answered, glad of the distraction. "I have a younger sister. My mom's a part-time nurse. My dad retired after forty years as an auto worker. We lived in a suburb of Detroit, so I had a typical middle-American upbringing."

"Tell me the best parts," he whispered.

Her vision turning inward, she tried to capture the flavor of her childhood. She told him about dressing as a princess for Halloween, camping with her family in Canada, winning ribbons in swim meets, and curling up in bed with a purring kitten snuggled beside her.

He sighed. "It sounds like 'Father Knows Best.'"

"That's one of the shows you've watched?"

"Yes. I like it. The people are happy. And the parents help the children solve their problems."

"Well, nobody's life is quite that idyllic. But I guess I was pretty lucky."

"Do you have a husband?" he asked suddenly.

She swallowed. "No, I don't."

"Why not?" he probed, leaning forward across the table.

She thought about it for a minute, trying to give him an honest answer. "I've dated my share of men. But I haven't met anyone who would complete my life the way Mom and Dad did for each other."

He nodded solemnly.

"Maybe I'm asking for too much."

"No. You should have a man who cherishes you, a man who knows how lucky he is to have you for his life companion."

"Maybe some day." With a jerky motion, she picked up her plate and carried it back to the kitchen. After several moments, he came after her and set his plate on the counter next to hers.

Then it was time for apple pie à la mode. The look on his face when he tasted it was angelic, and his sigh of pleasure was almost gale force. "It is fantastic."

"I'm glad you like it."

"It is warm and cool in my mouth at the same time," he enumerated. "And crunchy and gooey and creamy and sweet."

She could only nod, thinking how easy it was to give him a great deal of pleasure.

"Thank you." He concentrated on the pie for several more bites, then looked up. "You have taught me many things today. Can you teach me how to talk like everyone else?"

"What do you mean?"

"My speech is…wrong."

"Not wrong, just a little stiff."

"I know that. I hear it, but I do not know how to correct it."

"It would help if you used contractions."

"What are they?"

"You say 'I do not.' Most people would say 'I don't.'"

"Tell me more of them so I can hear the difference."

She gave him other examples, and he listened intently. After sitting for a while with his brow wrinkled, he asked, "Do you know the rhyme about Peter Piper?"

"Uh-huh."

"Well, *I'm* sure Peter Piper *didn't* pick a peck of pickled peppers because he *hasn't* found the pepper picking pot *that's* lost. *It's* in the toolshed."

She laughed. "That's good!" Impulsively, she reached across the table and pressed her hand over his. He went very still, his eyes lifting to hers. For several heartbeats, he didn't move, then he shifted slightly so that his fingers were pressed to hers along their length.

She felt a strong current flowing between them, a current that increased in intensity as he experimentally stroked her with his fingertips. He wedged his fingers between hers, then inched them up, and she knew from her own reaction he was testing the heated sensations generated by the simple touch.

"Can friends do this?" he said in a thick voice.

She should say no but she couldn't force the syllable out of her mouth as he flattened her palm against the table and delicately stroked it.

Such light contact, really, his hand on hers. Nothing more.

His eyes were closed, his lips slightly parted as if to shut out everything else but the slender link of flesh to flesh. Her own lids fluttered closed as she sat across from him, feeling heat pooling in her body—heat generated simply by his touch on her hand.

Then a noise from the front of the house made them both jump. The front door, she realized with a start as he snatched his hand back and prepared to push himself away from the table. He was looking over her shoulder toward the cabinet where he'd hidden the gun, she realized.

"No," she ordered. "Stay here."

Sam Winslow strode into the room. "What are you doing? Where the hell is the security team that's supposed to be outside?"

Hunter's face went blank as he sat back down in his seat.

Kathryn lifted her face toward the man who had rudely interrupted their supper. "To answer your first question, we're having dessert. Would you like a piece of apple pie?"

Winslow ignored the offer. "Where are the men who are supposed to be stationed here?" he clipped out.

"Perhaps they went to their quarters for dry clothes. But as you can see, we're doing perfectly fine by ourselves."

His gaze shot to Hunter. "He isn't accustomed to these conditions. He could leave."

"I would not...wouldn't do that," Hunter answered.

"This is ludicrous," Winslow muttered. "Are you playing house?"

"We're not playing anything. I've already taught him how to set the table." She swallowed, hating to demean Hunter. "And we've been working on his table manners and his speech patterns. I'm sure you'll be pleased with the results.''

"I'm moving a security detail to the porch," Winslow answered.

"Before you do, perhaps you can satisfy my curiosity about a matter of procedure.''

He raised questioning eyebrows.

"When I arrived back home from buying groceries, I found Hunter already here. But no one had informed him that I'd be sharing the cottage with him. That led to a little misunderstanding between the two of us. Were you responsible for bringing him over without adequate preparation?''

"Certainly not," Winslow growled. "Informing him was supposed to be taken care of.''

"But it slipped between the cracks?''

He gave a curt nod.

"Well, I appreciate your help," she said pleasantly.

"And I appreciate yours," he replied tightly. "Make sure he's ready for a field exercise at 0800 hours." Without waiting for an answer, he turned and strode from the room. Moments later, she heard the clump of heavy feet on the porch.

Hunter sat quietly for several moments. "You should not have asked him about that.''

"I know. But I wanted to see his face when he answered.''

"They do not...don't like to be caught making mistakes.''

"I know," she said again.

He took a deep breath, then let it out before pushing back his chair and standing. "I would like to be alone," he said.

When she raised her eyes toward him, he avoided her gaze.

"Why don't you finish your dessert?" she asked.

"The pleasure of it is gone."

"Don't let him spoil tonight for you."

Her words fell into an empty silence as he turned away and walked down the hall. She heard water running, doors opened and closed. Then nothing more.

THE TWO MEN MET in the shadows behind the gym. One was young and in his prime, a real hothead, who chafed at the bit when the rules kept him out of the action.

The other was older, wearier, more cautious. Yet desperation made him willing to take risks. They had disliked each other on sight and been unspoken enemies since coming to work on Project Sandstorm. Now they found themselves united in pursuit of a common goal—eliminating Kathryn Kelley. One was convinced she spelled the kiss of death to his plans. The other bitterly resented her interference.

"What happened?" the older one asked.

"He damn near broke my arm," his junior partner answered. "I was lucky to get away." He prudently didn't mention the missing gun. Thank God it wasn't his service revolver, but he'd have to retrieve it.

"I mean—did he kill her, like we thought he would?"

"He didn't do it."

"Maybe he hid her body," the older man said hopefully.

"No. She was alive and well and eating apple pie a half hour ago."

The older man cursed. "You checked on that personally?"

"You don't need to know that."

"Listen, we're supposed to trust each other."

"Yeah," came the gruff response.

"Do you have a plan B?"

"I'm setting up another opportunity."

"Good. Make it work this time."

"I can't give you any guarantees." Before he had to listen to any more whining, he turned and stalked into the night.

HUNTER GOT INTO BED in his briefs, just like on all the nights he could remember since they'd trusted him to get ready for bed by himself.

But this wasn't like all the other nights, he thought, as he lay staring into the darkness, mulling over the way his life had suddenly changed.

The mere fact that he was thinking in such terms astonished him. For a long time he had followed orders without questioning how they made him feel. In the space of a few hours he had been bombarded with more feelings than he knew existed. Now he was angry. Not with Kathryn Kelley. Never her. His ire was directed at his attacker and at Winslow—who had spoiled dessert by stamping into the house as if he owned it.

Hunter sighed. Winslow had the right to question training methods. And tonight was supposed to be part of that. Yet it had been so much more. He felt a hollow place open in his chest. He should have stayed at the table and finished dessert so he could have kept talking to her, touching her.

But he wasn't supposed to touch, he reminded himself, even if she said it was okay. Because simply pressing his fingers against hers had made him want to do things that were forbidden.

He tried to switch his thoughts to weapons, clandestine communications, the art of covert operations. Anything but Kathryn Kelley.

But he couldn't drive her from his mind. Too much had happened since that moment he had almost run into her car.

He clenched his fists, unable to cope with the unaccustomed emotions seething inside him. He was a warrior, destined for a specific purpose. His life would be short. He had come to realize that essential fact months ago and had dismissed it as irrelevant. For the first time he felt a kind of sadness. Not for the end of his life—for leaving her.

He looked toward the door, remembering the sounds of her walking down the hall, getting undressed. Now he imagined her lying on the bed, naked, her creamy skin against the white sheets, her wonderful red hair against the pillowcase.

His body tightened as he pictured her holding out her hand to him the way she had reached across the table tonight.

Her hand on his. He hadn't imagined anything could feel that good. Or that intense. The feeling flooded back through him as he lay with his eyes closed, thinking about her, and he had to gather up a wad of bedding in each of his powerful hands to keep himself from getting up and striding into her room.

He tried to drive her out of his mind by remembering the taste of the warm apple pie with vanilla ice cream. In its own way, the taste was almost as good as the sensation of tasting her. Almost, but not quite. Her effect on his senses was beyond imagining. Yet it brought pain as well as pleasure.

Once he had had the flu. He'd had a high fever, and his body had ached. He felt a little like that now. Hot and achy. It was because his body wanted to join with hers. The sexual urge was a powerful force. He had read that somewhere. Now he understood what it meant.

In the darkness, he gave a little snort. He might want her, but he didn't know much about how to do it. He'd probably hash it up. Nonetheless he kept picturing himself leaning over her, closing his mouth around the crest of her breast. Tasting her. Stroking her with his tongue. Probably she would think he was disgusting if he did anything like that.

Don't think about it, he ordered himself. *She's your friend. That's enough.* Yet he knew he was lying to himself. It wasn't enough.

KATHRYN SLEPT FITFULLY, waking and thinking about the man lying in bed across the hall. So much had happened since she met him that her mind was in chaos. It seemed no one at Stratford Creek—no one but her—thought of Hunter as a human being with needs and rights. He was their test subject, who might go berserk if not handled correctly, who might escape if given the chance. But he was too honorable to run from them. That was one of the complexities of the personality they had tried to obliterate.

Now that she'd gotten a chance to interact with him, she couldn't for a moment imagine that he was a convict volunteer. She had studied enough criminals to characterize their basic behavior—and it was the opposite of what she'd learned about Hunter. He was fundamentally decent, honest, ready to protect her whether that was to his advantage or not. Those were the hallmarks of a good man whose innate integrity had survived Swinton's hellish experiment.

She supposed the best thing to hope for was that they hadn't had him long enough to damage him permanently. Or, she thought with a strangled sound that didn't quite make it as a laugh, that he'd watched enough *Father Knows Best* reruns to have some sense of life beyond the confines of Stratford Creek.

Talk about grasping at straws, she thought, sitting up in bed and swiping her hand through her hair. Life as a fifties sitcom. She could be the mom. And what would he be? Not her son. And not her brother. That had become pretty clear. Pulling up her knees, she sat with her chin in her hands, contemplating her relationship with Hunter.

Basically, she'd been hired to work with him, and it was highly unprofessional to be considering anything beyond that. Yet she couldn't help being drawn to him. Or responding to him physically, just as he responded to her. Every time they touched, she could feel the heat building between them. But that didn't make it a good idea. Really, she had to figure out a way to cool things down—which was going to be difficult with them sharing the same house.

She wasn't going to ask for a change of quarters, though. Being near him suited her purposes too well. She had promised herself she was going to help him and somewhere along the line, she'd come to understand that meant getting him away from Stratford Creek. The trouble was, she didn't have a clue about how.

But she vowed she'd find a way to do it. And when

they were someplace safe, she could help him regain his memories, starting with the few things that seemed to have carried over from his former life. Which brought her to the topic she'd been avoiding, she silently admitted. He told her twice now that he remembered her. She was more convinced than ever that they'd never met. Yet she knew there was a kind of bonding between them. How else did you account for the instant physical response that was more potent than anything she'd ever experienced in her life?

She turned that around in her mind for a while, unable to come up with any answers. Around 6:00 a.m., knowing that she wasn't going back to sleep, she got up, showered and dressed in gray slacks and a turquoise knit shirt. Pulling aside the curtain, she saw two security men standing at the bottom of the front steps, close enough to come to her rescue if they heard a scream from inside. The thought made her laugh. Winslow had it the wrong way around. All her experiences here had taught her they were the threat, not Hunter.

When she came into the living room she found him sitting in front of the television set with the sound muted.

"What are you doing?" she asked.

"I didn't want to disturb you," he said, without looking up.

"But you can't hear anything."

"I can read their lips," he answered, his gaze flicking briefly to her before focusing on the screen again.

She nodded, no longer surprised by anything he told her.

He had barely looked at her, and instantly she felt the sting of his rejection—even as she reminded herself he had a perfect right to privacy. She should be grateful to him for putting some distance between them. Instead she felt hurt.

Very professional, Dr. Kelley. Annoyed at herself, she crossed to the kitchen and found a loaf of bread and some crumbs on the counter and a steak knife in the sink. On it were the dregs of some peanut butter. It appeared that he'd licked the knife. Another distinctive scent also lingered in the air. Peering into the trash, she found a banana skin and couldn't repress a grin. It looked like Hunter had fixed himself a breakfast sandwich.

She walked to the kitchen doorway. ''You like peanut butter and banana?''

He shrugged. ''Granger talked about it once. I wanted to see why he liked it so much.''

''What did you think?''

''It was strange.'' He glanced briefly toward the counter. ''I should have cleaned up better.''

''I'll do it later.''

When he turned back to the television, she pulled open the nearest cupboard. ''Did you leave room for some pancakes?''

That got his full attention. He focused on her with an undisguised look of naked hope. ''Do we have any?''

''I bought a box of mix. Why don't you get out the syrup while I start making them.''

He trotted into the kitchen and rummaged in the cabinet. ''I can set the table again,'' he offered.

''Thank you. And you can make coffee.''

''How?''

She handed him two of the packets next to the machine on the counter. ''Read the directions.''

He read quickly and followed instructions exactly, she noticed, as she mixed the batter.

"It takes a long time to make pancakes," he said, licking his lips.

"You can have the first two."

"No. You finish making all of them, then we can share."

"Why do you want to do that?"

He shrugged. "It seems like the right thing to do."

She smiled. "I told you you have good instincts."

He watched her work for a moment, then went back to the TV. As she often did when she cooked, she began to sing. She picked a folk song she'd learned long ago at camp, a song that took its words from the book of Ecclesiastes in the bible. *"To every thing there is a season and a time for every purpose under heaven."*

When the pancakes were cooked, she called him to the table.

"Are you angry at me?" she asked as she sat down.

"No," he denied.

"Why wouldn't you look at me this morning?"

"I—" He stopped. "I'm not used to conversation."

She knew that was part of the truth. She wouldn't press him for the rest. Silently, she watched him enjoy breakfast. Cooking for him on a regular basis would be very gratifying, she thought, then warned herself not to think in those terms.

After they carried their plates to the sink, she touched his arm and gestured down the hall toward the tape recorder. "Let's go outside so we can talk," she mouthed.

He nodded, and followed her into the yard.

Last night, she'd wondered about the wisdom of trusting him with her plans. This morning she'd decided that she needed his help. Yet she still didn't know how much she could tell him.

"What do you want to say?" he asked.

She ran a hand through her hair. "I need some background on the senior staff so I have a better idea of what's going on here."

"I can get that for you."

She stared at him. "How?"

"I have a computer session this afternoon. I can download personnel files onto a floppy disk to use in your laptop." He paused, considering. "Do not... don't transfer the files to your hard drive. Leave them on the floppy and erase the data when you are finished."

She grinned at him. "What other talents do you have that I don't know about?"

"I'm an expert mountain climber. I have a black belt in karate. I am qualified on many types of personal firearms and knives. I am certified as an emergency medical technician. I speak five languages fluently. I can drive a car. Once I heard Dr. Swinton say that I was a decathlon champion in one of my brilliant careers. Before I died that is."

Chapter Seven

"What?" Kathryn grabbed his arm. "What did you say?"

Patiently, he began again. "I am an expert—"

"No." She waved her hand for him to stop. "The last part. What did you hear Dr. Swinton say?"

"He said that—" he halted, his chest tightening as he realized what came next "—that I was a decathlon champion in one of my brilliant careers before I died."

"But you aren't dead!" she exclaimed with a combination of frustration and elation, her hands trying to shake him, the way Beckton sometimes tried to shake some sense into him. But her touch was very different.

"I—" He sucked in a deep breath and let it out in a rush as he considered the meaning of the words. His mind worked like that sometimes. He had information, yet he didn't know the significance. Holding up his right hand, he clenched and unclenched the fingers. "I feel alive."

"Of course you are! Are you sure that's what you heard? He used the word 'died?' He didn't say 'before his memory was erased?'"

"He said 'died.'"

Her palm flattened against his chest, feeling the beat of his heart.

"When did he say it?" she demanded. "When did Swinton say you were an athlete before you died?"

His eyes blinked open. "A long time ago, in the lab. He was lecturing Beckton. He said to push me hard because I had been a decathlon champion."

She stared at him, cleared her throat. "Only one of your brilliant careers!"

He shrugged. "I don't remember any careers." He had thought nothing came before waking up in Swinton's laboratory. Was it possible he was wrong?

"In your computer session, can you get onto the Web? Can you download me information on decathlon champions who died?"

He didn't let himself get excited about it. Hope could be dangerous, he had learned. "I can try."

"We can find out who you are." She sounded breathless. Transformed.

This morning had been bad. He had been cold with her, thinking that pretending he wasn't aware of her every move would make life easier. But he had been wrong. The sad expression on her face had made him want to hold her close, tell her he was sorry for making her feel bad.

Now she was happy, and he allowed himself the luxury of enjoying her enthusiasm.

"On television there used to be a show about the 'Six Million Dollar Man,'" she went on in a rush. "He was nearly killed in an accident, and scientists repaired his body using bionic parts. Then they trained him and sent him out on important missions.

It was just a story, but maybe they found a way to do it.''

He gave a casual shrug, sorry she had thought of it. "I have training," he said curtly. He didn't have to tell her the other things. That wasn't lying, he told himself firmly.

"I—" She stopped.

"What?" He waited, afraid that she was going to ask for information he didn't want to give.

"This is important for you."

Her eyes were bright. Her skin flushed. Like when he'd kissed her.

"Don't hope too much," he said, in a voice that was harsher than he intended.

"Don't be afraid," she answered.

She didn't know his fears. He wouldn't voice them, but he would remind her to be careful. "Winslow was angry when he left us last night. He will ask me what we talked about. You must order me to keep this conversation confidential."

Her face took on a kind of resignation. "Yes. I order you not to discuss this conversation with anyone."

"I will keep this between us, too. But now I must go." Abruptly he started back to the house.

"Wait!"

He pivoted, worried by the sudden panic in her voice. "What is wrong?"

She looked embarrassed. "I didn't mean to startle you. I only want to know what you'd like for dinner."

"Oh." He thought about the things he liked. "Could we have cherry pie with vanilla ice cream?"

"I'll see if they have it at the grocery store."

"And more steak. With a baked potato and lots of butter."

"Yes."

He paused, wondering how much he could request. "And something else I had once. A doughnut. With a honey glaze."

"I'll try to get some."

He wanted to pull her close against him. Devour her mouth with his. He only said, "Thank you. For everything." Then he turned and left to go with the waiting security men.

HE WAS REASSEMBLING a sniper rifle when Granger planted himself a couple of feet away and looked around to see that nobody else was in the vicinity.

"Heard about your new living arrangement," he said in a conversational voice. "You're a lucky S.O.B."

Hunter went on with the job at hand.

"So did you get any last night?" Granger asked with a smirk on his face.

From the talk he'd heard among the men, he was pretty sure he knew what that meant. He chose to give him an innocent look. "Any what?"

"I guess if you don't know, the answer is negative." The comment was followed by a nasty laugh.

He bent over the rifle, as much to hide his expression as to finish with the weapon.

"She's one good-looking babe," Granger insisted. "If I was living with her, I'd get in her pants, all right."

It took all his willpower not to surge up off the bench and sock Granger in the jaw. But he knew that would be a bad move. He'd already taken out his feelings on Beckton. He couldn't afford any more mistakes. So he kept blandly working, pretending that he wasn't seething inside.

Was Granger the man who had attacked him last night? he wondered, surreptitiously examining the man's muscular build. The attacker had been strong enough to wrench himself away, and he'd been a skilled fighter. Granger was a possibility.

The man made a few more choice remarks about Kathryn Kelley's body. When that failed to get a reaction, he switched tactics.

"I see Beckton is keeping away from you."

He didn't answer.

"He's afraid of you now."

He shrugged, determined not to get in any more trouble, because now he knew his behavior could affect Kathryn. When Granger didn't get any reaction from his victim, he lost interest and drifted away.

As SHE CLEANED UP the kitchen, Kathryn wondered what Hunter was doing. She had just finished washing the breakfast dishes when she heard a noise in the dining room and whirled. McCourt was standing by the table watching her.

"It's customary to knock before entering someone's home," she said.

"I did. I guess with the water running, you didn't hear me."

She was pretty sure he was lying, or he'd rapped so faintly that it would have been impossible for her to hear. She didn't waste her breath challenging him.

And he didn't waste any time getting to the point. "A sidearm is missing from the armory," he announced, watching her face for any reaction.

"And?" she asked, keeping her gaze steady, even as she felt her pulse speed up.

"I'd like to see if it turned up here."

"Are you asking permission to search the house?" she inquired.

"No. I'm just trying to show you I can be polite."

"Why should a missing weapon be in this cottage, of all places?"

"I'm checking various buildings. This one's on the list."

She forced herself to casually step aside and sweep her arm toward the kitchen. "Maybe it's under the sink," she said sweetly.

"Maybe."

Her mouth went as dry as sand when McCourt strode forward and opened several of the lower doors, moving aside cleaning supplies and loudly rattling pots and pans. When he straightened and started on the upper cabinets, she wanted to grab hold of the door frame to steady herself. Instead she only pressed her shoulder against the white-painted wood.

The gun was to the right of the sink. As if in a nightmare, she watched him open the cupboard and rummage inside. His fingers closed around the bag of flour, and she stopped breathing as she pictured him pulling it aside, revealing the weapon. It seemed eons passed before he removed his hand and slammed the cabinet.

"Are you doing this to harass me?" she asked in a voice that was almost steady.

"No. I'm doing it because I'm in charge of security, and if a weapon is missing, my neck is on the chopping block."

She managed a little nod as he strode past her and

into the dining room, where he paused to open a few drawers. Then he marched down the hall and into Hunter's room.

Kathryn pulled a paperback from the bookcase in the living room and took a seat in one of the over-stuffed chairs, pretending to read. McCourt was taking three times as long in Hunter's room as he had in the kitchen. Then he started on her room.

When he finally reentered the room, she looked up questioningly. "Find anything interesting—besides my preferred brand of toothpaste?"

"No," he snapped. Without another word, he crossed to the door and stamped onto the porch. She didn't relax until she heard a car drive away. Then she slumped in the chair. Her first instinct was to run to the kitchen and retrieve the gun. She stifled the impulse. McCourt hadn't found it, so it was safe for the moment.

HUNTER CAUGHT A FLASH of movement in the doorway. Keeping his head bent over the rifle, he slid his eyes to the right. It was Dr. Swinton. Why was he here today, when he hadn't come to the armory in weeks?

Although the research director stood watching him for several moments, Hunter didn't break his rhythm, even when he felt the man's gaze burning into the back of his neck. Then, thankfully, Beckton came over, and Swinton started asking low, brisk questions. Though Hunter couldn't hear, it was obvious from the expression on Beckton's face that he didn't like being quizzed. Still, he remained respectful as he showed Swinton some of the latest progress reports. Yet every so often threw a quick look over his shoulder, as if he were afraid someone would ask what he and Swinton were talking about.

If they had a secret, Swinton hid it better than Beckton. They finished talking and Swinton left. Beckton looked around nervously, then hurried out of the building.

Hunter finished with the rifle, completed a drill on the geography of Gravan—the country where he was going on his mission—and went outside to the paved area behind the building where a small truck was waiting. After studying a set of written instructions, he climbed into the driver's seat, started the engine and began to maneuver around an obstacle course that had been set up.

It was a normal day, yet everything had changed. He wasn't simply following orders anymore. He was noticing things around him, making assessments. He'd never tried to figure out if one of the men he worked with had killed Fenton, the ex-chief of security. Today he wondered if Fenton's death was connected to the attack last night.

When he came to no conclusions, he switched his thoughts back to the time with Kathryn Kelley—and found himself singing the song that she had sung. It was so different from the *1812 Overture*. He liked them both, but he liked this better—because she had sung it.

"To every thing there is a season and a time for every purpose under heaven."

Her voice was high and beautiful. His was a croak by comparison. But he sang anyway. What was his time? His season?

This morning he felt caught between two worlds. The old world where he did what he was told without question and without feeling. And the new world where his mind seethed with questions and emotions.

It was strange to admit that he took a kind of grim pleasure in Beckton's new fear of him. But he kept it well hidden, he hoped. He must not let them know how much he had changed since meeting Kathryn.

Kathryn. That was her first name. He didn't have to call her Kathryn Kelley, he suddenly decided. He could think of just the first name. The name her other friends would use.

If things were different, the two of them might—

He stopped the daydream before it could form. He would finish his instruction at Stratford Creek, then go on to his primary assignment, and that would be the end of it. But now he had another mission, as well. He must keep Kathryn safe while she was here. The problem was, he didn't know what would happen if he came to a juncture where the two aims clashed.

The worry made him lose his concentration, and he tapped the right front fender of the truck against a barrel. He had made a mistake, he thought as he forced his mind back to the obstacle course. He had taken this test before. He'd better not do worse than the last time or Colonel Emerson would ask questions.

LONG AFTER MCCOURT had left, Kathryn sat rigidly in the living room chair, afraid to trust her legs. She'd always been good about putting up a calm front. She hoped she'd fooled McCourt.

Ever since her arrival at Stratford Creek, she'd felt like a prisoner, but the security chief had just given her a vivid demonstration of his power over her. In a way he was worse than James Harrison. From Harrison she knew what to expect. She didn't know what to expect here anymore.

A glance at her watch, and she pushed herself out of the chair. She'd better pick up the groceries she'd promised Hunter. She started for the door, then stopped abruptly. Was it safe to leave the house, she wondered, looking uneasily toward the kitchen cabinet that held more than food. For a split second she thought about taking the gun. No, if she got caught with a gun tucked in her purse, she'd have some tough explaining to do.

HE'D BRAGGED to Kathryn that he could get personnel information. Now he realized that in his desire to please her, he had spoken too soon.

As he sat in front of the computer screen in a windowless basement room of the administration building, the chances of getting the files she wanted seemed slim.

Pushing the printer button, he half turned to look at the man sitting directly in back of him.

"You need some help?" the man asked. His name was Hertz. He was small and stoop-shouldered, and wore a baggy sweater in the chill of the basement office.

"No," Hunter answered, wishing that Hertz would leave the room. Apparently he'd been told to stay. In fact, he realized, someone was almost always watching him, except when he was being tested on a solo exercise. He'd never thought much about the lack of privacy. Today, however, he was vividly aware of the constant scrutiny—and a lot of other details of his life he'd never questioned.

He didn't know what Hertz had been told about him, except that he was preparing for a special assignment. Maybe Hertz had been told the same thing as Kathryn—that he was instructing a prisoner volunteer. They'd only worked together on a sporadic basis and always stuck strictly to business. Searching his memory, he decided that the man wasn't usually as conscientious as the regular instructors. Yet today he hovered nervously in the background like—

Like what? A fifth wheel? No, that was the wrong phrase. The wrong idiom.

Like a watchdog. That was better, he thought with a little grin. The grin vanished as he considered why the man was being so conscientious. Probably the incident with Beckton was being talked about around the compound.

Again he reproved himself for hitting the training chief. It was a mistake. But it was in the past, and he couldn't change it. He could only go forward, he thought as he booted up a government-restricted Internet search engine.

He had used the Net before and he had no problem locating a directory of the faculty in the physics department at the University of Stockholm and printing the biographies of selected department members. Then he went on to download and print out product specifications from an aircraft manufacturer in California.

But while he was doing the assigned work, part of his mind was on Kathryn's requests. She wanted Stratford Creek personnel records and a list of decathlon winners.

Perhaps he would have to make a choice between the two options. If he had time to get only one of the things, he would pick the personnel records. That was more important, he told himself. It would help her.

Finding out about dead athletes was another matter, he thought with a sudden prickle of fear at the back of his neck. He wasn't sure why he was afraid of putting a name to the face he saw every morning in the mirror when he shaved. He told himself that he didn't want to open a door that had always been closed.

After about forty-five minutes, he stood up. "I'm going to the men's room."

Hertz started to stand. "Okay."

"I know the way. I'll be right back." Without waiting for a reply, he walked into the hall. To his relief, the other man didn't follow him.

He hadn't been sure he could get out of the room alone. Making the most of the opportunity, he hurried down the corridor. After determining that no one was watching, he ducked into an empty office along the route and picked up a pack of matches and some cigarettes he'd seen lying on an otherwise empty desk.

The matches alone would probably work for what he had in mind, but if anyone checked to see what had happened, it was better to have a cigarette, as well.

He knew about smoking. He'd passed men clustered around exterior doors enthusiastically puffing on cigarettes when they were on their breaks. The smokers seemed to enjoy it. In fact, sometimes they sneaked into the men's room to smoke. Today he would find out how it tasted.

Locking himself into a stall, he struck a match,

pressed the burning end to the cigarette, and dragged in a deep breath through the filter tip the way he'd seen guys do it.

The moment the stinging smoke hit the back of his throat, he started to gag. When it reached his lungs, he began to cough violently. It was as if he'd breathed in poison gas, he thought as he wiped the tears from his eyes, thankful that no one else was in the washroom. After gasping in several lungfuls of air, he tried again—this time a lot more cautiously. Instead of inhaling the smoke, he only pulled it into his mouth. When he was sure the lit end was burning nicely, he exited the stall and poked the cigarette into the paper-towel-filled trash bin.

By the time he finished washing his hands and rinsing the foul taste out of his mouth, the trash was already beginning to smolder. For good measure, he dragged over a wooden chair from the corner with a sweatshirt draped across the back and dangled the sleeve in the trash. Then he hurried back to the office where Hertz was still sitting and reading a magazine.

Only part of the next Internet search was completed when the fire alarm began to ring.

Hertz jumped up and went to the door. "Maybe it's a false alarm," he muttered.

Lifting his head from the screen, Hunter loudly sniffed the air. "I think I smell smoke."

Fearfully, Hertz took another breath. "Yeah. Let's get the hell out of here." He started for the door, then looked back in consternation. "Come on," he urged.

"I must exit the Windows program," Hunter said, making his voice loud and mechanical.

"It's okay to leave it. Come on!"

In the hall, several sets of feet rushed past as the

workers assigned to the basement offices made for the exits.

"I am required to shut down the equipment properly," he answered, adding a stubborn note to the statement as he deliberately turned his back on the man and faced the console. His fingers were already moving over the keys. If Hertz approached, he'd discover that he wasn't shutting down the machine.

He felt the man hesitating behind him, apparently torn between escaping from a burning building and doing his job. The smoke wafting down the hall made the decision for him. After several seconds, he turned and dashed from the room.

Hunter bent over the keyboard, working rapidly. The smoke had begun to sting his eyes. Then he started to cough.

The spasm passed, and he peered at the screen through watery eyes. He had used the system many times. It was a simple matter for him to work his way into the personnel records. Quickly he typed in several names, along with records requests. As he waited for the information to download, he started to cough again.

Outside he could hear the wail of sirens. Fire trucks. He hoped everyone else had gotten out of the building all right.

He didn't have much time left, he thought, as he saved the personnel files onto a floppy disk. The smoke was getting thicker, and every breath made his lungs burn. It seemed like he was hardly getting any oxygen. He should leave now that he had the personnel information he had promised to bring. Yet something made him stay in front of the computer and switch back to the Internet search engine.

Long seconds passed during which he fought to not to pass out. Then he was into the Olympics web site. Trying not to breathe, he zeroed in on decathlon champions.

The smoke was so thick he could barely see the screen. Why was he doing this, he wondered. He didn't even want the information. Yet he stayed where he was, blinking to clear his vision as he downloaded the stats onto the disk. When he had them, he exited the Web site, then forced himself to shut down the program so that he'd have the right answer when they asked why he'd refused to leave a burning building.

He had stayed too long, he realized, as he ejected the floppy disk. Every breath he took now was agony, and his mind was enveloped in a gray haze, as if the cells of his brain were filling with smoke. With shaky hands, he stuffed the disk into his pocket, then dropped to his hands and knees to get below the smoke and dragged himself toward the door.

His trick had worked too well. The hall was filled with black, choking smoke that billowed from the direction of the men's room and made it impossible to see where he was going. Head bent, he lurched forward, hoping that he didn't crawl past the door at the bottom of the stairs.

Chapter Eight

Sirens shattered the afternoon quiet as Kathryn was on her way back from the shopping center. Two fire trucks and an ambulance sped past as she waited at the next cross street. Some sixth sense made her turn in the opposite direction from the guest cottage and follow the emergency vehicles.

When she caught up, they had pulled to a stop in front of the administration building. On the sidewalk and lawn, displaced office workers were milling around.

Craning her neck, she spotted Bill Emerson, who was conferring with an emergency medical technician. Another medic leaned over a man who lay on a stretcher on the ground. When the man moved, she felt a shiver cross her skin. It was Hunter—or her eyes were playing tricks on her. Her heart pounded as she tried to get a better view.

Then someone in the crowd blocked her line of sight. Unconsciously murmuring a little prayer under her breath, she maneuvered to the curb and leaped out of the car.

As she drew near the building, a fireman blocked her path.

"I'm sorry. You have to stay back," he said.

"I have to talk to Mr. Emerson." Ducking past the man, she made for the stretcher and saw with a sick feeling that she'd been correct. It was Hunter lying there, gray-faced, eyes closed. When she called his name in a high, strangled voice, he turned instantly toward the sound, his gaze searching for her in the crowd and zeroing in on her face.

She wanted to rush to his side, clutch his hand, hear his voice. She knew scores of eyes were watching her, so she remained standing where she was.

"What happened?" she asked, directing her question to one of the medics.

"Smoke inhalation," the man answered.

"Is he all right?"

"He crawled out of the building under his own power. But we're taking him to the hospital to check him out."

"I am fine," Hunter insisted. Although his voice was raspy, it sounded strong, and that reassured her.

He tried to sit up, but the medic put a hand on his shoulder.

Emerson came up behind her.

"How did this happen?" she asked.

"Some idiot started a fire in a trash can in the men's room," he clipped out. "Smoking. It's against regulations to light up inside. When I find out who it was, they're going to be damn sorry."

She noted the intensity with which Hunter took in the conversation. Near him, a stoop-shouldered little man in a gray sweater was also listening and looking sick.

"Who's that?" she asked in a low voice.

"Hertz. From computer support." Emerson made

no attempt to hide his annoyance. "He was supposed to be in charge of Hunter. He was supposed to stay with him at all times. He came running out of the building alone."

"He wouldn't leave the computer," the man said. "I wasn't going to stay in there and get turned into toast."

"The computer?" Kathryn asked, her gaze shooting back to Hunter.

"I had to shut down the program properly," he said in a flat voice, avoiding direct eye contact with her. She was pretty sure that it wasn't the whole story.

"What was I supposed to do, carry him?" Hertz whined.

"I made him go without me," Hunter wheezed.

"That was foolish," the chief of operations growled.

"I could not disobey orders."

"Your orders." Emerson nodded. "Yes, I understand."

Hunter's eyes flicked to Hertz. "I do not wish to cause trouble for him. He is a good computer instructor...he did his job every moment until the smoke began to fill the room."

The man looked relieved, and bobbed his head vigorously in agreement.

A fireman came up to Emerson, and they conferred briefly. Then the chief of operations raised his voice and spoke to the group of people who had turned toward him. "The fire's out," he announced. "And the damage is confined to the men's room where the blaze started and the hall immediately outside."

The crowd gave the firemen a round of applause. When they finished, the medics moved into position on either side of the stretcher, raised it to waist height, and began to roll it toward the ambulance. Kathryn wanted to follow. She wanted to ride with Hunter and stay with him. Yet she understood that showing too much concern wasn't prudent.

"I'll wait back at the house," she said.

"Good idea."

The last observation was made by Chip McCourt, who had come out of the crowd.

She gave him a little nod.

"We've been going along for months just fine." McCourt walked beside her as she left the crowd and headed toward her car. "Then you show up and our incident rate suddenly goes through the roof."

"Don't you mean *off* the roof?" she muttered under her breath, thinking about Fenton.

"What?"

"What incident rate?" she said more loudly.

"A fight in the gym. A missing weapon. Now we have a mysterious fire."

"Well, I think there are a number of witnesses who will swear that I was at the commissary when somebody tried to burn up the men's room."

"You think it was deliberate?" McCourt asked.

"I have no idea."

"It's interesting that you showed up so quickly."

"I heard the sirens. I was curious."

"I'll bet."

She raised her chin, gave him a direct look. "What are you getting at?"

To his credit, he kept his gaze steady. "Nothing."

"Good." Turning on her heel, she left, feeling several sets of eyes drilling into her back.

THE MOMENT KATHRYN walked into the dining room of the guest cottage, she knew something was wrong. Some of the knickknacks in the shelves had been moved, and the sweater she'd left on a chair was on the floor. A feeling of dread overwhelmed her.

Was the gun still in the kitchen?

She had to assume the tape recorder was still waiting to pick up sounds from its place behind the access panel. Suppose it was sensitive enough to tell the listeners that she'd made a beeline for the kitchen cabinet where the weapon was hidden?

She'd never had a devious mind. Now she forced herself to take a breath and consider how she would really act if she came in and thought her house had been searched.

Probably she'd check her personal belongings. With a grimace, she started down the hall to the bedrooms. Drawers had been opened and the contents moved about. Someone had poked through her and Hunter's things and hadn't bothered to hide the search. With shaky steps, she returned to the kitchen, opened the cabinet to the right of the sink and moved the bag of flour. She wasn't surprised that the gun and silencer had both vanished. Had McCourt waited for her to leave and come back for a more thorough search? Or had someone else done it? She couldn't discuss the possibilities with anyone but Hunter. And she wouldn't be discussing them with him, either, she reminded herself, barely managing to suppress anguish. He was in the hospital, and she didn't know when he was coming back. When he did they couldn't have a normal conversation because the house was bugged.

In an attempt to regain composure she began putting away the groceries. More time passed. The house remained quiet except for the sound of her own breathing. She ached to call the hospital and make sure Hunter was all right. She told herself firmly that he was, and that he'd come home when they released him.

Yet what if they didn't let him come back to the guest cottage? What if Emerson had changed his mind about the living arrangements? Fighting the clogged feeling in her throat, she sprinted across the room toward the telephone, but didn't make the call. In her present state she'd never be able to hide her feelings, and if Emerson knew she'd lost her objectivity, that would be the end of her access to Hunter.

She would have to wait for official word, she told herself firmly. Still, as the minutes turned into hours, she thought she would go crazy. Crazy with frustration. Crazy with worry.

Dragging herself into the bedroom, she slipped off her shoes and flopped down in her clothes, prepared to jump up the minute she heard the front door open.

It didn't, and she lay rigid, staring into the growing darkness, telling herself over and over that Hunter would surely be back soon and everything would be all right. But nothing could stop her mind from churning.

Finally, desperate, she staggered into the bathroom and splashed cold water on her face, trying to shock herself into steadiness. Feeling a little more in control, she called the medical facility. The woman who answered didn't know who Hunter was. When Kathryn switched to his old name—John Doe—she was told the information was classified. Now more upset than ever, she stood rocking back and forth with her arms wrapped tightly around her waist. Maybe Hunter was already out of the hospital, she told herself. Maybe he was already back in his old quarters. Maybe McCourt was supposed to give her the news, and he'd conveniently forgotten. A mirthless sound bubbled up in her throat. That would give him the last laugh, all right.

Only the sound of the front door opening saved her from hysteria. Her heart skipped a beat, then hammered into overtime as she barreled down the hall.

Relief flooded her when she saw Hunter standing there in clean clothes, the effects of the fire scrubbed away. Yet she came to an abrupt halt in the face of the two security guards flanking him. One was the guy named Reid—who probably didn't like her any better than she liked him.

"Here's your wayward boy," he said with a touch of sarcasm in his voice.

A sharp retort leaped to her lips. She bit it back and managed a simple "Thank you."

"Do you want us to stay?"

"No. I'd like the arrangement to be the same as last night," she answered in a cool, dismissive voice.

Reid nodded and the duo departed, leaving Hunter standing in the hall staring at her with his arms stiffly at his sides and a strained expression on his face.

She felt almost dizzy as she faced him. "Are you all right?" she gasped.

He gave a little nod.

"Thank God." Seeing him after the long hours of worry was like getting struck by a tidal wave. Struck from the back, so that she was propelled toward him. With a little cry, she flung herself across the space between them.

He took the impact of her weight, his arms coming up to catch her as she held on to him for dear life. Her hands slid possessively across his broad shoulders, up and down his back, as she assured herself that he was well and whole.

"I wanted to go to the hospital with you," she choked out. "I wanted to be there. It was hard to come back here and wait."

"They wouldn't have let you be with me there. But I'm here now."

"Yes." She reached up, tunneling her fingers though his dark hair so that she could bring his face within reach.

"Oh," was all he had time to exclaim before his mouth melted against hers. She sobbed as her lips moved frantically against his. There was so much she wanted to say to him. So much she couldn't say with the tape recorder ruling their lives.

But she could show him what she was feeling. Closing her eyes, she shut out everything but him, the taste of him, the feel of him. Each thing registered separately on her senses—the slightly coarse texture of his hair, the hard muscles of his shoulders as her hands came back to them, the clean smell of soap and water.

"Kathryn." Her name sighed out of him like a plea—like a prayer of thanks.

"I'm here," she answered. "Right here."

His mouth opened, perhaps in surprise, as she eased his lips apart so that she could taste him more fully. And as she drank from him, she taught him the ways that two people could express their deepest feelings to each other without words. Soon his mouth was moving hungrily over hers, tasting, sipping, nibbling at her tender flesh until she was shaking with the strength of her response.

His strong hands were under her blouse, burning the skin of her back, and then her front where he cupped her breasts through the sheer fabric of her bra.

He made a rough sound, half pleasure, half frustration.

"This thing is in the way," he said thickly.

"Yes." Reaching around, she unhooked the catch, and he pushed the fabric up, taking her breasts in his hands.

She heard him suck in a strangled breath, as he moved his fingers over her heated flesh.

"So soft." The words were almost a moan.

She was just as inarticulate. She could only gasp at the pleasure of his unschooled touch, a touch that made up in ardor and tenderness what it lacked in sophistication.

His hips moved against hers, instinctively, insistently. "I want to…" The sentence ended with a choking sound in his throat. In the next moment, he wrenched himself away from her, his hands balled into fists in front of him, his chest heaving.

She reached for him, but he stepped farther away.

"No," he ordered, his eyes fierce.

They both stood sucking in drafts of air.

"Friends can't do—" He stopped abruptly, looking over her shoulder.

She wanted to say he was wrong. Then with a start, she realized he was looking toward the tape recorder.

Oh God, how bad did his homecoming sound?

All she could do was shake her head in despair. What she had told him about the two of them was wrong. What she felt for him was a lot more powerful than friendship. She had tried to deny her feelings, but denial had become impossible when she'd seen him lying on the stretcher and then during the long anguished hours while she'd waited for him to come home.

When she felt a little more in control, she turned away and rehooked her bra.

She waited for the heat to fade a little from her cheeks before reaching for his hand and leading him into the dining room where the light was better.

The stark look on his face made it difficult not to clasp him to her again. That would only make things worse. After several shaky breaths, she touched her finger to her mouth. His eyes followed.

"Can you understand what I'm saying?" she asked, moving her lips slowly.

He nodded.

"You and I are more than friends," she said silently, knowing that she wasn't exactly helping the situation. But she'd vowed not to lie to him. And what had just happened between them had certainly passed beyond the bounds of friendship.

"What are we?" he spoke, but in a barely audible whisper.

"A man and woman who care deeply about each other," she told him silently.

When his face contorted, she realized she could only speak for herself. "At least I do," she said, forgetting not to vocalize the words.

"I—" He reached for her hand, drew her closer so that he could fold her fingers around his and bring her knuckles to his lips. Eyes closed, he kissed her hand tenderly, then carried it to his heart. Her vision clouded with moisture. She had never been so affected by a gesture, so affected by another human being. Silently, taking small steps, she moved closer so that she was standing with her cheek against his shoulder.

One of his large hands came up to stroke her hair, the other clasped her shoulder, and she stood with him, fighting tears. God, what a mess. They could hardly talk, and there was so much she wanted to say, so much she needed to tell him, she realized suddenly. Personal things. But the personal part would have to wait.

She brushed her lips against his cheek. "I have to tell you things that happened," she mouthed.

He nodded.

After giving him a flicker of a smile, she cleared her throat.

"Did you have dinner?" she asked in an almost normal voice.

"They gave me a turkey sandwich. It was dry and—" He stopped. "It doesn't matter."

"Well, you can have dessert. Cherry pie with vanilla ice cream."

His eyes lit up.

"Come into the kitchen and give me a hand."

He followed her toward the cabinets. Turning, she glanced at him, then opened the door where the gun had been and showed him the empty place behind the bag of flour.

His face took on a questioning look.

She turned her palms up and shrugged. "McCourt was here—officially," she mouthed slowly. "Looking for a gun from the armory. He didn't find it."

Hunter nodded his understanding.

"When I got back after the fire, the house had been searched again."

His eyes narrowed but he said nothing.

Turning she opened the box of pie she'd bought and warmed a slice in the microwave before topping it with ice cream.

"You have some, too," Hunter said when she handed him the plate.

Dutifully, she cut herself a small slice, although she had almost no appetite. She started to say some more about McCourt's visit, then caught herself. The strain of remembering not to speak was getting to her.

After a few bites, she gave up the effort and simply watched Hunter enjoy his dessert. He looked like a little boy who couldn't believe he deserved such a wonderful treat.

She was too keyed up to do more than nibble at her food. When she couldn't stifle a yawn, he nodded. "You...we...should sleep," he amended.

"Yes."

Standing, she started to carry the dishes to the kitchen, but he stopped her. "I'll do it."

"Thank you."

"Go to bed."

She shouldn't lie down, she told herself. But what good would it do the two of them to sit and stare at each other? Leaning over, she gave Hunter a small kiss on the cheek. She had intended it to be brief, but she clung for a moment, needing to hold him, touch him before she let him out of her sight again. Finally she headed down the hall to her bedroom.

HE PROWLED through the kitchen and felt a shiver of gratitude when he found the box of doughnuts she had bought. Slowly he ate two, savoring the sweet taste. He thought about finishing the box, then elected to save some for breakfast. He would eat them and drink coffee with a lot of milk and sugar, he decided as he licked his fingers.

He had never chosen what to eat. When to eat. What to do. It made him feel strange as he washed the dishes. Turning he looked toward the stereo, thinking he would like to hear the *1812 Overture* again if he couldn't hear Kathryn singing. But he didn't want to wake her up, so he hummed the song she'd sung.

"A time for every purpose under heaven."

He wished it were true.

He knew it was a lie for him. He had only one purpose.

The song died in his throat as he began to prowl the house, checking to make sure no additional sensors were monitoring their activities. There were only the tiny microphones he'd found before and the tape recorder. At least he hoped.

They were hard-wired, meaning that the system had not been updated to state-of-the-art technology. He had lain in his hospital bed thinking about what to do. If they could listen to the tape, so could he. Now he opened the utility panel, rewound the tape and fast-forwarded, stopping every minute to listen. He heard the sound of someone searching the house. Then the broken words and phrases from the frantic time in the hall when he had come home to her. He had to clench his teeth to get through that part. Methodically, he erased everything that had been said since he got home. The listeners wouldn't know how much was on the tape, because they wouldn't know exactly when it had been activated by speech or other noises.

After turning off the machine, he started down the hall. He and Kathryn had to talk. Now they could do it in privacy—at least for a few hours.

Quietly he pushed open her door and stood looking down at her in the shaft of light that came from behind him in the hallway.

She had fallen asleep on her back, with her flaming hair spilling across the pillow. The way he had imagined her.

Well, not quite the way he had imagined. The covers had slipped down to her waist, and he saw she was wearing a T-shirt. Yet as he moved quietly closer and waited for his eyes to adjust to the dark, he could see the outlines of her beautiful breasts against the fabric and the darker centers that had made his body tighten when he touched them.

He pressed his hands to his sides to keep from reaching for her.

"Kathryn?" he called out quietly.

She stirred a little on the bed.

"Kathryn?"

Her eyes fluttered open. When she saw him looming over her, she gasped and tried to climb out of his reach.

The terror in her eyes made him afraid she would scream and bring the security men. Flinging himself on top of her, he clamped his hand over her mouth.

She kicked at his legs and struggled to tear herself from his grasp. All he could do was try and hold her still as he told her over and over, "I didn't come to hurt you. I came to talk to you."

At first it seemed she didn't hear him, didn't even

see him, for her eyes were glazed and her frantic struggles continued.

Then, all at once, she focused on him. In the next moment, she went very still, except for the sobs that began to rack her body.

"I came to talk to you," he repeated.

She nodded against his shoulder but kept sobbing. When she clung to him, pulling him down beside her, he gathered her close and held her gently, wishing he knew what to do to make her feel better. He had frightened her badly, and sadness descended upon him. He had thought...well, it didn't matter what he had thought.

In that unguarded moment when she had wakened, he had discovered her true feelings.

He felt her struggling to get control of herself. When she fumbled for a tissue on the bedside table and blew her nose, he eased away from her and sat up, moving to the side of the bed.

"We can't talk," she whispered.

"Yes, we can. I turned off the recording machine," he explained. "Since it's voice-activated, they will think we are sleeping now."

She tipped her head toward him. "Are you sure?"

"Yes." He swallowed painfully, looking down so she wouldn't see his face. "I'm sorry. I shouldn't have come in. I frightened you."

She sat up and put her hand on his arm. "It wasn't you I was afraid of," she said quickly.

"Who?" he asked, hardly daring to hope he had been wrong about her terror.

She sucked in a deep breath and let it out in a rush. "I took the job Emerson offered me because I wanted to hide out from a man named James Harrison. He tried to kill me a couple of weeks ago,'' she said in a shaky voice. Moving her hand to his, she held on tight.

"Why would someone try to kill you?"

Her grip was almost painful, yet he didn't loosen her fingers.

"One of my jobs is testifying in court—in trials— as an expert witness. Three years ago, I gave an evaluation of Harrison. He lived at home with his mother because he couldn't sustain a relationship with a woman. He'd been fired from his job as a computer programmer, and he was depressed. His mother had a lot of money, and he wanted to get his hands on it. So he was holding her captive—starving her, hoping she would die."

"A person would do that to his mother?" he asked, hardly able to believe it.

"Not usually. He was sick—mentally sick. The mother didn't die, so he wasn't charged with murder. And she wouldn't press charges against him. I testified that he was a danger to society. Because of my testimony and another psychologist's, he was confined to a mental institution."

He listened intently, not sure he understood everything, but getting the gist of it.

"He escaped, but the authorities thought he was dead. He came to the apartment building where I live. He tried to kill me. I got away from him, but the police haven't found him yet. And sometimes I dream about him. I dream he's coming after me again," she ended with a little gulp that made his heart melt.

"Come here." He held out his arms to her.

She came into them without hesitation, and he felt

a wave of warmth and protectiveness sweep over him as she nestled her head against his chest.

On a deep sigh, he cupped his hands around her shoulders. He liked it so much when she gave herself into his care. It made him feel strong. Good. Able to protect her, although he didn't know if he really could.

"I thought I'd be safe at Stratford Creek. I didn't know I was jumping from the frying pan into the fire."

He repeated the phrase. He'd never heard it before, but he understood what she meant.

She burrowed closer to him. "It wasn't you I was afraid of," she said again, her warm breath seeping through his shirt to heat his skin. "I saw your shape in the doorway—a man's shape—but I couldn't see your face."

He stroked her hair. He had told himself he wouldn't touch her when he came to her room to talk. Still, it was impossible to deny himself the pleasure of running the silky strands through his fingers. He could feel his body getting hot and tight again. It was a strange combination of pain and pleasure that compelled him to seek more.

Remembering the kiss in the hallway, he turned his head. She opened her mouth for him, and he gave a sigh of gratification at the soft touch of her lips and the sweet taste of her. Some part of his mind knew this was the wrong thing to do. He shouldn't have come to her bedroom. Perhaps he had been fooling himself about his reasons.

The pressure of his lips on hers made him dizzy, hot, achy. His fingers shook as they stroked the tender line where her hair met her cheek. When she made a little sound of wanting in her throat, he answered with a growl of satisfaction.

Helpless to stop himself, he cupped one of her breasts and stroked his fingers over the tip.

It was hard. Touching it made him harden in response as if her body were giving a signal to his. The fabric between his hand and her flesh frustrated him. He wanted to pull the shirt over her head and push her down to the surface of the bed.

He wanted to make love with her.

He knew nothing of lovemaking, yet the image was very vivid in his mind—his body joined to hers so that it would be impossible to tell where one of them stopped and the other began.

He pulled her down, gathered her as close as he could with their clothing in the way. The tight, swollen part of him fit perfectly into the cleft between her legs. She must know it too, he thought, drunk with sensation as they rocked together on the bed. Blood surged through him in a roaring torrent. Need built, like a hot, raging river sweeping away sanity in its path.

He was caught and held in a spinning whirlpool of hunger—held by the soft sounds she made, the woman scent of her, the frantic little movements of her hips against his.

In a few moments he knew he would be unable to deny himself, unable to think beyond physical need. He would have to give himself over to the blinding, deafening desire for her.

But he couldn't let that happen. He had come here for another purpose. He must talk to her. Find out about the gun. Protect her.

That thought gave him strength he hadn't known

he possessed. With a strangled sound deep in his throat, he lifted his mouth from hers, moved a few inches away so that his aching body was no longer pressed tight to hers. Still, it was impossible to let go of her completely. His hand stayed clasped on hers as he spoke in a voice so thick that the words were barely articulate.

"We can't," he said, then more strongly, as he sat up and moved to the side of the bed. "We can't."

Her eyes were dazed, her face flushed. The color deepened as she focused on him.

"We have work to do," he rasped, knowing that if she held out her arms to him, he would go into them. "We must look at the disk—with the personnel files."

KATHRYN BLINKED, sucking in a shaky breath as she struggled to remember where they were, and why they couldn't do what both of them wanted so much. Sitting up, she ran an unsteady hand through her hair, pushing it back from her face, buying a few moments to collect herself. He was right, she thought as she forced her mind to start functioning again.

"The disk? You have it?"

He nodded and pulled it out of his pocket. "I brought it out of the administration building. In the hospital, I folded it into my clothes when they had me get undressed."

"Did you set the fire?" she asked, her fingers digging into his hand.

He kept his gaze steady. "Why would I do that?"

"You said you'd get me information from the computer. Then you realized it was going to be impossible. But you did it for me, anyway, didn't you?"

A flush crept up his cheeks. "How did you know that?"

"It was a guess. Hunter, you shouldn't have taken a chance like that!"

He shrugged. "It was like a field exercise."

She made a low sound of distress, and her fingers tightened on his.

"It was all right."

"You could have gotten killed."

"But I didn't."

Before she could lecture him on taking unnecessary risks, he changed the subject.

"McCourt was here? Tell me about that. And about the gun."

"He came in the morning after you left and said a gun was missing from the armory. He looked for it, but he didn't find anything. Then when I got back after the fire, I could tell that someone else had searched the house. The gun and the silencer were both gone."

"He could have come back."

"Or it could have been someone else."

"I heard the sounds of searching on the tape."

She nodded tightly.

"The gun may have come from the armory, but not the silencer."

"I—"

"We must make the most of our time," he interrupted. "You must read the computer disk and then erase the data. It's dangerous to keep the evidence if the house can be searched at any time."

She gave him a tight nod. Yes, the house could be searched. And men like Winslow and McCourt could burst in. Yet that didn't negate a basic fact that kept nagging at her. Why had she been given such un-precedented access to Hunter?

He must have seen the question on her face. "What?"

"The more I think about being left alone with you, the more I wonder why it's been arranged this way."

"I heard Dr. Kolb and Dr. Swinton talking about it when I was in the hospital."

"They were talking in front of you?"

"They were in the hall. I heard them. Dr. Kolb said this is the best field trial he could think of. If I pass this test, I'm ready to go off into enemy territory. Dr. Swinton thanked him. He said that he had thought Dr. Kolb was fighting him. But now they were working like a team."

"Enemy territory? Where?" she asked, hoping the answer might slip out.

"A country where Americans aren't welcome," he answered evasively. "A country where one man might be able to slip in."

"Who is funding Project Sandstorm?" she tried.

"The Department of Defense."

She kept her voice neutral. "And does the Department of Defense own Stratford Creek?"

"Yes."

When she tried to ask another question about his mission, he stopped her with a quick shake of his head.

"I can't tell you any more about it."

"I want to understand."

"You have to read the computer data tonight," he reminded her.

She knew he was right. They didn't have much time.

"What are you going to do?"

"Check the security at the motor pool," he said.

"Why?"

"Don't ask me that either." He made a quick exit from the room, and she stared after him. If he was checking the security of the motor pool, he must be thinking about leaving the base.

Could that really be true? Was he preparing to go against his training, after he'd told Winslow he wouldn't run away?

She couldn't answer the question, and she knew she was wasting time speculating. Taking the laptop off the dresser, she brought it to the bed where she propped up the pillows so she could sit comfortably. On the disk were two files. One was labeled "pers." The other "Olympics."

She ached to go right to the second file. But she knew the first one was more urgent. She had to see what she could find out about the men she was dealing with here.

An hour later, her head was swimming with information—information that didn't come entirely from reading dry personnel entries. Apparently Bill Emerson liked keeping track of his staff's peccadilloes and record the information in memos he'd attached to each man's record. Kind of like the J. Edgar Hoover method of personnel control, Kathryn thought with a shudder. If your employees knew you had something on them, they were likely to stay in line.

Among other things, she'd learned that Lieutenant Chip McCourt had a violent streak. He'd been thrown in the brig on several occasions. And he'd almost gotten himself court-martialed for assaulting a civilian worker on a tour in Germany. That time, Emerson had personally stepped in to get him off the hook. The lieutenant was allowed to leave the army with an honorable discharge, and he'd come straight to Stratford Creek to help set up Project Sandstorm.

Also enlightening were the confidential notes on Dr. Jules Kolb. According to Emerson, Kolb was an alcoholic who had badly mishandled a score of patients at a V. A. Hospital in Virginia, causing the deaths of several. The scandal had been covered up, and Kolb had been ordered into an alcoholic rehab program.

Reid, the man who had brought Hunter home this evening, had been jailed for selling supplies stolen from military bases. And then there was the brilliant Dr. Avery Swinton. His early reputation had been damaged by a scandal involving the fudging of test results in a scientific paper he'd published in the *Journal of Biological Sciences*. Still, he'd gone on to win a research grant at Berkeley—and then been dismissed for illegally experimenting with human fetal tissue.

Well, now she knew why she'd instinctively disliked most of the staff, she thought with a grimace. They were lawless and ruthless. And she had the data to prove it.

Was there some way she could use the information to her advantage? She didn't know yet. But maybe a plan would come to her. Closing the file, she switched to the information on decathlon winners.

At first she was disappointed because she didn't find anyone who could be the right man. None of the recent champions was dead, she saw as she went down the list. The first deceased medal winner she came to was a man named Ben Lancaster who had taken the gold seventeen years ago—when he was twenty-five, she noted, her brow wrinkling. That would make him forty-two, if he were still alive. And there was no way Hunter could be anywhere near that old. If she had to guess, she would say he was in his late twenties.

Still, Lancaster was the only one who fit the prime criterion—death. So she accessed the additional information Hunter had downloaded and found herself confronting the image of the man.

The hairs on the top of her head prickled as she stared at the picture. It was Hunter, but a different Hunter. The man she was looking at was at least fifteen years older than the man she knew.

Chapter Nine

Impossible. Nobody turned back the hands of time. The clock ran in only one direction. Plastic surgery? It might take years off your face, but it couldn't give a forty-two year old the body of somebody in his twenties. Could it?

Feeling strangely light-headed, Kathryn studied the man who could be Hunter's older twin, trying to dredge up some feeling of connection to him. But she could generate no emotions but shock at the remarkable resemblance. Perhaps if she read the information, she thought as her eyes began to scan the text. Lancaster had been a track and field superstar at the University of California at Berkeley in the early eighties before going on to the Olympics. He had given up his sports career, gone back to graduate school and ended up as a research physicist at the Sandia National Lab, of all places, working on cold fusion.

He had married a high school teacher, she read with a sharp pang. She had wanted Hunter to have a life before he lost his memory. She hadn't bargained for discovering a wife. But she should have been prepared, she told herself with a little inward stab.

However, two years ago, the Lancasters had been

killed on a New Mexico highway when a tractor-trailer had come around a mountain curve on the wrong side of the road. So the wife was dead, she thought, caught between relief and guilt.

And so was Lancaster...

She studied the picture and reread the short bio, trying to make sense of the startling new information. Ben Lancaster had been an athlete and a scientist—an unusual mixture that could account for the combination of multiple talents and high intelligence in Hunter. But he was much too young to be the same person. Could Lancaster have had a secret child—who had somehow fallen into Emerson's clutches? The possibility seemed remote. And it didn't explain the cryptic remark about previous careers.

A feeling that she was being observed made her look up to find Hunter standing in the doorway watching her. He'd slipped back into the house so quietly that she'd never even heard him.

"How long have you been standing there?" she asked.

"Two minutes."

"I've found something," she told him.

"I know. From the look on your face." His own face had hardened into a look of resignation as he watched her gesture toward the computer.

THE TWO MEN HAD ARRANGED another meeting—this time well past midnight in the woods behind the research center. The older one was angry—angry with himself for being reduced to working with morons. Angry with the way things were falling out. He usually hid his frustration well. Tonight, he took out his fury on his companion.

"Your dumb idea backfired. They're still cozied up
in that house like newlyweds."

The answer came as a sharp retort. "You thought
it was a great idea at the time. All you have to do is
sit back and let me take the chances."

"I'm paying you well enough."

"You're paying me peanuts, considering the risk.
Maybe I'll quit."

"The hell you will. We have an agreement."

The younger man cursed. He'd wanted to get back
at Kelley. Now he wished he'd thought before he
hooked up with this nut.

"Relax. I've got an idea that will do the trick."

"Oh, yeah?"

The more intelligent of the two began to outline his
plan. When he finished, the other one nodded.

"It might work—if we have the time. Deployment
has been moved up."

"Are you sure?"

"I heard Emerson talking to Beckton. By the end
of the week, John Doe is on his way to Gravan. And
you can take credit for a job well done."

In the darkness, the other man's fists clenched.
"And what about Dr. Kelley?" he asked.

"Come on. Do you really think Emerson is going
to let her leave?"

The younger one smiled to himself in the darkness,
thinking he'd imparted good news. The older one hid
his look of alarm. It appeared he was going to have
to speed up his own timetable, and he wasn't sure if
he could pull that off.

HUNTER MADE no comment as Kathryn stood between
him and the computer screen.

"I read some of the personnel files. Then I accessed the information on the decathlon champions," she said.

As she took in the tension in his face and body, she understood why he hadn't wanted to be the one to read the disks. He was afraid to unlock the secrets of his past. Well, she could help him deal with that. Stepping aside, she revealed the picture of Ben Lancaster, watching Hunter's expression as he scanned the image. He stared into the mirror over the dresser, then flicked his gaze back to the sports figure.

"He looks like me," he said. "But...he's older."

"Yes. He died at the age of forty-two in an automobile accident. He was a star athlete. Then he went back to school and got a Ph.D. in physics."

"He must have been smart."

"Yes. Like you."

"Am I?"

"Yes. You're very smart."

While he chewed on that, she took advantage of the light from the bedside lamp to examine his well-honed muscles, supple body and thick head of almost black hair. His face was almost unlined, and his skin was smooth and young-looking. There was no way he could be over thirty, even if he had kept himself in excellent shape.

She reached for one of his hands, turning it over and examining the pads of fingers. They belonged to a young man.

"You can't be him," she said. "But does the picture make you remember anything?"

He stared at the man on the screen for a long time. "No. I'm sorry."

"Why?"

"You want to know who I am."

"You don't?"

He swallowed. "You ask me too many questions. In some ways it was better before you came."

She turned her palms upward, unsure of how to answer.

"I was peaceful. I followed orders. I didn't get angry."

"McCourt warned me you attacked some of the instructors."

"Yes." He opened his hands in a helpless gesture. "In the early practice sessions, I didn't know when to stop fighting. I had to learn that."

She nodded, understanding.

"You stir up questions in my mind. I can't answer the questions, and they make my chest feel tight."

"Everyone has scary things they're afraid to face," she whispered, reaching for him.

"Everyone?"

"Yes. Even me. Like James Harrison."

She gathered him into her embrace, glad when his arms tightened around her. She drew strength from him, even as she gave him comfort.

His hands moved on her back, in her hair. "Feeling things is…" he paused for a moment, searching for the right word, "inconvenient."

"Yes, sometimes feelings are hard to deal with," she answered, "but that's part of being human."

He gave a low, mirthless laugh. "You are the only person here who thinks of me as human."

Her vision blurred, and she fought to keep from coming undone. "Because they can't let themselves!" she said vehemently, cradling him more tightly in her arms. "It's a defense mechanism. They know they've done things to you that are morally and ethically wrong. The only way they can protect themselves is by making you the enemy.''

"I didn't think about it like that.'' A shiver went through him. "I thought it was something wrong with me.''

"No!''

"But there *is* something wrong with me,'' he persisted. "You must know I'm not like other people. I have no history before I woke up in the research facility at Stratford Creek. I know how to be a fighter. I don't know the rest.''

"That's not true. You know more than you think,'' she insisted, her lips skimming his cheek. "Take my word for it.''

He moved back, his eyes bright as they searched hers. "What do you like about me?'' he demanded.

She raised her face, met his worried gaze. "I like your kindness. Your discipline. Your honesty. I like the way you haven't given up.''

"Maybe I did give up—before you came.''

She felt her heart squeeze painfully. "Then I'm glad I'm here.''

"You—'' He stopped, swallowed hard. "I think I have learned more from you than any of the rest of them.''

"I hope so. But I think we're learning from each other.''

"Like what?'' he asked incredulously.

She gave a little laugh. "Well, I didn't know much about turning off hidden recording systems until I met you.''

"Beckton could teach you that,'' he said dismissively.

"I'm not interested in interacting with Beckton. But seeing things through your eyes gives me a fresh view of the world." When his dark gaze continued to challenge her, she went on quickly. "You remind me how much enjoyment there is in simple things. Like music. Or cherry pie with ice cream. Or—" she stopped short, flushing as she realized what she had been about to say.

The flush gave her away. Hunter found her hand, stroked his fingers against hers, sending familiar currents of heat licking at her nerve endings. Her breath hitched as she stared at him.

"When I kiss you and touch you, what do you feel?" he asked with an urgency that turned the heat up several notches.

"The same thing you feel, I think," she answered softly.

His face was a study in stunned disbelief. "You want to…to make love with me?"

Dangerous ground. They were treading on very dangerous ground, yet she had vowed not to duck his questions. "Yes. I want to make love with you," she said, raising her face until their gazes were locked.

She saw him swallow hard. Another man would have reached for her then. Pulled her against him, fast and hard. Taken up where they'd left off in her bedroom. But he only stood with his whole body tight and stiff, fighting primal needs, proving once again that he had more strength of character than any other man she'd ever met.

She could be the one to do the reaching. She could be the one to do things that would break through his iron discipline. It was tempting to make it happen. For a little while they could blot out the intrigue swirling around them. But it would only be a temporary reprieve. And in the morning, their situation would be worse. Every hour they spent in this place made it worse.

"I should read some more of the personnel files," she whispered.

"Yes." He agreed, yet neither one of them moved.

When he spoke again, it wasn't of personnel files. "None of the men call it making love," he said in a thick voice. "They say having sex or—" He stopped, flushed. "They make it sound—dirty. But I can tell they are embarrassed, too. Why is that?"

"Because it's the most intimate thing two people can do together," she said, moistening her dry lips with her tongue. "It can be an expression of strong feelings—of love and commitment. Or it can be done as casually as scratching an itch. Men who don't value its deeper meaning generally make it sound cheap and dirty."

He took in the explanation, then spoke in a rush of words. "I don't know enough about making love to do it right."

His cheeks were bright, his eyes averted.

She inhaled slowly, knowing that few men would have the guts to make that confession. They always thought they were great lovers. "You're worried about that?"

He nodded.

"You're already good at it. Can't you tell I like the things you do?" she said softly.

"We have not done much." As he looked down, his gaze found the front of her shirt.

Her nipples had hardened while they talked. It

seemed he didn't need to touch her to heighten her response.

"I can see the centers of your breasts—standing out against the fabric," he said thickly.

His slow, husky sigh of frustration almost undid her. The temptation to press his hand against her aching breasts was almost unbearable.

When she didn't move, he dropped his hands to his sides. "I should not have asked you about...making love. We do not have much time left now for the computer files."

She closed her eyes for a moment and pressed her forehead against his shoulder. "It's not your fault," she whispered. "I keep letting my priorities get twisted up. I keep wishing we could be alone together, like two people who have nothing more pressing to do than get to know each other better."

"Yes," he said without hesitation. "If it were daylight, I could take you to the place in the woods where the stream makes a little waterfall. There are young spruce trees to make it private, and flat rocks where we could sit and talk—or do anything we wanted."

"You've thought about taking me there?"

"Yes. I found it once, when I was doing survival training. If you sit very still, you can see deer come down to the stream to drink."

"I'd like to go there with you."

"Sometime," he said in a wistful voice.

"Sometime."

"But not now."

She nodded, turned back to the computer, forcing her mind to business. "I want to ask you a question about these files."

"What?"

"Most of the men's duty assignments are listed on their personnel records. Dr. Kolb works at the medical center. Beckton and Winslow are at the training facility. McCourt is at the administration building. And there's a summary of their duties. But the only thing it says about Dr. Swinton is that he works in the research center and Building 22. It also mentions that the building is off-limits to everyone but the research staff."

"And?" Hunter asked carefully.

She had learned how to read him, and she knew he wanted to drop the subject.

"Maybe that's where Swinton keeps his records. Maybe I can figure out a way to check it out. Do you know where I can find that building?"

His gaze turned inward. It was several seconds before he answered, "Yes. But I don't think you should go there."

The way he said it made her even more sure that he knew something about the place, something he didn't want to discuss. And she preferred not to press him. Instead she said, "I'd appreciate it if you could draw me a map."

He gave her a long look, then picked up pencil and paper and began to work rapidly.

Building 22 was an annex to the research facility. When he handed her the paper, she saw his face was pale. All at once, she felt a sudden stab of guilt. He had been in the hospital this afternoon, and now she had kept him up half the night.

"I'm sorry. I wasn't thinking. You should be in bed—not up working half the night. I can finish with the files on my own."

"I'm all right."

"No. You need to get some sleep."

He considered the advice, then nodded. "First I must turn on the recorder."

"Yes." She followed him down the hall and watched him open the access panel that hid the listening device.

After he reactivated it, they returned to the back of the house.

He hesitated outside his door, his gaze dark and intense. That look was enough to make her blood turn molten.

Before temptation overwhelmed her, she gave his hand a quick squeeze and went back to work. But she found she was still thinking about Hunter. She had never met a man like him—such a potent combination of competence and naïveté. Strength and wonderment. A man with no memories because they had been taken away from him.

At least that was what William Emerson had told her when he described Dr. Swinton's research. At the time, it had sounded illegal and immoral. But what if it was actually worse than she imagined?

A terrible thought had been rattling around in her head since she had read the information on Ben Lancaster and seen his picture. Hunter was like a younger version of Lancaster. A younger identical twin.

Eyes narrowed, she went back to Swinton's file. He had earned a medical degree from George Washington University. After a residency in neurology at Johns Hopkins, he had gone back to school at Hopkins to get a Ph.D. in physiology. Then he had won a prestigious appointment to the National Institutes of Health where he had specialized in cutting-edge research in genetics. Next, he had taken a research post at Berkeley, but he had been dismissed for illegal work on human fetuses.

After that, he had switched to animal research at a remote, privately funded laboratory in the Colorado Desert. Not so far from Los Alamos, where Ben Lancaster had been working, she realized with a sudden start.

The lab had produced some notable successes in the cloning of animals.

Cloning.

She felt a wave of cold fear sweep over her as the force of the word hit her. Swinton had cloned animals. Would he dare to try it with human beings?

God, was she really thinking such things? Kathryn asked herself, her mind boggling as she tried to come to grips with the implications. It couldn't be true! She didn't want it to be true. Yet she'd always been a logical person, and against her will, logic forced her mind to move on to the next step.

Cloning was the only way she knew to produce identical twins of different ages. And to clone Lancaster, Swinton wouldn't have needed the whole body, simply a few cells. That she had progressed so far in her thinking in so short a time shocked her to the core. Her assumptions would make Swinton a lawless monster.

Silently, she got up and pulled on black sweatpants, T-shirt and running shoes. Before the sun came up in a few hours, she was going to check out Building 22. Maybe it would turn out to be like Area 51 in Roswell, New Mexico, she told herself, the place where the Air Force was supposed to be hiding a UFO. But she wanted to see for herself.

She took out the computer disk and held it in her

hand. Hunter had told her to erase it. But the information she'd just read on Swinton was electrifying, and she hated to give up the chance to find out more about the other key players—particularly since Hunter had almost gotten himself killed bringing her the files.

The thought made her struggle for composure.

God, she must be the only person on this whole damn place who understood his basic humanity, his basic goodness.

Her vision clouded. Emerson must have been struggling not to laugh in her face when she told him she wanted to give Hunter the experience of a normal life. Emerson didn't give a hoot about his welfare. Neither did any of the rest of them.

Her lips pressed into a grim line, she took another few minutes to carefully open a small hole in the seam of her pillow, stuff the disk into the middle of the foam rubber layers, and sew up the seam with the mending kit from her suitcase. Then, for good measure, she turned the pillow around in its case.

Satisfied with the hiding place, she took a small flashlight from her emergency kit and stole out through the sliding glass doors into the wooded area where she and Hunter had stood the night before.

The night was cool, and she shivered as she oriented herself to the map Hunter had drawn. Though she'd been to the research center before, she knew that things would look different in the dark. At least there was a gibbous moon, making it easier to pick her way through the woods. She came out onto a field about a block from the house and began to jog toward the research center. If anyone spotted her, she'd say she couldn't sleep and had decided to see if exercise would help. Still, when she saw the lights of a car coming down the road, she faded into the shadows under the trees.

It was a patrol car, she noted with a little shiver as it passed. Apparently the security force patrolled the grounds at night.

Staying away from the road as much as she could, she wound through the complex, stopping once more when she saw another vehicle approaching. With the two interruptions, it took her ten minutes to make it to the research building.

Building 22 was in back. The night patrol had made her careful, and she stood in the shadows of some oak trees, watching for activity, before cautiously moving forward and making a partial circle of the building. It was only one story, with a flat roof and metal doors on two sides. The moonlight did nothing to soften its stark lines, or the general impression that the exterior was in even worse repair then the rest of the facilities.

Now that she was here, she wished she had worked out a brilliant plan of assault. Probably it would be better to scope out the place tonight and come back tomorrow. That approach was sound, though she suspected that it had as much to do with a failure of nerve as anything else. She didn't want to prove her shocking theory. Yet she had to know one way or the other. So, after a nervous fifteen minutes during which she saw no sign of activity, she stepped cautiously forward.

She half expected the nearest door to be locked. But the knob turned easily. As she pushed the door open, she started worrying about a silent alarm. But why would Stratford Creek need one, since she was the only spy?

And not a very cool spy, she acknowledged, feeling

her pulse race as she tiptoed down a tile corridor with
painted cinder-block walls illuminated by dim lights.
Deep inside the building, she could hear air-
conditioning or other similar equipment running. After listening to the background noise for several moments, she crept ahead, feeling more and more
vulnerable the farther she progressed into the interior.

The dim, empty corridor was like the set of a
slasher movie. Ordinary—but filled with hidden danger around the next bend.

The intersection of the two hallways loomed directly ahead. Stopping a couple of feet short of the
juncture, she paused and listened intently, but heard
only the sound of the unseen machinery. When she
cautiously peered around the bend, she saw a desk
that might have been a guard station. At this hour in
the morning, it was empty.

Making a quick decision, she proceeded to her
right. Along the new route, she found several doors,
the first of which was locked. The second was open.
When she shone her light inside, she saw a small
office with another desk and a chair. But the surface
of the desk was bare, and the space looked unused.

Maybe the research center had been moved to another building, she speculated, ordering herself to
chill out. The advice only raised goose bumps on her
arms.

What if she got trapped inside this place, she wondered, as she continued down the hall, then tried to
cancel the frightening thought. Moments later, she realized the worry wasn't pure speculation. It had been
triggered by a tiny sound coming to her above the
whine of the machinery.

Voices. Someone talking in an angry tone. Someone answering. They were coming the way she had come. And they were getting closer.

She had only seconds to make a decision. Another door was several feet in front of her, but it might be locked. Going back toward whoever was coming along the hallway was terrifying, yet it was the best choice she could make. In a frantic dash, she turned and sprinted toward the oncoming sound, yanked the office door open, and leaped inside. The moment she was hidden from view, her knees turned to jelly, and she pressed herself against the wall to keep from melting to the floor.

Heart thumping against her ribs, she looked around the little room. There was no other exit, not even a window. If whoever was coming down the hall opened the door, she would be caught like a rat in a trap.

The voices came closer, and with a chill that went all the way to her bones, she realized that the angry person was Dr. Swinton.

"I don't understand why we're having this problem!" he growled. "We should be getting a much better success rate. But another one is going bad."

"I'm sorry, sir," the other speaker replied. "Perhaps, you've...uh...pushed the growth rate a little high. A few more weeks to maturity shouldn't hold up the project too much, and it might make the difference...."

She recognized this man, too. It was Swinton's assistant, Roger Anderson.

An ominous silence followed Anderson's reasonable-sounding suggestion. Then Swinton asked, his voice so sharp that Kathryn felt the words were piercing her flesh, "Are you sure you followed procedures exactly?"

"Yes, sir. It's not the fault of the life support system. It's the inherent problems with keeping genetic material viable."

The voices were receding now, and she dared to let out the breath she was holding.

"The genetic material is perfect!" Swinton growled.

"Yes, sir. But there are always problems. If you read the literature—" She didn't catch the rest of the response because the man's placating voice was now too far away. But she still heard Swinton loud and clear.

"I don't need to read the damn literature. I know more than anybody else working in the field. And I don't want to hear any excuses. You will prepare for a new trial. We will start on the next shift."

She stood silently in the dark, thinking about the conversation and the strained relationship between the two men. Things weren't going the way Swinton expected, and he was blaming his subordinate. But what type of experiments was he conducting?

After ten minutes without any further interruption, she decided it was safe to open the door. When she peeked cautiously out, the corridor was empty. Though the temptation to run for the nearest exit was overwhelming, she considered her options, finally deciding to retrace Swinton and Anderson's route in hopes that she might find out what they'd been doing.

Turning in the direction from which she'd come, she headed for the place where the hallways crossed. This time, she went left and found herself in a section of the building where the temperature was even colder than before. The only sound she heard was the constant whine of the machinery, which seemed to be coming from behind a door about ten feet along the corridor. She could see the red glow of a night-light shining along the bottom of the jamb. Somehow it made her think of fire seeping up from the depths of hell, and she had the sudden conviction that she didn't want to find out what was in that room.

Yet she kept moving forward until she could wrap her fingers around the door handle. In the back of her mind, she hoped it would be locked. Instead, it turned noiselessly, and she stepped inside. In the red light she could see several large tanks with glass walls. For a moment, she wondered if this was an aquarium. Then she saw what was floating in the rectangular containers, and a scream of mingled horror and protest rose in her throat.

Chapter Ten

Somehow she managed to stifle the scream so that it came out as a kind of helpless sob. She wanted to back out of the room and run headlong down the corridor, but her legs quite literally refused to move. Rooted to the spot, she stood in frozen horror, her eyes fixed on the closest tank. Inside, a naked man floated, a man lying on his side, with his knees pulled toward his chest and his eyes closed.

In the eerie red light, she could see tubes attached to his wrists and his mouth. For feeding and oxygen? Some detached part of her brain asked the questions, as she observed him. The rest of her fought horror at what she was seeing.

She stood breathing in gasps of the chilly air, trying not to pass out. The crazy thought ran through her head that she was watching a scene from a horror movie, except that special effects masters had not created this experimental laboratory.

It was an invention from the diabolic mind of Dr. Swinton. Aided by Anderson and Emerson and the rest of them.

Revulsion engulfed her, and it took every ounce of fortitude she possessed to keep standing in the doorway. But she had to know more, so she managed not to turn and run.

Stay calm, she ordered herself. *You have to stay calm.*

Taking a few steps into the room, she eyed the machinery attached to the tanks. There was monitoring equipment that looked like the kind used in intensive care units. Only this was no hospital.

Her eyes darted to the other containers ranked around the laboratory. Two were empty. Two others held men who looked like twins. The remaining four tanks held boys—or rather, what looked like the same boy—at different stages of development, ranging in age from a few years to a young teenager.

Clones? Started at different times. And growing at a much more rapid rate than any normal human child, she speculated, as she remembered the conversation in the hall.

Logic had forced her to consider the possibility that Swinton had progressed to cloning humans. The reality was more than she could cope with.

"No," she gasped as she backed away, out of the room, into the blessed solitude of the hall. Then she was running for the exit and freedom.

She was barely thinking, barely functioning at anything approaching a normal level. All she knew was that she had to get away from that place. Blind to caution, she staggered down the corridor. If Swinton or Anderson had still been in the building, they would surely have caught her.

Reaching the door through which she'd entered, she twisted the knob. For a few dreadful seconds it wouldn't open. Then the catch moved, and she stumbled out into the night. Moments later she found herself standing under the oak trees sucking in great gasps of air.

It was still dark, she saw with shock, since it felt as if she'd been in that terrible room for centuries. When she looked at her watch, she discovered that only half an hour had elapsed since she'd first entered the building.

Breath wheezing in and out of her lungs, she made for the cottage. Too late, she realized she had forgotten to pay attention to her surroundings. About a hundred yards from the cottage, a cruiser came gliding up behind her and gave her a blast from the siren, almost making her jump out of her skin.

She thought about fleeing, then imagined a bullet plowing into her back. Trying to wipe any expression from her face, she stood dragging in air as two security men got out of the vehicle and came toward her. She didn't recognize them, but they seemed to know who *she* was.

"Dr. Kelley?" the taller one asked.

"Yes."

"Do you mind telling us what you're doing out here at this hour of the morning."

"Running."

"You weren't moving very fast."

"I know." For a terrible moment her mind went completely blank. Then she raised her chin. "I had a stitch in my side. I've been walking for the last half mile, I think." As soon as she said it, she wondered if they'd been quietly following her. And how far?

"What was your route?" the one who seemed to be in charge asked.

"I don't know the compound all that well. I assume it's perfectly safe to be out at night," she said, pretending that the man's chief concern was for her safety.

"Of course," he agreed.

"Well, I probably should get home now. Thank you for stopping."

The guard looked at her consideringly.

As if she assumed the interview was over, she turned her back and walked toward the house. Then she remembered that the front door was locked. She'd have to go in the sliding door, the way she'd come out. Hoping they wouldn't wonder why she was disappearing around back, she hurried into the shadows under the trees.

It had taken every ounce of concentration to focus on the conversation with the security guards. Every ounce of concentration to sound sane and rational.

She was reaching for the door handle when Hunter appeared, slid the glass panel to the side, and stepped into the backyard. After her experience in the laboratory, seeing him was a shock. She made a muffled sound and stepped back.

"I frightened you," he said. "I'm sorry."

Her lips moved, but no words came out.

"I heard the siren," he said in a strained voice. "I looked out the window and saw you with the security guards. I didn't know what they were going to do. I thought I should protect you from them. Then I thought I would make things worse if they saw me."

"I'm fine," she said, although she knew she had broken her rule about lying. All at once, it was impossible to keep herself from shaking.

Hunter reached for her and wrapped his hands around the cold skin of her arms, rubbing the goose-flesh. "You're not fine," he said. "You're cold and shivering."

She tried to deny it, but gave up the attempt.

"Where were you?" he demanded.

Building 22, her mind screamed, as all the horror of the place came rushing back over her, swamping her, choking her, making it impossible to speak.

Hunter gave her a critical look. When she didn't say anything, he continued in a flat voice, "You asked me how to get to Building 22. Then you went there."

When she managed the barest of nods, his hands dropped away from her arms. "You saw the tanks."

Slowly she raised her head, hoping against hope that she had heard him wrong. "How do you know about that?"

"I've seen them. I tried not to think about it." When she continued to stare at him, he explained. "I—I guess I knew what they meant."

An involuntary shudder racked her.

"I hoped you wouldn't go there. I knew you would feel differently about me if you saw that place." When she didn't answer, he continued in the same strained voice, "I can see the horror in your eyes. Now you are like the rest of them. You know I'm not a real person."

She was still in shock, unable to think clearly. Her mouth was dry, so that her words came out rough and sharp. "You told me you never lie. Why didn't you tell me about Dr. Frankenstein's laboratory?"

He turned his face away from her and spoke rapidly. "Last night, when the storm came and we talked, you asked if I remembered my mother or my father. I said I didn't. That was a true statement. But

I didn't want to tell you I remembered waking up in the lab. Lying on a table, cold and naked and confused."

She sucked in a strangled breath. Her knees threatened to give way, and she locked them to keep standing. "Hunter—" She tried to speak, even when she didn't know what to say. But the memory of that nightmare place was too vivid. She had seen things that could drive a sane person to madness.

He closed his eyes for a moment, then focused on her face. "The time with you was good," he whispered. "Like nothing else in my life—before or after. You were my friend—and more." She saw his hands clench and unclench. "I will remember all of the things that happened between us. The alligator toy. The steak. The sound of you singing." His voice hitched. "Holding you. It was all good. But I understand that you will no longer have anything to do with me." He reached toward her, then his arm fell back to his side. "For a little while, with you, I had the things you said people need. But at least now it will be easier to go on my mission."

"No," she whispered, unsure of what she meant. Yet after the shock of Swinton's lab, it was impossible for her to respond in any kind of normal fashion. She had been stunned past her capacity to function, and she truly didn't know what she felt.

"I can't—"

"I know," he answered. "It's all right. I understand. I've been waiting for you to change." With that, he turned toward the house and in moments he disappeared from view.

On legs that barely supported her weight, she tottered forward and gripped the door handle, somehow finding the strength to pull herself inside and slide the heavy glass panels shut behind her.

The ten feet to the bed might have been ten miles, but she made it across the vast distance and collapsed. As soon as her legs no longer had to carry her weight, her shoulders began to shake uncontrollably. The shaking turned to sobs, and she pressed her face into the pillow to muffle the sound.

HE GOT UP at the usual time, dressed and neatly made his bed the way the orderly had taught him. Outside Kathryn's door Hunter stopped and imagined he could hear the sound of her breathing. She had been crying last night, now she was sleeping. He was glad, because he didn't want to see her now—see the look of fear and disgust in her eyes. He wanted to remember the relief and joy on her face when he came back from the hospital, but the scene kept slipping out of his mind.

Quietly he walked down the hall to the kitchen. He warmed a little of yesterday's coffee in the microwave and drank it as he eyed the box of doughnuts on the counter. He could eat more of them. As many as he wanted. Instead, he picked up the box and pitched it into the trash.

Moisture blurred his vision. Like when Beckton had slapped him. But this pain was different—not physical, but worse.

He had thought he could deaden himself, the way he had been dead before Kathryn. But banishing the anguish churning inside him was impossible. He had told himself he didn't care what she thought of him, just the way he didn't care what any of them thought. With them it was true, but with Kathryn, it was a lie.

Quietly he walked back to his room and packed the clothes he had brought from his quarters. He had never asked Beckton or anyone else to do him a favor. He would ask for something now.

In the living room, he hesitated in front of the bookshelves. The green alligator was where he had left it. Before he could stop himself, he snatched it up and stuffed it in his bag.

When the security men came to pick him up fifteen minutes later, they eyed the duffel bag slung over his shoulder.

"Hey, what are you doing?" the senior one asked.

"I am going back to my quarters."

"You don't make those kind of decisions."

"Living here is interfering with my work. I will tell that to Major Beckton."

"Oh, yeah?" The man laughed. "I guess Dr. Kelley would interfere with my concentration, too."

Hunter kept his expression blank. He would not talk about the things he and Kathryn had done. That was a private memory he would lock away in his heart for the rest of his short life.

He climbed into the car, and set the duffel bag on the seat beside him. The driver started the engine, and they rode to the training center. But leaving the house didn't help. The pain rode with him.

It wouldn't go away. He had invested too much of himself in the feeling of being connected with her. In the talks, and the sharing, and the touching and kissing, and all the little things.

The song she had been singing while she worked in the kitchen began to run through his mind. He liked the song. It had words that talked about life.

He had thought that he and Kathryn might have

a little more time together before he fulfilled his purpose.

He had been wrong. But he knew his duty, and he hoped now that they would deploy him soon. He could go off and assassinate General Kassan, the dictator of Gravan. Kassan was evil. Colonel Emerson had explained many times that the man was destroying the lives of everyone in his country. Killing him would be a good deed. But nobody could get close enough to kill the general and escape. So the clone Swinton had made was going off on what Colonel Emerson called a kamikaze mission. Like the Japanese airplane pilots in World War II who dive-bombed American ships and sacrificed their lives for the glory of the empire. He would be killed, too. But that was good, because then the pain would stop.

KATHRYN FOUGHT against waking, fought against the need to face reality. But once awareness returned, it was impossible to slip back into the blessed oblivion of sleep. The images from the night before came back like demons sent to carry her off to hell.

With a small sound of protest, she tried to push them out of her mind. But the pictures were too vivid. Over the course of her career, she had seen shocking things, like the miserable conditions that could prevail in a state mental hospital. But nothing had prepared her for the laboratory in Building 22.

Who had given the approval for the research here, she wondered. Did the President know Dr. Swinton was growing men in tanks? Or had permission come from some madman in the Pentagon?

She shuddered, then thought of Hunter. Oh, God, Hunter. He'd been worried when he'd heard the siren and come out to meet her. Then he'd seen the horror on her face, and she'd been too upset to talk to him coherently.

She'd been in shock, and much of the scene between them was now a blur. But she could remember some of the things. His words. Her totally inadequate responses.

Leaping out of bed, she rushed to his bedroom. It was empty, with the bed neatly made. A drawer was slightly open. He never left anything out of place, she thought, as she crossed the room and looked inside. The drawer was empty.

With a feeling of dread, she ran down the hall. The front of the house was also deserted.

Hunter was gone.

Eyes stinging, she sank into a chair, thinking about what she'd done to him. For the first time in his life, someone—she—had reached out to him on a human level. At first he'd been wary. But she'd worked hard to make him understand she cared, and finally he'd let himself trust the warmth and sharing growing between them. Last night she had shattered that trust, destroyed the private world she and Hunter had built.

She felt her heart being ripped from her chest as his words came back to her. He had said that he would always remember the things that had happened between them.

Oh, God. What have I done?

He seemed so strong in many ways. Yet he didn't know what to expect from himself, she realized, as she remembered the way he kept checking his reactions with her—checking to see if he was normal. And he certainly didn't know what to expect from her.

Trying to block out the look on his face, she covered her face with her hands, her body rocking back and forth. But she couldn't hold back the tears welling up inside her. They leaked from between her fingers and ran down her cheeks as her shoulders began to shake.

BECKTON CALLED Emerson. Thirty minutes later, they had a staff meeting in the little office off the training area. Emerson, Beckton, Swinton, Anderson, and Kolb.

While the five of them argued, Hunter was sent off to clean his spotless automatic weapon. But he could hear the loud discussion. Kolb wanted him to move back into the cottage. Beckton and Winslow had always thought it was a stupid idea. Emerson said that Hunter had changed—his request to leave the guest quarters proved it.

They called him in and asked questions about what Kathryn Kelley had taught him. They watched to see if he could eat a sandwich neatly. They made him pretend he was sitting in an airport waiting area, then asked what he would do if someone accidentally bumped against him.

He said, "Excuse me."

They asked him to talk about other things. He remembered to use the contractions. They asked why he wanted to change the living arrangements. He told them he wanted to concentrate on his assignment.

He was pretty sure that he did everything right. He showed them he had learned a lot of important socialization skills. Really, he had known many of the things already. He simply hadn't thought of them as important—because nobody had made them important before Kathryn. Now he demonstrated that he could pass for human. He hoped he had convinced them he was ready for his assignment.

They let him put his clothing back in his quarters. He unpacked everything and softly touched the green fur of the alligator before shoving it into the back of a drawer. If anyone asked, he would say it was a souvenir.

That night he would sleep in the narrow bed where he had slept since he had left Swinton's laboratory— except for the two nights he had lived with Kathryn. Only two nights. It seemed like longer. His whole life. The meaningful part of his life. He clamped his teeth together, trying to hold back any sound. But he couldn't hold back the feeling of emptiness inside.

KATHRYN COULDN'T GET an appointment with the chief of operations until well into the afternoon. She entered his office braced to argue that she could still be of help in Hunter's training.

To her surprise, Emerson concurred immediately. "You've done a tremendous job with him in a very short time," he complimented her.

"Thank you."

"I was hoping you'd stay at Stratford Creek in case we need some further assistance."

"I'd certainly be willing to do that," she agreed, both relieved and elated that she wasn't being dismissed.

"And I'd like to see the report on the sessions you had with him," Emerson added. "Could you start writing it up?"

She nodded, wondering exactly what she was going

to say. Some double-talk or other. But at least making it up would give her something to do.

When she left the office, she almost ran into Dr. Kolb, who was pacing back and forth in the waiting room.

He looked up when he saw her, his face gray-tinged, his upper lip beaded with perspiration. "Are you leaving us?" he asked.

"No. Mr. Emerson wants me to stay."

He relaxed a fraction. "I was hoping we would get a chance to talk."

"Uh, yes," she said, unsure of what they had to say to each other.

"Maybe we—" He stopped and glanced at the secretary, then ushered Kathryn into the hall.

She eyed him questioningly.

"I was wondering if we could meet somewhere private."

"Where?"

"You jog. What about the woods at the end of East Road?"

She thought about rendezvousing with this man she didn't trust in an isolated patch of woods. Too dangerous.

Before she could politely decline, Emerson's voice rang out. "Kolb, where the hell are you? We have an appointment."

The doctor went rigid. Giving Kathryn an unreadable look, he squared his shoulders and marched into the outer office, leaving Kathryn staring at his back.

THE NIGHT WAS THE WORST, Hunter thought. He missed being with Kathryn. Missed her smile, the little jokes she made, sharing food with her, the warm looks she gave him. He had said he would lock those things away, that they could no longer be part of him.

But as he lay alone in his narrow bed, he found he needed them. In his mind, he brought them out, one by one, like jewels from a treasure chest.

She had sung while she had made the pancakes. When he came home from the hospital, she had leaped into his arms. Later, they had talked about making love. They would never do it now, but he had held her close in her bed—kissed her, felt her body rocking against his. That had felt so good—even the tight aching part of it. Better than anything he could imagine.

In the darkness, he could relive the moments with her, pretend they were happening again. In the daylight, as he ate runny eggs and drank cooling black coffee, he knew he was only fooling himself.

But it helped a little to focus on the training sessions, and to remember that he wouldn't have to stay here for long.

Reid came to get him after weapons drill and took him down to the lake to practice setting plastic explosives. Usually Reid was in security, but it seemed he had also been an explosives expert, so he was on the instructional team today.

It was odd for Reid to be working with him alone, he thought. But he didn't ask questions. He simply followed orders.

"Have you detonated these before?" Reid asked, holding up two plastic bricks.

"Yes."

"What is the explosive power?"

He recited the specs, until Reid stopped him with another question. "What do you think about using a transmitter instead of fuses to blow up the cabin at the end of the pier?'' He pointed to a weathered house that sat about fifty feet from the shore.

"No problem," he answered, thinking this was like a test, only he wasn't sure that Reid knew the answers.

KATHRYN SAT with her laptop computer at the dining-room table, working on the report Emerson had asked her to write, trying to make it sound as if she and Hunter had focused exclusively on business.

But her mind kept wandering. She wondered where Hunter was, what he was doing, whether he was thinking about her as much as she was thinking about him. But probably that wouldn't be good for him, she decided with a pang as she pictured the tortured look on his face two nights ago.

She clenched her fists, trying to wipe away that scene. She had messed up badly. But it was Swinton's fault, damn him. Swinton and his Frankenstein lab. And as she contemplated his research, she couldn't stop her mind from starting to form a terrible hypothesis—a hypothesis based on what she already knew and what she could guess.

This was a secret DOD research center, and they must have invested millions of dollars in a project to develop clones and train them for special assignments. Why?

Well, suppose you had a human test subject, she thought. But you didn't think of him as a man, because you'd grown him in a laboratory, so you could send him off on a dangerous mission. Would you care about bringing him home when he finished the job? Or would you figure that you didn't need him anymore, because you could always produce another one to fit your specifications?

Maybe you didn't even care if he succeeded in his assignment, because you could always try again with an equally expendable subject.

She almost gagged, then thought of something equally sinister—something that helped confirm her hypothesis. You didn't have to kill a man to clone him. If you had his cooperation, you could ask him for cell samples. There were lots of guys at Stratford Creek Swinton and Emerson could have used. But they had wanted a particular blend of brains and physique—combined in the person of an ex-athlete and physicist named Ben Lancaster. She'd bet they hadn't asked him for cell samples. Or maybe they had, and he'd refused. Then they'd been afraid he'd blow the whistle on the project, and they'd murdered him. Maybe that so-called accident that took his life was anything but.

Unfortunately, Lancaster wasn't going tell her what had happened, because he was dead. And now they had Hunter to send off on a one-way trip. The whole theory made a kind of awful sense, once you added up all the other factors.

She told herself there was still time to wreck their plans, but how?

Feeling trapped and helpless, she got up and paced restlessly around the house. It had become impossible for her to work on the report, so she wandered back to the bedroom and picked up her pillow with the disk sewn inside. She might as well get it out and read about the pack of criminals who ran this place.

To her relief, the pillow was still stitched the way she'd left it. After ripping the seam, she pulled out the disk and brought it back to the dining room where she inserted it into the floppy drive.

She had planned to go over the personnel records. Instead she was drawn back to the biographical information on Ben Lancaster, avidly reading the details of his life and his career. He had been a strong, capable man. Like Hunter, she thought with a pang. So many athletes never went on to achieve anything noteworthy after their early successes. Lancaster was different. He'd been one of the outstanding researchers at the Sandia Lab, and he had traveled widely. Maybe his personality was part of Hunter. Maybe in some unaccountable way, some of his memories had also come through.

But at least they'd picked the right candidate for cloning, she thought with bitter irony. A man with a superb body and an IQ to match. Her thoughts switched easily from Lancaster to Hunter. She had to figure out how to get to him as soon as possible, how to regain his trust, and how to get him out of Stratford Creek. Small stuff, she thought with an edgy laugh.

If she had more specific information on Lancaster, maybe that would help her figure out how to approach Hunter. She knew she was grasping at straws, but it was better to have some constructive focus for her thoughts than to simply sit and worry.

Perhaps she could get what she wanted from Dr. Kolb. He had proposed a meeting. What if she could use that to her advantage?

She was about to call him when the phone rang, making her jump.

A man with a stuffed-up nose said, "Dr. Kelley?"

"Yes?"

"This is Bob Perry calling about Hunter."

As he started to speak again, she'd thought she recognized the voice that was muffled by the nasal congestion. But she'd never talked to a Bob Perry, as far as she could remember.

"What can I do for you?" she asked, waffling between hope and caution.

"There's been a change in plans. Mr. Emerson wants to know if you would you be able to work in a session with Hunter at noontime."

She tried to hide her burst of elation as she answered, "No problem."

"He's on a field exercise at one of the cabins down by the lake. He'll be having a lunch break in forty minutes. Would that be convenient for you?"

"Of course."

"The cabin is a little unusual. It's on the end of a pier that juts out into the water. You should recognize it right away."

"I'll need directions." Opening the drawer under the phone, she found a notepad and a pen.

"It's about a ten-minute drive," the caller said, then went on to give her precise directions.

He was more civil than most of the other staff members she'd had contact with, she thought, as she replaced the receiver and headed for her bedroom. She needed a shower and clean clothes.

As she hurried to get ready, she started worrying. Did Hunter know she was coming? It wouldn't be good to take him by surprise.

Praying that they'd let her talk with him alone, she got into the car and headed toward the woods. When she'd jogged down here, the road had had a security barrier blocking off traffic. Now the gate was open, and she drove through, into an area she'd never seen before. There were no buildings, only virgin forest and then a lake sparkling in the sunshine at the base of the hill.

Another quarter mile and she came to the parking lot Perry had indicated. There was only one other vehicle in the lot, a jeep sitting at the far end. She pulled in next to it and scanned the woods. Several paths led downhill—presumably toward the lake. She took the middle one and came out facing a stretch of pristine beach. No one was in sight, and the only sign of habitation was the weathered pier with the cabin Perry had described.

"Hunter?" she called, but the noise of a jet overhead blocked the sound of her voice. If he was there, he couldn't hear her, she thought as she stepped onto the worn boards and started toward the cabin.

The footing was uneven, and she picked her way, hoping she wouldn't step through rotten wood.

OVER THE NOISE of the jet, Hunter thought he heard Kathryn call his name and looked up in surprise. He and Reid had set the explosives on the underside of the shack at the end of the pier. Then Reid had gone off to do something, leaving him alone to wait for additional instructions.

He'd been sitting with his back against a tree, holding a flower by its stem and stroking the petals against his mouth, remembering the wonderful softness of Kathryn's lips against his. If he closed his eyes, he could imagine she was with him, and they were in the place where the deer came to drink from the stream.

Now he heard the sound of her voice. Was she really here?

He saw her step onto the dock and start walking tentatively toward the doomed little house. The charges were in place, expertly positioned to blow the structure into oblivion. All somebody had to do was press the buttons on the detonator.

"Get back," he shouted at Kathryn above the drone of the jet. She didn't hear him, and he started running, calling more loudly and frantically waving his arms.

She stopped at the sound of his voice and tipped her head to the side, but she was looking in the wrong direction and didn't see him. After a moment, she started moving again, along the pier toward the enclosure with its deadly charges.

At the same time, from the corner of his eye, he saw Reid running down one of the other paths from the parking lot. He broke into the clearing along the shoreline and dashed toward the spot several hundred yards away where they'd set up the detonators.

Hunter's eyes narrowed. "What are you doing?" he called.

The man didn't answer. Instead he kept moving toward the firing mechanism. If he'd wanted to get Kathryn Kelley out of danger, Hunter reasoned, he would be running in the other direction—shouting at her to get away from the pier.

Instead, he was hurrying to set off the charges!

Reid was farther away than Kathryn. There was no chance of intercepting him before he could get to the detonators. All Hunter could do was dash toward Kathryn, sprinting with every ounce of power he possessed, knowing that he had little chance of getting to her in time.

Chapter Eleven

Kathryn reached the cabin and stooped to peer in a broken window, but there was no one inside.

"Hunter?" she called, turning away in perplexity from the dilapidated building.

Had Perry been mistaken?

Then she saw Hunter dashing madly toward her and heard him shouting, "Get away from the house. Get away."

He came toward her at full tilt. Behind him she saw a man running toward a little stand of trees. It was Reid, she realized. The security guard who had cursed Hunter in the locker room.

At that moment, Hunter gained the end of the pier, leaped onto the worn boards and came straight at her. He plowed ahead like a freight train speeding down a mountain, and she knew that when he hit her, the impact would be painful. Cowering back, she stiffened her body against the inevitable crash.

She screamed as he struck her with the weight of his muscular frame, screamed again as he took her over the side of the flimsy railing and into space.

They fell toward the lake, her body under his. And

she had time for only a partial gasp of air before they hit the cold water.

As they splashed down, she heard an explosion like a dozen thunderclaps coming together in the air above them. Then they plummeted below the surface, and she felt a shock wave hit the water.

Hunter held her down, at the same time kicking strongly and towing her away from the spot where they'd gone over the side. She hadn't taken in much air, and she felt as if her lungs would burst. Then suddenly he tugged her to the surface, where she dragged in grateful drafts of air.

"Breathe. We must go down again," he gasped.

Pieces of wood were raining down around them in the water. One hit her shoulder and she winced as Hunter dragged her under again, pulling her parallel to the shoreline and into a stand of water grass that swayed wildly in a sudden pounding of waves.

They surfaced among the quaking stalks, and she sucked in oxygen, shivering in the cold water.

Hunter put his arm around her. "Stay low."

She ducked into the greenery, lifting her head only enough so that she could breathe.

"Did I hurt you?" he asked urgently, his hand gliding along her arm. "I saw you on the dock, and I didn't know what else to do."

"I'm okay," she assured him as she swung around and stared at the spot where she'd been standing moments ago. It no longer existed. In fact, only the first quarter of the dock was still visible, listing at a steep angle toward the water. As she watched, it fell sideways and hit the surface of the lake with a large splash, adding to the fury of the churning waves.

Wide-eyed, she gaped at the scene, her mind trying to make sense of the destruction.

"What happened?" she asked in a strangled voice.

"He waited until you were out on the pier. Then he set off the explosives. Why were you here?"

"A man named Bob Perry called me. He told me to meet you here. He described the location. But just now, I saw Reid."

"When did this Bob Perry call you?"

"Around eleven-thirty."

"That was one of the times when Reid left me alone."

She nodded tightly, remembering that she had thought the voice was familiar. It might have been Reid.

As they watched, the man in question moved along the beach near the ruined pier, shading his eyes and scanning the wreckage.

"We must get away from here," Hunter said. "When he doesn't see our bodies, he'll look for us farther from the explosion."

She made a small sound of agreement, gripped his arm. The last time they'd met, she had been too shocked to speak coherently. This morning she'd come prepared with explanations and apologies. The words still raged inside her. She wanted desperately to make him understand what was in her heart, but it would have to wait.

"Follow me," he said, "and stay down."

Her legs felt shaky, but she managed to keep up with him as they moved farther from the site of the devastation.

She imitated his crouched posture as they moved

through the reeds. When a small black snake slithered past, she gasped.

Hunter turned and looked at the creature. "It won't hurt you. There are no poisonous snakes in this lake."

"Glad to hear it."

"But watch for snapping turtles."

Right. She didn't tell him she wasn't an expert at turtle identification. She simply kept following him, her teeth chattering both from the cold water and from reaction.

"It will take longer if we climb out of the water," Hunter told her. "And you will be colder in the air."

"I'm fine," she lied.

Hunter paused, then gestured toward a point of land in the distance. "Can you swim that far?"

She eyed the peninsula, telling herself it was well within her range. Never mind that she'd never been in worse shape for a long swim.

"I can make it." To prove the assertion, she pushed off and started stroking. Hunter came after her, caught up, and kept pace easily as they crossed the open water.

She was a good swimmer, but not today. By the time she was three-quarters of the way across, she was breathing hard, and her arms were aching.

"Are you all right?" Hunter asked.

She nodded and kept moving, then finally she reached a point where her limbs simply wouldn't work.

"I—" She started to slip below the surface but he grabbed her around the chest and pulled her up.

"It is only a little farther. Rest for a minute."

She let herself go limp, holding on to his arm, relying on his strength to keep her afloat. She thought she felt his lips brush her cheek. "You are very brave," he whispered. "Very determined."

"I've tried to be," she answered, then gulped, her vision blurring as his murmured praise rekindled the deep feelings of guilt that had haunted her since he'd fled the guest cottage. All at once it was impossible to hold back the unspoken words pressing on her heart. "Hunter, the other night...I was too shocked and frightened to act normally. I hurt you. I'm so sorry. I don't feel the way you think I do."

His grip on her stiffened, but he said nothing. When she tried to twist around so she could see his face, he held her fast.

His reaction made her take a gasping breath so that she could keep talking, force him to understand. "When I got up the next morning and found that you had left, I felt so awful. I wanted a chance to explain what happened—that I'd been frightened. And upset. But not with you. Then Reid called, and I was so glad I was going to see you again..."

"We cannot stay in the water," was all he said, sounding as if he hadn't heard anything she'd tried to tell him.

"Hunter, please."

"This is a dangerous place for a discussion." Stroking strongly with his free arm, he began to tow her toward shore. She wanted to dig her fingers into his flesh and force him to listen, but she knew he was right. She also understood that he wasn't prepared to let her hurt him again.

"I can swim," she managed.

"I'll do it," he said in a gruff voice.

Though pride made her want to insist, she knew it

was better to save her strength for walking when they got out of the water. So she let him tow her.

Finally, she realized he must be standing on the bottom. After climbing out onto a flat boulder, he pulled her from the water. In the chilly air, she began to shiver again.

His look of concern made her clamp her teeth to try and stop their chattering.

"We can't stay here," he said. Taking her arm, he guided her toward a stand of pines.

While she propped herself against a rock outcropping, he went back to scatter pine needles over their trail.

She watched him numbly. When he came back, he took her hand and led her farther along the rocks, searching the edge of the cliff.

His face took on a look of satisfaction as he pointed to a spot where a narrow trail wound upward.

"I thought this was the right place."

He helped her up the rocky trail to a low door hidden in a crevice. The door looked like it was secured with a padlock, but it wasn't really locked. Hunter twisted the hasp open, then helped her through the doorway. They crawled about ten feet down a dark tunnel.

"Where are we?"

"I think this is what they used to call an atomic bomb shelter," he said, switching on a powerful portable light. "It must be from the time when Stratford Creek was a military base."

In the shaft of light, she could see a small room cut into the side of the mountain. Various supplies were ranged on metal shelves around the wall.

Too worn-out to stand under her own power, she

leaned against the wall, breathing hard and making little pools on the plastic floor where the water dripped off her clothing.

"Are we safe here?"

"Yes. I discovered this place when I was on a survival mission. I come here sometimes, when I am supposed to be hiding in enemy territory. Nobody has ever found me here. I brought some lights and emergency rations." He switched on another large flashlight, then swung the door shut, dropping a stout metal bar in place to seal the entrance.

"Is the air all right with the door closed?" she asked.

"There are ventilators," he said.

After turning a crank in the wall, he eyed her critically in the dim light. "You are cold. You must get warm and dry." Briskly he crossed to the wooden boxes on the shelves and rummaged through them until he found blankets. Then he turned back to her and began to unbutton her shirt, his fingers a bit clumsy as they struggled with the wet buttonholes. Where he touched her chilled flesh, he left a trail of heat.

He finally got the buttons open, then slipped the shirt off her shoulders and down her arms.

A moment ago she had been wilting with fatigue and aching with the knowledge that he didn't want to hear her explanations. Now she felt a new burst of energy and hope. Although he hadn't listened when she'd tried to tell how she felt, perhaps a more basic approach would get through to him.

"Maybe we'd better make a comfortable place to sit down," she suggested.

"Yes." He spread blankets on the floor before

turning back to her and tackling the snap at the waistband of her slacks. Then he worked the zipper open
so that he could kneel and skim the wet pants down
her legs. When she stepped out of them, she was
wearing only panties and a bra and feeling a good
deal warmer than she had when she'd come into the
shelter.

He stayed on his knees for a moment, his warm
breath fanning her belly. She lifted her hands as she
gazed down at his dark head, wanted to tunnel her
fingers though his hair and press his face against her.
But she bided her time, letting him stand and drape
her soggy clothing over the edge of a box.

"You're as wet as I am," she said, trying to sound
objective.

He looked down at his clinging knit shirt and chino
pants, then tugged the shirt over his head. Unselfcon-
sciously, he unzipped the pants and stepped out of
them.

He was still wearing his wet briefs, but the knit
fabric left little to the imagination. As she regarded
him through half-closed lids, she wondered when it
would dawn on him that there was more than one way
to get warm.

"We should dry my hair," she said in a thick
voice.

He searched the storage boxes again and found a
thin towel, which she took from him. Briskly she began to rub the long strands of her hair between her
towel-covered hands, observing him through heavy-
lidded eyes. He was watching her intently.

"My arms are tired from swimming," she said, in
a languorous voice. "Could you help me?"

He took the towel from her and began to work on

her hair, rubbing the way she'd demonstrated. With a deep sigh, she let her head drop to his naked shoulder.

Her eyes were downcast, not with modesty but with interest. He might be a whirlwind of activity, but the clinging briefs gave him away.

His hands became a bit shaky, but he kept at the drying until she made a small sound in her throat.

"Am I hurting you?" he asked anxiously.

"No," she answered, silently admitting she enjoyed shredding his composure. "But I'd like to get out of this wet bra." Reaching around, she opened the catch and pulled the garment away from her body. Straightening, she tossed it in the general direction of the boxes.

She could hear the uneven breath rushing in and out of his lungs as he stared at her breasts.

Her nipples were already hard. They tightened further under the heat of his scorching gaze. Silently, she lifted the towel from his hands, dropped it onto the floor, and took a step closer, so that her naked breasts touched the hard wall of his chest.

His strangled exclamation was as gratifying as the feel of his flesh against hers. For long seconds he seemed too stunned to move.

"Touch me," she whispered. "Please touch me."

In slow motion, his hands came up to cradle her breasts. When his fingers began to knead and stroke, she made a high sound of pleasure as she arched into his caress.

Silently she raised her hands to his chest, combing through the crisp mat of hair and finding his nipples, drawing a sharp gasp from him as she showed him ways to touch—ways that he might imitate.

He did just that, to her delight.

"I don't think I can stand up much longer," she murmured.

His hands stilled. His breath drew in sharply. "I should stop doing this to you."

"Not this time."

"Kathryn, when you came back from Swinton's lab, you...had changed. I saw the look on your face." His eyes were bleak as he put distance between them.

"Hunter." She grabbed his arm and held tight. "I saw things there that upset me. And I was in shock."

"Yes. You saw. You know."

The look on his face made her eyes sting. "Please believe me. It hasn't changed the way I feel about you."

"It must." His lips hardened. "Emerson told you I was a man who had lost his memory. When I heard it, I wanted it to be true, but I knew that was just a fantasy. I knew that you would find out the truth."

"I did, and I was angry with Swinton. Angry with Emerson and Beckton and all the rest of them. But I wasn't angry with you, Hunter. I wasn't frightened of you. Or...or offended."

The doubt in his eyes made her hurry on. "My feelings for you are the same as they were when we were talking about making love, both of us wanting it so badly we ached. The other night, we both knew we couldn't give in to that wanting. But now we're alone. And safe. And I think I can show you how I feel better than I can tell you." She prevented further discussion by pressing her mouth to his, using her lips in ways that would stop him from thinking.

She knew to the heartbeat when she had won. For several seconds he remained absolutely still, then his lips began to move against hers with a hunger she felt in every cell of her body.

He made a low sound in his throat as her tongue entered his mouth, sliding over strong teeth and sensitive tissue before withdrawing slowly, inviting him to try out the same technique.

When he raised his head, he was shaking. But she suspected he still wasn't quite convinced.

She skimmed her hand along his ribs, down to his hips, drawing him against her, as she found his eyes with hers, held his gaze. "I want the same thing you do. Please. If we don't make love now, I think my body is going to self-destruct."

"You feel that way, too? Like a volcano about to explode?"

She managed a little laugh. "Oh, yes." Taking his hand, she tugged him down to lie beside her on the blanket, then rolled so that she was facing him as she held out her arms.

He stared at her with a kind of wonder, touching her face, her shoulder, her breasts, as if he couldn't quite believe they were finally together like this, both aching with desire.

"I want to do the right things," he said in a thick voice.

She moved her lips lightly against his. "Anything we do together will be wonderful. It's already wonderful."

"Yes. Everything with you is perfect for me." Tenderly, he stroked his thumb against her lips, tracing their outline. "But I think that's because you know how to make it that way. I want to do the same for you, but you must tell me what I need to know."

His eyes were so serious that she took his face in

her hands and gave him a soft kiss. Again she marveled at his candor. His caring.

"You only need to know one thing," she told him gently between tiny kisses. "Men are ready for joining more quickly than women. But a woman needs a little more time if she's going to reach sexual climax. She needs to be kissed and touched first."

"Sexual climax?"

"The burst of pleasure that comes at the end."

She didn't know whether he understood all of that yet, but she had no doubt that he would. "So kiss me. And touch me," she whispered, kissing the warm place where his neck joined his shoulder as her hands stroked his cheek, his neck, his chest, down the flat plane of his stomach, over his thighs, and finally to the rigid flesh straining behind his briefs.

He drew in a quick, sharp breath when she cupped her hand around him, and she permitted herself only a few brief caresses, knowing that she could bring this to completion too quickly.

Instead, she tugged off her panties so she would be completely open to him. With a little smile of reassurance, she lay back on the blanket, her arms bent upward, her body and soul open and vulnerable to him.

"You are perfect," he said with awe. He stroked the hair on her head, then touched the triangle of red hair below.

"It's the same beautiful color against your creamy skin." He rose over her, kissing her mouth, then moving his lips to her shoulders and then to the tops of her breasts.

"Can I?" he asked in a thick voice, his lips hovering above one taut nipple.

"I was hoping you would," she told him, curling her hand around his head and bringing his lips down to her breast. His mouth opened around her nipple, and she melted under the exquisite tugging sensation as he drew on her.

"That's good," he said, raising his head to look at her in wonder. "I was afraid you wouldn't want me to do it."

"I told you. I want the same things you do," she whispered.

And perhaps that gave Hunter confidence, because he set out on a journey of exploration that left her aching with arousal. No one had ever focused on her like this. No one had ever devoted himself so completely, so unselfishly to pleasing her. Each thing he did brought her delight, and that delight was multiplied by the light in his eyes as he learned the secrets of her body.

"Here. I need to feel you here," she told him, taking his hand and guiding it to the hidden warmth between her thighs.

He watched her face again as he stroked her, learning what she liked best.

Still, his touch quickly became shaky and his breath ragged, and she knew that she'd better end the preliminaries.

"There are lots of ways to manage the last part," she whispered. "This time, let me do most of the work."

She asked him to lie back, then dragged his briefs off and straddled him, her eyes locked with his.

His face was a study in awe as his hard flesh touched her softness, as she brought him inside her.

"That is—" He seemed to have no words to finish the sentence.

Then she began to move, finding a rhythm that captivated them both. She saw his features tighten as his body trembled in its climb, heard his shout of surprise and gratification, felt him spasm within her. Then she was driving for her own completion, moving in a frantic rhythm that brought her to heights she had never reached. She called his name, feeling her whole body convulsing above him in tremors of raw pleasure that went on and on.

Afterwards, she lay on top of him, her skin slick with perspiration, her body boneless as she felt him stroke her hair and shoulders.

"Thank you for that," he whispered.

She moved to lie beside him, snuggling against him, and he held her close.

"The thanks are mutual," she answered.

His fingers skimmed her lips. "You're a good teacher."

She laughed. "Well, you forgot one thing I tried to teach you."

His eyes clouded in alarm. "What?"

"Didn't I warn you not to get undressed in front of a woman?"

His cheeks colored. "This was different. We were wet and cold. I was trying to get us warm."

She gave a little laugh. "Well, you did that, all right."

"I guess I did. Very warm," he said, his lips breaking into a grin.

She smiled back.

"I like this," he said.

"So do I. I like making you happy." Finding his

hand, she stroked her fingers against his. "I like being happy with you."

He didn't answer, and she suspected he was still afraid to trust anything good coming into his life. She would teach him differently, and teach him how much a man and a woman could mean to each other.

But for the moment, she was exhausted.

"How long can we stay here?" she murmured, her lids fluttering closed.

"Until dark."

"Good."

"Then I will get you away from Stratford Creek."

Her eyes opened, searched his. "And you'll stay with me, get me to—to a place of safety," she clarified.

"Yes."

Perfect. If he could get them off the grounds, she would make sure Emerson and Swinton never got their hands on him again.

She wanted to talk about escape plans, ask when he had made the decision. But emotional turmoil and lack of sleep had finally taken its toll. For the time being, it was enough to know she was safe with him and that he would take her away from Stratford Creek. She closed her eyes, snuggled close to him, and drifted off to sleep.

DR. JULES KOLB'S face was set in hard lines as he slipped through the trees in back of the guest cottage. His breath coming in painful gasps, he waited under the shade of the branches, watching the house. He was too old and used-up for this. And he knew it would be disastrous for him to be caught inside, but he was going to take the chance. Because there was no better time than now, with every available security patrol out searching the grounds.

News of the explosion had taken him by surprise when he'd been writing up notes on a patient's records. He'd heard two of the nurses babbling excitedly and was about to yell at them to keep it down so he could work. Then he'd caught the name "John Doe." Slamming his pen down on the desk, he'd run out into the hall to find out what in the name of Sam Hill was going on.

Everybody was talking about it. But nobody was sure what had actually happened. A team had gone out to the site of the explosion, but they hadn't found anything. Now they were searching farther along the lake and in the woods.

He couldn't repress a high laugh as he wondered whether he should be excited or upset. It all depended on whether Reid was telling the truth. He'd told Emerson that the clone had set explosive charges on the cabin at the end of the pier in order to kill Kathryn Kelley. Reid had tried to stop him, but he'd been too late. How many people had believed that absurd story?

The staff meeting had been a zoo, he thought, with everyone pointing fingers. Swinton was angry that Kelley had ever been brought into the project and Anderson kept saying that the fault was in the basic specifications of the program. That was one of the little bastard's constant themes. Luckily, that had turned Swinton's wrath on his subordinate. Emerson had tried to quiet things down. But it was obvious he'd lost control of the meeting.

Kolb sighed. At least no one had turned on him.

But now Emerson would go back through the records.
And that was bad news.

He had to press his hands against his sides to keep
them from shaking. Muttering under his breath, he
began to move toward the sliding glass door in one
of the bedrooms. Weeks ago, he'd discovered the de-
fect in the doors. One of them had a faulty locking
mechanism. All you had to do was lift the glass panel
upward, and you could disengage the latch.

Grasping the handle with shaky fingers, he pulled
upward, straining with the effort, uttering an explosive curse when the panel refused to come free. Then
it suddenly gave, and he almost hit his damn hands
against his chin.

Yanking the door open, he stepped inside. Quickly
he checked the bedroom. Finding nothing of interest,
he made his way down the hall and spotted the computer sitting on the dining-room table. When he saw
what was on the screen, he sucked in a sharp breath.
So she'd found out about Ben Lancaster! With a
shaky hand he reached out and closed the file, then
removed the disk from the machine.

WHEN KATHRYN OPENED her eyes again, she sensed
that time had passed. Turning her head, she looked at
Hunter. He had covered them with an extra blanket
and lay with his arm possessively around her.

"Hi," she said.

"Hi," he answered, reaching to touch her cheek.
"Did you sleep?"

"A little. Then I got up and went out to set alarms.
I want to know if someone comes near this place."

"I would have worried if I'd woken up and found
you gone," she murmured.

"You were very tired—after the explosion. And the swim." He swallowed hard. "And making love."

She nodded.

"You didn't wake up even when I got back under the covers and held you," he said, his voice full of tenderness and a kind of wonder. "I watched your face. It was peaceful. And your breathing was even. You felt safe here with me."

"Of course," she answered, kissing his chest, snuggling against him. She looked around the small room. It was dark and bleak, and the bed was only a couple of blankets on the floor, yet she was more content than if she'd spent the night in the world's most sumptuous honeymoon suite.

His hands drifted over her. "I was thinking about the time we lay together on a blanket in the desert," he said. "With the sunset making everything glow."

"That sounds like a nice idea," she said dreamily.

"It isn't an idea. I mean, it is one of the memories in my mind. I can bring it back. The way I can bring back the look on your face when I came back from the hospital."

She turned her head toward him. "Ben Lancaster lived in New Mexico. Maybe he did that. Maybe it's his memory."

"You are part of it. I see your face. Your hair."

"It can't be me. I would be too young for him. And he had a wife."

He nodded.

She stroked the side of her hand along his beard-stubbled cheek. "We need to know more about him," she said. "And about how you can remember things he did. Maybe you have a stronger connection to his life than you think. Maybe it helped you survive in this place."

He looked as if he didn't think it was possible, and she didn't want to spoil this time together by making him worry. So she changed the subject. "Did you say you brought field rations here?"

"Yes." He slipped out of bed, and she saw he'd dressed in sweat pants. He opened a canvas pack. "They're not very good."

"I'll manage. And while you're at it, maybe you can find me something to wear."

"I like looking at you the way you are."

She blushed and pulled the covers over her breasts as she sat up.

"I like to see your face get warm, too."

"You'll see a lot more of that unless you find me some clothes. I'm not used to lounging around like this."

He got up, looked through the boxes, and handed her a T-shirt, which she pulled over her head. When he rejoined her on the bed, he brought protein bars and bottled water.

They ate sitting with their backs propped against the wall.

"While you were asleep, I was thinking."

"About escape plans?"

"Yes. And about Reid. He could be the same man who came into the cottage that first night. But I don't think he could have made elaborate plans by himself." He hesitated. "I think he was supposed to kill me after the explosion. Otherwise I could tell what happened."

She gave an unwilling little nod.

"Someone wanted us both dead," he continued.

She struggled to think objectively. "Not Swinton. At least I don't think so. This project is important to him. On the other hand, he didn't want me working with you in the first place. I guess he thought I would make you start asking questions and refuse your assignment."

"That's possible," he conceded.

When he stared into the distance without saying more, she touched his arm. "What are you thinking?"

"About living in the guest cottage with you. I think they wouldn't have let me do it if they were planning to let you leave afterward."

A shudder swept across her skin.

"I shouldn't have said that," he muttered.

"No. It's best to be honest about the danger."

"Staying is more dangerous to you than trying to escape. But—"

"It's not going to be easy," she finished for him. "But if anybody can get me out of here, you can." She couldn't hold back another laugh. "Because Beckton and his team taught you everything they know."

"Damn right!"

She raised her face toward him. "I've never heard you use that kind of language."

"I'm experimenting."

"You're loosening up."

"Is that good?"

"Yes."

He bent toward her, his free hand gently stroking her arm, her shoulder. "There's only a little time before we have to leave, but I want to talk about so many things."

"You'll have to make a choice," she said, wondering what he would decide.

"Can I ask you questions?"

"Of course. I like answering your questions."

He reached for a lock of her hair, wrapping it gently around his finger, playing with it. "Is making love always that good?" he asked.

So he had been thinking about their lovemaking. "I don't think so," she answered. "Only when a man and a woman—" she stopped. "Well, I can only speak for myself. For me, it was wonderful because my feelings for you are very strong."

After the easy give-and-take of a few moments earlier, his reaction wasn't quite what she'd expected. She'd thought he'd be pleased. Instead, he looked sad.

Raising her head, she searched his face, knowing she should say what she really meant. "Why do you think I can't love you?" she asked.

"Love," he said softly. "You should not love me. I'm not a real person."

"Of course you are!" She grabbed his arm. "Don't say things like that. Genetically, you are a man named Ben Lancaster. Maybe you even have some of his memories."

He made a dismissive sound. "It's not that simple. What about the other men Dr. Swinton is growing in his tanks?"

She shivered at the memory, then watched as his face took on a sad, angry look.

"I am like them," he said with sudden vehemence. "And none of us has a soul."

Chapter Twelve

Hunter's words brought a strangled feeling to her throat. "Where did you get that idea?" she managed.

"Dr. Swinton said it."

"The bastard!" she hissed. "He knows that raising men in laboratory tanks in order to send them off on dangerous assignments is morally wrong. He's frightened by the consequences of what he's done so he's shifting the blame to the victims."

"Yes, I come from his laboratory, and I'm not a human being," Hunter said.

She cupped her hands over his naked shoulders, feeling the flesh and muscle and bone. "You're a better human being than Dr. Swinton," she said with conviction. "When you saw me standing on the dock, and you knew Reid was going to set off the explosives, you could have moved out of danger. Instead you came running toward me. So why did you do it?"

"I—" His features took on a look of remembered pain. "I saw you standing there, and I—I couldn't let him kill you. What happened to me didn't matter. I had to save you if I could."

She folded back his hand and brought it to her

mouth, stroking his flesh with her lips. "You put my welfare before your own. If you had no soul, you wouldn't have done that."

He raised his face toward hers, his expression achingly hopeful, and she knew that he wanted to believe her.

"Swinton may be expert at illegal biological experiments," she said, "but I have a lot more experience with people. I've worked with all kinds. I know what kind of man you are. You are good. Moral, honest, intelligent, giving. All the things I value."

"That can't be true."

"It is. Or I wouldn't have wanted to make love with you." She kissed his fingertips.

Emerson and his men had done their best to damage Hunter. Yet there was a deep well of strength and of resilience within him. She knew it was true, or they wouldn't be sitting here talking so intimately.

"Who do you believe?" she asked softly. "Swinton or me?"

After a long time, he answered, "I want to believe you, more than anything, but—"

She lifted her face to his, found his mouth. At first he held himself like a man turned to stone. Then with a strangled sound of wanting, he began to respond. She gave him a long, desperate kiss, her hands moving over his naked chest and shoulders.

"Hunter, never doubt yourself. Never doubt that you are a good man. A normal man, and an extraordinary man, too. Very few people could have survived what they did to you. But you have. And from now on, everything will be better for you. For us."

There was still uncertainty in the depths of his dark eyes.

She pulled his mouth back to hers, and her hands began to move urgently over him again, trying to show him the truth of her words. Trying to show him how much she cared.

A sigh of gratification went through her when she felt him surrender to his need for her.

"Yes. Make love with me," she murmured.

This time there was no way either of them could go slowly. This time was hot and sharp and full of the desperation of two people caught in a trap that might destroy them both.

A RUMBLING VIBRATION made her raise her head and look anxiously around.

Beside her, Hunter sat up, his gaze fixing on the door.

"What is it?" she asked. "What's happening?"

"One of the alarms I set out while you were sleeping. We must leave here quickly." He pulled the cover from a screen that sat on a low shelf and stared at what looked like a round green target with a series of concentric circles. At the bottom left, several small blips moved toward the central area.

"Four men," he said, watching the screen. "They are heading straight in our direction. Maybe somebody dug into the old records and found out about this place."

She felt a shiver go through her. After they'd made love again, Hunter had urged her to get ready to leave. She was dressed, except for her shoes, which weren't quite dry. Now she pulled them on.

"We must assume they are looking for us," he said as he checked the packs of supplies he'd gathered earlier.

Handing her the lighter one, he silently moved the bar away from the door.

"We can't use a flashlight. Someone might see," he whispered. "So stay close to me."

"You can count on it," she murmured, following him down the tunnel and waiting while he scanned the immediate area before they both slipped outside into the cool evening air. He closed the door and used another lock he'd found inside to reseal the entrance.

She looked around her in the gathering darkness, half expecting an attack from someone poised on the rocks above their heads, but she saw no one.

Quickly and silently, he led her down the path they'd taken earlier. There were large rocks and tree roots under foot, and she would have fallen several times if he hadn't been gripping her arm.

It was hard to keep up with the pace he was setting, but she didn't voice a complaint. About halfway down the trail, she heard footsteps, then a gruff voice.

Hunter went stock-still, his fingers digging into her arm as he brought her to an abrupt halt.

"This must be the place," a man said.

"Anyone home?"

"The door's locked," the first speaker answered, and she knew he was talking about the shelter they'd vacated only minutes earlier.

"I guess this is another dead end."

"Maybe they were here. I'd like to look for footprints, but it's too dark to see much."

"All right, we've got another couple of hours before we can report back to the chief of operations. Let's head back toward the lake," another voice ordered. "See if we can spot anything along the shoreline."

The feet started down the path, directly toward them. Kathryn went rigid as she stared at the rock walls hemming them in. Now what? Run for it? They'd never make it. At least, she wouldn't, she silently amended. Hunter could probably get away if he didn't have to wait for her. But she knew with absolute certainty that he would never leave her. He had vowed to get her to safety, and he would do everything in his power to keep his promise.

He tugged on her hand, and she came out of her trance, following him around a boulder. He pulled her into a crevasse on the far side, shielding her body with his and pressing her into the shadows. She buried her face in the front of his shirt, breathing in his familiar scent, trying to match his apparent calm, though her heart threatened to pound its way through the wall of her chest as the search team moved closer and closer.

To her vast relief, they didn't leave the trail, didn't stop as they descended to the lake.

In a few minutes, Hunter tugged at her hand again and whispered, "We will go the other way."

They retraced their steps up the hill. Before they reached the shelter, Hunter led her down a branching path. In the fading light, it was even slower going than before.

When they reached the bottom of the hill, she stood dragging in air.

"We can't stay here long," he said in a barely audible voice. "But we can take a shortcut through the woods," he added as he scanned the area and began to edge forward into the forest.

He moved with caution, stopping to listen every few minutes, but they met no more patrols. She was starting to relax when she saw flashlight beams cutting through the gloom.

Hunter swiftly pulled her behind the trunk of a tree as the lights and the sound of moving feet drew closer. Swallowing a little moan, she melted against him, resisting the urge to close her eyes. Unable to look away from the lights, she watched them approach, feeling like an animal being stalked.

She felt Hunter's muscles tense as he prepared for a confrontation. But at the last moment the men passed a few feet to their left and moved into the distance.

The air frozen in her lungs hissed out. Stratford Creek might not be a military base anymore, but it looked like Colonel Emerson commanded a small army. "That was close," she said, when she dared to speak.

"Yes. Lucky for us none of them have night scopes." He made a low sound. "I should have made a better evaluation of the situation. We have less time than I thought."

Before she could answer, he started off again, moving faster, but watching to see if she could keep up. When he heard her breath coming in little gasps, he slowed his pace.

"I'm sorry. This is hard for you."

"I'll manage."

"You can rest here for a little while," he said, gesturing toward a dark hulking building just visible against the night sky. Cautiously, he led her to a high window. "I need something in here. I can get it if you boost me up to the window."

She eyed the building. "What is this place?"

"The garage where they store auto parts, and vehicles that need repair. There is no guard."

We hope, she silently added. After their two close calls, she wanted to beg him not to go inside, not to leave her alone. But she knew her best option was relying on his judgment, so she made a cradle with her hands and boosted him up to the window frame. She watched him open the window, then disappear into the darkness beyond. Straining her ears, she thought she heard him drop to the floor inside, but she wasn't even sure of that.

After standing and staring into the opening for several moments, she decided it was foolish not to take his advice and get as much rest as she could. Sinking to the ground, she pressed her back against the cold metal wall and tried to relax.

But all her senses were on red alert.

A dry twig cracked in the underbrush, and she went rigid. Then the sound of movement through the woods receded, and she figured that some nocturnal animal was as wary of her as she was of it.

Minutes dragged by, and she felt her tension mount. Then she saw the figure of a man running toward her. For an awful moment her heart blocked her windpipe, until she recognized Hunter's shape and realized he had probably exited through a door she couldn't see. As he drew closer, she saw he was holding a set of license plates.

"We will put these on the car we take," he said. "That will make it harder for anyone to figure out which one we have stolen."

"How did you think of that?"

He gave a low laugh. "*They* taught me to be devious—to use tricks to hide myself."

"Good."

"Now we must go to the motor pool, where the working vehicles are kept." He hesitated. "We could circle around the main buildings, but we'll lose time. It would be faster to go straight across the compound."

"Won't there be people?" she questioned.

"Yes. But they won't be looking for us there. And they won't recognize us." He pulled two jackets and caps from his pack and handed one set to her. "Put these on. In the dark we will look like men who work here. Walk as if we have somewhere to go—but not as if we are afraid of being discovered."

She nodded as she donned the jacket and twisted her hair into a knot before pushing it under the cap. Hunter looked at her critically, then reached to tuck in several wayward strands that had escaped her attention.

He stroked his finger against her cheek, and she turned her face to brush her lips against her hand.

"We will be away from Stratford Creek soon," he said in a gruff voice.

"Good. I don't like it here. The only good thing about it was meeting you."

His face contorted, and he gave her a quick, rough embrace. "It's the same for me."

Before she could say more, he turned and started toward the end of the garage. Her eyes widened as they rounded the corner. She hadn't known how close they were to the center of the action. Now she saw they were only fifty yards from several low buildings where lights shone through the windows.

Hunter started off at a purposeful pace. Trying to imitate his masculine gait, she strode along the road, swinging her arms briskly and keeping her eyes straight ahead.

They came to a sidewalk, and he stepped onto the pavement. She followed, feeling exposed and vulnerable. When a man emerged from one of the low structures and stood at the top of the steps staring into the darkness, she imagined he was looking directly at them. She wanted to dart around the side of a building, but she realized that would be a fatal error, so she forced herself to keep pace with Hunter. To her relief, they walked on past the watcher without being challenged. But before she could relax, she saw two men coming directly toward them on the sidewalk. And each step closer seemed to increase her heart rate.

She barely heard Hunter over the roaring in her ears.

"This way." He gave a little tug on her arm. Stopping short, she followed him onto a side road, fighting not to turn and look over her shoulder to see if they were being followed. Several minutes later, she spotted a parking area ahead of them, surrounded by a chain-link fence with razor wire at the top. Moving onto the grass, Hunter stopped under the shadows of some trees and ran his hand over her arm. "You did perfectly."

She let her body relax against his. "I'm scared spitless. How can you act so calm?"

"I was trained for espionage."

"But even trained agents have nerves."

"What happens to me is not important," he said dismissively.

She turned him toward her, clasped his shoulders,

wished she could see him better in the darkness. "It is to me."

He didn't answer and she added, "You're going to have to adjust your thinking."

"Right now, I have to get you away from Stratford Creek." He paused, and she heard him swallow. "If anything happens to me, you must try to escape. This time *I* am giving *you* an order."

"I—"

"Do not go to Colonel Emerson," he clipped out. "Do not trust him."

"I don't."

"Kathryn," he said in a thick voice, folding her close. "What I feel for you is very strong. If it's possible for a man created the way I was created to love, then I love you."

"Hunter," she whispered, holding on to him for dear life.

"This isn't a good time to speak of my feelings. But I want you to know. In case I don't get another chance to tell you."

"You will," she vowed.

"You make me want to believe that." For several heartbeats he clasped her tighter, then eased away from her.

She shivered as the warmth of his body left her. When she saw him watching her closely, she stood up straighter, determined to show him she wasn't going to fall apart.

"Wait here. I will put the plates on a car and come back for you."

She gave a tight little nod and watched him walk toward the parking lot. As he drew abreast of the gate, a guard stepped out of a small building.

A guard. She hadn't even been thinking about that, she realized. But she was sure Hunter had grasped the situation when he'd checked the motor pool earlier. She couldn't hear what the man was saying, but she heard the note of challenge in his tone.

Kathryn held her breath.

"I have orders to report to the administration building with a sedan," Hunter said, reaching inside his jacket. Instead of pulling out a piece of paper, he brought his hand out in a lightning-quick stroke that connected with the guard's neck.

The man gasped, yet he also was well trained. At the last second, he moved a fraction of an inch, deflecting the worst of the blow. Then he spun around, coming back at Hunter with his own martial-arts move.

As they circled each other, Kathryn wondered if somehow she could tip the odds in Hunter's favor. What if she caused a distraction, she thought, starting forward. Before she had taken two steps, another man materialized silently out of the shadows. She bit back a tiny sound as he raised a gun and landed a hard chop on the guard's head. Confused, she tried to figure out what was happening.

Before the combatant hit the ground, the newcomer took a quick step back and pointed the gun squarely at Hunter. Until that moment, she hadn't gotten a clear view of his face. When he raised his head, she saw it was Reid, the security man who had lured her down to the cabin, then set the fuses and tried to blow her up.

Hunter started forward.

"Don't come any closer." Reid gestured with the

gun. "Just pick him up nice and easy and dump him behind a car."

When Hunter hesitated, he gestured with the gun. "Do it. Then turn around slowly."

Hunter complied.

"Don't move a muscle except to put your hands up," Reid hissed.

Slowly, Hunter raised his hands. He was facing in her direction, but he didn't once look at her, and she knew he was doing it to protect her hiding place.

"Where's the Kelley woman?" Reid demanded.

"You wanted to kill her," Hunter said in a flat voice. "You did an excellent job of setting the explosives."

"You'd better not be lying to me."

"I never lie," Hunter said in the same unemotional tone.

And he wasn't, Kathryn realized. But he had done a masterful job of twisting the truth to make it sound like she was dead. Yet even as she admired his resourcefulness, she watched in sick horror as Reid held the gun leveled at his chest.

God, what was she going to do now?

"I bet my pension you'd come here and try to get a car," he said in a voice that rang with triumph.

"Yes, you are clever," Hunter complimented him without a trace of admiration.

"That's right. Like when I told everyone you set off the explosives that killed the broad. That puts me in the clear. It's all the fault of the clone run amok."

"Why did you lure Kathryn Kelley to the shack?" Hunter asked.

"I was well paid. And I'm going to do even better when I bring you in."

"In where? To Colonel Emerson?"

"Hardly."

"Swinton? Beckton?"

"Stop asking questions," Reid growled. "Get moving. And don't try any sudden moves. I know all the defensive gambits they taught you in those fancy martial arts classes."

Hunter's jaw was tight.

"Move. Down the sidewalk along the fence," Reid clipped out. "I'll be right behind you. And hope we don't meet up with one of those search parties out beating the bushes for you. Because if I have to, I'll shoot you in self-defense."

Kathryn fought to stand unmoving and silent. Still not glancing in her direction, Hunter followed orders. She watched him and Reid head along the edge of the parking area.

When she tried to take a steadying breath, it rattled in her throat. Hunter had told her to leave Stratford Creek if something happened to him. But she couldn't do it by herself. More importantly, she wasn't going to leave him in Reid's clutches. She had to follow, and find out where the security man was taking him.

When captive and captor turned the corner, she leaped from her hiding place. Sprinting along the fence, she prayed they wouldn't disappear from view before she reached the end of the parking lot.

Panic roared in her ears when she thought she was too late. Then she spotted them in the shadows at the edge of an unkempt field that bordered the research center.

Hunter had wondered if Reid was working for Swinton. He must be right, she decided as she followed behind the pair, darting from shadow to shadow.

She was about to step into the light again, when Reid suddenly stopped at the edge of the lawn and spun around, scanning the open area behind him. Kathryn froze in mid-stride. Thank God he hadn't waited a few seconds longer, she thought as she pressed herself against the wall of the building, hardly daring to breathe.

She sagged back against the wall when Reid issued a gruff command to Hunter and started moving again. They were skirting the front door of the research center, aiming for another destination. Building 22, she realized, feeling the blood drain out of her face. *Please, not Building 22.* But her guess was confirmed as they made directly for the low structure, with Hunter in the lead and Reid right behind him with the gun.

As she watched in horror, Hunter pushed open the same door where she'd previously entered, and stepped inside. Reid followed, pulling the door closed behind them.

For long moments she was rooted to the spot where she stood, fighting the urge to scream. Her first trip inside that building had been the most terrifying experience of her life. And she'd silently vowed never to go back. Now here she was again.

About thirty yards back, she had passed a telephone box on a utility pole. It wasn't an outside line, she knew. It was only connected to the base phone system. Uncertainly, she turned and stared at it. She could call for help, and a security team would come on the double. Yet she didn't need Hunter to tell her she couldn't trust Emerson. Worse, if Reid was telling the truth, everyone now thought Hunter was a killer. Maybe they had orders to shoot him on sight. For all she knew, they had orders to shoot her, too.

She was on her own. If she couldn't save Hunter, they were both doomed. Clenching her teeth, she forced her legs to carry her toward the building. But when she reached the door and tried the knob, she discovered it wouldn't turn. The entrance was locked. Reid had shut her out.

For endless moments she stood making little sounds of distress in her throat as she tried to force the knob. Finally, with a sob, she gave up the futile effort. Stifling the impulse to pound her fist against the door, she straightened and started along the perimeter of the lab, searching for another entrance.

She had almost made a circle of the entire building when she heard the sound of someone muttering in a low, angry voice. Freezing in place, she looked wildly around, but there was nowhere to hide.

The voice sounded frustrated, but it grew no louder. Realizing that the speaker was hidden from view around the corner of the building, she crept cautiously forward and peered around the wall. A man was standing hunched over, trying to insert a key into the lock of another door. When he met with no success, he cursed, then switched to another key on the same ring.

The man was a disheveled Dr. Kolb, she saw. Apparently he too was trying to get inside and having little success. Emerson must have tightened security all over the base and ordered doors locked.

What was Kolb doing here? she wondered as she peeked around the corner. Hunter had told her Reid wasn't capable of carrying out elaborate plans. Maybe the security man was supposed to deliver Hunter to Kolb, and maybe the physician had accidentally gotten locked out of the building. He looked like he was coming unglued, Kathryn thought as she watched him try several more keys. His fumbling hands dropped them on the grass. Cursing furiously, he went down on his knees and scrabbled frantically until he found them again.

With a groan, he heaved himself up. Squaring his shoulders, he attacked the lock again, still muttering to himself. It seemed to Kathryn that he was taking half the night to accomplish a relatively simple task—if the ring he'd brought held the right key.

Finally he let out a growl of satisfaction, pulled open the door, and stepped inside.

The hinges were cushioned by air cylinders. Praying that she wouldn't be too late, Kathryn sprinted forward and caught the edge of the metal just in time to give her fingers a sharp pinch. Repressing a gasp of pain, she pushed her shoulder through the opening and saw Kolb scurrying down a hallway.

If he glanced over his shoulder, he'd spot her. But he appeared too preoccupied to check his surroundings. She mouthed a little prayer of thanks when she realized he was heading away from the room with the tanks. At least she wouldn't have to see that awful sight again.

About thirty paces down the hall, he stopped and stepped through a door. As silently as she could, she crept forward. Pausing to listen, she heard muffled voices. When she cautiously stuck her head around the corner, she found she was staring into a vestibule that led to three more doorways. Kolb had stepped through the one on the right.

In his hand was a gun, pointed at a man whose face she couldn't see. But she could tell he was standing in what looked like a medical supply room and was wearing a white lab coat.

Afraid to approach any closer, Kathryn strained her ears as she tried to figure out what was going on. The guy in the lab coat wasn't tall enough to be Swinton. When he turned to face Kolb, she saw with a little jolt that it was the research director's assistant, Roger Anderson, the man who had let her look at the videotapes of Hunter.

Anderson drew himself up to his full five feet eight inches. "What's the meaning of this intrusion?" he growled. "You're not supposed to be in this building unless you have direct orders."

"I'm not going to let you and Swinton go any further with this," the doctor said, his voice quavering, the gun shaking in his hand.

"Any further with what?" Anderson demanded.

"With your diabolical experiments."

"Then we're on the same side," Anderson said in an even tone. "I've been trying to stop Dr. Swinton ever since he began growing human cells in a petri dish."

"It will be a cold day in hell before I believe that," Kolb said, moving farther into the room so that Kathryn had a better view of the interior of the lab.

Chapter Thirteen

Hunter was slumped in a chair, his elbows resting on a narrow table in front of him and his head cradled in his hands. From the tension in his arms and body, Kathryn judged that he was in considerable pain.

Kolb and Anderson were too absorbed in their little drama to look at him, or to be aware that she was on the scene. But as she stood in the shadows beyond the doorway, Hunter slowly raised his head. As if some sixth sense told him she was behind the doctor, he raised his face and stared in her direction. When his gaze focused on her, his face contorted into an expression of such anguish that she had to press her fist against her mouth to keep from crying out. Then a pleading look came into his eyes.

"Go away," he mouthed.

She gave a small but emphatic shake of her head.

He kept his gaze on her for several more heartbeats. But it was clear that keeping his head up was too much of a struggle. With a grimace, he dropped his face back into his hands.

It was almost impossible to contain her anger as she took in his appalling condition. He had been through so much. Now what torture had they devised for him? Her own hands clenched into tight fists. It was all she could do to stop herself from rushing to his side. But she forced herself to stay where she was. All she'd accomplish by going to him would be to get them both caught.

In desperation, she glanced around the anteroom, looking for some sort of weapon. A long metal pole leaning against the wall. Not even sure of how she could use it, she began to move across the room.

"At first I thought you were on my side," Kolb was saying. "Like Fenton, when he was chief of security. He had the guts to complain to Emerson about this hellhole."

"Look where it got him," Anderson growled. "Somebody pushed him off a roof."

"Probably McCourt." Kolb's voice rose an octave. "I thought after that that you were afraid to speak up, even though you wanted to close down this obscene project. But I kept my eye on you. Finally, I realized you didn't give a damn about the subjects of the experiment. You were only trying to discredit Swinton so you could take his place. You don't like playing second fiddle. You want the glory for yourself."

"That's right," Anderson answered mildly. "I hate doing the dirty work of a pompous ass who thinks he has all the answers. I can do a lot more for this project than he ever could—if I just get the chance to prove the flaws in his methods."

The physician made a noise of disgust.

"If you think cloning human beings is obscene," Anderson asked in a conversational tone, "why are you part of the jolly little team at Stratford Creek?"

"Not by choice. That bastard Emerson's got something on me, just like he's probably got something on you. That's his specialty, digging up garbage and using it to his advantage. I wanted to atone for my sins, but he forced me to come here. Now the joke's on him. It turns out I'm not going to live long enough to enjoy my retirement. So I don't have to do his dirty work anymore. I'm taking Hunter out of here. I thought Dr. Kelley could turn him around. If she's gone, I'll have to do it myself in the time I have left.''

As she heard her name mentioned, Kathryn stopped in the act of reaching for the pole.

"You had her killed, didn't you?" the doctor demanded. "And you wanted it to look like Hunter did it."

Anderson shrugged. "That was my plan," he said, laughing, as if he were enjoying a private joke.

"What did you have against her?"

"Nothing personal," Anderson shot back. "But she gave me the perfect opportunity to prove that Swinton's methods produced unstable subjects unsuitable for secret missions. You need to use more brain-altering drugs to control their reactions."

Kolb answered with a low curse.

"While we're discussing Dr. Kelley," Anderson said, "would you mind telling me why you moved heaven and earth to get her on the team here? And why you arranged to have her shacked up with our friend in that nice cozy cottage?"

"Because I thought if anybody could get through to him on a human level, she could. She looks a lot like Ben Lancaster's wife."

"Oh, really?"

Hunter's head jerked up, and his unsteady gaze fixed on the doctor.

"Yes," Kolb said. "I was willing to do anything to get her. Even—" He stopped short.

Kathryn felt a trail of shivers travel across her skin. She looked like Ben Lancaster's wife? Kolb had done *what* to get her here?

Anderson sneered and glanced at Hunter. "So what was the big deal? Hunter doesn't have any of Lancaster's memories. Or do you think he's genetically disposed to get the hots for blue-eyed redheads?"

"You're wrong about his memories," the doctor shot back. "You may remember Lancaster wasn't dead when he arrived here. I was able to save some of his brain cells; I transferred them to Hunter."

"What?" Anderson practically shouted. "How dare you!"

"Maybe you should thank me. You haven't exactly had a tremendous success rate bringing your subjects to maturity. Maybe the brain cells were crucial to his survival. Maybe they're the reason he's the only one of your Lancaster clones to make it."

Anderson started toward Kolb, his hands balled into fists. "You've invalidated our tests."

"I don't give a damn about your precious tests, you moron. I care about the dignity of human life."

Anderson made a low sound and raised his fist.

"Stay where you are," Kolb ordered as he moved toward Hunter. "I'm taking him with me."

"I don't think so," Anderson answered in a voice that had turned surprisingly mild.

To the doctor's right, a door that had been cracked an inch quietly opened to admit Reid, holding a gun. It appeared he'd been there most of the time, waiting for a signal from Anderson.

In the space of a few heartbeats the whole situation changed.

"To your right!" Kathryn shouted.

The doctor whirled, saw Reid and fired. But the security man had also pulled the trigger. The noise of two sidearms being fired reverberated in the close confines of the room even as both men collapsed to the floor.

The shots seemed to reverberate through Hunter as well. He had been sitting at the table as if he were no longer capable of free movement. The gunfire released him from the paralysis. He sprang to his feet, leaped across the space that separated him from Anderson, and struck the researcher on the back of the neck with the side of his hand.

Anderson crumpled, and Kathryn found herself moving toward Hunter across a room where bodies sprawled across the floor. She reached him and fell into his arms, folded him into her embrace.

"Thank God you're all right," she gasped, too overcome with relief to say more.

His arms tightened spasmodically around her, then he pushed her from him.

"No," he said.

"It's all right now."

"No."

She stared up into his face. "What's wrong? What did they do to you?"

His mouth opened, but no words came out.

"Hunter?"

"A time to kill…" he said in a thick voice.

"What?"

"The song you were singing," he said.

"Yes. I sang that. But…"

A groan from the floor made her turn. Reid was sprawled unconscious, but Kolb was lying on his back looking at her. A red stain spread across his shoulder.

"Dr. Kelley," he said in a weak voice.

She knelt, felt the pulse at his neck. It was shallow but steady.

He closed his eyes for a moment, then asked, "Where were you—"

"Hunter saved me from the explosion," she explained quickly. "We were hiding out—waiting for a chance to get out of here. Then Reid caught Hunter."

The doctor gave a tiny nod. "Were you listening to us?" he said.

"Yes."

"I saw your computer file."

"My file?" She blinked. She'd been so careful to hide the disk in her pillow. Then the call about Hunter had come from Reid, and she'd forgotten all about the incriminating evidence.

"It's safe," he said. "After the explosion, I came to your cottage and took it. Now you take Hunter. Get him out of here. You can save him."

"I intend to."

He was silent for several seconds. "Emerson dug into my records. He knew..." He stopped and started again. "He forced me to come here. Work for him."

"I understand," she said.

"Go. Before somebody comes," the doctor said.

"What about you?"

"It's not a fatal wound."

"But you said— Are you sick?"

He gave her a steady look. "Stomach cancer."

"I—"

He didn't let her finish. "My car...at the side of

the research building.'' He swallowed, then continued, ''A silver Honda.''

''Yes. Thank you.''

''There's a pass on the passenger seat that will get you out of this damn place.'' He stopped, sucked in a breath. When he spoke again, his voice was weaker. ''Keys....'' He gestured toward his right pants pocket.

Kathryn reached inside and retrieved the keys.

''Go. Then I can send a message to the media about Stratford Creek.''

She wondered what he was planning.

''Go,'' he repeated.

''Thank you,'' she said.

He gave her a long look, then sighed and closed his eyes.

She stood, found Hunter leaning against the wall, his arms folded tightly across his chest and his pupils dilated. Beads of sweat stood out on his forehead. He focused on her as she hurried toward him, but he didn't change his position.

''Are you all right?'' she asked urgently.

''No.''

''What did Anderson do to you?''

''He...orders to...'' His face contorted and he raised his hands, pressing them to the sides of his head. She could see him fighting to say more, but no words came out. And the pain on his face deepened.

She waited with her heart pounding, wondering what the hell Anderson had done to him. When he lowered his hands, she pressed her fingers against his cheek. ''We have to leave. Come on.''

When she gripped his arm, his whole body jerked. ''I...love you...'' he said. ''I...don't want...''

''I love you, too,'' she whispered.

GET 2

HOW TO GET YOUR
2 FREE BOOKS AND FREE GIFT!

1. Peel off the MIRA® sticker on the front cover. Place it in the space provided at right. This automatically entitles you to receive two free books and an exciting surprise gift.

2. Send back this card and you'll get 2 "The Best of the Best™" books. These books have a combined cover price of $11.98 or more in the U.S. and $13.98 or more in Canada, but they are yours to keep absolutely FREE!

3. There's <u>no</u> catch. You're under <u>no</u> obligation to buy anything. We charge nothing – ZERO – for your first shipment. And you don't have to make any minimum number of purchases – not even one!

4. We call this line "The Best of the Best" because each month you'll receive the best books by some of today's most popular authors. These authors show up time and time again on all the major bestseller lists and their books sell out as soon as they hit the stores. You'll like the convenience of getting them delivered to your home at our special discount prices . . . and you'll love your *Heart to Heart* subscriber newsletter featuring author news, horoscopes, recipes, book reviews and much more!

SPECIAL FREE GIFT
We'll send you a fabulous surprise gift absolutely FREE, simply for accepting our no-risk offer!

5. We hope that after receiving your free books you'll want to remain a subscriber. But the choice is yours – to continue or cancel, anytime at all! So why not take us up on our invitation, with no risk of any kind. You'll be glad you did!

6. And remember...we'll send you a surprise gift ABSOLUTELY FREE just for giving THE BEST OF THE BEST a try.

Visit us online at
www.mirabooks.com

® and TM are registered trademark of Harlequin Enterprises Limited.

BOOKS FREE!

THE BEST OF THE BEST™ — Here's How it Works:

"Then...leave me...here." The words were torn from him. When he finished speaking, his whole body was shaking.

"I won't go without you." She tugged him away from the wall, watching anxiously as he swayed on his feet. Picking up the cap that had fallen onto the floor, she put it back on his head. Then she felt to make sure her own hat was still in place. Miraculously, it was.

Pausing, she looked at the gun lying beside the doctor. Hunter's eyes followed her gaze.

"No gun..." he said in a hoarse voice, his fingers closing tightly around her arm.

"Okay." He was obviously in no shape to handle a weapon. And maybe he thought that having the gun would increase their chances of getting shot.

Hunter let her lead him across the lab. At the door to the hall, she paused, listened, then stuck her head out. The corridor was empty, so she hurried them toward the exit. Thank God the building was off by itself. And the lab was deep in the interior. It looked like nobody had heard the shots.

"James Harrison," Hunter gasped out as he stumbled along beside her. "Remember James Harrison?"

"Of course. The man who tried to kill me."

"Kathryn," he said in an agonized voice. "What... if someone had given James Harrison drugs that...that filled up his mind and made him follow orders."

"That didn't happen," she answered quickly.

"Kathryn...listen to me. I can't..."

"Please, Hunter," she begged as she pulled open the door. "You have to be quiet. Someone might hear us."

He stopped talking, and she led him around the building. To her relief, a silver Honda was waiting where the doctor had said it would be.

Hunter was silent for a little more than a minute. Then he started to mumble again. He was saying the words to the song she'd been singing while she'd fixed breakfast. Only they were all jumbled up. God, had he totally lost his mind? she wondered with a sick shudder.

When she opened the back door and picked up the blankets she found on the seat, he stood with his legs stiff, his shoulders rigid.

"Get on the floor," she told him.

He made a strangled sound but obeyed, and she pulled the covering over him, eyeing the camouflage critically. In the dark, it might work.

Inspecting herself in the mirror she adjusted her cap so that the visor hid most of her face. Then she started the engine.

Hunter was still mumbling under the blanket as they pulled onto the road.

God, she needed help. Even if they made it off the base, Emerson would send men after them. They needed a place to hide. If she called some of her Light Street friends, could they tell her where to hole up?

Blocking out Hunter's rambling speech, she picked up the portable phone on the console and dialed an emergency number at Randolph Security. Jessie Douglas picked up on the first ring.

"Kathryn, thank God," she said.

Jessie was a social worker with the Light Street Foundation, and Kathryn wondered why she was the one answering the call. "What are you doing on this line?" she asked.

"Cam has been trying to figure out a way to get in touch with you for days. He did some research on Stratford Creek, but it was too late to warn you. We've been praying that you'd call us."

A profound feeling of relief washed over her.

"I'll put you through to Cam," Jessie said.

It took several seconds to transfer the call. Then Cameron Randolph's deep voice came over the line. "Kathryn, are you okay? Where are you?"

"Driving toward the main gate of Stratford Creek. Hunter and I have a car and a pass that should get us through."

"Who is Hunter?"

"The man I was hired to work with. It's a long story."

"You can tell me about it soon. We have a unit stationed in your vicinity, headed by Jason and Jed."

"They're up here?" she asked incredulously, picturing the two men who had both been covert agents before joining Randolph Security.

"Yes. Jo wanted to go in and get you. I pointed out that if we got caught on the grounds of a U.S. government preserve we'd risk getting shot and branded as traitors or saboteurs."

"I understand," she whispered.

"They should be in position a couple of miles down the main road. Turn left when you leave the grounds."

"Thanks." She hesitated, then asked in a strained voice. "Could you have a doctor available?"

"Are you all right?" Cam asked anxiously.

She glanced at the back seat, seeing the large bulk shaking under the blanket. A shiver of fear went through her as she lowered her voice. "It's Hunter."

"Is he wounded?"

She gulped, gripped the wheel, fighting not to let the fear swamp her. "Shell-shocked, or something like it. I can't say any more."

"I understand. Good luck."

"Thanks." She was overwhelmed as she hung up. While she'd been at Stratford Creek, her friends had been putting out an enormous effort on her behalf.

Hunter was still talking to himself in the back seat.

"We're almost to the guard station," she told him. "You've got to be quiet, and don't move."

Thankfully, he stopped his babbling as the car slowed.

A sentry stepped smartly into her path as she approached the guardhouse. The gate beyond it was closed, blocking her exit.

As she came to a stop, she willed her hand to steadiness and rolled down her window.

"I'm sorry, ma'am, you can't leave the grounds," the sentry said as he approached the car.

"I have a pass," she replied, struggling to keep her voice even as she prayed that Hunter would keep quiet, prayed that the guard wouldn't glance into the back seat and ask what she was hiding under the blanket.

Quickly, she handed the laminated plastic card through the window.

He inspected it, then gave her an appraising look. "I'm sorry," he said again. "There's been an incident. All passes have been temporarily suspended. Didn't you hear the directive from the chief of operations?"

"I was out jogging," she improvised.

"Please step out of the car and come with me."

She looked again at the gate. If she'd thought she could ram her way through it, she would have. But she knew that a frontal assault wasn't possible with the doctor's car.

"Come with me," the man said again, leaning down to open her door. When she sat frozen in place, he reached inside and efficiently unbuckled her seat belt.

Before he could straighten, the back door of the car shot open and Hunter sprang out. In a flash of motion, he leaped toward the sentry. Catching him by surprise, he landed a powerful, two-handed blow on his back.

The guard went down, just like Anderson. Kathryn watched in a daze, hardly believing the sudden reversal of fortune. Hunter might be practically disabled, but every time she needed him, he came through for her.

She was still standing there, wondering what to do next, when he turned and sprinted inside the guardhouse. Moments later she heard a whirring noise, and the gate began to swing open on well-oiled hinges.

"Go!" he shouted to Kathryn as he stood breathing hard and holding on to the edge of the door frame, looking as if he would fall over without the support. It was obvious that the sudden violent activity had drained him again.

"Not until you get in the car," she shouted back.

He made a grating sound of protest. "You cannot stay here. Colonel Emerson will send men. And...and Anderson knows you are not dead. He knows...I want to get you...away."

She folded her arms across her chest and bluffed

through her teeth. "If you don't get in the car, I'm not leaving."

His features contorted as he remained clutching the door frame. Either he was holding himself up, or he was trying to keep from moving forward.

"Do you need some help?" she asked, starting toward him.

"No." He sucked in a strangled breath, then let it out in a rush. Slowly, dragging his feet, he walked toward her. The misery on his face made her throat constrict. He looked like a man in great pain, or a man walking the last mile to his execution.

"Everything's going to be all right now," she told him quickly. "As soon as we meet up with my friends, we'll get you to a doctor and find out what Anderson did to you."

He shook his head as he slid into the passenger seat and leaned back against the headrest, eyes shut, teeth clenched.

The moment he closed the door she gunned the engine. They shot through the open gate, turning left as Cam had directed.

She glanced in the rearview mirror, half expecting another vehicle to materialize out of the darkness. But hers were the only headlights on the road, in front or back of her. It looked as if they were in the clear so far. And if Jed and Jason were really just around the bend, she and Hunter could make a swift escape.

They were on a stretch of rural highway that wound through deep woods. There were no street lamps, and her headlights stabbed through the dark, illuminating a sharp curve ahead. Narrowly avoiding a tree that loomed in her path, she slowed her speed as she leaned forward, searching for signs of the rescue team. Probably she was still too close to the grounds, she told herself.

Beside her, Hunter sat rigidly, his hands clasping and unclasping in his lap.

"Can you tell me what's wrong?" she asked.

"No. I cannot tell you."

"Is it something you don't want me to know about?" she asked gently.

She heard his breath rattle in his throat. "Kathryn, listen to…me," he gasped out. For long moments he was silent, breathing rapidly. Then he began to speak again. "Listen hard," he said in a voice that was thick with agony. "What if someone—what if Anderson pumped drugs into Harrison—drugs that made him do what Anderson told him to do. What if Harrison…wanted to tell you about it, but he couldn't say it?"

"What?"

He gasped, twisting in his seat, his hands clamped to the dashboard. "Drugs. Can't tell…you," he managed, then made a strangled sound of pain that seemed to well up from the depths of his soul.

"Hunter?"

"I…love…you. Think! Think!" he demanded, turning toward her, his eyes fierce, his face distorted by some inner agony she could only imagine.

Staring into the darkness beyond the headlights, she tried to make sense of what he had been saying since Kolb and Reid had shot each other. She'd thought he was out of his head. What if he was desperately trying to give her a message?

"Drugs…Harrison…a time to kill…"

Suddenly, in a blinding flash, the pieces of the puzzle dropped into place. God, Emerson had told her from the beginning that they'd used drug therapy on Hunter. Apparently he hadn't been lying. They used drugs to reinforce his orders. And tonight Anderson had given him an extra big dose, along with some specific instructions. Instructions to kill *her*. And instructions not to tell her what had been done to him.

Her gaze slid to the man sitting next to her. The man she had come to trust above all others. She was hoping against hope that her theory was wrong. Yet as she looked at him, she knew the truth. His body was shaking, and his hands were clasped tightly in his lap as if he were trying by brute force to control his actions.

Anderson had given him something all right. A lot of something. And Hunter had been fighting it with every cell of his being, fighting not to follow the directions zapped into his mind. And doing his damnedest to let her know she was in danger—from *him*.

The anguished look on his face and the tension in his strong hands told her he was losing the battle for control.

Fear shot through her. What the hell was she going to do now?

Her foot bounced on the accelerator. If she slowed the car, maybe she could jump out. Run for help from her friends who were supposed to be just up the road. Unless Hunter caught her first.

But it was already too late. Beside her, Hunter made a sound that was part protest, part growl, and lunged across the space between them.

Chapter Fourteen

Hunter's body twisted. His large hands angled toward her neck, brushed her skin in a parody of a caress. She tried to dodge away from his grasp, but there was nowhere to go in the close confines of the car as it hurtled along the darkened road.

"Don't," she gasped. "You don't want to hurt me."

"I don't," he sobbed out. Tear tracks ran down his cheeks. The hands in front of her shook, and his face twisted with the force of his resistance as he tried to pull away.

But the compulsion had been too deeply embedded in his mind. He had been fighting it since she came into the lab, she knew, and now he had all but lost the battle to resist.

"I...must," he gasped as his powerful fingers closed around her flesh. Even as he began to squeeze, he made a moaning sound.

"Hunter, don't," she said with her last bit of breath. Desperate to free herself, she jerked her foot off the accelerator and slammed it onto the brake pedal.

Her hands on the wheel kept her in place. Unprepared, Hunter was thrown forward. For a few seconds the pressure on her neck lessened. Then it was back, tighter than before.

The car skidded sideways as she raised her hands, trying to pry his fingers loose, but she might as well have been prying at large metal hinges that had snapped shut. Her fists pounded his chest and shoulder, but it was like pounding against a brick wall.

She could hear his breath rasping in and out of his lungs, even as she struggled to drag in air. But there was no oxygen getting to her brain.

She felt the car dip as the wheels on the right side left the road. Maybe they'd slam into a tree, she thought with some part of her mind while her vision swam, and the blackness of the night closed in around her.

As she felt consciousness slipping away, she dimly heard Hunter make an agonized sound of protest. Then the tension on her neck was suddenly gone, allowing her to drag in a grateful draft of air.

With a mighty effort, Hunter swung away from her and yanked on the door handle beside him. As the door slammed forward, he threw himself from the car and into the darkness.

She screamed, even as her foot found the brake again and mashed down. The car ground to a halt, and she leaned against the wheel, hearing the shrill sound of the horn as she gasped for breath.

''Hunter,'' she sobbed out as she threw her door open and scrambled from the car into the darkness. Standing made her head spin, and she had to grab the top of the vehicle to stay erect.

Her throat felt like raw meat, and it was agony each time she swallowed.

She had seen a flashlight in back when she'd covered Hunter with the blankets. Opening the back door, she fumbled along the floor, found the light and switched it on. Then, still drawing in strangled breaths, she turned and staggered back down the road, training the light on the shoulder as she searched frantically for Hunter.

Behind her she heard footsteps pounding. Moaning, she tried to run but only succeeded in stumbling. Strong hands caught her, and she started to struggle.

"Kathryn, it's all right. It's Jed. It's all right," a familiar voice assured her.

Finally, the words sank in. "Jed, thank God," she wheezed, the effort to speak making her throat ache.

"I saw your headlights. Then you stopped, and I heard the horn. What happened?" he asked.

"Hunter threw himself out of the car. Back there." She pointed in the direction from which she'd come.

"Why?"

She hesitated, wondering what kind of explanation she could give that wouldn't sound like she'd lost her mind. Then she remembered that the Light Street Irregulars were used to dealing with crazy situations. "They were experimenting on him at Stratford Creek. They put a—a compulsion in his mind that made him want to kill me. He was trying to stop himself. The only thing he could do was try and get away from me."

"Then he still could be dangerous. You stay here."

"No."

Jed started off, training his own light along the shoulder and into the underbrush.

She hurried to catch up.

About twenty-five feet down the road, they found

Hunter lying in a tangle of vines that looked like they'd cushioned his fall.

She ran toward his limp body. "Hunter!"

His head moved, and he stared at her.

"Are you all right?" she asked urgently, coming down beside him on the leaves.

"Get...away...from me," he gasped in a broken, desperate voice.

She reached to grip his arm as she gazed down into his horror-filled face. "I know what happened. I understand what you were trying to tell me, what Anderson did to you. I figured it out," she said. "He didn't believe Reid. He thought I was still alive and that he could make you finish the job. But it's all right. We can help you. It's going to be all right."

"No." He tried to shake his head and grimaced.

Jed was beside her, kneeling. He pulled a phone out of his back pocket and spoke in a low voice. "Get the van up here immediately. And be prepared to—"

Before he could finish the sentence Hunter reached out and yanked the pistol from the holster riding at Jed's hip. With no hesitation, he turned the barrel toward his own head.

"God, no," Kathryn sobbed and lunged at him, yanking his hand up as she braced for the impact of the bullet.

"Kathryn!" Hunter screamed.

Instead of a shot from the gun, the sound of a distant explosion tore the air, and a ball of fire erupted, turning the night sky an eerie orange over Stratford Creek.

Hunter stared at the fire leaping into the blackness.

Jed pushed past Kathryn, wrestled the gun hand to the ground, and landed a solid blow to Hunter's chin. He went limp.

WITH EYES DARK-RIMMED from lack of sleep, Kathryn sat in an armchair that someone had been thoughtful enough to put beside Hunter's hospital bed. Her hands were clenched in her lap. Sometimes she prayed, sometimes she simply watched Hunter's face for any sign of change.

They were at the Randolph Security Research Center, where they had been flown by helicopter two days ago. Two days during which Hunter had been unconscious and she had been in turmoil.

First he'd been sedated because she knew that if he were awake he'd try to kill either himself or her. Then they'd stopped the medication, but Hunter hadn't regained consciousness. Instead, he'd sunk into a coma.

With a sharp pang she watched him lying on the bed, his strong body clad only in a hospital gown, his arms strapped to the sides of the bed. Cam had insisted on the straps for her safety, if she was going to stay alone with Hunter. If he woke and the drugs had damaged his brain, he might go after her again.

She touched one of the thick restraints, then glanced toward the door. If Hunter wasn't all right, it didn't really matter what else happened, she thought. With fingers that were amazingly steady, she unbuckled the straps and clasped one of his large hands in her smaller ones. Turning his palm up, she saw the half-moon gouges where his nails had dug into his flesh as he'd tried to keep from attacking her. Softly, she kissed the healing wounds, thinking about the tortures he'd put himself through to save her.

She had never met a man like him before. She knew she would never meet another. He hadn't grown up with all the cultural cues and restraints that hemmed most people in. For better or worse, that made him unique. Although Emerson and the other devils at Stratford Creek could have broken his spirit or turned him into a monster, she was betting that she'd gotten him out of there in time, and that they hadn't had him long enough to do permanent damage. Her heart told her that must be true. So had her own observations, because every time he'd had real choices, he'd proved his goodness—his moral superiority.

But now she was faced with something she didn't know how to handle.

Her fingers clenched around his strong hand. "Hunter, I love you. Please, come back to me," she whispered.

But he lay without moving. And she felt the knot of fear in her stomach tighten. She'd been in a kind of limbo since they'd brought him here. Mostly she'd sat in the chair beside the bed. Sometimes she'd flopped onto a nearby cot when she was too exhausted to remain erect. She'd watched his pale face, touched him, talked to him. But he'd remained unresponsive. And from the expression on the faces of the men when they came in to check him, she knew that his failure to awaken was a bad sign.

Lifting his hand, she pressed his fingers against her cheek. They were strong, and warm. Like the man who lay there unconscious, she thought.

"Hunter," she whispered softly as she looked at his still face and began to repeat things she'd told him many times since they'd brought him back to her. "Hunter, everything's all right. You didn't break any bones when you...fell out of the car. You're only a little banged up. You're going to be fine." She gulped, then, and quickly went on with her periodic news bulletins. "Dr. Kolb blew up the lab to stop Project Sandstorm. The media swarmed up to Stratford Creek like bees to a honey pot. It's the latest government scandal. The reporters got the whole story, except the part about you." She paused to draw a shaky breath. "Emerson let them think that you were in the lab. Swinton and Anderson are in custody for conducting illegal experiments. Emerson is saying he only followed orders. I think he's going to end up testifying on Capitol Hill. And something else important. The police caught James Harrison. He can't hurt me now."

Hunter didn't answer. The small, comfortable room at the end of the hall was quiet except for his breathing. Leaning down, she laid her head on his shoulder, watching the rise and fall of his chest, refusing to give in to despair.

Perhaps exhaustion made her doze for a while. But she knew the moment his breathing changed, knew that something was different.

Suspended between heaven and hell, she raised her head and watched his eyes flutter open. For several seconds they were unfocused. Then they found her and filled with panic.

"No!" His whole body jerked as he tried to push himself away from her.

Anguish rose in her throat. *God, no.*

Even as a terrible sense of loss threatened to swamp her, she reached for him and held on for dear life. His fingers squeezed her arm painfully, spasmodically.

"Hunter, it's all right. Everything's all right," she repeated over and over, praying that she spoke the truth.

He went very still as if listening intently for some sound that he couldn't catch. "It's gone," he said in a hoarse voice.

"What's gone?"

He turned his head, focused on her face, really seeing her. "I—" He sank back against the pillows, sweat glistening on his pale skin.

"Talk to me," she begged, her heart pounding.

After a long, long time, he raised his hand to his forehead and pressed his fingers against his flesh. "The pain is gone. From the drugs."

"Was it very bad?" she whispered.

"Yes. I felt like my head was splitting in two, and it got worse when I tried to tell you what Anderson had done."

"I'm so sorry he did that to you." She wrapped her arms around him and held tight, as she dared to hope that he had come through the worst.

"They used drugs when they first started my training. Then Dr. Kolb made them stop. He said they were going to fry my brains. I hadn't had them in a long time—until Reid brought me to Anderson."

"They're out of your system now. Nobody will ever do that to you again."

He nodded, then looked thoughtful. "Dr. Kolb blew up the lab to end Project Sandstorm. It's finished."

She raised her head, stared at him. "How do you know all that?"

"You told me. Over and over. You told me the police captured James Harrison."

"Yes, but I didn't think you heard," she managed.

"I heard," he said with a deep sigh. "I thought it was a dream. I thought if I woke up, I would try to..." He gulped. "I tried to stay asleep."

"You shouldn't have done that. We were all worried. I was so worried."

She saw a shadow cross his features.

"What's wrong?"

"I tried to kill you," he said brokenly.

"It wasn't your fault! Anderson pumped you full of drugs and instructions."

"I should have—"

"You did everything you could. You tried to tell me what he did to you. Then you threw yourself out of the car. You grabbed Jed's gun."

"I had to." There was still uncertainty in his eyes. She couldn't stand his self-reproach. Leaning toward him, she brushed her lips softly to his. She meant it to be a light kiss because she knew he should rest after the ordeal he'd been through. But he demanded more, reaching up to pull her into his arms.

"Kathryn." Her name was a shaky sound as he settled her onto the bed with him. She forgot about restraint as he slid his hands up and down her back, over her hips, pressing her to him with the uncensored abandon that she had come to expect from him. When his hand worked its way under her loose knit shirt and found her breast, she exhaled in a low, pleading sigh that matched his deep exclamation.

"I want to feel your skin. All of your skin next to mine," he gasped.

"Yes." She helped him pull the shirt over her head. Standing, she kicked away her sweatpants and panties, then remembered with a strangled laugh that she'd better lock the door. When she turned back to Hunter, she saw he'd torn off the hospital gown.

She returned to the bed, kissing him, touching him, showing him what he meant to her, even as he did the same.

"I love you," she told him. "So much."

"Yes. So much."

Caught in a spiral of passion, they drove each other to a high plane where the air was almost too thin to breathe.

"Do it the way you did the first time," he gasped. "So I can see you. See your beautiful body above me when I'm inside you."

The request seemed to vibrate through her. She shifted her position so that she was straddling him, her legs clasping his hips as she came down on him. She liked it this way, too, because she could see the pleasure on his face as their bodies joined, as she began to move above him.

She wanted to make the sheer euphoria of it last. But the joy of being with him like this again was too intense. Urgency overtook her, and she drove for her satisfaction, her breath coming in gasps. He shuddered beneath her and she followed him over the edge into a place of rapture.

For long moments, she lay limply on top of him. His hands stroked through her hair, then stilled.

Rolling to the side, she reached down to pull the covers over them, then nestled beside him. But his silence and his stillness worried her, and when she raised her head so she could look into his eyes, she saw that his expression was sad.

"Didn't you like that as much as I did?" she asked softly.

"It was wonderful. But I am very selfish. I wanted to be close to you like that one more time," he answered, his fingers playing with the edge of the sheet.

"Hunter, you're the most unselfish man I ever met!" The tears that had been threatening her earlier gathered in her eyes and began to spill down her cheeks.

"I am not good for you, Kathryn," he said in a raspy voice. "You must leave me."

She couldn't believe she had heard him correctly. "I wasn't planning to leave you."

"You have your life to live."

"So do you! I thought we would do that together."

"I—"

"You said you loved me," she reminded him, hearing the quaver in her voice. "Did you stop?"

His face contorted. "Of course I didn't stop." He sucked in a quick breath and let it out. "But..."

Behind her, she heard the doorknob jiggle.

Both she and Hunter tensed, and she laid a hand on his arm.

When the knob didn't turn, the door rattled. "Kathryn, are you all right in there?" an anxious voice called. It was Cam.

"We...we're fine. Hunter's awake."

"He's all right?" Cam asked.

"Yes. We're talking," she said, flushing as she imagined her friend checking on them a few minutes earlier.

His footsteps departed and she turned back to Hunter. "What's changed about your feelings?" she demanded.

"Not my feelings. Everything else."

When she questioned him with her eyes, he contin-

ued, "At Stratford Creek, I always knew there would
be no future for me. Emerson was going to send me
on a mission to Gravan to assassinate its leader.
Whether I succeeded or not, I knew I wasn't coming
back."

When she made a sound of protest, his hand
stroked gently through her hair. "I accepted that, and
I knew the time with you was precious, that it was
only for a little while."

She reached for his hand and knit her fingers with
his. "I didn't know which country you were going
to, but I figured out what Emerson had planned for
you."

"You did?" he asked, incredulous.

She nodded gravely. "Yes. That morning, after you
moved out of the guest cottage. I was thinking about
you, wanting to tell you I was sorry about the way I
behaved when I came back from the lab. Then I
thought about the whole Stratford Creek project, and
it made a kind of awful sense. If you had a man who
didn't exist, you wouldn't have to bring him back
from his dangerous mission. But I didn't accept it. I
realized that somehow I had to get you out of there."

His head turned toward her, and his fingers stroked
her lips. "You are a remarkable woman. And you
deserve everything good in life."

"Damn right! And I think I've found the thing that
makes me happiest," she told him.

"What about—" He stopped, started again. "I
think a man is supposed to support his wife. Take
care of her. I can't do any of that. I have no skills to
earn a living. I don't know the right things to do and
say. I have no place in your world."

She pressed her fingers to his lips. "Where did you

get your view of domestic life? From 'Father Knows Best' reruns?''

He shrugged. "Is 'Ozzie and Harriet' better?''

She gave a little laugh. "They're both a little out of date. Women today aren't looking for men to support them," she told him vehemently. "They can do that themselves. What every woman dreams of is a man who will love her as an equal, a man with the same values as hers. A man who will share the joys and the responsibilities of life with her. A man who's strong but not afraid or embarrassed to show his tender side. I've had a lot of time to think about it while you were sleeping. You fit that description better than any other man I ever met.''

He looked overwhelmed as she continued, "And I promise you, you have skills my friends will value.''

"Killing?" he asked in a hoarse whisper.

"Undercover operations. Jed, the man who decked you when you grabbed his gun, isn't so different from you. And Jason has a similar background, too. They were both secret agents with training a lot like yours. Now they work for Randolph Security, one of Cam's companies. And when you meet our friend Thorn, you'll find out he has an even stranger background than you. You'll be surprised at how well you'll fit in.''

"I could...work with them?" he asked, unable to conceal his astonishment.

"Yes.''

His eyes told her that he still wasn't convinced. "You told them where I come from? You told them everything about the Stratford Creek project?" he asked carefully.

She nodded.

"They don't think that makes me..." He turned his head away, and she saw him swallow painfully. "A copy of a man. Not a real person."

Her expression was fierce as she caught his chin in her hand and guided his dark eyes back to hers. "They'll accept you on your merits, just the way I have. And they'll help you learn about the world, just the way I have. We can do things gradually. Each thing when you're ready."

She felt some of the tension seep out of him as he shifted his position beside her. He had never had a home or a family who cared, but he was about to find out what it was like to be part of a warm extended family of people who were there for you in good times and bad.

He raised himself on one elbow so he could look down at her. "To have you for a wife would be a miracle."

She gave him a playful little grin. "Not to be pushy, you understand, but is that a proposal?"

"A what?"

"Are you asking me to marry you?" she said, half teasing, half serious.

He flushed as he realized the implications of his words. "I want to. More than you can ever know. But I think we should wait."

"Why?"

"I want to make sure that it's the right thing for you."

When she started to object, he shook his head.

"Let me see if I fit in first."

She nodded. Hunter was cautious. And honorable. But she'd have plenty of time to make him comfortable with the idea of marriage.

He brought her hand to his lips, tenderly kissed her fingers. "Dr. Kolb said you looked like Ben Lancaster's wife," he whispered. "Ben Lancaster had excellent taste."

"Thank you."

"I don't know much about her, except that she was beautiful. But she isn't the same as you. No other woman has the warmth and strength you have. No other woman could have seen Swinton's laboratory and still loved me."

When she tried to deny the statement, he shook his head and plowed on, "No other woman has your bravery. No other woman could have gotten me out of Stratford Creek." Tears misted his eyes. "No one else would have cared enough about me. Why did you care so much?"

Her own vision swam. "At first I knew you needed me. Then I knew I needed you, too."

They lay holding each other silently for several moments, then he spoke again. "Would you...would you go to the desert with me? See the places I remember—the memories from Ben Lancaster?" he asked in a tentative voice.

"I'd like that."

"It's a good place to start, but I have a lot to try and understand now."

"I know. But you'll have my help. And my love."

"I couldn't do it without your love," he said simply. "Meeting you was like waking from a bad dream to find that there was a bright, warm light piercing the darkness around me."

"Oh, Hunter."

He folded her close, even as she wrapped her arms around his neck and surrendered to the joy of the moment, the joy awaiting them in the future.

HIJACKED BRIDE

B.J. Daniels

This book is dedicated to Ethel Witmer Fisk.
From those days at Montana State University
we have remained good friends even across the miles.
Thanks, Ethel, for your faith and encouragement
over the years.

Prologue

September
Houston, Texas

"And with the power vested in me, I now pronounce you husband and wife."

Patrick turned from the altar with his new bride, more pleased with himself than he'd ever been. He'd pulled it off—against incredible odds, too.

Finally, he'd beaten Jack Donovan at something. He'd not only gotten the girl—he'd gotten *Jack's* girl.

He took his bride's hand as they started down the aisle. By this time tomorrow he would finally have everything he wanted.

Now it was just a matter of getting Angie out of town—and killing her.

He glanced over at his new bride. Angie *was* a beauty. Too bad she was so damn rich. And too bad for her that the last thing he wanted was a wife. Mostly, he knew he couldn't keep up the pretense much longer and he wasn't about to let her leave him and take all her money with her.

So he'd come up with a plan to get rid of her on their honeymoon.

She looked at him. He squeezed her hand, reassuring her, just as he'd had to do for weeks. He'd seen her start to waver, becoming more uncertain as the wedding grew closer. It helped that Jack Donovan was locked up in jail and would have a hell of a time making bail at all, let alone getting out to spoil the wedding.

"Angie!"

At least, that had been the plan, Patrick thought as he looked up to see Jack burst into the church, yelling Angie's name.

"Angie?"

The look on Jack's face was priceless as he saw the bride and groom coming down the aisle. *Too late, Jack.*

Patrick felt Angie stumble at the sight of Jack framed in the doorway. The bitch had been *hoping* Jack would stop the wedding! Patrick tightened his grip on her. Amazing the way she trembled, just seeing Jack again. She still loved him—even after all the trouble Patrick had gone to, the weeks of planning and pretending, holding her hand and letting her cry on his shoulder.

He could feel her slipping out of his control as if her blind love for Jack Donovan was even stronger than the drugs and lies Patrick had numbed her with.

Patrick put his arm around Angie—just in case she had any idea of going to Jack—as four security guards cut Jack off. He was a little disappointed Jack didn't put up more of a fight, but then, it was four against one.

By the time he and Angie reached the church door, the guards had restrained Jack in a room out of sight—and hearing. There was no way Jack was getting near the bride. Not today. Angie didn't need to hear any more of Jack's wild stories about being framed. *You lose, Jack.*

Everything was going just as planned. Patrick felt his smile slip, though, as he looked over at his bride. Too bad she didn't appreciate all he'd gone through to get her. He'd always been second to Jack. Just the little friend from the poor family in the old neighborhood. The guy Jack always had to help out when Patrick failed. Well, not this time.

This time he'd outsmarted Jack. But that didn't mean he wouldn't always be second to Jack when it came to Angie. But not for long, he reminded himself.

By tomorrow Angie would be dead. Jack would be devastated—and back in jail for violating the restraining order Patrick had against him.

And Patrick would be rich and free. And there was nothing Jack could do to save Angie. Not a damn thing.

Once in the limo, Patrick poured the champagne and handed a glass to his pale and obviously shaken bride. Did she realize yet the mistake she'd made? Fortunately, he wouldn't have to keep up this pretense much longer.

At his sweet insistence, she took a sip of the drug-laced champagne. Later, when she complained she didn't feel well, they would leave the reception early.

She thought they were flying to Hawaii. Wouldn't she be surprised when she realized that wasn't the case? By then, though, she would be in no shape to protest.

He glanced over at her, afraid he wouldn't be able to get her out of town quickly enough. Tendrils of her dark hair framed an unusually pale face. Her brown eyes shone with unshed tears and her hand shook as she held the champagne glass to her lips. Damn Jack for showing up.

A stab of anger pierced Patrick's practiced facade. He had bent over backward to try to make her happy, had spared no expense, but she still wanted Jack. He had to turn away, to look out the window. He couldn't blow it now. Just a few more hours of pretending and Angie would be dead and he would be a very rich widower. He did like the sound of that.

He turned back to his bride and smiled sympathetically. "I know how hard this is for you. We both loved Jack. It's…heartbreaking to see him mess up his life like this. Drink up," he said as the limo pulled up to the country club where the reception was being held. "It's almost over."

Chapter One

Angie woke to the roar of the small jet touching
down. She opened her eyes, instantly confused as to
where she was. Worse, who she was with. She'd been
dreaming about Jack and a wedding. She'd foolishly
expected to see Jack in the seat beside her.

But instead it was Patrick. Just the sight of him
brought it all back. Jack's lies. Jack's betrayal. She
turned away, feeling sick. Out the small window all
she could see at first was darkness, then the inky black
line of high mountains etched against the night sky.
The tops of the mountains gleamed in the moonlight.
Snow?

"Where are we?" She sat up straighter, suddenly
afraid. "I thought we were flying to Hawaii." The
confusion in her mind was scaring her.

"Don't you remember, sweetheart?" Patrick asked,
looking concerned.

She'd been forgetting things the past few weeks. A
lot of things, it seemed. She often felt as if she were
walking around in a fog.

That's what she got for falling in love with Jack
Donovan. Hadn't her father always warned her not to
mix business and pleasure? She'd broken all the rules

she'd lived by for twenty-eight years—and paid the price.

Jack had lied, cheated, broken the law. If that wasn't enough, he'd betrayed her with another woman. *That* she could never forgive.

"We're in Montana," Patrick said patiently, as if speaking to a child.

"*Montana?*"

"Remember, we decided a cabin in the mountains of Montana would be much more romantic than Hawaii, where everyone honeymoons."

The plane slowed to a stop. She looked out the window and felt a chill run up her spine as she saw that they hadn't even landed at an airport. Instead, the small jet had put down on what appeared to be an old highway surrounded by pine-dark mountains. She could see weeds growing up through wide dark cracks in the pavement, as if the highway hadn't been used in years, and shivered as she looked around and saw nothing but mountains and pine trees.

She didn't remember Patrick saying anything about a change in their honeymoon plans. Nor about flying to Montana right after the reception to stay in a cabin. A cabin in the woods was so...not Patrick.

Her head ached as much as her heart. She felt Patrick take her hand and she wondered if she was losing her mind. She must be. Why else had she married Jack's best friend?

As she let Patrick lead her off the plane, Angie drew in the cold night air, filling her nose with the scent of pine. She felt her head begin to clear a little.

"The car is right over here," Patrick said. "I have champagne chilling just for you."

She could hear a motor running, and moved toward the dark vehicle parked off the highway.

He opened the door and ushered her into a large, warm Suburban SUV. The heater was on. She could hear the whirl of it, feel the waves of heat rising around her. She glanced out into the darkness but didn't see another soul.

"Here, have some of this while I get our luggage," Patrick said, pouring her a glass of the champagne. "Drink up, sweetheart. It's only a short drive to the cabin."

She took the glass he pressed into her fingers as he closed the car door. She saw that he was waiting just outside the car. She lifted the glass to her lips.

He winked. Over the rim, she watched him walk down the road away from her. She knew he'd look back, but she didn't know how, any more than she knew how she'd ended up here.

He glanced over his shoulder, smiled as if pleased with her, then continued toward the plane.

Her lips touched the cold champagne. She shivered and lowered the glass, staring down into the sparkling liquid as if she could read the future in the bubbles.

He'd be angry if she didn't drink it after he'd gone to the trouble. The thought shocked her—not that Patrick would be angry; he was always put out with her when she didn't seem to appreciate the things he did for her—that she could be manipulated like that.

What was wrong with her? She'd never let any man force her to do anything she didn't want to do. Quite the opposite.

But here she was married to Patrick, a man she didn't love. About to drink a glass of champagne she didn't want. About to go to a cabin she had no desire to go to on a honeymoon she didn't care about.

This wasn't like her. At least, not like the woman she had been before she started falling for Jack Donovan.

That's when she changed, wasn't it? Or was it when she found out that Jack had betrayed her? Wasn't that when she started letting Patrick make decisions for her?

She lowered her window and poured the champagne onto the ground. The night air felt good. She turned down the heat and breathed in, as if imbibing sanity.

Patrick started back toward her with the luggage, the bright starlight bathing him in cold whiteness. She stared up at the sky, startled and afraid she was losing her mind. A new moon. She couldn't have agreed to be married on this night. New moons were bad luck.

Instinctively, she reached up to touch the good luck charm around her neck.

It was gone! In its place was something cold and foreign.

Panic filled her. She never took off the talisman. Never. Had she lost it? Or had Patrick talked her into removing it for the wedding? What else had he talked her into?

This marriage.

She opened the car door and stumbled out. She didn't know how this had gotten so out of hand, but she couldn't let it go any further.

"Stay in the car," Patrick said, sounding irritated. "I can get the luggage."

"I don't want to go to the cabin." It surprised her

how unsteady she felt on her feet. "I'm sorry, Patrick. This is a mistake. I want to take the plane back—"

The roar of the jet drowned out the rest. She lurched toward the small plane.

Patrick dropped the luggage and grabbed her arm. "Are you crazy?" he yelled at her over the sound of the jet taxiing down the old highway away from them.

She tried to shake him off, but she felt dizzy and weak and her strength was no match for his.

"Most women get cold feet *before* the wedding, not after," he said, letting go of her because there was no place to go now.

She realized that beyond the old road, there were no lights. No towns close by. Why did she get the feeling that Patrick had planned it that way? He'd wanted her alone, just the two of them, because he thought he could make her forget Jack. Had she let him think that was possible? She must have.

"Where is my necklace?" she asked. Her grandmother had given her the amulet to ward off evil spirits, although she'd never told anyone that except Jack. He'd laughed and hadn't believed her. He'd never had to worry about bad luck—until he met her.

"You're concerned about that stupid, cheap charm?" Patrick snapped. "Really, Angie, a woman with your money shouldn't be wearing costume jewelry. Especially the dime-store kind."

"That necklace brought me luck," she said, feeling close to tears, as the small jet roared over them and headed south, the lights becoming dimmer and dimmer.

"Luck? What is it with you and this superstition thing?"

She shook her head. She didn't have the energy to

explain it to him. "Just give me my necklace." She remembered now his coming into the bride's room with a present for her. He'd laughed when she told him it was bad luck to see the bride before the wedding; then he'd come up behind her, taken off the amulet and put the bright white gold chain around her neck, a large diamond pendant dangling from it. Against her protests, he'd pocketed her amulet.

She shivered. "I want my necklace."

"So much for my wedding present." Patrick shoved his hand into his jacket pocket and tossed her the amulet.

She caught it and saw at once in the starkness of the starlight that the chain was broken. Her gaze came up. She glared at him.

"It broke when I took it off," he said, sounding angry and disgusted with her. "Do you have any idea how much that diamond around your neck cost me? Oh, I forgot, money means nothing to you."

She leaned against the side of the car, clutching the talisman in her fist, exhausted. "I appreciate everything you've tried to do but—"

"Angie, I'm sorry," he said, softening his tone. "It's late and we're both tired. Look, if you still feel like you've made a mistake tomorrow, I'll take you into Missoula and you can catch a plane back to Houston, all right?"

She breathed deeply in and out, trying to clear the fog from her brain. She had to find that old inner strength that had got her this far in life. She had to take control of her life again.

He stepped to her and brushed a lock of her hair back from her forehead, his fingers warm against her skin. "I know I'm getting you on the rebound, but I don't care. I thought my love for you would be enough for a while, until… I guess I was kidding myself that you could ever love me as much as I love you."

She closed her eyes, too tired, too confused, too wounded by what Jack had done to her.

"The plane is gone and it's getting so late," Patrick said, his tone soothing. "The closest real town is Missoula, and to get there you have to go down a narrow, winding mountain road. Can we just go to the cabin tonight? It's not far. I'll build a fire. We can have a late supper. I'll sleep on the couch. In the morning, if it's still what you want, I'll drive you to Missoula. I'd hate to drive the road tonight considering I've never been on it before. But I will, if it's what you want."

He sounded so reasonable, so caring. She opened her eyes. She could see his face in the moonlight. How could she have let him think she could fall for him the way she had for Jack? And marriage? Why couldn't she remember his asking her, her agreeing? She couldn't even recall most of the wedding ceremony—except for Jack bursting into the church. The look on his face.

"Angie, it's just one night," Patrick said, his voice thick with emotion. "If I'd known earlier that you felt like this…" He shook his head, picked up the luggage and stood waiting for her to tell him what she wanted.

She felt weak and sick to her stomach. She couldn't remember the last time she'd eaten. Her head still ached and she felt as if she needed to sit down before she fell down. She needed something solid to eat. She needed to get her strength back, to get her edge back.

She looked at him, telling herself this wasn't his fault. He'd been there for her during those horrible days after Jack's arrest, after she'd found out about Jack Donovan's crimes against her. Patrick had thought he could make her forget Jack. Maybe at some point she'd hoped he could.

"There is food at the cabin?" she asked.

He smiled. "Everything we need."

"You'll take me to this…Missoula in the morning?"

He nodded, looking miserable but resigned. "If it's still what you want."

"Thank you. I'm sorry—"

"Let's not talk about it tonight," he interrupted. "You're tired. Get in the car where it's warm. I don't want you catching your death of cold because of me."

She climbed into the Suburban. The heat did feel good. She rolled up her window, leaving a crack at the top to allow in fresh night air, even though she was chilled to the bone. It was a cold that had little to do with the temperature and everything to do with Jack Donovan.

She closed her eyes and leaned back against the seat. The fog seemed to be clearing a little from her mind, as if she was coming out of a long, fitful sleep.

Breathe. And don't think about Jack. Don't think about the look on his face at the church.

She didn't open her eyes as she heard Patrick load the suitcases in the back, then climb behind the wheel, nor when she heard the *clink* of her empty champagne glass as he picked it up from the floor.

"Why don't you have another glass of champagne? It will make the drive go faster and then I will cook you a wonderful dinner. All you have to do is rest in front of the fire.''

"I really can't drink any more al—"

"No arguments. Let me take care of you for tonight. Give me at least that.''

She heard him pour the champagne. She could almost feel the fine cool spray against her lips. She still didn't open her eyes even as he pressed the glass into her hand. It was just one night. Just one more night of letting Patrick take care of her. Tomorrow she'd fly back to Houston. Tomorrow she'd put her life back together. Tomorrow.

Chapter Two

"Are you sure this is the right road?" Angie asked, growing anxious as the Suburban's headlights exposed what looked more like a trail than a road through the pines.

Patrick turned onto it and started up the mountainside, the beam of the headlights bobbing through the dense woods that formed a wall on each side. "This might surprise you, but I know what I'm doing. Have a little faith, Angie."

Faith. Faith wasn't something she'd ever been strong on. She'd always depended on skill—and the survival lessons her father had taught her.

She tried to relax but couldn't. The rutted road switchbacked upward like a jagged scar cut in the mountainside. The suffocating darkness of the thick pines pressed in on her. Overhead, the starlight glittered in the moonless sky above the pines, like an omen that her luck had taken a turn for the worse.

She squeezed the amulet in her wedding suit pocket, wishing she'd never laid eyes on Jack Donovan.

The pines suddenly opened, and in the clear, cold starlight, Angie saw that the road fell away into a deep, narrow gorge on her side of the car. A twisting ribbon of silver wound its way through the canyon below.

"Take a look," Patrick said as he drove the Suburban along the road's edge.

"Be careful!" She let go of the amulet in her pocket to clutch the grip handle over the door.

"Angie, I thought you'd appreciate this. It isn't like you to be afraid."

No, it wasn't like her. Because she'd always been the one at the wheel. But she didn't see him looking down into the canyon, either.

"I didn't mean to scare you," he said. "It's just that you may never see the gorge again in starlight."

She hoped not. She pressed back against her seat, staring straight ahead at the road. It seemed to climb ever higher up the mountainside.

Out of the corner of her eye, she noticed that Patrick's knuckles were white from gripping the steering wheel so hard. Hadn't Jack once told her a story about Patrick having a horrible fear of heights? So why would Patrick pick a place like this for their honeymoon?

"How much farther is the cabin?" she asked, regretting now that she'd let him talk her into this. How could the road into Missoula have been any worse than this?

Patrick sighed. "I thought you'd love this."

She could hear the disappointment in his voice. "It's spectacular. Just a little scary."

"Only if you were to fall down in there."

She shuddered at the thought and took one last look at the canyon, wondering again what Patrick had been thinking in bringing her here.

A short distance along, the road veered back into the trees, straightening a little but still climbing upward, then leveled out some. Patrick slowed, turned right onto a dirt lane that looked even less traveled. A half dozen turns through the trees later, Angie got her first glimpse of the cabin in the headlights.

"Rustic, isn't it?" he said. "No phone. No electricity. We even have to pump our own water from the well out back." He parked in front, the headlights shining on the small log structure surrounded by dark pines. "Not even a cell phone works up here."

Off to the side, she saw an outhouse with a crescent moon cut in the door. If Patrick was trying to shock her, he was wasting his time. She'd roughed it before—but then, he had no way of knowing that. Or did he?

She looked over at him, anxiety prickling her skin. He'd picked this place because he wanted to make sure they were completely alone! He was afraid Jack would find them.

"I'm surprised this would appeal to you," she said, remembering the gorge and Patrick's fear of heights. Patrick seemed to like the finer things in life. She couldn't imagine him "roughing it."

He flashed her a rueful smile. "I guess you don't know me. Nor I you, as it turns out." He glanced pointedly at the expensive bottle of champagne chilling in the ice bucket next to her. "It seems there are a lot of things you don't like."

She had poured out the first glass and spilled the second, the alcohol making her nauseated. He must have seen the wet spot beside her car door earlier at the airstrip. Just as he must have noticed she hadn't drunk much at their wedding reception. Patrick didn't seem to miss much. Nor did he pass up an opportunity to try to make her feel guilty. Hadn't he realized by now that she would always disappoint him? Telling him she felt sick and didn't want any more would only make him angry with her.

"I'm just not thirsty."

"No, I guess not."

Just before he turned off the headlights, she spotted another vehicle parked off in the woods. An older model Jeep Wagoneer. Someone was here! Someone who knew the road and could take her to Missoula tonight rather than in the morning.

"The cabin owner left us an extra car," Patrick said, dashing her hope in one fell swoop. "We're so far from civilization, he was worried that if we had car trouble of any kind we would be stranded up here."

So they were alone…far from civilization…

Patrick turned off the engine. Silence and darkness settled around them. "I'll go light the fire and the lanterns—why don't you stay here." He got out, taking the car keys with him, and unloaded a large cooler from the back of the Suburban.

She watched him carry it up the steps to the cabin in the moonlight. He put it down, dug out a key from his pocket and unlocked what appeared to be a padlock. The cabin didn't even have a real lock. A few minutes later, lantern light flickered on inside.

The car cooled down, the engine ticking. It was the only sound. She looked around, seeing nothing but trees and darkness. When she glanced toward the cabin again, Patrick was on the porch, motioning impatiently for her to come inside.

She opened her door and got out. The air was cold

and smelled wet. Her head ached as if she had been
drinking champagne for days. Maybe she had. She
couldn't remember.

Patrick had gone back inside. She couldn't see him.
She looked over at the Jeep parked in the trees, then
back at the cabin, half expecting to see Patrick watching her. He wasn't—for once.

She hurried over to the Jeep and tried the door. It
wasn't locked. The dome light came on. The keys
were in the ignition! She quickly extinguished the
dome light and pulled the keys, pocketing them.

Relieved, she closed the car door. If Patrick
wouldn't take her to town in the morning, she'd drive
herself. The thought made her feel a little better. If
she didn't feel so weak and tired and sick, she might
go now. Except she couldn't imagine trying to find
her way to Missoula in the dark.

"Hope you're hungry," Patrick said, as she
stepped into the cabin and closed the door behind her.

She could already smell food—precooked, no
doubt. The cooler she'd seen must be one of those
that also kept food warm. Someone had left the Suburban—and the food—parked off the old highway.
Didn't that mean a town couldn't be very far away?

"Starved."

That seemed to please him. "Make yourself comfortable. Rest. It won't be long. I have everything
under control."

She didn't doubt that.

The cabin was nicer inside than she'd expected. A
fire crackled in the stone fireplace with a large leather
couch, end tables and several club chairs circled
around the inviting blaze. But the fire did little to take
the chill out of the cabin.

She moved to stand directly in front of the grate, warming her hands first, then turning to survey the cabin as she heated her backside. Three rooms. Kitchen, living room and bedroom. Through the partially open door, she could see part of a patchwork quilt covering the antique iron-framed double bed. There was a back door, but it was padlocked from the inside. That seemed odd.

Patrick went out to the Suburban and came back in, putting his suitcase and some other items by the door. She didn't pay any attention to what he'd brought in. She felt chilled and tired and, even as hungry as she was, she wished she could just go to sleep now and skip dinner.

"We're having steaks, baked potatoes, salad and a nice merlot," he said as he went back into the kitchen. He was certainly pushing the alcohol. Did he think he could get her drunk and change her mind?

"Sounds wonderful." She didn't have the energy to argue.

Sitting down on the hearth, the fire warming her back, she watched him add wood to the old-fashioned stove. He took out several foil-wrapped containers and set them on top of the stove.

When she was sure he was too busy to notice, she took off the diamond pendant and put it in her pocket. Quickly threading the amulet onto the gold chain, she clasped it around her neck, buttoning her blouse so it was hidden from view. What Patrick didn't know wouldn't hurt him.

Through the cloth of her blouse she rubbed the good luck charm, pressing it against her bare skin. It felt wonderfully familiar. She closed her eyes, feeling at peace for the first time in weeks.

"There are some clothes for you on the bed. Change while I finish dinner. You'll be more comfortable."

She glanced toward the bedroom. She didn't have the energy to play dress-up. But neither did she have the energy to argue with him about this any more than she did the wine. She got up and walked toward the bedroom, afraid to see what he wanted her to put on.

With relief, she spotted a pair of flannel-lined jeans, a sweater and a fleece-lined canvas coat. It all looked wonderfully warm. She hurriedly changed, noticing that some of her own things were hanging in the closet along with several pairs of her shoes, including her warm winter boots.

She felt a little guilty. It had been thoughtful of Patrick to consider her comfort. The new clothes he had bought her were all the right size and felt good. And he'd brought some of her things from her Houston hotel room—

An owl screeched outside the cabin, making her blood curdle. *"When you hear the screech owl, honey, in the sweet gum tree, it's a sign as sure as you're born a death is bound to be."* She clutched the amulet at her neck for a moment, remembering the new moon outside, suddenly afraid.

When had Patrick put her things in the cabin? She hadn't seen him bring anything into the bedroom from the Suburban. He'd either mailed the items up here or—

Was it possible he'd been here before tonight? But he said he'd never been on the road to Missoula before.

She moved to the chest of drawers and opened the top one. Several more new items of clothing for her.

Some still had the tags on. She lifted out a bright red teddy, read the name of the store on the tag. Little Lil's Boutique? She'd never heard of it.

She closed the drawer and glanced in the closet. At the far back, she spotted a wadded-up pale blue plastic bag. Squatting down, she reached in and pulled it out. Printed on it was "Little Lil's Boutique, Missoula, Montana." Missoula?

Several other plastic bags had been stuffed into this one. She pulled them out, not recognizing any of the store names. All of the bags had receipts in the bottom. She dumped them onto the floor and glanced over her shoulder, expecting to find Patrick standing behind her.

Why did she think he would be upset to find her checking the dates? After all, he'd bought the clothing for her.

She picked up the receipts. They all had the same date on them. Three weeks ago. All signed by Patrick.

The receipts blurred in her trembling fingers. How was that possible? She'd only agreed to marry him a little over a week ago. Even now, she couldn't recall why. And she remembered distinctly Patrick promising to take her to Hawaii. She hadn't been to Hawaii in years and the distance from Houston had appealed to her. She'd wanted to get as far away from Jack Donovan as possible, someplace warm and tropical.

Her heart began to pound. Patrick had been planning to bring her to this cabin for *weeks*. He'd bought this clothing and rented this cabin *before* Jack was arrested. *Before* he'd asked her to marry him. He'd been that sure he could get her here.

And he had.

Her head ached, but the fog was clearing, leaving

in its wake a growing fear that stole her breath and filled her mind with panic.

My God, what had Patrick done to get her here? And why?

Chapter Three

Jack Donovan swept past the reporters, covering his eyes to keep from being blinded by the camera lights and the flash of bulbs.

"Mr. Donovan! Are the allegations against you true?"

"Jack! How long have you been ripping off low-income homeowners in your old neighborhood? What else is the investigation going to uncover?"

Jack ducked into the back of the black limo parked at the curb and slammed the door on the reporters and their questions. He still couldn't believe any of this was happening and it only kept getting worse.

"Going to that church was beyond stupid," snapped the distinguished gray-haired man sitting next to him, as the limo driver sped away from the jail. "You knew there was a restraining order against you. Do you have any idea how hard it was to get you out tonight? What in blazes is wrong with you?"

Jack Donovan shook his head as he looked out at the darkness. He wouldn't know where to start. "Montie, you've known me all my life. You don't believe these allegations against me, do you?" He turned to look at the elderly man on the wide leather seat next to him.

"It doesn't matter what I believe, Jack—"

"It does to me," Jack snapped. "How can you defend me if you believe I'm guilty?"

Montague Cooke shook his head. "You really aren't that gullible, are you? Lawyers defend guilty clients all the time, Jack."

"We're not talking about any client. Or any lawyer. You've been a family friend all of my life."

"I'm your lawyer, Jack. I was your father's lawyer. It's my job to defend you. Even if you're guilty."

"That's comforting," Jack said sarcastically.

"Someone put a gun to your head and make you go to that wedding?" Montie said sharply.

What had Jack thought he could do? Stop the wedding? Convince Angie of...what? That all the charges against him were fabricated? That she could trust him? Maybe. Maybe he'd just needed to see for himself that Angie was really going to marry Patrick.

Well, he'd seen it and he wasn't even sure that if he'd gotten there sooner it would have made a difference. She'd done it. She'd married Patrick. She was Mrs. Patrick Ryerson now. And he still couldn't believe it.

He leaned back and closed his eyes. The limo smelled of pipe tobacco and leather, a familiar and comforting scent. He'd been riding in the back of one of Montie's limos for almost as long as he could remember.

Still, it felt strange that his father wasn't here. It had been over a year since Kelly Donovan died, but Jack still expected to open his eyes and see his father sitting across from him, leaning back into the leather as if born to it, long legs stretched out and a big smile on his handsome face. Kelly Donovan loved riding in a limo.

"The point is, you have to quit acting so damn stupid," Montie said, tapping fresh tobacco into his pipe as the limo cruised the streets of Houston. Traffic was light this late at night, and they had temporarily lost the media. "What were you thinking?"

He hadn't been thinking—nor paying attention to his business, not for months—that was the problem. He should have been worried about clearing his name of the charges now against him instead of thinking about Angie, but that wasn't possible.

"I know she didn't want to marry him," Jack said, shaking his head.

One of Montie's thick white brows shot up. "What makes you think she didn't want to marry him?"

"Because. She's in love with me," Jack said, holding on to what he believed to be the one truth in his life right now.

Montie grunted and took his time lighting his pipe. "Who is this woman, this Angelina Grant, that you think is in love with you?"

"You met her that night at the restaurant."

"Just in passing—"

Montie had run into the two of them at a local uptown restaurant. What had they been celebrating that night? Their one-month anniversary? They'd been like teenagers, everything feeling so new, so wonderful.

"I remember she was beautiful."

Jack nodded. Beautiful and funny, sweet and innocent in a way that had stolen his heart.

"But what do you actually know about her?" Montie persisted.

"She's the heir to some fortune. Import-export, I think." It hadn't mattered. He'd fallen for her in spite of her wealth, always having been leery of women with a lot of money. Too much money could corrupt.

"You never asked?" Montie shook his head.

"It didn't matter. Also, she was never involved in the actual business end of it, from what I gathered. Her father died recently, but by then he'd sold the businesses and put everything into stocks and bonds and a trust fund for her, his only heir."

"How nice for her," Montie commented. "How exactly did you meet this woman?"

"In the park this spring. Angie was trying to flag down a cab not far from my office building when some idiot driving too fast practically ran her down. I pulled her out of the way and she bought me dinner." He shrugged. "As they say, the rest is history."

Montie shot him a look. "You saved her life?"

"It wasn't quite that dramatic."

The older man grunted. "So you know nothing about her other than what she told you?"

He knew the important things. Like how her green eyes sparkled in candlelight, how her dark hair felt running through his fingers, how she made *him* feel. "I know her—all right?"

"Jack, how can you be sure this woman is even rich?" Montie demanded.

"I don't care if she's rich or not," he snapped.

"She could have been after your money."

Jack shook his head. "You saw the way she dressed. She was staying at the Carlton Arms." Montie looked ready to argue. "Anyway, I saw a report from her accountant one day when I was in her suite. It was lying on the coffee table. I didn't really look at it—''

Montie groaned. "She just left it out where you could see it?"

"It wasn't like that." But maybe she had purposely left it there. Maybe she'd wanted him to know she wasn't after his money. "You don't know Angie."

Montie grunted again. "I know she's married to Patrick."

"He was there for her after all this stuff came down about the housing and me." But even as Jack said it, he knew something else had happened. Somehow Patrick had turned Angie against him, talked her into marriage. It wasn't what Angie wanted. Jack had seen that in her eyes at the church. In her expression when he'd burst in before the security guards had hauled him away. Angie loved him, not Patrick.

"So much for her undying love for you," Montie noted.

"She never said she loved me." Jack looked out the tinted side window, the lights of Houston blurring by. "It never got that far."

Montie shook his head. "And you never told her how you felt, did you?"

He'd been planning to, but then there was a fire at one of the houses his construction company was building in his old neighborhood, and the next thing he knew he was arrested for arson and fraud.

"You didn't ever happen to see her social security number, did you? Or the name of her financial advisor?"

Jack frowned. "Why the interest in Angie?" He hadn't been paying attention to anything but Angie that day when he'd seen the financial report. She had come back into the room dressed in a black sheath, a tiny string of pearls at her slim throat.

"She married Patrick and they have both left town. That pretty much says it all."

Jack shook his head. Montie was convinced Patrick was behind the kickbacks and the arson. "I still can't believe Patrick would do something like this."

Montie growled. "Jack, open your eyes. You put him in charge of those homes."

"I know, but it was our old neighborhood where we grew up, we know those people. I never thought he'd cheat them."

The press was having a field day with the story, saying Jack had been taking kickbacks—the difference between the materials that should have been going into the houses and the inferior ones that actually were. And that Jack had burned down a house under construction to try to cover his crime when it looked like he was going to get caught.

Montie puffed on his pipe for a moment. "The buck stops with you since you own the company. Patrick, of course, says he quit when he became aware of what you were doing. I suspect he's the concerned citizen who turned you in. I'm just worried the investigation will turn up more substandard housing down there."

So was Jack. He hadn't been involved in that part of the business in the year that he'd turned the project over to Patrick. They'd built a lot of houses during that time. "I need to talk to Del." Del Sanders was the general contractor on the project, a man who'd worked for Jack's father.

Montie was already shaking his head. "I told you

I don't want you going near Del or any of the workers. I don't want anyone thinking you paid them—or threatened them—to lie for you in court. Patrick has already said you threatened him.''

"You know better than that.''

"A judge and jury might see it differently since you violated the restraining order today at Patrick's wedding.''

Jack raked a hand through his hair. He was bone weary, exhausted and sick with regret. He never should have put Patrick in charge of that housing project. He should have paid closer attention to what was going on down there. He should have told Angie he loved her.

"Jack, you have to let me handle this,'' Montie was saying. "It's a legal problem. That's what you pay me for. We'll get Patrick, don't worry.''

Don't worry? What a joke. The hardest part was sitting back and doing nothing. "It's my reputation at stake here.''

"It's your *reputation* that's going to get you off with probably little more than a slap on the hand,'' Montie said. "Sure, there are people who are going to believe you cut corners. You wouldn't be the first contractor to get rich that way. Your only crime is bad judgment for hiring Patrick and letting him run the project.''

Even if Montie got him off, his reputation would be tarnished. He would have to forget the housing project, maybe even sell his construction business. The majority of people would think he "bought" his way out of the charges, and he knew it.

They rode in silence for a few minutes, and Jack realized they were almost to his penthouse.

"I tried to warn you about Patrick," Montie grumbled.

Jack glanced out at the city and the darkness, remembering when he and Patrick were kids. They'd been close as brothers growing up in a poor section of Houston, the same part of town where Jack had been building low-income housing for the past year.

"You've always been too trusting, Jack," Montie was saying. "And Patrick has always been too competitive when it came to you. He pretended it didn't bother him when you prospered and he didn't. I'm sure you got him started in his first business, the one he lost—maybe the others, as well. I would imagine he resented the hell out of you because of it."

Jack didn't deny he'd helped Patrick. Why not? Jack had the money. Patrick didn't. And they were friends.

"I saw that hungry look in his eyes when that story came out about you in *Fortune* magazine. He was jealous as hell of you—more jealous, obviously, than either of us realized. You giving him a job overseeing construction of nice homes in your old neighborhood was probably more than Patrick could take."

Jack shook his head. "I thought he'd appreciate the fact that we were building houses for families we used to know, trying to help people who were just like us."

"Just like the way you *used* to live," Montie pointed out. "I have a feeling it isn't something Patrick likes to remember."

"Life can only be understood by looking back," Jack said, trying to remember where he'd heard that.

"At least now you realize what Patrick is capable of," Montie said.

Yes, Jack thought. He was capable of stealing Angie from him and leaving him facing criminal charges. Jack was now in danger of losing his business, his reputation, his freedom... And yet the loss that was killing him was Angie.

"You're sure this was all Patrick's doing?" Jack just didn't want to believe it. "How could he pull it off without the general contractor and the job foreman not knowing what was going on? He couldn't. That means Del and Leonard both knew." Leonard Parsons was the job foreman, someone Del had hired. Jack had only seen the man a few times. Not paying closer attention to what was happening down there was another mistake.

"Jack, I told you. Don't concern yourself with this," Montie said. "I talked to Del. Patrick was running things. Del was pretty much stuck in his office. As for Leonard, well, he said he thought you knew about the cheaper materials being used in the house. In fact, he thought the orders had come directly from you."

Jack swore. "So Patrick had to be the one behind this." He couldn't help but think about the day of his father's funeral, when Patrick had suddenly appeared after a five-year absence. He and Patrick had had a falling-out over a business Jack had helped him start. But when Patrick had shown up for Kelly Donovan's funeral just over a year ago, Jack had been grateful and glad to see him.

He had thought Patrick had changed and wanted to give him another chance. So he'd given him the job. Patrick had seemed overwhelmed by Jack's generosity.

The limo stopped at a traffic light. Jack realized that Montie was staring at him.

"You still want to believe that Patrick isn't behind this?" He sounded incredulous. "Jack, the man just married the woman you were in love with, framed you and took off. I wouldn't be surprised if he and this Angie woman were in on this together."

Jack scoffed at the idea. "You don't know Angie."

"It doesn't sound like you did, either," Montie said as the limo pulled up in front of Donovan Inc., a large, glittering monolithic structure in the heart of Houston. The offices for his many businesses were housed on several floors, with his penthouse apartment on the seventeenth floor.

"I want you to lay low," Montie said. "Try to stay out of the public eye. I know you're upset, but don't make matters worse."

"How could things be any worse?"

"If you jumped bail and went after Patrick and this woman," Montie said.

The thought had crossed Jack's mind—except, what would be the point? It wouldn't prove Patrick had framed him. Or prove that Angie hadn't been in on it. Bursting in on their honeymoon would only make him look like a bigger fool—and get him thrown in jail for jumping bail and ignoring for a second time the restraining order against him.

"We'll get the proof we need against Patrick," Montie said. "He isn't smart enough to get away with this. But you are to have no contact with him. I can't have you violating that restraining order again."

Jack's attempts to talk to Patrick after the arrest had led to the restraining order. Patrick had said he feared for his life for testifying against Jack.

"Patrick has you right where he wants you," Montie said. "Anything you do to fight this will only make you look more guilty."

But how could he not fight it?

"Do the clothes fit?" Patrick called from the cabin kitchen.

Angie leaned against the bed, so shaken her legs felt as if they wouldn't hold her. "Perfectly," she managed to answer.

"Everything all right?" he called back, obviously hearing something in her voice that warned him.

She cleared her throat and pushed herself up, fighting for her old strength, her old courage. "Fine. I thought I'd just rest a while until dinner is ready. I'm a little tired."

"Good idea," he called back to her, sounding more cheerful over the clatter of dishes and silverware.

He didn't seem to hear her come up behind him. He was humming, his back to her, as he put a single red rose beside one of the plates at the table he'd just set.

She watched him turn back to the counter and had to lean against the kitchen doorjamb, she felt so weak and sick. The smell of steak and baked potatoes made her stomach growl with hunger. How long had it been since she'd eaten? She couldn't remember.

Patrick had one of the potatoes split open. He bent over something on the counter, grinding it with the edge of a glass.

Her gaze went to the reflection in the corner window. He methodically dumped several white pills from a prescription container onto the counter and pulverized them to dust with the bottom edge of the drinking glass, then ground several more.

To her horror she watched him brush the white powder into his palm and then into the open baked potato. Without ever turning in her direction, he topped the potato with sour cream and chives, then set it on the table beside the plate with the rose on it. *Her* plate.

She couldn't move, couldn't breathe. The headaches, the fogginess, the forgetfulness. How long had Patrick been drugging her? From that first night when he'd come to her with the news of Jack's duplicity? He'd made her a drink. It had tasted bitter, but no more bitter than what Patrick had told her about Jack.

Had it all been a lie? Jack had sworn he was innocent, but she hadn't believed him. Because it had been easier to believe Jack lied, being a liar herself.

She watched Patrick pocket the container of pills. He'd manipulated her from that first night. That's how he'd gotten her to turn her back on Jack, to marry him so quickly, to come to this cabin with him. That's how he'd known weeks in advance that she would be coming here with him as his wife.

But why? Why go to so much trouble to—

Oh God.

She stumbled back, bumping into the edge of a bookshelf along the wall.

Patrick turned, surprise flashing in his eyes. He looked to the table where he'd put the baked potato. She could see the question in his gaze. How long had she been standing in the doorway? Long enough to see him put the drugs in the food? Or just long enough to see him pocket the pills?

"I thought you were going to rest for a while," he said.

Her expression must have given her away. She'd

definitely lost her touch. She used to be able to hide her feelings without any trouble. It was one of the first things she'd had to learn.

Whirling, she bolted for the front door, but he was on her in an instant, bringing her down hard on the wooden floor, knocking the air from her lungs. She gasped like a fish thrown up on the beach as he dragged her to her feet.

"This isn't the way I wanted it," Patrick yelled, angrily shoving her backward. "If you had cooperated it would have been painless. All you had to do was drink the damn champagne. You would have been out cold by now and it would be over."

"Why?" she gasped, stumbling back from him.

"*Why?*" he parroted, shoving her as he advanced on her. "Why? Because I was sick to death of things always coming so easy to Jack. He wasn't getting you and your money on top of everything else."

"You did this for the money?" she cried, the irony killing her.

"Don't tell me you really believed I *loved* you?" He shook his head. "I just wanted to win for once. Do you have any idea what it was like growing up in Jack's shadow? No, a woman like you couldn't understand that any more than Jack could. But now I'm going to be the one with the money, the power. I'm the winner for a change." He smiled. "And poor Jack's the loser."

She stared at him, too shocked to speak, as she inched backwards, trying to stay away from him but running out of room in the small cabin. "You were Jack's best friend."

Patrick smirked. "I was just do-gooder Jack's pet project. He deserves what he got."

Anger bubbled up inside her and she wanted to lash out at him, but she knew he was waiting for her to do something stupid like that. She had to be calm. To think. But her head ached and she felt light-headed from lack of food, from the drugs she now realized he'd been using to neutralize her. "Patrick, you've made a terrible mistake."

"The only mistake I made was in not killing you on the way up here," he said as he advanced on her. "But how would I have explained that—you still dressed in your honeymoon suit? I've put too much into this to have it spoiled now."

She stumbled back, bumping into one of the chairs, as her mind reeled. Jack had tried to tell her it was all lies, but she hadn't listened. She thought he was just lying to save his skin. That was something she could understand. Just like she expected men to betray and disappoint her, didn't she?

She moved around the chair, furtively looking for something to use as a weapon against him. She was too weak to fight him off and they both knew it.

"Patrick, I'm not who you think I am. I'm not rich. I'm not even—"

"Not rich? Nice try, but I'm not stupid. I checked you out. You're loaded."

She was shaking her head. "If you kill me, it will have been for nothing. Those financial reports were fakes. I was just after Jack's money." She was near the door now but he was too close. She'd never be able to get through it before he caught her. Nor could she outrun him even if she did.

"It isn't going to work, Angie." Patrick stepped toward her. "You're a lousy liar. After Jack's money!" He laughed. "You were in love with him.

Don't you think I know that? You'll go to your grave loving Jack. But at least *I'll* have your money.''

A lousy liar? That was a first. ''Patrick, there is no money.'' She was trapped. She couldn't possibly get out the front door before he grabbed her. Nor would running in front of the fireplace buy her anything but a little time. Either way, she knew he'd catch her in an instant. And no matter how much she protested, he wasn't going to believe that he was killing her for nothing.

''Do you realize what you've put me through this last week, all the whining about Jack, all the reassuring I've had to do? I just wish I could see Jack's face when he finds out about your death.''

The raw bitterness and hatred in his voice cut through her like a blade. How could she not have seen this? Because Patrick was more than adept at deceit.

She tried to clear her mind, to think. Out of the corner of her eye, she spotted the ice bucket, the neck of the expensive champagne bottle sticking out, where Patrick had put it on a small end table next to the couch.

She hadn't noticed before that he'd brought it in from the Suburban. Just as she hadn't noticed the sediment at the bottom. How could she have been such a fool? Love and betrayal. Falling for Jack was about to cost her her life.

She glanced toward the fireplace tools on the other side of the fireplace, knowing Patrick was watching her every move.

He followed her gaze, just as she knew he would. The poker handle gleamed in the firelight. He smiled, sure she could never reach it before he caught her, but wanting her to try.

She lunged toward the tools.

Patrick gave her an extra second of a head start—no doubt to make it sporting. It was all she needed. He sprang at her, still so sure she was going for the poker that he was taken off guard when she swung around to face him suddenly, her hand closing over the neck of the champagne bottle full of drugs resting in the ice bucket.

He was off balance and not expecting the blow. She swung, aiming for his head. It caught him on the temple, a glancing blow, but enough to drop him to his knees.

She raised the bottle, ready to strike him again, and saw him reach into his jacket pocket. Even before he withdrew it, she knew he was going for a handgun.

She hurled the champagne bottle. It caught him in the shoulder. He let out a grunt of pain as the gun clattered to the floor, and for just an instant, she thought about diving for it. But he was closer and stronger.

She grabbed the ice bucket as Patrick groped for the gun. Using both hands, she hurled it at his head. The bucket hit with a *thud,* making him shriek and fall to his back on the floor as the ice and water cascaded over him.

Just before she turned to run for the door, she saw him try to get to his feet, swaying, blood running down into his left eye from the cut on his forehead where the ice bucket had split his skin open.

Her only hope was that it would slow him down. She burst out of the door, slamming it, frantically fumbling with trembling fingers to padlock the door behind her. The lock clicked closed.

She could hear Patrick banging around inside the

cabin. The paned windows weren't large enough for him to get through. With luck, he would try to break down the door—and that would give her more time.

Once he had realized she'd padlocked him in and he couldn't break down the door, he'd go for the back door. That door was also padlocked, but from the inside. It should take him a while to find the right key.

At best, she'd bought herself a few precious minutes. She hoped it would be enough.

She ran to the Jeep, jerked open the door and threw herself behind the wheel, afraid this was another of Patrick's tricks—giving her hope and then snatching it away. She dug the key out of her pocket and shoved it into the ignition. As she pushed in the clutch and turned the key, she prayed it would start. A first. Praying.

The cold engine coughed and backfired like a shot, making her jump. She pumped the gas pedal and tried the engine again, as she heard Patrick crashing angrily into the front door. Then silence.

The Jeep engine sputtered to life, running rough, but running. She slammed the car into reverse, groping for the headlights switch. As the lights flashed on, she saw Patrick come barreling around the side of the cabin.

She swung the Jeep around and hit the gas, the tires throwing dirt and pine needles as she left him behind in a cloud of dust and darkness. It wasn't until she was headed down the road and saw the headlights behind her that she realized the mistake she'd made. Why hadn't she thought to try to disable the Suburban? She told herself there hadn't been time. Her father must be rolling over in his grave. Everything he'd taught her—wasted.

The Jeep rattled and bounced as she barreled down the narrow, rutted road, the dark pines flashing by. She didn't dare drive too fast for fear of crashing into the trees. The Jeep couldn't outrun the newer Suburban, anyway, and Patrick had the advantage: He knew the road.

Not that she wasn't determined to make this as hard for him as she could. Even if he caught her, she was going to do her damnedest to make him work at killing her. At least she would have that satisfaction.

She tried to remember the road from earlier, when Patrick had been driving. Behind her, the lights of the Suburban closed the distance between them. It was all downhill now—to the big curve and the gorge.

She knew she stood little chance. Not only did he have the larger, more powerful vehicle and know the road, but also he hadn't spent the past couple of weeks being drugged out of his mind. Mostly, though, she knew that Patrick couldn't let her get away. Just as she knew with sudden certainly where on the road he would try to kill her.

He was gaining on her, the blazing headlights of the SUV growing brighter and brighter, closer and closer, until they filled the interior of the Jeep, blinding her.

With a teeth-rattling jar, the Suburban crashed into the back of the Jeep. She gripped the steering wheel, desperately trying to keep the Jeep in the narrow tracks between the trees.

Ahead she could see where the trees ended—and the gorge opened. Patrick dropped back a little. This would be the spot. The headlights were growing brighter behind her, the Suburban picking up speed.

Her hand went to the amulet at her neck as the

black gaping hole of the river gorge opened before her. The lights of the Suburban filled the Jeep and she knew it was only a matter of seconds before he rammed into her again—driving her into the gorge. Angie hit her brakes and swerved.

The SUV crashed into the passenger side of the Jeep. The Jeep rocked under the force, rolled onto its side, slid a few yards, then dropped over the edge into the canyon and darkness.

Chapter Four

Patrick hadn't realized how fast he was going. He laid into the brakes, his heart suddenly in his throat. The bitch was going to take him with her.

At first, it seemed to be happening in slow motion. The brake lights flashing on the Jeep, Angie trying to swerve out of his way. Fool woman.

He had hit the Jeep hard, rattling his teeth, and watched it rock up on two wheels, flop over, slide and drop over the edge.

Now everything was moving too fast. *He* was moving too fast. There was nothing between him and the gaping gorge.

The Suburban began to skid toward the canyon rim. He could see it in his mind's eye. The Suburban dropping over the edge into the blackness of the gorge just as the Jeep had done. Angie's revenge. The bitch.

The brakes on the Suburban were screaming. Or maybe it was Angie. He couldn't be sure it wasn't him as he stood on the brake pedal, fighting to stop, the canyon looming in front of him, setting off his horrible vertigo. The bottomless chasm pulling him—

The Suburban came to a jarring halt, the front tires

only inches from the edge of the canyon wall. He gripped the wheel, afraid to move, afraid to breathe.

He hung on, fingers cramping, as he tried to catch his breath. He was shaking too hard to do anything else right now. His chest ached from the pounding of his heart and his pulse buzzed like a swarm of wasps in his ears. He felt physically ill, nauseated and dizzy, and blood kept running down into his eye. He closed his eyes, afraid he was going to be sick.

Too close. That had been way too close. But he'd wanted her so badly. Just the thought that she might get away—

Without looking at the gorge, he carefully eased the Suburban into reverse. He was scared to take his foot off the brake. But he had no choice. He jerked his foot from the brake to the gas. Too hard. The Suburban leapt backward. He slammed on the brakes again, snapping his neck painfully. Damn Angie. This was all her fault.

The engine died. He sat in the quiet darkness, wiped blood from his eye, then slowly cut the lights, popped open his door and got out.

The last thing he wanted to do was go near the edge of the canyon. He had a deathly fear of heights and became violently ill when more than a few feet above the ground. But he had to make sure she was dead.

His shoulder ached where she'd hit him and he was still bleeding from the wound on his forehead, both spurring his anger. He wanted to hurt her. This didn't feel good enough. Cautiously he stepped to the edge of the gorge and, bracing himself, peered down.

In the starlight, he could see the battered Jeep in

the river far below, water rushing over the top of it, through it.

The vertigo hit him hard and he stumbled back, queasy and light-headed. He was disappointed the car hadn't exploded. That would have made him feel better. He told himself that the fall alone had to have been terrifying, let alone the landing, and assured himself she had suffered all the way to the bottom for making this so difficult for him.

A cold breeze came up the sheer canyon wall, chilling him with a thought. What if she wasn't dead?

Impossible. No one could survive a fall like that, could they? Swearing, he edged to the rim of the gorge, forced to take another look.

All he could see was the Jeep. No mangled, dead body that he could make out from here with only stars for light. But he wasn't going down there. He couldn't even if he'd wanted to, which he didn't.

He stumbled back on legs as weak as water. No, he would let the local authorities find her body in the morning. Once he'd gotten rid of the Suburban and made sure he'd covered his tracks.

This wasn't the way he'd planned it. She'd forced him to improvise. Damn her to hell. He'd have to come up with an explanation for his injuries. She had made this so much harder than it should have been. Not that he'd ever killed anyone before.

He wobbled back to the Suburban, trying to reassure himself. He would have her fortune soon. In the meantime he had the stocks and bonds he'd talked Angie into putting in his name before the wedding.

But even better than that was knowing how devastated Jack Donovan would be when he heard about Angie's unfortunate accident. Both thoughts cheered him. *I win, Jack.*

LATE THE NEXT MORNING Patrick forced himself to take a quick look down into the canyon. Far below him, he caught a glimpse of the search-and-rescue team scouring the banks of the river downstream for Angie's body, then lurched back to a safe spot to wait.

He was cold and tired, miserable with rage and sick with the damn vertigo. He'd been up all night, forced to cover his tracks. Then, early this morning, he'd driven down to Missoula to report his wife's horrible accident. Since then, he'd had to hang around for hours above this damn canyon, waiting for them to bring up her body.

As the backwoods sheriff approached, Patrick could tell by the look on his face that the news would not be good.

"Well?" Patrick demanded.

Sheriff Jeff Truebow rubbed his stubbled jaw and looked down into the canyon for a moment before speaking. "I'm sorry, Mr. Ryerson, but we haven't been able to find your wife's body yet."

"How is that possible? I mean, where is it?"

"Well, she must not have been wearing her seat belt. I'd imagine her body washed out of the car, and we'll find it downriver."

"How long will *that* take?"

"Oftentimes a body will get hung up in a tree limb or wedged against a rock and won't float up until it starts to…decay. Sorry," the sheriff added quickly, obviously having seen Patrick turn three shades of green.

"What are you saying? That her body might be

trapped down there for days?'' Without a body, he couldn't get to Angie's money for seven years!

"Hard to say how long," the sheriff informed him. "The water's pretty cold this time of year."

Patrick couldn't believe this. "I can't wait...here."

"No, I guess it's pretty painful," Sheriff Truebow agreed. "On your honeymoon, huh? I'm real sorry. I know how hard this must be on you."

The man had no idea.

"You say she was a sleepwalker?" Truebow asked.

Patrick nodded. "That's what's so horrible about this. She's done this sort of thing before—just got up in the middle of the night and wandered outside. The other times I stopped her before she could leave in the car." He buried his face in his hands. "The worst part is, I took the keys out of the rental car, but I didn't think to check that old Jeep the owner of the cabin had left up there."

"Sleepwalking," the sheriff said with a shake of his head. "I had a cousin who walked out a two-story bedroom window one time and landed in the lilac bushes. Just skinned him up good. Crazy, huh?"

Patrick nodded. The sleepwalking story might sound crazy, but it was the best he could do on short notice.

"You look like you landed in some lilacs yourself," the sheriff commented. "That was a fool thing you did, trying to go down there."

"I know, but when I realized she was missing and the Jeep was gone and then I saw it down in the canyon—" He'd explained his cuts and bruises by telling the sheriff that he'd tried to climb down into the canyon and had fallen. He could just kill Angie all over again for making this so difficult.

He turned away from the sheriff. It was damn hard playing the grief-stricken husband under the circumstances. He had thought it would all be over by now. That Angie would be at a local funeral home. He'd planned to have her body cremated. He would dump her ashes on his way out of town.

"Why don't I give you my cell phone number," he said now, thinking there was no way he was hanging out here any longer.

The sheriff nodded and took down the number in the little notebook where he'd written Patrick's story about poor Angie's accident.

"I'll go into Missoula and find a place to stay," he said. Missoula wasn't large; by Houston standards it was a hick town.

He'd already been to Missoula several times. Last night he'd been forced to drive down there to get rid of the banged-up Suburban and pick up another car. He'd paid cash for the Suburban since it, and not the Jeep, was supposed to have ended up in the bottom of the canyon.

He would have liked to go even farther than Missoula, but he had to at least look like he gave a damn about Angie, and her body had to float up soon. He was running out of money fast. The wedding had cost him a bundle, what with the private jet to Montana and buying cars and jewelry and champagne the bitch then wouldn't drink.

Damn Angie. He hadn't planned on letting her get away with that diamond pendant, either. That had just been for show, just like the wedding. He'd had cheap duplicates made of both the pendant and her diamond wedding ring and had planned to replace the good stuff.

"I'll call you on our progress," Sheriff Truebow assured him.

Patrick nodded and braved one last look at the mangled Jeep in the water below. The search-and-rescue workers had disappeared around a bend in the river. Where the hell was Angie? He felt all the color leave his face and he stumbled back and threw up in the grass.

The sheriff handed him a clean white handkerchief and made sympathetic noises, no doubt thinking it was grief that forced Patrick to sit down on a rock until the nausea passed.

JACK HAD BEEN MAKING a pot of coffee—out of habit more than desire—when the phone rang. He felt like a zombie, walking around the penthouse, lost. Feeling useless. If he didn't do something soon—

"Turn on the local television news station," Montague Cooke said without preamble.

Jack hit the remote control on his wide-screen TV, afraid of what he was about to see. Patrick's face appeared in some old footage outside the courthouse taken after Jack's arrest.

Fortunately, the news station didn't rerun Patrick's speech saying how shocked he was that his friend had cheated poor people in their old neighborhood. Jack didn't need to hear that speech again.

The screen jumped from Patrick to live footage of a newscaster standing at the edge of a river canyon with pine-forested mountains in the background. Jack turned up the sound.

"...Jeep Wagoneer went off the road at this point

and plummeted into the gorge.'' The camera swung from the newsman down the canyon wall to what appeared to be a red Jeep in the river at the bottom. ''The body of the driver hasn't been found yet. Search-and-rescue workers are looking downstream, believing the body was washed from the vehicle.''

Jack stepped closer to the television screen, his heart in his throat.

''Authorities believe the twenty-eight-year-old newlywed was going too fast and either didn't have time to brake before her vehicle went into the gorge or might have been asleep at the wheel. The two were on their honeymoon. I'm Sally Chambers, live, here in Big Pine, Montana, outside Missoula.''

''Jack? Jack?''

He lifted the phone to his ear again.

''Oh God—'' Jack said, his voice breaking. ''Angie was in that car?'' He slumped onto one of the stools at his breakfast bar and lowered his head into one hand, still gripping the cordless phone with the other.

Angie dead.

''Jack, listen to me. I don't like the feel of this,'' Montie said. ''Are you listening to me? I think Patrick staged this.''

''What?''

''Jack, I ran a check on this Angelina Grant. She doesn't exist. You understand what I'm telling you?''

He raised his head slowly. He didn't understand any of this. ''What do you mean she doesn't exist?''

''Obviously Angelina Grant isn't her real name. I'm sending someone over to try to get some latents from your apartment.''

"You're going to try to get her fingerprints?" Jack couldn't believe Montie was serious.

"We need to know who she is, Jack. I need to prove that Patrick fleeced and framed you, and my money's on this woman as his accomplice."

"You're wrong," Jack said wearily. What did it matter now, anyway? Angie was dead. How could Montie think Patrick would stage her murder? For what possible purpose?

"Just open the door when my man shows up, and stay out of the way. You hear me?"

Stay out of the way? Jack was damn tired of staying out of the way, standing back, waiting, letting the legal system try to save him. He had to do something.

He walked down the hall to his office and, still cradling the cordless phone against his shoulder, pulled out his atlas.

Angie had lied about her name? Why?

"Jack?"

He remembered their last night together. There was something she had been anxious to tell him. Patrick had interrupted them. And then all hell had broken loose with the arson and discovery of kickbacks and inferior materials in the house.

Had she been going to confess that she'd lied about who she was?

Or was he just kidding himself? He'd been so sure that she was falling in love with him—just as he was her. Could he be wrong about that, too?

Look how wrong he'd been about Patrick. And Patrick had been jealous of Jack's relationship with Angie from the start.

"Jack? Are you still there?"

"What did Patrick say on camera?" he asked Montie as he opened the atlas. "All I saw was old stuff about me and the investigation."

"He wasn't interviewed on camera. They said he was too distraught and had to leave the scene."

"The son of a bitch," Jack said. He hadn't stayed at the scene while they looked for Angie's body?

"Just calm down. I've got my best investigator on this. You sit tight. We'll find out what happened."

Jack flipped through the atlas to Montana. He found Missoula on the map but it took him a while to find Big Pine. It indicated there were no services there, just a wide spot on Fish Creek in the Lolo National Forest. The closest larger city was Missoula. No way would Patrick have thought that a cabin in the woods was the perfect place for a honeymoon. Especially with a gorge nearby, given Patrick's fear of heights. Everything felt wrong about this.

"I've got to go."

"Jack, don't do anything stupid like run off to Montana. You won't find Patrick there, anyway."

"I'll find him."

"Jack, Patrick won't be there."

Still cradling the phone against his ear, he opened his safe and took out all the cash he had on hand. "What do you mean, he won't be there?"

"I told you I'd put my best investigator on this. An hour ago, Patrick bought a ticket to Seattle with Angelina Grant's credit card. His flight leaves Missoula in two hours."

Jack frowned. "He's not waiting for a body to be found?"

"No. And he's using her credit card. You see what I mean? She could be alive and they're meeting up later. If I'm right about this woman, she could be running from something other than this mess with you.''

"Did Patrick use the credit card to make a room reservation in Seattle?"

Montie groaned.

"Where?"

"What the hell do you think you can accomplish by chasing after him, Jack?"

"Don't make me have to check every motel in Seattle."

Montie sighed. "It's down by Pike's Market, the Seafarer. You're just going to end up in jail, and this time I won't be able to get you out."

"I'll keep that in mind."

"I'm serious, Jack. Have you given any thought to what you're going to do when you find him?"

"Kill him with my bare hands."

"Wait until we get the prints on the woman. My guy should be there any minute. You don't want to go off half-cocked because I'm putting my money on the two of them being in this together."

No way, Jack told himself. Not the Angie he'd fallen in love with. "I'll wait for the investigator, then I'll call you from Seattle to see what you've found out." He hung up.

Once Jack had made up his mind to jump bail and go after Patrick, it didn't take him long to get ready. He changed out of his suit into jeans and a cotton shirt, and packed, not sure how long he'd be gone. Or even if he'd be back. The thought surprised him more than he wanted to admit. It wasn't like him. He'd always played by the rules. Faced the music.

But he was going after Patrick and the truth. And he had a bad feeling he wasn't going to like what he found out. If Angie was really dead…well then, he had nothing to lose. He just hated that he hadn't gone after her sooner. Now it was too late…but not for Patrick.

Jack had his bag by the door and a taxi called when the desk phoned up to announce he had a visitor. Jack buzzed up the investigator Montie had sent, a nondescript man by the name of Harvey Ford.

"Where would be a good place to find one of her latents?" Ford asked, getting right to business.

Jack pointed toward the breakfast bar. "I haven't had a chance to pick up." What with being thrown in jail and his maid quitting in disgust because of the charges against him, Jack hadn't been back to his apartment except to shower and change clothes so he could try to stop a wedding.

"You should be able to get a print off that wineglass," he said. Her glass was right where she'd left it when they were interrupted by Patrick's arrival to accuse Jack.

God, Jack wished he could turn back the clock, let Angie tell him whatever it was she seemed so anxious to talk about that night. If only he'd told her that he loved her—before everything else happened.

He stood back while Ford dusted the wineglass.

"There's at least one good one. We've got her."

Whatever her reasons for lying about her name, it wouldn't change how he felt about her.

"What are the chances her prints will even be on file?" Jack said, more to himself than to the investigator.

Ford smiled and shrugged sympathetically as he

carefully tucked the glass into an evidence bag and left without another word.

"I guess we'll find out soon enough," Jack said under his breath.

Chapter Five

Patrick was on his way to the Missoula airport when his cell phone rang, making him jump. He hurriedly pulled it from his jacket, hoping desperately for good news.

"How ya doin'?" the sheriff said.

Patrick really didn't have time for pleasantries. "You found her body?" Silence. He heard the sheriff chewing on something. A toothpick? Gum? He had to get out of this backwoods state or he'd go stark-raving mad.

"I'm afraid not," Truebow said finally. "But we did find a shoe."

A shoe? That was good, right?

"It's brown with white stitching. Does that sound like what she was wearing the last time you saw her?"

As if he had noticed what shoes she was wearing when she hit him with the champagne bottle. "I really wouldn't know, Sheriff. I was asleep when she left, remember?" *Idiot.*

"Yes, sorry. I thought you might have recognized it from the description. How about size? These are seven and a half. That sound about right?"

"Yes," he said, not having the foggiest idea what size shoes Angie had worn, nor caring. The shoe had to be hers. He'd talked a maid into letting him into her room at the hotel in Houston and taken some of her shoes, randomly grabbing a few pairs from the back of her closet, ones he thought she wouldn't miss.

He'd put them in the cabin when he'd rented it on his first visit to Montana, long before Angie had any idea she would be coming here. At the time, he hadn't even been sure himself that he could pull this off.

He'd never planned on Angie wearing any of the shoes. But if one of her shoes had been found, that was good news, wasn't it?

Now, if they would just find her body. "All you found was the shoe? That's the only reason you called?"

"No, actually, a thunderstorm blew in up in the mountains this afternoon, muddying up the river. We're suspending the search until the water clears up."

Patrick almost wrecked the rental car as he fought to contain his rage. "How long will that take?"

"Depends on whether or not there is more rain. The thing is, Mr. Ryerson, bodies can travel a long way in that kind of current and get hung up on all kinds of things—old car bodies, tree roots, rocks. Also, we don't know what time for sure she went into the water. She could have left the cabin any time after midnight, you said?"

"That's right."

"So we have no way of knowing how far the body washed downstream, but don't worry, eventually it will come up. They always do. But until then…"

Patrick couldn't believe what he was hearing. "Are

you telling me you're calling off the search indefinitely?''

"To be honest with you, Mr. Ryerson, there is just too much river and not enough volunteers. The search-and-rescue team can only do so much. We've got a couple of lost bird hunters we're looking for now. In cases of drownings, the bodies are usually found by fishermen. We had a case just last month where—''

Patrick quit listening. He turned into the airport parking lot and concentrated on the future. Seattle. It would be nice there this time of year. It wasn't the Riviera, but at least it was far from here.

Angie would turn up. Eventually. The bitch.

"Look, Sheriff,'' he said, interrupting the man's long-winded story. "You have my cell phone number. I can't stay here. There are just too many memories. I need to work. It's the only thing that will take my mind off…this horror.''

The sheriff sounded a little surprised but asked, "So I can reach you in Houston?''

God, no, not Houston. He was never going back there. "Actually, Angie and I were relocating after the honeymoon. We hadn't really decided where.'' He pretended to break down for a few moments. "I'm sorry, but you understand why I can't stay in Montana? I'll be in Seattle for a few days.'' He repeated his cell phone number. "You'll call me the minute you find her?''

"Of course.''

He clicked off and, grabbing his bags, walked toward the airport terminal.

Four hours later, Patrick was sitting under an umbrella drinking a scotch and water at a picturesque

little sidewalk bistro in Pioneer Square and going
through Angie's address book. He needed to talk to
her attorney, her stockbroker and her accountant. He
needed to cash in those stocks and bonds and start
that whole probate thing so he could get his hands on
the rest of her money.

At least he'd been smart enough to take the address
book from Angie's purse before throwing the bag into
the canyon this morning on his way to town to call
the sheriff.

Using the cell phone, he now dialed her lawyer.
The phone rang and rang, then an operator came on
to say the number had been disconnected.

He called information and double-checked the listing. Directory assistance didn't show anything for a
Bob Carpenter. That was odd. Nor was there a listing
for Brainard, Benjamin, Carpenter and Harris in New
York.

Frowning, he leafed through her book until he
found the number for her financial advisor, a man
named Ralph Tinsley. As with the first number, the
line rang several times—only this time an operator
came on to tell him the number had been changed
and no forwarding number was listed.

What the hell? He'd heard Angie talking to Tinsley
just a few weeks ago. In fact, that's when he'd come
up with this plan. He had been damn tired of working
for Jack, that was for sure. Then he'd heard Angie on
the phone and in a flash a plan had leapt to mind to
pay back Jack and get Angie and all her money.

Patrick looked at the name in the address book
again. Ralph Tinsley. He was sure that was the name
he'd overheard Angie use. Patrick wouldn't make a
mistake about something that important.

Sweat broke out on his forehead and he could feel it soak through this shirt under his jacket. He took off the jacket and tried to calm himself.

Angie hadn't had any family—just lawyers and accountants and financial advisors, people who handled all her money. Maybe she'd made a change and had just forgotten to tell him about it. He'd kept her doped up, after all.

In the address book, he found more numbers and names. People with last names that sounded like money, old family friends she'd talked about, friends from college, several close friends he was afraid she'd want to invite to the wedding, friends that might try to talk her out of marrying him.

He'd convinced her not to contact any of them, saying it was short notice and promising to throw her a big party when they returned from their honeymoon so he could meet them all. She'd gone along with it much more easily than he'd anticipated. A little short on friends himself, he'd had to hire guests to fill the church.

He started dialing the numbers of her old friends listed in the book. He was sweating profusely now, his heart hammering in his chest, making it hard to breathe.

He tried all of the numbers. In every case, the line had been disconnected or was wrong in some other way. Often the person who answered the phone swore he or she had never heard of an Angelina Grant.

He picked up his drink and downed it, the alcohol like a fire running through him. Maybe this was an old address book.

But he knew better. This was the one she had used when she'd made the calls to her attorney and financial advisor to inform them of her upcoming nuptials. Patrick had reminded her to make the calls—and had overheard her end of the conversation as she told them to make the necessary arrangements.

He remembered being amazed that they hadn't advised her to get a prenuptial agreement. Funny, too, that Angie hadn't ever mentioned one, either.

He looked up, motioning with his glass for the waiter to bring him another. "Make it a double."

He didn't like the feeling he was getting. He kept remembering her saying in the cabin what a mistake he was making in killing her.

JACK HAD CAUGHT the first flight out of Houston to Seattle, a nonstop that put him in the city before Patrick. He'd found the Seafarer, had confirmed Patrick was registered and had waited in a bar across the street.

He hadn't had to wait long. Patrick had checked in, then walked down to Pioneer Square where he'd ordered a drink and settled in at one of the tables on the sidewalk. He wore an expression of satisfied arrogance that Jack couldn't wait to wipe off the man's face.

Either he didn't give a damn about Angie and her death, or Montie was right—Angie's alleged death was some kind of scam and she was alive and going to meet up with Patrick later.

Jack didn't want to believe Angie was dead. But he also couldn't stand the thought that Montie might be right about the two of them working together. Not Angie. Angie had lied about her name, though, he reminded himself as he watched Patrick from a coffee shop across the street. Why was that? The coffee shop was almost empty, most customers, at this time of the afternoon, getting coffee to go. No one paid Jack any mind.

Now that he was in Seattle and had found Patrick, he just wanted the truth. About Patrick. About Angie. What Jack wanted was a confession. He wanted his name cleared. And it was all he could do not to go over to Patrick's table and try to beat a confession out of him.

But good sense prevailed. Accosting Patrick in a public sidewalk café in front of a dozen people would only get Jack thrown back in jail with little chance of bail. No, he had to bide his time. Wait for an opportunity to get Patrick alone.

From the coffee shop, Jack watched his former best friend order another drink. Patrick was visibly upset. Jack was pretty sure that Patrick had Angela's little red address book and was going through it, trying numbers. Odd.

Patrick was trying another number and seemingly becoming more agitated with each attempt. Who was he trying to reach? Angie?

Jack's cell phone rang. "Hello?" Jack said into the phone, almost afraid it would be Patrick calling.

"Her name is Angelina all right," Montie said on the other end of the line. He sounded excited. "Angelina LaGrand."

"Who?"

"She's the daughter of Addison LaGrand, granddaughter of Isabella LaGrand. Do you realize what this means?"

"Am I supposed to know those names?" Jack asked, obviously not realizing what it meant, but hoping it meant Angie had a good reason to change LaGrand to Grant.

"Jack, the LaGrands are a notorious family of thieves, con artists, swindlers. Very high-class, mind you. They steal from the very rich and usually get away with it. We're talking confidence men, Jack. In Angie's case, confidence woman."

Jack couldn't breathe. "There must be some mistake."

Montie didn't seem to hear him. "This is exactly what we need to nail Patrick. He was working with a known confidence woman. This is the break we needed."

Jack stared across the street at Patrick. He was thumbing through Angie's address book again, frowning. "It's just not possible." But even as Jack said the words, he knew it was. Angelina Grant was Angelina LaGrand, a swindler and crook. Could it get any worse?

"I'm sending the dossier I've put together on Angelina and her family by express messenger. You'll get it tonight. Read it. If you still think you met Angelina LaGrand by accident, then you need your head examined."

Jack felt numb. "Why me? You said they go after the very rich. I'm not that rich."

"Obviously you're rich enough," Montie said. "The way this family works is they find a mark, study his habits, and then one or more of them work their way into the mark's confidence. When did you meet her?"

"May."

"So it was right after that article came out about

you in *Fortune* magazine.'' Montie swore. ''Still think she and Patrick weren't in this together?''

Fortune magazine had called him a ''financial genius'' because he'd taken what his father had left him and quadrupled it into a small fortune.

He was a genius, all right. Except when it came to women—then Jack Donovan was the biggest fool on earth. He shouldn't be surprised that the first woman he'd really been interested in was a con artist and had wanted nothing from him but his money. So why couldn't he believe that she was in on this with Patrick?

''If this woman is such a crook, why isn't she in jail already?'' he asked Montie.

''Confidence men rarely see jail. They choose their marks carefully, reel them in, sucker them and often involve them in schemes that might not be exactly aboveboard. So the marks are either guilty of something or too embarrassed to go to the cops and admit that they'd been hoodwinked.''

Jack knew the feeling. He'd been fleeced and framed along with being publicly humiliated and left holding the bag—and all he was guilty of was stupidity.

''Read the dossier when it arrives. I don't want you to have any illusions about this woman. Or what we're dealing with,'' Montie said, and asked where he was staying.

Jack told him the name of his hotel—one right across from Patrick's.

''I'd bet you Angelina LaGrand is alive and will try to contact you,'' Montie said. ''If a con works, oftentimes a confidence man will double back and try to play the mark again, for even bigger stakes.''

"How could she possibly pull that off?" Jack asked, resenting the hell out of being anyone's mark, especially hers. He might have been fooled once, but twice?

"She could pretend she wasn't in with Patrick, might even come to you for help, tell you she was in danger. This woman is a LaGrand and she's attractive. I would imagine she could convince a man of damn near anything."

Oh yeah, Jack thought. He rubbed his hands over his face. Angie had been incredibly convincing.

"Don't feel too bad. The LaGrands are the best there is," Montie was saying. "You wouldn't believe the well-known people they've swindled. And you're certainly not the first man to fall for a pretty face and a good line. You had no reason not to believe she was as wealthy as she pretended."

The irony was, he'd fallen for her in spite of her fortune. What a laugh.

And to think he'd been considering marriage and a family with her. He'd even been thinking Christmas would be a great time to give her a ring. Maybe sooner, say, Thanksgiving. What a fool he'd been.

"I'm wondering if Patrick knew Angelina before they both showed up in Houston," Montie was saying. "Patrick could have hired her to distract you while he stole you blind and framed you."

Well, if that had been the plan, it had worked like a charm.

"My money's on this accident being a scam," Montie said, still sounding excited. "I'll bet she meets up with Patrick in Seattle. They are so confident we aren't onto them. Patrick made one big mistake: hooking up with that woman. I'm going to send Ford out—"

"No," Jack interrupted. "Let me handle this."

"Do I have to remind you, you weren't even supposed to leave the state? And anyway, it's a bad idea for you to be the one who catches them together, given your…feelings about this woman."

"If you're right and Angie is alive, I'll find her," Jack said. "I'm watching Patrick as we speak. He's been trying to reach someone on his cell phone and becoming more irritated by the minute."

"Be careful, Jack. And don't do anything stupid."

"No problem," Jack said, and clicked off, wondering how he could be more stupid than he'd already been.

He caught movement out of the corner of his eye. Patrick suddenly stumbled to his feet, overturning the table in front of him and sending everything crashing to the brick sidewalk. He looked stricken, his shocked gaze riveted down the block from him.

Jack looked down the street in the direction Patrick was staring. A taxi turned the corner and started down the block toward him—and Patrick.

Jack's shock turned quickly to anger. Angie sat in the back seat, staring straight ahead as if she didn't see Patrick, but Jack saw the satisfied smile on her lips as the taxi cruised by.

She didn't notice Jack. Nor did she see him leave the coffee shop, hail a taxi and follow.

Chapter Six

Patrick stood staring after the taxi as waiters and guests crowded around him.

"Sir, are you all right?"

He barely heard them picking up the table and the broken glass from the bricks. His ears buzzed and he felt light-headed, as if he might pitch headlong into the bricks himself.

Angie is alive! That's why the search-and-rescue team hadn't found her body. Because she'd gotten away.

Impossible. She couldn't have survived the crash.

Unless she'd gotten out of the car before it dropped into the gorge. He swayed, dizzy, knees weak.

"Here, please sit down. Can I get you something? Another drink? A glass of water?"

He braced himself, palms down on the table that the waiter had righted for him. He felt sick as he watched the taxi disappear into the traffic. He could feel people staring, whispering. He didn't give a damn.

"Sir, are you all right?"

Hell no, he wasn't all right.

"A drink. A double scotch," he managed to say to

the annoying waiter. The sidewalk café came back into focus. He sat down, told himself to calm down. He was making a scene.

That couldn't have been Angie. But it was her double, her doppelganger, then. Just a bizarre coincidence. Angie was dead. The sheriff had found her shoe. Didn't that prove she was dead?

A shoe was not a body. But even if she had jumped from the Jeep before it went into the river, how could she have made it down the mountain in the dark last night? She didn't have any idea where she was. And she was wearing only one shoe.

Unless the shoe hadn't been hers—had been left by someone in the old Jeep. He hadn't thought of that.

She could have jumped free of the Jeep, hidden in the trees, walked on the road. Except, there was no moon. But the stars were bright last night. And she was just enough of a bitch to walk out with only one shoe. He had a sudden image of her limping into Missoula barefoot.

He fought to remember every detail, looking for any time she could have escaped the Jeep before it went over the cliff into the canyon.

When she'd swerved! The driver's door had been on the opposite side, out of view. She could have jumped out. Or rolled out. And he wouldn't have seen her.

But the dome light hadn't come on! He was sure of that. And it would have if she had opened the Jeep's door. So how the hell—

"Your drink, sir."

Patrick took it, his hands trembling.

"You're sure you're all right?"

He waved off the waiter and took a long drink of the scotch. It burned all the way down.

Wait a minute. If she'd survived, wouldn't she have gone straight to the cops? Of course she would have. A woman like her. If Angie was alive, he'd be in jail right now.

The thought calmed him a little. He took another drink. Angie was dead. The woman in the taxi was just someone who looked like her. If he'd seen the woman up close, had gotten more than a brief glimpse, he would know she looked nothing like Angie. He'd only imagined the resemblance—and all because Angie's body hadn't floated up yet.

"DON'T LOSE THAT CAB," Jack ordered as he reached over the seat to stuff a hundred dollar bill into the cabbie's shirt pocket.

"You got it." The driver sped up, swerving as the cab ahead of them slipped into the right-hand lane.

Traffic was bumper-to-bumper this time of the day, with everyone getting off work. His cab followed the other one, several car lengths back, as it worked its way through the downtown area and onto Interstate 5 north, the Space Needle a shining spire in the evening light. The traffic was dense and fast.

It had been Angie in that cab, hadn't it? All that talk of Angie being alive— Jack wondered now if he'd just imagined seeing her. But Patrick had obviously thought it was Angie. The expression on his face had been one of shock. He had looked as if he'd seen a ghost.

Ahead, Jack could make out the woman's dark head in the back of the taxi. She appeared to be on a cell phone—Jack had a terrible thought. What if this too had been staged? What if Patrick had spotted him in the restaurant across the street? What if Patrick's being surprised to see Angie was just an act—one choreographed just for Jack?

Suddenly the cab ahead of them increased its speed, the driver zipping in and out of the traffic.

"He's spotted us," Jack said. Or more likely, given her past, Angie had spotted the tail. "Stay with him and there's another hundred in it for you."

His driver hit the gas, changing lanes, weaving in and out of the afternoon rush-hour traffic.

They were going close to eighty when the taxi they were tailing suddenly cut across three lanes and hit the Aurora exit, causing brake lights to flash across all four lanes.

For a moment Jack's taxi was trapped in the slowed traffic, then the driver started honking and motioning to the drivers to his right as he pulled in front of them.

"Seattle people are so polite," the driver said, as the cars allowed him to cross until he'd reached the edge of the highway—but there was no way he could get back to the exit.

Jack could see the other taxi stopped at a light below the interstate. He tossed the driver the extra hundred and leapt out, sprinting down the grassy incline straight for the cab, praying the light wouldn't change before he could reach her.

She was turned in her seat, staring back up the ramp. No doubt looking for his yellow cab. She didn't see him until he jerked open her door and slid into the seat next to her. He'd caught her. And if she thought he was going to fall for her lies again, Angelina LaGrand was sadly mistaken.

PATRICK TOOK A GULP of his drink, still shaking inside as he picked up his cell phone and started to dial Sheriff Truebow's number. Maybe they'd found her other shoe, at least. Maybe the sheriff had some good news for him. He could use it right now.

The number wasn't ringing. He shook the phone. Something inside rattled. Damn. It must have broken in the fall from the table.

Angrily, he threw it down, causing the other patrons to eye him again. *Go to hell.* He picked up Angie's address book. It was wet and smelled of scotch. He tucked it into his pocket anyway, telling himself there had to be a good explanation for the wrong numbers in the book. She probably had a new address book with more current numbers—just like the new checking account.

His pulse leapt. What was wrong with him? He had completely forgotten about their new joint checking account. Just before the wedding, he'd gone to the bank with her, insisted she close out her checking account and move her balance into the joint account he'd set up for them.

She'd had over eight thousand in her account. While most of her money was in stocks and bonds, money market accounts and a huge trust fund, there should still be a nice chunk in their joint account to tide him over. He felt weak with relief.

But it did worry him a little that he'd forgotten about the joint checking account. He'd been so focused on the *real* money. The other had been chicken feed in comparison.

In hindsight, he thought again, it did seem odd that she hadn't even mentioned a prenuptial agreement.

But then again, she'd been drugged out of her mind and grieving over her disillusionment with Jack.

Just the thought of Jack fired his anger at Angie all over again. Like Jack, the woman deserved everything that had happened to her.

As he drained his drink, he spotted a taxi coming up the street. He froze. It inched toward him in the heavy traffic. He could feel his heart laboring in his chest. The taxi came to a stop in the traffic right in front of the café.

For just an instant, he thought it was her again. But the woman turned her face toward him. Not Angie. Not even a look-alike. He released the breath he'd been holding and laughed, causing the now uneasy patrons to steal glances at him. He couldn't quit smiling he was so relieved.

Angie was dead. Everything was going to be all right. He got up and headed for his hotel. He'd call the automated number at the bank from his hotel room and have the money in the joint account wired first thing in the morning to a bank here in Seattle.

But first, he'd touch base with Sheriff Truebow. He needed to hear that Angie's body had been found.

"WHAT THE—" The cabdriver let out an oath as Jack jumped into the back seat. The light changed.

Jack looked over at Angie, momentarily stunned by the sight of her, alive, sitting next to him. "Just drive," he ordered the cabbie. "The lady and I have some unfinished business. Although 'lady' might be stretching it."

"You want me to call the cops?" the driver asked, swiveling around to look at Angie. Cars behind them started honking.

"No, that's not necessary," she said. "I can handle this." Her voice had an edge to it that could have cut glass.

"Aren't you the cool one, Angie," Jack said, really looking at her as the taxi began to move along in the traffic.

She smiled at him icily, but her brown eyes flashed with anger. "I'm *not* Angie."

"Right."

She wore her long dark hair up, accentuating her lovely features, her makeup perfect—just like the large diamond stud earrings sparkling at each ear. She was dressed in a dark skirt and matching jacket with a pale silver blouse—all expensive, all fitting her body wonderfully. He would have known that face and body anywhere.

But the dead giveaway was the amulet on the chain around her neck, her good luck charm. Well, her luck was about to change for the worse.

He felt that old ache as he looked at her, but realized there was something different. Probably the fact that she was no longer acting the part she'd played with him. She seemed slicker, more chic and sophisticated, more ruthless. Obviously, things she'd hidden from him in Houston.

"You've been busy, Angie. Conning me. Helping Patrick destroy my business and get me arrested. Marrying him. Faking your own death. And now turning up in Seattle. I can't wait to hear what game you're playing now."

She glared at him. "Who are you?"

He laughed. "Jack Donovan, the man you and Patrick framed. Oh, let me guess. Amnesia? Is that the new game?"

She appeared to be surprised. "Jack?"

"Ah, you *do* remember," he said sarcastically. He felt torn between being glad she was alive, and furious that she'd tricked him into falling in love with her—and all just for his money. It didn't help that she was pretending she'd never laid eyes on him before.

She licked her lips and leveled her dark gaze at him. "I couldn't possibly *remember,* because we've never met."

"So the Texas accent is real?" he said with a shake of his head. "I figured that would be a lie, too."

"I was born in Dallas," she said haughtily.

He nodded, wondering if that were true. Not that he would believe anything she ever told him again.

"Angie, I know. I know all about you, all about your family. I know *everything,* Ms. LaGrand."

"Obviously not or you would know that I'm not Angie. I'm her sister, Maria. Her identical *twin* sister, Maria LaGrand."

"Angie doesn't have an identical twin."

She raised a brow, then opened her purse and pulled out her wallet. From a hidden compartment, she withdrew a photograph and handed it to him. The paper appeared to be old, the edges worn smooth and rounded, the surface cracked and discolored.

He stared down at two smiling little dark-haired girls with Angie's face. Identical right down to their pretty yellow dresses. Except, the one on the right had her leg in a cast.

He must not have looked convinced because she sighed and lifted her skirt to reveal a black garter belt above her silk stockings—and a three-inch scar on the inside of her thigh in the shape of a half moon. "I fell out of a tree and broke my leg when I was five."

She pulled her skirt back down and took back the photo to return it to her wallet. "So I guess you don't know everything about me. Or my family."

"That photo may not be any more authentic than you are. And as for the scar, you might recall that I wouldn't have any knowledge as to whether you have a scar on your inner thigh since you and I have never been that intimate."

She raised a brow as if surprised.

His throat tightened. "What? You normally sleep with your other marks?"

She sighed. "I'm surprised you and Angie never made love, considering how she felt about you."

"I'll just bet."

She met his gaze. "The last time I talked to her, she said she was falling for you and wasn't going through with her previous plans."

"Don't, okay? You helped Patrick frame me. I'm on my way to prison if I can't prove the two of you set me up."

"You're wrong. My sister would never have fallen in with a man like Patrick Ryerson."

"Excuse me? You *married* him."

"Patrick tricked my sister." Anger made her voice as hard and cold as ice. "He killed her."

He stared at the woman beside him, remembering the look on Patrick's face when he'd seen Angie get into the cab at the corner of the street by the hotel. Was it possible Angie really did have an identical twin and Patrick hadn't known about it?

Jack smiled. "You're good."

She nodded.

"You almost had me buying your act. Again," he said. "What's your game this time? You double-cross

Patrick? Or is he in on this and just pretending he didn't know you were still alive?"

"You don't get it, do you?" Anger flamed her cheeks. Her eyes snapped. "Patrick murdered my sister. You think it's a coincidence I just happened to be on that street corner, a coincidence that Patrick saw me?" She scoffed at that and narrowed her gaze as she shook her head.

He studied the woman as the cab slowed. She was so damn convincing. He was starting to think he could see dissimilarities between this woman and Angie, as if Angie really did have an identical twin.

He felt the anger return, like a balm against the pain, remembering how Angie had fooled him the first time. He wouldn't be fooled again.

"Enough lies," he snapped, grabbing her. "You're going with me back to Houston to clear—" His gaze locked with hers. He saw the truth at the same time he felt it. He let go of her as if he'd been burned.

Maria LaGrand smiled a slow, told-you-so smile.

"You really aren't Angie," he said as the cab pulled to the curb and stopped.

"What have I been trying to tell you?" she said, stone-cold serious again. "My sister is dead."

He was shaking his head, not wanting to believe it.

"I'm her twin. I know."

He felt the blow of that news stagger him again as if just hearing of her death for the first time.

The cab had stopped in front of an old brick hotel. He looked out at the building, then at the woman next to him.

"I'm sorry if my sister hurt you," she said.

"She did more than hurt me. She and Patrick framed me for a crime I didn't commit."

"So you say. But if you're really innocent of the crimes, it wasn't my sister who framed you."

"And I should take your word for that?" he asked, the anger back. "Don't even try to con me, all right? I've been conned by the best."

Her laugh sounded so much like Angie's it hurt. "See, you're wrong again. *I* am the best. Angelina was an amateur compared to me."

He hated to hear her say "was." Past tense. "They haven't found her body. Maybe…"

Maria met his gaze, her eyes shiny with tears. She shook her head. "No one could have survived that." She opened her door and swung her legs out.

He started to follow her, had gotten out of the car and gone around to her side, when he saw the gun. It was small, but deadly enough. She had it hidden from the cabdriver's view, pointed straight at Jack's heart.

"This is where we part company, Jack Donovan. Go back to Houston. Let me handle this. You're out of your league."

"Handle what?"

"Vengeance, of course."

"So Patrick doesn't know Angie had a twin?"

She smiled. "No, few people do. And what could be worse than Angie coming back from the grave to make her killer suffer?"

So that's why Maria had been in front of Patrick's hotel. She'd wanted him to think she was Angie. She hadn't planned on Jack seeing her, too.

"Sorry, but you're not the only one who wants Patrick Ryerson to suffer. Remember, he framed me with your sister's help—"

"Don't be a fool. My sister was in love with you."

"Sure she was. The point is, I'm going to prison unless I can prove I was set up."

"And you thought you could do it by following Patrick to Seattle?" That seemed to amuse her.

"Actually, I came here to kill him, but you distracted me."

She laughed. "You aren't the killer type."

"I might surprise you."

"Don't. If you really are innocent of the charges, then go home before anyone realizes you've jumped bail. Leave Patrick to me." She slammed her door as the cab quickly sped away.

He stared after her, still stunned by how much she looked like Angie. Stunned also by how much she knew about him and Angie. He figured Maria had been in on the con job Angie had done on him. He realized she could have been driving the car that supposedly had almost run Angie down that spring day by the park. He had thought he'd saved Angie's life that day. The joke was on him. He'd just fallen into her trap. What a chump.

He flagged down another taxi and headed back to the wharf. Maria LaGrand didn't really think she'd gotten rid of him that easily, did she? Not when he knew where she'd turn up next—wherever Patrick was.

Chapter Seven

Back at his room, Patrick still felt a little off balance. He couldn't believe he hadn't thought of the joint-checking account before this. Seeing that woman who'd looked so much like Angie had thrown him.

It just wasn't like him to forget money. Maybe killing Angie had rattled him more than he'd thought. Especially since it hadn't gone anything like he'd planned and it was his first time. And last, he hoped.

He called Sheriff Truebow's number. The sheriff wasn't in, so he left the number at the hotel where he could be reached. Then he dialed the automated bank number to wire funds to a bank down the block here in Seattle.

He knew there couldn't be enough in the account to live on for long, not the way he planned to live, but it would definitely make things easier for a while. And Angie's body was bound to turn up any day.

Punching in the appropriate numbers, he waited for the balance, doodling on the scratch pad by the phone, hoping to be surprised—he had no idea how much Angie got from her trust fund each month.

"What!" His pen froze over the pad. There had to

be a mistake. Fingers shaking, he hit the star key to have the transaction request repeated.

The automated voice said, *"Your balance of...one dollar...cannot be transferred as per your request."*

He hit the star key again and again until, in frustration, he slammed down the phone and threw it across the room. Of course there was a mistake. One dollar? He'd personally had *two thousand* in his account—let alone what Angie had contributed. And her trust fund check should have gone in there the day before yesterday. There should be thousands of dollars in that account.

He raked his hands through his hair, wanting to scream. Was it possible that Angie had cleaned it out *before* the wedding? That cheating, lying bitch! She must not have been as upset and doped up as he'd thought.

Too angry to sit, he prowled the room, and tripped over the phone cord. As he put the receiver back on the hook and returned the phone to the desk, he saw that the message light was flashing. He must have got a call either while he was on the phone—or while the phone was on the floor, off the hook.

Sheriff Truebow! It could be the call he'd been waiting for. Truebow must have called to say they'd found Angie's body.

Relief washed over him. All his troubles would be over. He could quit imagining that he'd just seen Angie riding in a taxi in downtown Seattle. Even if she'd cleaned out their joint accounts before the wedding, he'd still have the money from the stocks and bonds she'd signed over to him. He could get out of the country until her estate was finalized.

He was thinking about someplace tropical as he

retrieved the message, anticipating the sheriff's slow, western drawl.

"Hello."

His heart seized up in his chest at the sound of Angie's voice. He dropped onto the bed, his hand holding the phone jerking spasmodically.

"I can't wait to see you—" Angie's laugh "—soon."

WHEN JACK GOT BACK to his hotel, a large thick brown envelope was waiting for him. The LaGrand dossier.

He took it up to his room, unlocked the door and dropped the envelope on the bed. Without turning on a light, he went to the window and peered across the street at the Seafarer—and Patrick's room. The drapes were drawn, a light glowing behind them. Through a crack between the drapes, he saw movement every few moments as if Patrick was pacing.

Going to the small courtesy bar, Jack poured himself a stiff drink, then scooped up the file and carried it to a chair by the window and turned on the small light next to it.

He didn't want to read what was inside it. He didn't want to know that everything with Angie had been a lie. Everything Angie had ever said or done. All to get his money. Where exactly Patrick fit in, Jack wasn't sure. But he intended to find out.

Maria swore that Patrick had tricked Angie and killed her, but Jack knew better than to take anything Maria said at face value. He couldn't trust this woman from a known con artist family with Angie's face and body. Why hadn't Montie mentioned that Angie had a sister—let alone an identical twin?

He glanced down at the envelope, knowing he was going to have to read it. He had to know the truth. He had to know why. Why Angie had picked *him*. Had it been Patrick's doing? Or her own? He had to know if Patrick and Angie had been working together.

He opened the envelope and dumped the contents into his lap and began reading, all the time keeping an eye on Patrick's room.

When Jack finished, he shoved all the papers, newspaper clippings and photocopied articles from the Internet back into the envelope, made himself another drink and turned out the light to stare across at Patrick's hotel room window. The light was still on. Patrick still appeared to be pacing.

Jack didn't want to think about what he'd read. It was all there—the truth about Angie, the truth about her family. Except, there was no mention of identical twin sisters. He closed his eyes for a moment, then put down his unfinished drink.

That wasn't all that was missing from the dossier on the LaGrands. It didn't tell him why Angie picked him. Or if she'd been in on it with Patrick.

Jack saw now that there was only one way he would ever get those answers. He headed for the door. He had to see Maria LaGrand again.

PATRICK PROWLED HIS hotel room back at the Seafarer, more worried about money than about the Angie look-alike he'd seen in the cab.

Antsy, he went to the window and dragged back the drape. He still couldn't believe Angie had cleaned out their joint checking account. She'd been ripping him off. And all this time he'd thought she was putty in his hands.

He stared down at the street, surprised it was so late. When had it gotten dark? Pools of light glowed under the street lamps and in the windows of the shops and restaurants. A flurry of pedestrians still moved quickly along the sidewalks. He couldn't help looking for Angie. He knew he would continue to imagine seeing her until her body was found. Would imagine she was watching him right now from the shadowed darkness.

He shuddered, the feeling of being watched was so strong. His gaze raked the street even as his mind argued that Angie was in a watery grave back in Montana and not standing out there in the darkness watching his hotel room. He didn't see her, but that didn't mean she wasn't there.

Across the street, diners sat at candlelit tables in the ferny little courtyard along the sidewalk, sipping good wine, eating seafood or grade A prime beef, enjoying themselves while he— He was starting to close the drape when a familiar face caught his attention.

His heart leapt to his throat. Jack! He sat at a table off to one side in the shadows, his candle extinguished. Patrick could barely make out his features, and thought for a moment he'd just imagined seeing Jack, the same way he'd imagined seeing Angie.

But then Jack sat forward, watching the street, watching for someone, then looking up, looking right at Patrick's hotel room window!

Patrick jumped back from the window, pulse pounding. Jack was in Seattle! Looking for him! What was Jack doing here? He wasn't allowed to leave the state.

My God, he'd jumped bail. He'd come after him!

Panic short-circuited his brain, making his thoughts erratic and crazy. He stormed around, only the light by the desk providing any illumination in the slowly darkening room.

He knew he needed to calm down, but all he could think about was the message Angie had left on his phone, the wrong numbers in her address book, the money missing from their joint checking account, and now Jack in Seattle, Jack coming after him with blood in his eye. Patrick was sure of that.

A flash caught his attention. He turned slowly, already knowing what it was before he saw the small red message light on the phone at the desk.

No, not again. He stared at the phone as if it were a snake that could bite him. He'd only left the room for a moment, just long enough to check the hallway and see if anyone was in the elevator because he thought he'd heard someone outside his door.

Slowly, he picked up the receiver, put it to his ear and hit the message button, his chest aching as he waited to hear Angie's voice again, fearing that somehow she *was* alive and coming after him, as well.

Instead, he heard Sheriff Truebow's hick drawl on the recording. "Sorry, I don't have any news for you. The river's still running muddy. I'll call as soon as I have any word. Seems your cell phone isn't working?"

Patrick hung up and began to pace again. If that really had been Angie's voice earlier— It *had* been her voice. Who was he kidding? Angie was alive, and the sheriff and his search-and-rescue team wouldn't be finding any body in the river. Somehow, she'd managed to get away. Oh God. She and Jack were both after him now.

Unless— He stopped pacing, remembering a movie he'd seen where a cassette recording of a woman's voice had been cut and spliced together to trap the murderer into believing she was still alive.

Yes, that was possible. But who would have a recording of Angie's voice and go to the troub— "Jack." The word came out on a puff of air. Jack!

Patrick burst out laughing. Of course, Jack had to be behind this. The look-alike in the cab. The message. Jack had jumped bail, no doubt looking to get even. What better way than trying to make Patrick think Angie was still alive and seeking revenge for her murder? Jack was trying to trap him into admitting what he'd done.

Patrick laughed harder. Now that he was calmer he realized Angie's message hadn't said anything about murder. She hadn't even mentioned him by name. The tape had been so generic that—now that he replayed it in his mind—it was almost comical.

Jack could easily have gotten it off his answering machine from before, when he and Angie were together.

"Jack, old buddy, you had me going there for a minute." He held out his hands. They were still shaking. It had almost worked; he'd almost believed Angie was alive. He'd almost panicked. "Jack, you son of a—"

But how had Jack found him—and so quickly? He slapped his forehead with the heel of his palm. Angie's credit card! Of course.

Unfortunately, he realized he would have to use the credit card again—to skip town. He had no choice, since Angie had cleaned him out and he hadn't had a chance to cash in the stocks and bonds.

It was clear he couldn't stay here and let Jack leave him any more Angie messages. Even knowing Angie wasn't really alive, he still didn't want to hear her voice again. It was too creepy hearing a dead woman's voice like that.

So that meant he had to get the hell out of Dodge. But first, he would take care of Jack.

He glanced out the window. Jack was still at the table, away from the light, watching the street and the hotel. Patrick was surprised now that he'd even seen Jack down there in the dark. If he hadn't had the feeling that someone was watching him...

He smiled and, picking up the phone, dialed 911. Jack wouldn't be following him anymore. *You just can't win for losing, old buddy.*

SHE SPOTTED JACK about the same time she saw the police car pull up at the other end of the street. She should have known he wouldn't go back to Houston and let her handle this. And to think that at one time he'd been so predictable it had made him an easy mark.

Two officers got out of the cop car and started toward the restaurant. She'd bet Patrick was watching from his room. This had his name written all over it.

She had changed into jeans, a sweatshirt and sneakers, her dark hair hidden beneath a Mariners cap and she wore no makeup and had a backpack slung over one shoulder. She knew Patrick hadn't seen her again. He would only see her when she wanted him to. Unless Jack made her blow her cover.

She debated letting the cops arrest Jack. At least in jail, he wouldn't be in her hair. But she couldn't be sure he wouldn't just get back out on even higher bail.

The last thing she needed was him messing up her plans. But even as she thought it, she knew that that wasn't the reason she couldn't send him back to jail.

Jack was sitting at one of the outside tables farthest from the front door of the restaurant. The other tables were full, the large dark umbrellas folded down for the evening and candles flickering on all tables except Jack's.

The two cops were coming down the sidewalk from the opposite direction. All she had to do was keep them from reaching him. Otherwise, he was on his way to jail.

Piece of cake, since Diversion was her middle name, she thought as she glanced around, spotted her mark and moved in quickly. The two police officers were about twenty yards behind her when she rushed past an exquisitely dressed woman exiting the restaurant and simply bumped into her.

Relieving the woman of her Gucci bag was child's play. Daddy would have been so proud.

Nor did the wealthy matron fail her.

"Help! Help! My bag!" the woman shrieked. "Someone stop him!" She must have seen the two cops then. "Police! Police! Stop that boy! He stole my bag!"

With the bag tucked under her arm, she dove into the traffic, darting between moving cars, to reach the other side at a run. She had a head start and excelled at a quick getaway—and she had reconnoitered the area as soon as she'd found Patrick so she knew exactly where to go to ditch the cops.

She raced down the alley between buildings, leaping trashcans and dodging parked cars and Dumpsters, sticking to the darkness. Not far down the block, she swung over a fence and through the back door of a deli. She ducked into the ladies' room. No one inside the deli had seemed to pay her any mind.

Once inside, she pulled off her baseball cap, shook out her long hair and stripped off the sweatshirt down to the white cotton top she wore beneath. After discarding the cap and sweatshirt in the bottom of the trashcan, she took her purse from the backpack and put on a pair of large silver earrings and a little eye shadow.

She could hear some commotion outside the bathroom door and quickly stuffed the stolen purse into her own bag, along with the cheap nylon backpack, flushed the toilet and washed her hands, then put on her cool, calm and collected expression and walked out to find two policeman banging on the door of the men's rest room.

She showed only mild interest as she glanced at them. She could feel their eyes on her as she entered the busy deli and stood in line, studying the menu on the wall.

Out of the corner of her eye, she watched the cops wait outside the men's room. They seemed both surprised and disappointed when an elderly man came out. The two policemen glanced into the packed deli, evidently didn't see what they were looking for and went back out into the alley.

After a few moments, she pretended to lose patience with the long line and left. Once outside, she hightailed it as quickly as she dared back toward the restaurant.

One of the policemen was inside with the wealthy matron, trying to calm her. The other was moving through the restaurant, obviously looking for Jack.

Jack was gone, just as she had hoped he would be. But she also knew Patrick would be watching from his third-floor hotel room window across the street.

She looked up at Patrick's room. It was dark—no lights on. She smiled up at him, knowing he was standing there, watching her. Leisurely she walked past the courtyard restaurant, slid the Gucci bag from her purse and stealthily dropped it onto the seat of an empty chair across from an honest-looking elderly couple, the purse and her movements covered by the checked tablecloth.

She knew Patrick had seen her. Just as she knew he would follow her. She started down the street, turning at the corner to head toward the wharf and the darkness, drawing in her prey.

Wisps of fog swirled around her as she walked, growing denser as she neared the water. She shivered, wishing she still had her sweatshirt. There were no other pedestrians in the industrial area this late. Only a few cars sped past, headlights piercing the darkness, then fading to black again.

She wanted to look over her shoulder but forced herself not to. She knew why she was feeling vulnerable and it had nothing to do with the soft footfalls behind her. She'd wanted Patrick to follow her, dared him to. He would come to prove to himself that she wasn't real. She liked the idea of his thinking she was a ghost, and the fog would be ideal for her purposes.

She thought of Jack. No doubt he'd taken off when he'd seen her—and the cops. Maybe he had the sense to catch a plane back to Houston. She could only hope.

She wished now that she'd had Jack arrested back at the restaurant. The safest place for him right now was a Houston, Texas jail. She feared that moment of weakness would come back to haunt her.

She cut through the now deserted industrial area of the wharf, the fog thick as chowder, the street lamps glowing like diffused sunlight overhead. In the distance she could hear the sound of a boat out on the water, but couldn't see it, couldn't see six feet in front of her.

But she could hear the footsteps behind her, closer now, gaining on her. A few more feet and— She heard a sound off to her right, turned, seeing nothing but blackness in a narrow space between the two buildings.

A hand shot out, closed over her arm. Before she could react, the other hand clamped over her mouth as she was dragged back between the buildings.

"SHH," JACK WHISPERED next to her ear. He could hear the sound of footfalls on the street just beyond them, moving stealthily through the fog and darkness in their direction. He held her to him, breathing in the sweet scent of her hair, her body warm against him.

Jack saw a dark shadow flicker past through the fog. Patrick? It was all he could do not to go after the man. The only thing that kept him from it was the woman in his arms. He had her right where he wanted her.

The sound of footsteps stopped. Silence settled as thick as the fog. A boat horn sounded. Water lapped at the docks nearby. Jack heard Patrick let out a curse. He was coming back this way.

The footsteps picked up speed, the shadow sweeping past in a blur. Jack listened until he was sure

Patrick was gone before he let go of the woman, turning her around to face him.

She'd saved him back there at the restaurant, but right now he wasn't feeling much gratitude. He wouldn't need saving if it hadn't been for her sister.

"Give me the gun you're carrying, Maria," he whispered.

"What gun?"

He grabbed her purse, opened it and dug around for the weapon she'd pulled on him earlier today.

"Don't you believe anything I tell you?" she asked as she leaned back against the side of the opposite building, only inches from him.

"No." This close he could feel her gaze on him, fired with defiance. She was right. No gun.

He looked up at her. The sleeveless, white cotton top she wore accented her curves nicely. So did the jeans. Few places to hide a weapon, and damn distracting. He knew those curves too well. It threw him, seeing them on another woman.

She spread her arms wide against the side of the building. "Go ahead, frisk me if you still don't believe me."

He stared at her, too many emotions coursing through him. Her dark hair curled around her face, falling to her bare shoulders. She looked so much like Angie....

"Well?" she asked softly.

He met her gaze. *Don't underestimate this woman.* He had underestimated her twin and look where that had landed him.

He stepped forward, covering her hands with his own as he flattened her against the rough brick. He saw a spark flash in her dark eyes. Anger? Or something even hotter? What he didn't see was whatever truth he was looking for in all that bottomless darkness.

She didn't move, didn't seem to breathe, as he let go of one of her hands to run his fingers along the top of her hip-hugger jeans, down her long legs to her sneakers. No weapon. Could he be that wrong about her?

She shot him a sly smile.

He let go of her, then, surprising her, he grabbed the front of her shirt and the bra she wore beneath it and pulled, his other hand palm up at her waist.

Her eyes widened, the smile disappearing as the Derringer, warm from her bare skin, dropped from between her breasts and into his palm.

"Well, how about that." It was his turn to smile as he stuffed the weapon into his jeans pocket. "Lying must come as naturally to you as breathing," he said, pressing her to the wall again.

"It's genetic."

"Obviously."

He could almost hear her heart pounding. Smell her perfume rising from the spot where the Derringer had rested, the scent something exotic and potent that dazed his senses. Feel her lush curves pressed against his larger, stronger, harder body.

She seemed to be holding her breath. Afraid of what he'd do next? Or waiting for it?

He reached up to cup her face in his hands, her skin silken cool on his fingertips. He felt her pulse jump under his thumbs. She looked so much like Angie, felt so much like her— Her lips parted, a soft sigh escaping as she closed her eyes.

The kiss was inevitable.

Chapter Eight

Jack drew her closer, his mouth dropping to hers. She moaned against his lips and he pulled her to him, deepening the kiss, his body molded to hers.

He felt her tremble against him, her fingers digging into his shoulders as he lost himself in the taste and feel of her, swept away without reason or thought or realization of just whom he was kissing.

Suddenly she shoved him away.

He stumbled back, his heart in his throat as he looked at her, emotions roller-coastering inside him.

The woman in the alley with him wasn't Maria LaGrand! She was Angie! Angie was alive! He wanted to wrap her in his arms, to strangle her, to kiss her, to shake the truth out of her.

He stared at her, his mind racing, battered by conflicting emotions: shock and relief, anger and joy. Angie was alive and she was pretending to be Maria.

The idea came in a flash. Why let her know he knew the truth? If she wanted to masquerade as Maria, he would play along. He wouldn't let on that he even suspected. Not yet, anyway. First he'd get her to help him clear his name. Then, when he didn't have to worry about being sent to prison, he'd deal with Angie.

"Do you think you can just exchange one sister for another?" she demanded, sounding shaken by the kiss.

He shook his head. "It's just that you are so much like Angie...." He shrugged, his pulse still pounding. "I'm sorry. I won't make that mistake again."

She stared at him for several moments. He had a pretty good idea what she was worried about.

"You can see why it's best if you go back to Houston and we don't see each other again," she said, still sounding a little breathless.

He tried to calm his racing heart. What did he want from this woman aside from help clearing his name? Oh, where did he begin?

"I'm not going back to Houston," he informed her. "You and I will just have to get used to being around each other, I guess, since you're going to help me clear my name."

"That isn't part of the plan."

"There's been a change in plans. Otherwise," he continued, "I'm going after Patrick and when I catch him, I know he will try to blame everything on you—" He quickly added, "And Angie. You did help her set me up, didn't you? You and Patrick and Angie. And while I doubt you're worried about your family name being dragged through the mud—"

"I told you—" anger sparked in her eyes "—if you were framed, Angie had nothing to do with it."

"So you say," he replied, ignoring the "if you were framed" part. "But then, I have no reason to believe anything you tell me, do I?" He stared at her, reminded again what a liar she was.

"You're wrong about my sister."

He laughed. "What is it? Some strange kind of family pride that makes it all right for your sister to be a crook who was conning me out of my money, but heaven forbid she would ever stoop to framing me for fraud and arson?"

"I don't expect you to understand," she said, lifting her chin in obvious indignation. "My family are not *crooks*. They only take from those who have stolen from someone else."

"Ah, modern-day Robin Hoods?" he said with a laugh. "Nice. I'm sure that helps you and your family rationalize being thieves, but I didn't steal my money from anyone and your sister came after me."

She raised one fine brow. "I know you claim you're innocent of the fraud and arson charges against you—"

"I am."

"Even if that is true—"

"Angie came after me *before* it had even come out about the substandard housing, *before* the arson," he said. "So that proves she was just after my money."

She met his gaze. "You inherited the money from your father."

"What are you saying?"

She shook her head and looked away.

He grabbed her arm and swung her around to look at him again.

Her eyes filled with anger and defiance as she jerked free of him. "Haven't you ever wondered how your father was able to go from dirt poor one day to rich the next?"

"You think my father *stole* the money?" he demanded.

"I don't think. I know he did," she said, and tried to step past him.

He blocked her exit. "I don't believe you."

"I'm sure you don't," she said. "You don't believe anything I tell you, right?"

"Right."

She shoved past him into the empty street along the wharf and headed in the direction she'd originally come from, almost disappearing into the fog.

He caught up to her. "You're going to drop a bombshell like that and just walk away?"

"What does it matter now?"

"It matters to me."

"Angie is dead," she said, wisps of fog whirling past as they walked. "All that matters now is getting Patrick."

He walked beside her in silence, thinking about what she'd said. Of course she had her facts wrong.

But she was right about one thing. Clearing his name and getting Patrick had to be the top priority right now.

Later... Later he would get answers to all his questions.

PATRICK RUSHED BACK through the fog and darkness to the hotel, wondering what had possessed him to follow the woman in the first place.

Obviously, she wasn't Angie. Angie was caught underwater on a limb in the Clark's Fork River, waiting for the water to clear so some fisherman could find her.

He had followed the woman only to prove to himself that Angie was dead. He knew the moment he saw the double up close, it would be clear she wasn't

Angie. The truth was, he wouldn't mind a little re-assurance.

As he neared the hotel, he couldn't shake the feeling that he was being followed. And yet every time he turned around, he saw no one tailing him.

Where are you, Jack? What do you have planned now?

He watched the faces of people coming out of the restaurants and stores, half expecting to see Jack again. Or the Angie look-alike. He couldn't wait to get back to the hotel, get packed, get out of Seattle.

Maybe he could catch a flight out tonight. It wasn't that late. But once he used Angie's credit card, Jack would be right behind him.

"Then again…" Maybe he could use that to his advantage, he thought as he pushed open the door to the hotel lobby and stepped inside. He could set a trap for Jack.

"All I have to do is go somewhere and wait for him to show up again," he said to himself as he entered the empty hotel elevator and hit the button for his floor. "Only this time, I'll make sure the cops get him."

As the elevator door closed, he didn't see Jack or the look-alike follow him into the lobby. He took that as a good sign.

Once in his room, he went straight to the phone and was extraordinarily relieved to see that the message light wasn't flashing. The last voice he wanted to hear right now was Angie's.

He called the airport. There were flights to Las Vegas, Palm Springs, Los Angeles or San Diego tonight. Eenie, meanie, minie, mo. He bought a ticket to Palm

Springs. Maybe he would have better luck trapping Jack there. It was smaller. Fewer places to hide.

He wondered what Jack's game was. Did he just plan to try to "gaslight" him? Make him think he was going crazy and somehow trick him into confessing all?

Killing Jack had never occurred to him as part of his original plan. But the thought was starting to appeal to him. If Jack kept chasing him... It would be self-defense, right? Wasn't that why he'd gotten that restraining order against Jack? Because he feared for his life?

Patrick felt confident he could get any jury in the country to believe killing Jack had been self-defense. Jack was a loose cannon. A man who had jumped bail to come after him. A man who couldn't stand the thought of Patrick being with Angie. At least that part was true.

The judge and jury would be sympathetic to Patrick, who had obviously had some bad luck lately. Of course, Jack's attorney would try to muddy the waters by trying to pin Angie's death on him. The husband was always the first suspect. Unless the sheriff was not the brightest bulb in the store.

But maybe Angie Grant Ryerson hadn't really been asleep at the wheel the night she drove off into the canyon. The tire tracks proved she'd never even tried to brake. Maybe she had killed herself over Jack! That would be a nice touch.

What the judge and jury wouldn't know is that, while Jack might want to kill him right now, it just wasn't in Jack Donovan's nature. No, Jack could never kill anyone. Jack just thought that by trying to intimidate him, he could get a confession. *Good luck, Jack.*

So basically, Patrick told himself, he had nothing to fear.

THE FOG DISSIPATED as Jack and Angie left the water. Buildings rose out of the darkness. Stars twinkled overhead. The moon climbed up through the city, blindingly bright. Jack told himself that he'd make Angie tell him everything. And he'd set her straight about a lot of things. This woman had no idea who she was dealing with. And she thought he didn't, either.

"Help me clear my name and you can have Patrick," he said.

She laughed softly. "I will have Patrick either way." She shot him a challenging look. "So what's in it for me?"

"Mercenary, aren't you? You remind me more and more of your sister all the time."

She glared at him. He could see cold anger coursing through her. It made her eyes blaze, her body seem to vibrate.

"Fine. I'll prove to you that you're wrong about my sister."

"Good luck."

"Do you hate her that much?"

He didn't hate Angie at all. That was the problem. Even knowing that she'd only been after his money, he still couldn't hate her.

"I'm sorry she hurt you."

"Yeah. I'm sure that's what you say to all her marks."

She didn't slow her stride as she looked away from

him. They were almost to Patrick's hotel. "Angie was going to tell you the truth."

He smiled, hiding his surprise and disbelief, reminding himself of the night she'd said there was something important she needed to tell him. The night they'd been interrupted by Patrick.

"But instead she decided to marry Patrick."

"She was a fool to believe him. Patrick took advantage of her. He...conned her."

"Ironic, isn't it?" he said. "The con getting conned."

"She fell in love with you. It made her vulnerable."

He laughed. "So it was *my* fault."

She didn't answer, just stared straight ahead and kept walking.

He studied her profile, reminding himself who this woman was. A professional liar, a thief. So why did he desperately want to believe her? Because his heart couldn't believe it was all a con. Angie had felt something. But how would he ever know that for certain?

He heard the sound of the traffic on Interstate 5, just a few blocks away. The fog was gone, but the air felt damp. He could see Angie more clearly in the glow of the street lamps as they passed under them.

"Here," he said, taking off his jacket and draping it around her shoulders. "You look cold."

Her expression was one of surprise. And something he couldn't put his finger on.

"I think I understand what Angie saw in you. You're a nice man."

"I used to be," he said, looking into her dark eyes. He knew what he was looking for and quickly glanced away. "Let's find Patrick. I want this over with." He felt her gaze on his face, but he didn't look at her—couldn't.

He would have to be on guard all the time around her, keep her at a safe distance and yet never let her out of his sight.

It would be hell, he thought and smiled to himself. He really did have Angie right where he wanted her.

As Patrick started to repack his suitcase, Angie's address book—scotch-stained and bloated from being wet—fell from his jacket pocket. His stomach roiled at the sight of it. All the numbers wrong or disconnected.

If she'd cleaned out their joint checking account, then maybe she'd hidden her fortune from him, as well. No wonder she hadn't asked for a prenuptial agreement.

Suddenly he recognized that bad taste in his mouth. Fear. Angie's money was now his. But what if he couldn't find it? *Wait a minute.* He knew just the man who could.

He picked up the phone and got the number for a low-life lawyer he'd hired last year by the name of Burns. Lester Burns.

"Ryerson, sure I remember you," Lester said when he'd introduced himself. "I got you out of that scrape in Dallas last year. You never paid me the rest of what you owe me."

"I've been meaning to do that."

"Call me when you do."

"Wait!" Patrick cried. "Do you take credit cards?" He could almost hear Lester smile.

"Give me the number slowly, and the expiration date."

Patrick did, trying not to let his annoyance come across in his voice. "Now, here's what I need." He started to ask Lester to track down Angie's financial advisor, but realized there was a faster way. "I need to cash in some stocks and bonds and find out how much my wife is worth." He couldn't tell Lester the truth. The man would blackmail him, sure as hell. "I think she's cheating on me and I—"

"Save me the gruesome details, all right," Lester said. "Just give me her name, social and some information off the stocks and bonds. I assume they're in your name. I'll let you know what I find out—if your credit card clears in the morning."

So much for trust. "Angelina Grant." He read off her social security number and birth date. He'd gotten both from the forms they'd had to fill out to get married. Then he pulled out the stocks and bonds and gave Burns that information.

"I'll call you first thing in the morning."

"Eleven. Don't call before eleven." Lester hung up.

Patrick slammed down the phone with an oath and took a taxi to the airport. No sign of Jack along the way. Or the Angie look-alike. So far so good.

Tomorrow he would buy a new cell phone and call Sheriff Truebow to give him the number. He'd call Lester Burns. If anyone could help him it was Lester.

In the meantime... He didn't bother to check out, just went out the back and flagged down a taxi to take him to the airport.

Patrick went straight to an airport bar, ordered a drink and tried to think only about Angie's money, his first big score, but he couldn't relax. Wouldn't relax until Angie's ashes were strewn across Montana. Until he had his hands on at least some of her money and was flying off to Tahiti. Once Lester told him just how much Angie was worth—and how to get his hands on some quick cash—

He heard his flight being called over the P.A. system. As he walked toward his gate, he watched for Jack. And the Angie look-alike. He quickened his step, telling himself that by the time he woke up in the morning, his life could be all wine and roses. Or in his case, scotch and tropical beaches, women in string bikinis and—he smiled to himself—word that Angie's very dead, very bloated body had floated up still wearing the too-expensive diamond pendant and wedding ring he'd given her. A man could dream, couldn't he?

ANGIE STEPPED INTO THE hotel lobby phone booth, the door shutting behind her with a soft *whoosh,* and closed her eyes. She fought to still the trembling— worse, the tears. What had made her think she could pull this off?

Years of experience in deceit and lies, she thought bitterly. But her feelings for Jack Donovan had made her lose her edge—and almost cost her her life. The game she was playing now was deadly.

She opened her eyes, the taste of him still on her lips, the scent of him clinging to his jacket, which he'd insisted she wear.

Pull yourself together. It was just a kiss.

What a laugh. No kiss was just a kiss with Jack.

He doesn't know. He can't know.

She turned to look out through the phone booth glass at him. He stood over by a potted plant, waiting, watching her, watching for Patrick. She knew he would die trying to protect her. That's what worried her.

He glanced over at her. Her heart leapt as his gaze met hers. How would she ever be able to pull this off? She should have let the police arrest him. She turned away, took out her cell phone and hit speed-dial.

Maria answered on the first ring. She'd obviously been expecting her call. "How did it go?"

"Fine."

"Fine? What happened?" she asked, sounding worried.

"Nothing. It all went according to plan." Angie had known Patrick would follow her down to the wharf. She hadn't thought Jack would, though. He'd been smart enough to circle around and cut her off. He just kept surprising her. And that was the problem. Like that blasted kiss.

"And Patrick?" Maria asked.

"He's rattled and on the move again," she said. "He didn't even bother to check out, but I had the maid peek into his room. He's gone."

"You're sure Jack doesn't know that we made the switch?"

Angie glanced over her shoulder again at Jack. He was watching her intently. She turned back to the phone. "No. He thinks I'm you. I can handle this."

"Can you? You'll have more than Jack to worry about if Patrick realizes you really *are* alive—"

"You don't have to remind me what Patrick is capable of," she said, recalling his trying to kill her last night. She had hit the brakes and swerved, tucking and rolling as she bailed out of the Jeep. It had been so close that she'd felt the rear tire brush her pants

leg. She'd scrambled on all fours into the darkness of
the trees, amazed she was alive.

Ironically, the heavy coat and jeans Patrick had told
her to put on were the only things that saved her. She
had wondered why he'd wanted her to change into
them, but realized his plan must have called for her
to be dressed in something practical—not her wedding suit. He'd have enough suspicion on him as it
was.

She had listened to the shriek of the Jeep's tearing
metal as it tumbled down into the canyon, all the time
knowing that she could have been inside it.

As she'd huddled in the cold and pines, she'd
watched Patrick get out of the Suburban. She'd seen
how hard it was for him to near the rim of the canyon,
let alone to look down. She'd watched, vowing to get
out of the mountains alive—and make Patrick wish
he had never been born.

Well, she'd gotten out of the mountains. And now
she intended to keep the second part of that vow. As
soon as she took care of Jack.

She could hear the clatter of computer keys.

"Patrick used your credit card to book a flight to
Palm Springs," Maria said. "He'll be staying at the
Rancho Vista del Norte."

He had no choice but to use her credit card, since
she'd cleaned out their joint checking account. It
made him easy to track. His own cards were maxed
out from courting her, not to mention the cost of the
wedding and the plot to kill her at the cabin in Montana. That must have cost him a bundle.

"So you got Jack out of your hair," Maria said.

Angie took a breath and let it out slowly.

"Don't tell me you didn't send Jack packing to Houston," Maria ordered.

"He's going back to Houston," Angie assured her. "I'm going with him."

"What?"

Her twin knew she couldn't turn Jack in to the authorities. Wasn't her style, even if she hadn't been in love with him. "I'm going to help Jack clear his name."

A sigh. "How did I know you'd do that?" Silence.

"He thinks I was working with Patrick."

"I know," Maria said. "So you're going to pretend you're me and prove to him he was wrong about you." She chuckled. "What is wrong with this picture? Angie, you don't really think you can change his mind about you, do you?"

"That isn't what I'm doing. I just don't want him believing that I had anything to do with sending him to jail."

"Maybe he belongs in jail," Maria said. "You can't change who you are," she said more kindly. "What does it matter how much you lied to him or how good your motives were? Do you really think he could ever trust you again? Worse, what if you find out that Patrick didn't frame him? What if Jack is guilty of those charges?"

Angie glanced back at Jack again. At one time, she would have argued that she knew the con business so well she could spot a lie at fifty feet. When she'd started falling in love with Jack, she had become a mark herself. And now she couldn't trust her instincts, not when it came to Jack.

"I hate to see you get your heart broken again," Maria said quietly.

Again. Yes, Angie hadn't forgotten the first time. She'd been much younger then, but it hadn't hurt any less. And it had taught her a lesson she'd thought she would never forget. Until Jack.

Wasn't that why she'd believed all the horrible things Patrick had told her about Jack? Because she'd been burned by a man before? Because she didn't have faith in happy endings? And she knew what Jack's father had done. Of course Jack too would be flawed. Of course he would break her heart. And there was the "evidence" Patrick had provided.

"If Jack is innocent, I can't let him take the fall. I suspect Patrick really might be behind this. Worse, that he used me to distract Jack while he was busy framing him." Her heart argued Jack's innocence while her cynical nature held out little hope. But a little hope was better than none.

"You get too close to the truth and you might have to fear not only Patrick, but also Jack," Maria warned.

Angie smiled to herself. Maria didn't realize just how much of a threat Jack Donovan was. Just not in the way Maria was imagining.

She hoped Patrick had left something that they could find to clear Jack. Before Patrick tried to stop them from discovering the truth. They would have to move fast.

"I suppose there is no talking you out of this?" Maria asked.

"No." She didn't deceive herself that she could turn back the clock and change everything between her and Jack. He knew now why Angelina Grant had come into his life. Or at least enough of it to hate her.

He would never trust her again. Nor could she blame him—if he was as innocent as he claimed.

"As for Patrick, I don't want you doing anything without me," Angie told her twin. "Let's allow him to think he's gotten away for the next forty-eight hours. I'll take care of things in Houston, then meet you in Palm Springs. Just keep an eye on him?"

"Gladly," Maria said.

"But no more than that. It's too dangerous to move forward on the plan without a backup." Angie doubted even her sister knew just how dangerous Patrick was. You had to look into a man's eyes to see the depth of his depravation. And Angie had. "Just let me know if he runs again."

"Don't worry, I'll be watching him like a hawk," Maria said. "You think forty-eight hours is enough?"

"Any more will be too dangerous if I'm right about Patrick. Promise me, Maria, that you'll stay out of sight," Angie said. She remembered only too well the expression on her twin's face when she'd flown to Montana to pick her up and had heard Angie's story.

Maria had wanted to drive up to the cabin right then and kill Patrick. Forget any plan for LaGrand-style revenge. She wanted vengeance, the clean, simple, permanent kind.

"Promise?"

"Promise," Maria said.

"Why don't I believe you?"

"Because I'm a con artist." Maria laughed. "I told Jack I was better than you."

"You are such a liar," Angie said good-naturedly.

"See?" Maria said with a laugh.

Angie disconnected, still worried Maria might decide to take matters into her own hands. She dialed the airport.

When she hung up, she turned to find Jack standing outside the phone booth. She pushed open the door, wondering how much of the conversation he'd overhead. "Patrick's on his way to Palm Springs."

"Then why did you just book us seats on a jet to Houston?" he asked, making it clear he'd heard at least the last conversation.

"Patrick will be fine in Palm Springs. I want him to think he's safe—at least temporarily—so he stays put. We're going to Houston to clear your name." She'd learned from an early age that nothing was impossible—with the right attitude and the right connections. Her daddy had taught her well.

"Just like that?" He chuckled.

She raised a brow. "Only if you're really innocent."

A muscle in his jaw jumped, his eyes narrowed. "I'm innocent. As for Angie…"

She stepped past him and headed for the door, refusing to take the bait. There was only one way to convince him that she hadn't had anything to do with the charges against him.

"Chartering a private jet to Houston isn't cheap," he noted, catching up to her.

He still seemed to think she was broke and that she'd targeted him last spring for his money and nothing more.

"Vengeance is never cheap." She looked over at him, meeting his gaze. "Sometimes the price can be too high, though."

He met her gaze. "Not in this case."

Chapter Nine

As the plane banked over Palm Springs, Patrick looked down and thought it a sparkling jewel—the glittering lights illuminating turquoise pools, towering palms and red-tiled roofs.

He smiled. This was more like it. He felt that old excitement shoot through his blood. This was the life he should have been born to. Not some slummy part of Houston. Not taking favors from Jack Donovan.

Patrick put down his window on the cab ride to the Rancho Vista Del Norte and breathed in the dry rich scents of desert night. The cab cruised down the main drag under a canopy of backlit palms.

He thought he might take a late swim in the pool. Tomorrow he would catch some rays, get a good tan. He couldn't wait.

Once he got to his room, he was feeling so good he decided to call Sheriff Truebow's after-hours number, feeling lucky. Maybe the sheriff had tried to call the broken cell phone. He left his room number, then began to unpack his suitcase, looking for his swimsuit.

The aquamarine pool right outside his sliding glass doors was just too inviting. Majestic palms swayed in the warm breeze, bathed by golden light. He could hear the alluring lap of the water in the pool, the rustle of the palm fronds, the sweet voices of several hotties in skimpy bathing suits as they glided through the water like young playful seals. Oh yeah, this was more like it.

Where was his swimsuit? He couldn't wait to get in the pool. His fingers brushed something unfamiliar. He looked down and let out a startled cry as he jerked his hand back.

It was a woman's brown shoe with white stitching—just like the one Truebow had said was found in the river.

ANGIE SAID NOTHING on the short taxi ride to her hotel but she didn't seem surprised when, true to his word, he didn't let her out of sight for an instant as she quickly packed her things for the flight to Houston.

It was obvious from her expression that she regretted not letting the cops arrest him back at the restaurant tonight.

"I told you I would help you," she snapped at one point.

He smiled. "Angie too told me a lot of things."

"I'm not my sister!"

"As far as I'm concerned, you're the same. Two of a kind. No difference."

"You're wrong about that. Angie and I are very different. Right now, I can't imagine what attracted her to you."

"My money," he said with a laugh. "Nothing but my money."

She groaned as they left her hotel. "You don't have

that much money. And I told you, it wasn't about money.''

He caught up to her. "Sure it was about money."

"It was about righting a wrong," she said without looking at him as she walked out to hail a taxi.

"Right. Come on, there must be dozens of guys LaGrands could have conned whose fathers were much more crooked than mine. Why me?''

She shook her head, trying hard to ignore him. Good luck.

"Look, I don't know how my father went from rags to riches, but I can't imagine he did something so horrible to your family that it would make you go after his son. My father's been dead for over a year."

She finally looked at him, for an instant her gaze unguarded. Then her eyes narrowed and darkened. Her lips parted. He could see the pink of her delicate tongue, remember the taste of her on his lips. Her eyes locked on his, daring him to look away. Not likely.

Did he just imagine it? Or in that instant when her gaze was unguarded had he glimpsed the Angie he'd fallen in love with? Or did she even exist? Maybe everything about the LaGrands was smoke and mirrors.

"You were right earlier," she said. "We *are* mercenaries. We work as a family on behalf of people who were bilked or wronged, people who didn't get proper justice.''

"You're telling me that your family specializes in revenge—for a fee, of course."

Her smile was rueful. "I knew you wouldn't understand." A taxi pulled up. "We have work to do." She jerked open the door and started to get in.

He caught her arm. "Is the truth so hard for you?" he demanded. "Who did my father wrong?"

"We don't have time for this."

"We will before this is over," he whispered as he let go of her, then slid into the dark intimate back seat of the cab next to her. "Count on it."

He gave the driver the address of his hotel. He needed to pick up his suitcase and the thick envelope with the dossier on her family.

Her features weren't quite distinguishable in the darkness. Once a mark, always a mark, he thought angrily. Anger and frustration warred with emotions he no longer wanted to feel for this woman. He told himself that he had never known her—only what she wanted him to see, which was all a lie.

She was lying to him right now, pretending to be her twin. She thought he was buying it, that he couldn't tell the difference between them.

That gave him an advantage he planned to use in his favor, even if he did feel guilty about it. He owed this woman nothing, certainly not the truth. And yet he hated the thought of lowering himself to her level, of becoming her. A liar.

He could tell that once she helped him clear his name—or prove that he was guilty of the charges—she thought she'd be rid of him and could deal with Patrick on her own. Fat chance.

But right now he was more worried about what she may have planned for him. Was going to Houston with him nothing more than leading him on a wild-goose chase? Or was she just trying to cover her own tracks?

He breathed in the sweet scent of her perfume and

told himself he could do this, whatever it took. Only, this time, he'd be the one calling the shots.

But even as he thought it, he wondered if Angelina LaGrand wasn't already one step ahead of him and leading him into a trap far worse than any others she'd laid.

"WHAT THE HELL?" Patrick stared down at the shoe, his throat contracting. How could this shoe possibly have gotten into his suitcase?

He had to sit down before he blacked out. Moving to the glass doors, he pulled the blinds and stumbled over to one of the chairs at the table, dropping down, his gaze locked on the bag.

Of course he had to have put the shoe in there himself. No one else had access to his suitcase, right? He'd packed so quickly back at the cabin in Montana, maybe he'd accidentally put some of Angie's stuff in by mistake.

Right. The other shoe from the river? Like Angie had taken off wearing only one shoe.

Maybe the sheriff had found the shoe, flown to Seattle, come into his room and put it in the suitcase to scare him. Ridiculous.

Jack. It had to have been Jack. But how could Jack have gotten the shoe?

Patrick shook his head as he got up, moved to the suitcase and removed the shoe gingerly. He clutched it in both hands and tried to snap it in half, succeeding only in breaking off the heel.

Angrily, he threw both shoe and heel into the wastebasket and covered it with some crumpled-up brochures and advertising pamphlets from the desk. *There.*

But now he didn't feel like swimming anymore. Just moments before, he'd felt safe, content here. Later, after the hotties were out of the pool, he'd get rid of the shoe in the Dumpster in the alley behind the resort. He'd never be able to sleep with that damn shoe in his room.

ONCE THEY WERE ON THE JET and winging toward Houston, Jack asked, "So what are you planning to do to Patrick?"

She shook her head. "It's better if you don't know."

He'd seen the bruises on her arm earlier. What had happened up at that cabin in Montana? Had Patrick really tried to kill her? Or did she just want everyone to think that? Especially Jack Donovan.

Montie had warned him that Angie might have faked her death. He'd even predicted that she would come running to Jack for help. Show up swearing she hadn't been in on any of it with Patrick.

Except, she hadn't come running to him for help. In fact she had tried to persuade him to return to Houston and let her take care of Patrick alone.

But then again, she knew he wouldn't. So maybe he was playing right into her hands, letting her take him back to Houston. For all he knew, the police would be waiting at the airport to arrest him.

"Just let me handle everything," she said now, and leaned back as if to sleep away the flight.

"Excuse me? My entire life was messed up when your twin waltzed into it, not to mention when she and Patrick ripped me off and framed me. I'm sorry if my being here is inconvenient for you, but I'm part of this. It's my reputation that is shot to hell, my freedom that's at stake. I want to know what the hell you have planned. Start with what's happening when we land at the airport in Houston.''

She opened her eyes, glared at him and sat up. ''I could have let the cops catch you back in Seattle if my intent was to have you thrown in jail. I could have saved myself the cost of this flight.''

''Why didn't you?''

She let out a sigh. ''I did it for Angie, all right? Whether you believe it or not, she had feelings for you.''

''If you're looking for gratitude—''

''I'm not looking for anything from you. I thought I made that clear. You're nothing but trouble to me. And if I'm not careful, you'll get us both killed. Unless you are still of the mistaken presumption that Patrick isn't a killer.''

''There was a time I certainly wouldn't have believed Patrick capable of violence,'' he admitted. ''Now? I'm not sure of anything.''

''That's a start, I guess. It helps if you know what you're dealing with.''

How true, he thought studying her. ''I thought I knew Angie. But the woman I knew wouldn't have married Patrick.''

She raised a brow. ''When you knew her she wasn't being drugged.''

Anger ripped through him. ''Patrick *drugged* her? That son of a—''

''It wasn't just the drugs, Jack. What really changed her mind about you was the photographs.''

Jack stared at her. ''What photographs?''

She didn't answer.

''What photographs?'' Jack demanded again. His

blue eyes were hard as ice chips and just as cold. Whatever had made her think when she first met him that his eyes were the color of warm denim?

"Photos of you and another woman. In bed."

He stared at her. "What woman?"

"Your former fiancée."

"Constance?" He sounded surprised. "How in the hell did someone get photographs of—" He scrubbed a hand over his face. "The photos aren't real."

She lifted a brow.

"Okay, when were they supposedly taken?"

"Recently."

Jack scoffed. "I broke it off with Constance last spring and I know of no photos—"

"That isn't what Constance says."

He narrowed his gaze at her.

"Angie confronted Constance, and she admitted the two of you had been having an affair—while you were dating Angie."

"That's a lie. I haven't been with Constance since before I met Angie."

But she could tell he was surprised she had—that is—Angie had confronted his former fiancée.

"The photos are quite convincing."

"I want to see them," he said between gritted teeth.

"No problem." She opened her purse, took out a color snapshot and handed it to him. "I found this in Angie's hotel room."

He stared down at the shot of him and Constance in his bed at the penthouse. "Is this all?"

She shook her head. "Angie told me Patrick had the rest at his apartment."

Jack swore and crumpled the photo in his fist.

"This photo was obviously taken before I broke it off with her. But what I'd like to know is who the hell shot it."

"Why *did* you break off the engagement with Constance Whitaker?" she asked, way too curious.

He swept her with a look that said it was none of her damn business.

She waited.

"I found out Constance lied to me. Satisfied?"

"That's it?"

"That's it. I abhor liars."

She looked away. "Even liars sometimes tell the truth."

"Right. It's just impossible for people around them to know when that is."

How in the hell had someone gotten photographs of him and Constance? That's what Jack wanted to know. And why would Constance lie about recently sleeping with him?

Well, the second answer was easy. Spite. Constance had been furious when he'd broken off their engagement and had threatened to get even with him. It seemed she'd found a way.

He glanced over at Angie. He forgot sometimes that he had no secrets from the woman beside him. She knew things about him and his family that he didn't even know himself, it seemed. But he promised himself he'd know everything there was to know about her before they parted ways.

He smiled to himself, just thinking about her confronting Constance. That must have been something to see. He wished he hadn't missed it.

But there seemed to be a lot of things he'd missed while she and Patrick were framing him.

He studied Angie, wondering why she'd kept that one photograph. "Tell me how the con works," he said, and saw her flinch. "Tell me how the one you and Angie cooked up for me worked. Really. I'm dying to hear. And we have lots of time before our plane lands in Houston."

And he needed to be reminded right now just how dangerous the woman next to him really was.

JACK SETTLED INTO HIS SEAT, the look on his face making her uneasy. It was clear that he wasn't going to take no for an answer.

"Tell me how Angie set me up that day in the park," he said. "You were in on it, right?"

Her heart ached as she met his gaze. "Yes, I was." The memory of that day filled her with so much regret, it hurt to look at him. What ever had made her think she could pull off this charade? Just being this close to Jack and still lying to him was killing her.

"Well?" he said, crossing his arms over his chest and waiting as if he had all night. He did.

She thought back to that day, the first day she came face-to-face with Jack Donovan in the park. A beautiful spring day in early May.

"READY?"

Angelina adjusted her earpiece as she glanced out the hotel suite window. "Ready." After all this time, she was more than ready.

"He's on his way down," Maria said into her ear. "Ten minutes and counting."

"Got it." She checked her watch, then glanced across the street at the mirrored steel monolith of

Donovan, Inc. It gleamed in the morning sun. Such an easy target. Just like the man behind the building.

She watched Jack Donovan come out the front door, stop to talk to the doorman for a moment and walk south, just as he had every day for the past week. His step was brisk and light. He unbuttoned his suit jacket as he walked and looked around, the sun on his face. Thirty-six, successful and a paragon of virtue, he was a man on top of the world.

She checked the time. Jack Donovan was also a creature of habit. Didn't he know that being this predictable made him an easy mark?

Picking up her purse, she took one last look in the mirror by the door of her hotel room and smiled at the image staring back at her as she made sure her long, dark curly hair hid the earpiece. She even smelled of money, she thought, breathing in the expensive perfume she'd dabbed behind her ears. She ran a hand over the fine fabric of the suit she wore, the gray skirt cut just above her knee, modest but accentuating her legs.

Jack's ideal woman. He just didn't know it yet.

She took the elevator down, in no hurry. She knew exactly where to find him. The same place he was every day at this time. The park. It was only a short walk.

She followed the scent of the lunch cart and saw Jack lathering his daily hot dog with mustard, relish and sauerkraut. He took a big bite, closing his eyes, chewing for a moment, then smiling, making the hot dog vendor laugh.

Jack ate as he walked toward the duck pond, careful to save some of the bun. The ducks welcomed him, all waddling or swimming toward him for the treat he threw them each day. He walked on, nodding, smiling, stopping to throw back a ball to a young boy and his dog.

"This guy is too much," Maria replied in her ear, after Angie had described his movements.

A man who loves hot dogs, ducks, kids and mongrel mutts. She glanced at her watch and headed for the other side of the park, circling from the opposite direction.

She'd walked this stretch at least two dozen times to get her gait down. Timing was everything. And luck, she thought, unconsciously reaching for the amulet she always wore on the chain around her neck, hidden under her blouse today. Her father had taught her to plan for every possible occurrence. But her grandmother knew the importance of luck when it came to a good con. Her grandmother had given her and Maria each an amulet when they were just girls. Angie had never taken hers off.

She glanced at her watch, then up at the next park entrance. "Mark in sight," she said quietly. Jack Donovan was just coming out of the trees. She should intersect with him in one minute.

"Right on time. We're rolling. Good luck."

She kept walking, keeping Jack in sight as the two paths of the park intersected at the busy street. This is where Jack always turned to the left and circled back around through another portion of the park, returning to his office and work.

Today, with luck and years of practice, Angelina planned to change Jack's routine, change his world forever.

As he reached the sidewalk and started to turn, she stepped across the sidewalk and grassy boulevard, pretending to look for a taxi. Being the noon hour, it was next to impossible to get a cab on this side of the park. It was the reason she'd chosen this spot. Along with two lanes of busy bumper-to-bumper traffic, there was a narrow road that cut through the park and merged at this very point. That road had been closed by a repair crew ten minutes ago. Leave nothing to chance.

She stepped out into the street, arm raised as if she'd seen a cab in the traffic. The car came out of the park road, tires squealing, making Jack look up.

He saw her. Even with her back to him, she could feel his gaze on her, his concern for her almost palpable. Predictable Jack Donovan. This was almost too easy, she thought as the car bore down on her.

He tackled her an instant before the car would have hit her, taking her down in the grass along the boulevard. All those years of playing football. Jack Donovan had also stayed in shape.

She'd known that he would save her. The risk this time had been minimal. After months of study, she knew Jack Donovan better than he knew himself.

"Are you hurt?" he asked anxiously as he pushed himself up on one elbow to look down at her.

She actually did feel a little dazed. This was the first time she'd been this close to him. She'd known his eyes were blue—just like his father's—but they were a light denim like soft, worn jeans. His lashes were like his hair, blond as sunshine.

"What happened?" she asked, trying to sit up.

"Some fool came around that corner going way too fast."

Jack still sounded shaken. It must have been closer than she had planned it.

"I could have been killed," she whispered, and met his gaze.

"Are you really all right?" he asked, concern in his expression, in all that blue denim.

She nodded as he helped her to her feet. "Thank you. I owe you…my life."

He almost blushed as he handed her the purse she'd dropped. "Let's not get carried away. I'm just glad you're all right."

She nodded and looked down. Her suit was grass stained, her silk stockings torn at the knee and one of her high heels broken off. A hole in a stocking was bad luck. She pushed the thought away. Her luck was going fine. Better than fine, she thought, looking up into Jack's handsome face.

"I can't tell you how lucky I feel right now."

He laughed at that, a laugh filled with relief. Then he noticed that she was limping.

"It's just my shoe," she said, and pulled off the broken shoe as well as the other expensive high heel.

"I hope you don't have far to go," he said as his gaze moved from her stockinged feet to her face. He seemed much shyer than she would have thought. He glanced toward the street. "I'll get you a cab."

"Actually, I've changed my mind. I was going to the Institute of Art Museum, but under the circumstances…" She held up her broken high heel shoe. "I think I'll just walk back to the hotel."

"Where are you staying?"

"The Carlton Arms." She looked up at him, knowing exactly what he would say.

"Let me walk you, then—that is, if you don't mind."

"No," she said with a small laugh. "I'd love the

company, and maybe people won't think I'm crazy for going barefoot if you're with me.''

There was only a moment's hesitation. He quickly slipped off his shoes and socks, stuffed his socks into his pocket, and, his shoes dangling from his fingers, grinned at her. ''Let them think we're both crazy. It's spring and I can't remember the last time I went barefoot and felt new grass between my toes.''

Angelina was seldom surprised. It was bad for business. But for such a predictable man, Jack Donovan seemed to be capable of surprising her. That should have warned her. Instead, it delighted her.

She smiled up at him. ''It is a beautiful day for a walk in the park, isn't it?''

''Do you like ice cream?'' Jack asked, sounding as excited as a boy. ''What's your favorite?''

She laughed and had to think. ''Rocky Road.''

He studied her, then smiled. ''Rocky Road, it is. By the way, my name's Jack. Jack Donovan.''

''Angelina Grant, but please call me Angie,'' she said, returning his smile.

''Angie,'' he said, repeating it softly, his smile broadening. ''I like that.''

Jack held out his hand and she took it as they cut through the grassy park toward the ice-cream vendor.

''Nice work,'' Maria said in her ear.

Just like that, Angie had changed Jack's routine—and was about to change his life, as well. And not for the better. Even then the thought had given her an odd feeling, one she had little experience with: guilt. Vengeance always comes at a high price, her father used to say. But in the end, all debts must be paid. And Jack, like all marks, was going to pay dearly.

He had bought them each a double-scoop ice-cream

cone and they ate them as they sat and talked on one of the park benches. She wasn't surprised when he had asked her to dinner. But she had been surprised when he suggested a small barbecue joint he knew of, instead of a four-star restaurant. Her surprise should have put up another red flag.

But she'd ignored it, blinded maybe by the spring day. More likely, by the man.

Even later, when Jack's friend Patrick Ryerson had showed up unexpectedly at dinner, she hadn't been worried. Patrick wouldn't be a problem because she knew that within no time she'd have Jack Donovan right where she wanted him.

Getting to Jack had been easy. In fact, it had almost been too easy.

She smiled ruefully at the thought. She should have known that nothing was going to go the way she'd planned it. Well, she did now.

Now that it was too late.

Chapter Ten

"So it had nothing to do with money," Jack said sarcastically when she'd finished. "It was just a job."

She heard the edge to his voice, part anger, part fear that she knew more about his father than he did. "It is seldom about money, although money is usually the exchange medium."

Jack laughed. "You fleece people. Why don't you just be honest? It isn't about vengeance or settling a score. It's about you taking some poor sucker for everything he's worth. I became your mark because your family saw the article in *Fortune* magazine about me. It had nothing to do with my father."

"You inherited the construction company from your father," she said calmly. "He started with nothing, right? First remodeling one of the houses in your area, then starting his own business as he began buying run-down buildings, getting low-income housing loans and rebuilding the neighborhood."

Jack's gaze narrowed. "That's right."

"Later, he moved the two of you out of the neighborhood and started building new subdivisions, but he made his money in your old neighborhood, building houses for the poor—just like you started to do a year ago, after your father died, and taking kickbacks from substandard construction and materials.''

''That's a lie!''

''Did your dossier mention that I had relatives who came from that Houston neighborhood?'' From his expression it was clear he hadn't known. ''I had a great-aunt on my mother's side who lived in one of the houses your father built. She was killed in a fire. The fire department found a short in the electrical wiring. That's when it first came out about the substandard materials.''

Jack was shaking his head. ''If that were true—''

''Your father hired a lawyer, paid off some people and nothing ever came of it. But part of the deal he made was to stop building houses in our neighborhood and never return.''

Her dark eyes met his, hers warm as honey. Jack thought he glimpsed regret in that gaze and something far worse, pity.

''It would be smart for you to stay away, as well,'' she said.

''Don't worry about me, okay?''

''Fine,'' she said, and looked away. ''I just don't think you have any idea how ugly it could get.''

''I grew up on the streets of Houston in a rough neighborhood. I was pretty much on my own from the time my mother left and my father…'' He stopped and smiled ruefully. ''Oh, I forgot, you know all of that.'' And more. ''At least, you think you do.''

Jack frowned and looked out the plane window at the darkness. He'd been eleven when they'd left the old neighborhood. It had always bothered him that they never went back. When he'd missed his friends and complained to his father, Kelly Donovan had told him to make new friends. When he'd insisted on seeing old friends, Patrick had been brought to their house in the new neighborhood. Jack wasn't allowed to go back to the old neighborhood. He'd thought it was because the place held too many bad memories for his father. Apparently, if Angie was telling the truth, it did.

"So why didn't your family go after my father then?" he asked.

"Angie and I were only five and my father was busy raising us and making a living," she said.

"Your father had bigger fish to fry," Jack said. "Talk about the pot calling the kettle black."

"The difference is that my father didn't swindle innocent, trusting people," she snapped. "A confidence game only works if the mark has thief's blood."

"Thief's blood?"

"You can't cheat an honest man," she said simply. "A mark must have larceny in his veins. Oh, he thinks he's honest. He's rationalized his behavior to the point where he never admits, even to himself, that he's not. The mark has to be a willing participant. All confidence men do is play upon the mark's weakness."

Well, Jack knew what his weakness was: Angie's lies. "So after all these years your family decided I should pay for my father's alleged sins?"

"My family hadn't forgotten about your father or what he did," she said. "Vengeance to the LaGrands is a fine art. It can sometimes take years. We have extraordinary patience."

"So it was just a matter of time," Jack said. "You

were waiting until I had enough money to make it worth your while.''

She shook her head. ''One of my distant cousins hired us. He's related to the great-aunt who died in the fire and still has friends who live down in that neighborhood. He saw the article in *Fortune* magazine—and heard you had started building substandard housing down there, just like your father.''

He shook his head, more out of disbelief than denial. ''So everyone thought the acorn hadn't fallen far from the tree.'' He was dumbfounded. ''Was the plan to ruin me financially?''

''We were going to make you an offer we believed you wouldn't refuse.''

''A way to make even more money,'' he said. ''And when I went for that, I'd lose my shirt, right?''

''Right. We would put you out of business for good.''

''And make yourself a nice, tidy, little profit,'' he noted. ''Only Angie never made me an offer.''

''No.'' She looked away. ''Angie started falling in love with you and having doubts about your guilt.''

''Until Patrick convinced her I was even worse than she'd first thought.''

She nodded. ''That about sums it up.''

He could see now why Angie had fallen for Patrick's lies—if what she'd told him was the truth.

As the plane began its descent to the Houston airport, he asked, ''What was the name of the lawyer who allegedly got my father off?''

''Montague Cooke.''

IT WAS LATE, dark and raining in Houston. With only carry-on luggage, they caught a cab right away.

Angie felt tense, her skin feverish, nerves raw, fearing the slightest touch or look from Jack would give her away. Their verbal sparring on the plane had left her with a headache. Lying to him about her identity was exhausting. She wanted desperately to reach out to him, to tell him everything.

But she knew her words would be wasted. He had branded her a liar, a cheat, a con. And his disgust of her kept her silent. She'd seen his expression when she told him about his father. *He hadn't known.* She'd stake her reputation on that. And although Jack wouldn't understand this, a good reputation was very important to a confidence woman.

But even if Jack really was innocent—every instinct told her he was—and she could clear his name, she didn't kid herself that he could ever forgive her.

She tried not to think about that, concentrating instead on the task at hand. From an early age, she'd learned to focus on one problem at a time. It had always seen her through rough times before. She knew it would this time, as well.

As long as she didn't forget she was Maria. That wasn't hard because in her mind the old Angelina LaGrand truly was dead. As soon as things were settled with Jack and Patrick, she was going off the grift. Going straight. Let Maria continue with their family's legacy. Angie was done. Too bad it was too late as far as Jack was concerned.

"I need to make a stop," he said, his head turned toward the passing city streets outside the taxi.

She was too tired for another stop. "You could drop me at a hotel—"

He swung his gaze to her. Even in the darkness of the back of the cab, she could see the hard blue of his eyes. "I told you. I'm not letting you out of my sight. This shouldn't take long and there's no reason to stay at a hotel. I have a perfectly adequate guest room at my penthouse."

She looked away, wondering where they were going first. She hadn't heard what address he'd given the driver. Twenty minutes later, the taxi pulled into the circular driveway of a large brick house in a better part of Houston.

Montague Cooke opened the door in his robe, looking as if they'd gotten him out of bed. Not surprising since it was now nearly two in the morning.

"What in the—" Montie's gaze went past Jack to Angie.

"I need to talk to you," Jack said, and Montie moved to one side to let them both in. "You've met Angelina LaGrand."

"I would advise you not to say anything in front of this woman," Montie said, closing the door behind them.

Jack smiled. "There isn't anything I could say that would surprise this woman. She knows me better than I know myself. I just need to know one thing. How did my father make his money?"

"Your father?"

"Answer my question."

"He built houses, you know that," Montie snapped. "You woke me up to ask me that?"

"Did you get him out of a mess in the old neighborhood involving substandard construction and another fire that caused some deaths?" Jack asked.

"Lawyer-client confidentially doesn't allow me to—" Montie glanced toward Angie. "Jack, I warned you about this woman."

"He was my father, dammit, Montie," Jack said tersely. "It's true, isn't it? That's what you were trying to tell me the other day. All that talk about how I wouldn't be the first contractor to make my fortune through kickbacks and substandard work and materials." He let out an oath, anger and disappointment like a vise around his chest.

"When did you become my father's lawyer?"

"Your father and I were friends, you know that, from the old neighborhood," Montie said.

"Before you became a lawyer, before he made all his money?"

Montie met his gaze. "What are you asking me, Jack?"

He knew what he was asking, but did he really want to hear the answer? "My father put you through law school. Where did that money come from?"

"I think you already know the answer, Jack," Montie said softly.

Jack stood looking at the lawyer, each breath a labor, his heart hammering so loudly he could barely hear himself speak. "Thief's blood. Like father, like son, right?"

"Jack, this sort of thing is done every day," Montie said sharply. "Your father knew that building nice homes down there was a waste of good money. Those people don't appreciate anything you do for them. Look how—"

Jack was shaking his head as he backed toward the door.

"—those people live. They crowd a dozen people into those houses and live like animals. Jack, your father was no different than other businessmen—"

Jack opened the door and looked over at Angie.

The pain he saw in her eyes hurt him worse than his own. Thief's blood. Now, finally, he knew why Angie had come after him.

THE TAXI WAITING outside Montague Cooke's took them to Jack's penthouse. It was nearly three in the morning. Rain drummed on the roof of the cab and the wipers flap-flapped into the silence that had settled like concrete between her and Jack in the back seat.

Jack hadn't said a word since they'd left Montie's. Angie wanted to reach out to him, to say something that would make him feel better, but didn't know what it would be. She could tell that he was devastated to learn that everything she'd told him about his father was true.

"Jack—"

"Don't," he said, and looked over at her. "Just don't, okay? This doesn't change anything between us. I'm not my father. I didn't take kickbacks. I didn't know I was building substandard housing. I'm a fool, but I'm not a crook."

At the penthouse, Jack showed Angie to the guest room.

"I'll be right across the hall with my door open. Leave yours open. Don't worry. Your virtue is safe." His look said he questioned if she had any virtue to lose.

"Do you intend to sleep with one eye open all night?" she asked.

"A man would be crazy to let down his guard around a woman like you."

"I'll take that as a compliment."

"*You* probably would."

She hadn't realized how hard this was going to be.

Jack kicked off his shoes and sprawled on his bed. She could see him watching her. She locked herself in the bathroom and took a hot shower, standing under the water, trying hard to forget that Jack was just yards away from her, listening to the water cascading over her.

He thinks you're Maria.

Yes. If only she could tell him the truth. But that would only make proving she hadn't helped Patrick frame him more difficult.

Dressed in silk pajamas and a matching robe, she stepped out of the bathroom, hoping she'd stalled long enough that he was asleep. He wasn't. Both blue eyes were open.

Jack took her in, from her wet hair to the silk that clothed her to her bare feet. She felt her face flush. Desire shot through her.

She moved to her bed, made a project out of turning down her sheets. She didn't look at him, but she knew he was still watching her. She climbed into bed and turned out the light.

He turned out his light without a word.

She wanted to tell him everything. How she'd wanted out of the con because she'd fallen in love with him. How she had been planning to tell him. How vulnerable she'd felt at even the thought of admitting her love for him—and how afraid.

So much so that when she heard that he'd lied and cheated she'd believed it. All her life she had gone after dishonest, corrupt men to con out of their illegally gained fortunes. It had left her distrustful and wary.

She wanted, too, to admit to him how Patrick had

conned her. She was glad her father wasn't still alive to see how she'd blown this.

"Jack? Are you asleep?" No answer. "There's something I have to tell you. I'm not Maria. I'm Angie and…" Her voice dropped to a whisper. "I love you."

In the bed across the hall, Jack lay perfectly still, staring up at the ceiling, pretending he hadn't heard, afraid to believe there might actually be a little truth in her words. He wasn't ready to trust her. He wondered if he ever would be.

Chapter Eleven

Patrick woke the next morning with a start, sitting up in the bed, confused for a moment as to where he was. Palm Springs. That's right. He thought of the shimmering pool just outside the glass doors, the palms, the tanned hotties in their string bikinis, and laid back into the pillows on the bed.

Against his will, the empty wastebasket drew his gaze. Still empty. What did he think? That the shoe he'd taken out to the Dumpster last night would find its way back? He smiled at how ridiculous that was and looked over at the clock on the bedside table to see the time.

His heart stopped. Lying curled up like a deadly snake right next to his head was a silver chain. At the end of it was the pendant that had been around Angie's neck when she'd plummeted to her death in the canyon. Next to it was the wedding ring that had been on her finger—the diamond winking mockingly at him.

Panicked, he threw back the covers and leapt from the bed, staggering backward, his hand covering his mouth for fear he might start screaming. Or throw up.

He had to get out of here. But where could he go? She'd found him every place he'd gone.

The wedding ring winked at him again from the bedside table. He frowned and stepped over to the night table, cautiously picking up the ring. Cheap glass. He hurriedly scooped up the pendant. Also glass.

They were the fake pair he'd planned to put on Angie *before* she died. No reason to let her take real diamonds with her. He'd hidden the fake duplicates in his shaving bag. So how had they ended up on the nightstand?

The phone rang, making him practically jump out of his skin. He grabbed the receiver to keep it from ringing again and said hello without thinking that it might be Angie's voice.

"Mr. Ryerson?"

"Sheriff Truebow." Patrick's legs buckled and he had to sit down. "I hope you have some good news for me."

"I'm not sure there is any good news in a case like this," the sheriff said soberly.

"Yes, yes—you know what I mean. Tell me you've found Angie so I can lay my wife to rest," Patrick said.

"I wish I could. But we did find her purse," Truebow said.

Her purse? The one Patrick had thrown into the gorge yesterday morning. "But you still haven't found her."

"Not yet. I'm sorry. The river is running muddy still, and with a bird hunter still lost in the woods... Can I reach you at this number for a while?"

"Sure," Patrick said, and moved to open the drapes so he could see the pool and the palms.

He hung up and picked up the jewelry from the nightstand, no longer fearing any of Angie's superstition about bad karma. Cheap glass. Definitely not the pendant or the ring that Angie had been wearing. Too bad, though. He would have pawned both pieces if he had them.

He glanced toward the pool. Still no body. Because she was alive? Or because her body was caught in a limb under the Clark's Fork River in Montana?

Looking down at the jewelry in his hand, he figured Jack had either found out about its existence or just stumbled across it in the shaving bag. Either way, it meant Jack was here in Palm Springs. Had even been in Patrick's room.

He felt a chill as he glanced outside. This should have been paradise. He should be lounging by the pool right now. Jack should be in jail in Houston. Angie should be decomposed and floating past a couple of fishermen in Montana. Patrick should have his hands on at least some of her money by now.

He looked around the room, wanting to break something. Smash it to smithereens. His head ached from the fury. He couldn't stand still. Needed desperately to get out of here, out of this town, out of this state, out of this.

But where would he go? He had no money and even Angie's credit card would soon be maxed out. Then what?

He couldn't think, couldn't just keep running. He would call his lawyer in less than an hour. He would get this all cleared up. He took a breath. It couldn't possibly be as bad as it seemed right now, he thought, glancing again toward the pool.

The water shimmered in the morning sunlight, the palm trees swayed in the warm desert breeze and a couple of bikini-clad cuties giggled and splashed at the edge of the pool.

It was paradise. He took his swimming trunks from his suitcase and changed. He'd go for a swim, catch some rays, clear his head. When he came back, he'd call the cops on Jack. Then call Lester for the good news.

Going into the bathroom, he admired his reflection in the mirror. He looked damn good. Angie should have been crazy for him. Instead the stupid woman only had eyes for Jack.

He tried not to think about that as he grabbed a towel, crossed the room and threw open the sliding glass door. As he started to step out, he spotted a woman in a bright-red, one-piece swimsuit standing beside the pool.

Angie. He froze, heart seizing up in his chest. She waved at him and dived into the water.

THE NEXT MORNING it was still raining in Houston. Angie woke from a restless night to find Jack up and dressed and standing at the living room window.

"I want to see Constance first," he said.

She nodded, a little surprised he was going after the infidelity part first. She pulled the silk robe around her as she headed for the bathroom. "I'll get a shower and won't be a minute. Unless you want to go get some breakfast?"

He smiled at that. "I wouldn't dream of going anywhere without you."

"You're too sweet."

"Aren't I, though."

CONSTANCE WHITAKER was an attorney with Harper, Johnson, Curtis, Whitaker and Whitaker. Angie thought she couldn't dislike Constance Whitaker any more than she had after seeing the photographs of her and Jack together—and confronting her a few weeks before. She was wrong.

"Jack!" Constance said, blue eyes wide with surprise when she saw them enter her office unannounced. She came around her desk, blond and beautiful, tall and slim, carrying herself with an air of privilege.

Angie knew more than she ever had wanted to know about the woman. Constance was from old money and a respected family. She'd gone to the best schools, was smart and enormously successful—and ruthless. She'd lost only one case—the case she'd been working on when Jack had broken off their engagement.

Had she loved Jack that much? Or was Constance Whitaker more upset because their breakup was as highly publicized in the press as their engagement had been?

Jack stood stony straight as Constance embraced him and gave him a kiss on the lips.

She seemed amused when he didn't respond, and turned to Angie. "And who do we have here?"

Before Angie could speak, Jack said, "Don't you recognize her?"

Constance looked at him with total innocence, but Angie saw a muscle in her cheek jump. "I'm sorry, you'll have to refresh my memory."

"She had a talk with you a few weeks ago about some photographs," Jack said.

Constance lifted one finely shaped brow and flicked

her gaze at Angie. "Oh yes. Then I guess we've already met." She turned her attention again to Jack and smiled. "Darling, I hope you're here to ask me to represent you in this little mess you've gotten yourself into."

"Not exactly," Jack said. "Constance, when was the last time you and I were together?"

"What?" Her smile slipped a little.

"It's a simple enough question," he said.

"One that you should know the answer to."

"Oh, I do. I just want to clear it up, in case there is any misunderstanding," he said.

"Jack, are you sure you want to discuss this—" she shot a look at Angie "—in front of *her?*" Her gaze shifted back to him, her look suggestive and sensual.

Angie gritted her teeth.

"I know you couldn't have really forgotten the last time we were together," Constance purred.

"When."

The attorney's blue eyes narrowed, her features hardening. "Nine days ago, Jack. Why? Did you think I'd been counting them? Well, I haven't." She turned and went around her desk to sit in the large leather chair that blocked out the sun from the bank of windows behind her. "I know I'm not the only one you sleep with. It isn't like I think you will ever be happy with just one woman."

Jack laughed, surprising Angie. "Constance, you missed your calling. You should have gone into theater. Oh, I forgot, you're an attorney. You specialize in theater, don't you?"

She leaned back in the chair and crossed her legs.

"Jack, I'm disappointed in you. Ripping off people who are desperate for a decent place to live. Stealing from the poor to line your own pockets. And this from a man who hates liars and cheats—"

"I know you didn't do it for money," Jack interrupted. "You're greedy, God knows. But you did this purely out of spite. Payback, right? You couldn't stand the thought that I might have found a woman I actually wanted to marry."

Angie shot him a look. Was he serious? He had wanted to marry her?

"I made the mistake of telling Patrick," Jack continued without looking at Angie. "I had picked out a ring and was going to ask her on Thanksgiving."

Angie's pulse pounded. She tried not to look stunned. Or heartbroken. But she was both. He'd planned to ask her to marry him. The damage was much worse than she'd thought.

But neither Jack nor Constance seemed aware of her shock or disappointment. They were glaring at each other.

Constance had gone rigid in her chair, her cheeks two angry slashes of red. "You got me back into your bed knowing you were going to ask another woman to marry you?"

"You always were a lousy liar, Constance," Jack said with a humorless laugh. "But we both know there is no way I would have invited you back into my bed. No chance in hell."

"Get out of my office," she snapped. "I hope you rot in prison."

"If you were my lawyer, I'm sure I would," he said. "Come on," he said to Angie. "We're finished here."

"Charming woman," Angie said once they'd left the office building and were heading for the rental car, trying to sound like Maria.

"You still believe I slept with her while I was with...Angie?" Jack asked as he climbed behind the wheel.

He looked over at her. There was hope in his eyes, a need for her to believe him.

She didn't want to believe anything that woman said. She especially didn't want to believe that Jack had slept with her nine days ago. "I don't *want* to believe her."

"Well, I guess that's a start." He smiled. "I get the feeling sometimes you're trying to convince yourself I'm worth helping."

"You could be right about that."

He started the car. "Let's see if Patrick left those photographs at his apartment. I assume you still have a key?"

PATRICK SCRAMBLED OUT of his room, pushing his way past a horde of vacationers to race to the place where he'd seen Angie dive.

The pool area was cluttered with bodies in swimsuits of every color, both in and out of the water. He kept glimpsing flashes of red material or long dark hair, but when the swimmers surfaced, they were never Angie.

He worked his way hurriedly along the side of the pool. It was long and curved in a graceful sweep around the side of the building, connecting with yet another pool and another, circling the resort.

He stumbled over the chair of one sunbather,

pushed past a half dozen screaming, wet children and leapt over several people lounging at the edge of the pool, feeling their glares.

Where was she? He hadn't just imagined her. Of that he was certain. This was no hallucination. Nor had she been any look-alike. It had been Angie.

He slowed, suddenly afraid he was wrong, suddenly frightened. The hot desert sun lolled in the blue sky above the palms, dazing him with its brightness. He felt dizzy, confused, disoriented in a sea of tanned bodies and a kaleidoscope of bright-colored swimwear.

He glanced around. All the rooms looked the same. Glass and tan stucco. Palms and blue-green pools. He felt lost, like a man who couldn't remember where he'd left his car. Or worse, how to drive it when he found it.

Some kid did a cannonball next to him. Water shot out in a drenching tidal wave, soaking him. He swore loudly, now wet and angry.

As he moved away from the pool, he saw that one of the sliding glass doors to the rooms stood open just as he'd left it, and that lying on the floor where he'd dropped it was his towel.

He had run all the way around the building and was back where he'd started. Relief made him weak. Needing to sit down, he rushed toward his room, stopping short at the doorway.

His heart leapt to his throat. He tried to swallow, but couldn't. A trail of small, wet footprints led from the edge of the pool directly into his room. *Angie.*

ANGIE'S LATE-NIGHT confession was still killing Jack as she opened the door to Patrick's apartment. It was

the last place he wanted to go—especially with her—
but he wanted those photographs, wanted them destroyed. As if that would change anything.

"Well, hello, Ms. Grant," said the doorman. "I'm
sorry, it's Mrs. Ryerson now, right?" The man obviously didn't watch the news.

"No, I kept Grant," Angie said, smiling. "How
are you today, Henry? That arthritis still bothering
you?"

"Not so bad today, Ms. Grant," he said, holding
the door open. "But thanks for asking."

Jack felt the man's gaze shift to him.

"Will Mr. Ryerson be joining you?" Henry asked
pointedly.

"No, I had to come back on business. I'll be re-
joining Patrick out in Palm Springs tomorrow," she
said smoothly as she walked through the open doorway. Jack followed her with a nod to the doorman.

"Give him my regards," Henry said.

"I will." She swept into the small lobby and went
right to the elevator, and stopped to dig in her purse.

"Did you forget something?" Henry asked.

"My keys. Can you believe it?"

Obviously Henry could. He smiled and left his post
to go to a small office off to their right. He opened
the door and brought out an extra key.

"I'll return it in a few minutes," Angie promised.

"No need. You just keep it," Henry said.

Jack could feel the man's gaze on him.

Angie thanked him and pressed the button for the
fifth floor. The doors closed and the elevator began
to rise slowly.

"You know about the doorman's arthritis?" he
asked, not looking at Angie.

"It's my business to know everything Angie knew," she said.

So it seemed.

"Patrick close to the doorman?" he asked, already knowing the answer.

"I would imagine Henry is calling Patrick's cell phone as we speak," she said. "Patrick pays him for information on the other tenants."

Jack shot her a look.

"Information is often as good as money," she said.

"That sounds like a confidence woman's motto."

"I have it embroidered on a pillow at home," she quipped.

"Where's home?"

She shook her head as the elevator door opened on the fifth floor. "Wherever I am."

"Homey."

She shot him a look. "Like your penthouse is a home."

"I don't spend much time there," he defended, then wondered why he felt he needed to. It was a penthouse, for crying out loud, decorated by a professional interior designer, and she was right. It had never felt like home.

He noticed her hesitate after she unlocked Patrick's apartment. What was she worried about? Something they would find? Or memories from the days before the wedding, when she stayed here with Patrick?

He tried not to think about that as he followed her into the apartment. The air was warm and muggy as if the place had been closed up without air-conditioning for longer than a few days. It was instantly clear that Patrick had planned never to return.

The place was a mess of empty boxes and newspapers, everything he might have valued packed up and gone.

The apartment was small, with an open floor plan: small kitchen, living room, bedroom, bath. It looked as if the place had come furnished, the furniture all big and bulky and drab.

Angie moved straight through to the bedroom. She obviously knew the way. The thought did nothing for his disposition.

Jack could see that the bed had been stripped. He turned away and heard Angie come back out.

"The photos are gone."

He wasn't surprised. As she walked past the couch, she picked up a white blouse. Hers? That's when he noticed the stack of bedding at the far end of the couch. This was where she'd slept? The realization hit him like a brick.

He glanced up to see her looking at him. He tried to hide his surprise, but obviously failed.

"You thought Angie was sleeping with Patrick."

"That seemed the logical conclusion, since they were getting married," he said, sounding as defensive as he felt.

She gave him a look that made him feel small.

"I guess you're out of luck on the photos."

"I think I know where at least the one photograph was shot from. Constance had the entertainment center built for me." He nodded. "Want to guess who had a carpenter friend of his build it for her?"

"Patrick," Angie said on a breath.

Jack nodded. "He must have known Constance was cheating on me." He shook his head, amazed.

''It looks like Patrick knew more about what was going on than I did.'' The story of his life.

''Blackmail. That must be how Patrick got her to go along with this,'' Angie said. ''That means she won't give up Patrick to us.''

Jack agreed. He hated to think who Patrick might have photographed Constance with. Someone significant enough that Constance would still lie to protect herself. ''Let's get out of here.''

PATRICK FOLLOWED THE WET prints slowly into the shadowy room. Angie could still be in here, waiting for him. Or maybe she'd only stopped by to leave him something.

The room was cool and dark after the hot morning sun, and he was still wet from that damn kid splashing him. He blinked, blinded for a moment. There was nothing on the bed. Nothing new beside it on the nightstand. He stepped in farther and stumbled as he caught the heady scent of her perfume.

She *had* been here! He was breathing hard again, each ragged breath taking in the smell of her. The carpet was wet where she'd walked. He could make out her tracks, see where she'd wandered through his room, stopping at the bed and the nightstand, then at the closet and finally the bathroom.

He followed the tracks, seeing the telltale droplets of water where she'd touched his things. He trembled with rage, cold to his very soul, feeling violated and powerless.

What did she want? Had she taken something? Or left something? What was she doing alive?

The carpet was wet as he slowly moved toward the

bathroom, the only room he hadn't checked. The image of Angie's drowned body floating in his bathtub flashed into his mind. He thought for a moment that he heard the drip of the bathtub faucet.

Bracing himself, he peered around the corner of the door into the bathroom. The tub was empty. He gripped the doorjamb, sick with relief. This woman was trying to drive him crazy and it was working.

He was starting to turn back to the room when he felt the dampness on the rug, the tracks headed for the door to the breezeway outside.

He rushed over, opened the door and looked out. No woman in a red swimsuit, though the damp footprints on the terra-cotta tiles were undeniable.

He closed and locked the door, then leaned against it. She was gone. He could almost pretend she'd never been here, if it weren't for the wet spots on his carpet and the scent of her lingering in the air.

Worse, he thought surveying the room, she'd left him something. He was sure of it. And it wasn't a shoe. Or cheap jewelry. No, not this time. Fear gripped him as he imagined a bomb under his pillow. Or a deadly snake. Or— He stepped cautiously toward the bed.

The phone rang, and he clutched his chest. The phone rang again. He hurriedly picked up the receiver.

"Patrick, you son of a bitch."

He jerked back at the vehemence in the voice. "Constance? What the hell are you doing calling me?" he demanded. She knew better than to contact him. Their business was finished. "I told you not to—"

"Jack was here, in my office. Just minutes ago. With Angelina Grant," Constance spat out.

His hands began to shake. "That's impossible."

"I saw them both with my own eyes. He wanted to know about the damn photographs. He knew, Patrick. Damn you, he knew. How long do you think it's going to take him to find out everything else, as well?"

"Settle down," Patrick said, more to himself than to Constance. His heart was racing, he was having trouble breathing again. At this rate he'd have a stroke. "You're sure it was Jack? And Angie?"

"I just told you—"

"The woman was a look-alike," Patrick said, wondering if that were true. But then, who had he seen dive into the pool? Who had left the wet footprints on his carpet?

He tried to focus on the larger problem: Jack was in Houston. Patrick had been so sure Jack would follow him to Palm Springs. Damn. There went his plan to have Jack arrested.

"This woman was no look-alike," Constance snapped.

"I've seen her. The resemblance *is* uncanny," Patrick said. "Jack hired her to try to scare me."

"What?"

"That explains how she cleaned out the checking account," he said to himself, and swore. She must have a fake ID or something. "I knew Jack was behind this."

"Behind what? Patrick, you slimy little weasel. You told me you'd destroyed the other negatives and removed the camera equipment."

"Calm down," he ordered. "I did." A lie. "I have

everything under control. You just keep your cool, damn you. Jack isn't going to find out anything. There is *nothing* to find out. Do you understand?'' He took a breath, the sound of his heart too loud in his ears. "How did you get this number?'' he demanded, suddenly not sure of anything.

"I saw the news report on television about Angie's alleged death. I called that sheriff up there. He gave me your hotel number when I told him I was your lawyer.''

"That was a stupid thing to do,'' he said. The sheriff would think he was guilty of something, having a lawyer trying to reach him. Damn her.

"Getting me involved in this was a stupid thing to do,'' she said, her words pelting him like stones.

"I don't remember you kicking up too much of a fuss at the time,'' Patrick noted. "In fact, you were quite keen on the idea of sticking it to Jack.''

"You know damn well why I did it. And I wouldn't have if I'd known you were going to get Jack arrested for arson and your wife was going to take a nosedive off a cliff,'' she said. "If she's even really dead. Jack introduced her as Angie.''

"Yes, you would have. You didn't have a choice,'' Patrick retorted. "Believe me that wasn't Angie you saw.''

"If I find out that you lied to me, you little bastard... You better hope to hell I don't get dragged into this. I know enough about you to get your ass fried.'' She hung up.

He slammed down the phone. How dare that bitch threaten him! She had as much to lose as he did. Well, maybe not quite, considering she hadn't been in Montana at the time Angie died. If she truly was dead.

He told himself not to worry about Constance. She was too smart to open her mouth about any of their dealings.

It was Jack he was worried about. Jack was trying to scare him—and it was working. His heart was still banging in his chest. "You expected this," he said to himself. "So stop panicking. There is nothing to find. You covered your tracks. And it isn't like Jack would even know where to begin to unravel all the lies and deceptions you laid for him."

Damn Jack. Why couldn't he have just stayed in jail? Now he was asking a bunch of questions and dragging that look-alike around with him, freaking people out. And that's what worried him, that Angie look-alike.

He took a breath and glanced at the clock. One minute to eleven. Time to call his real attorney, Lester Burns. He picked up the phone, shaking with anticipation.

"Yeah," Lester Burns answered. "Too bad you're not as prompt on paying your bills."

Two things were clear. Lester had caller ID and Angie's credit card had gone through.

"Well, what did you find out?"

"Are you sitting down?"

He was too excited to sit down. Too anxious. "What?"

"What did this woman tell you?"

"That her family made their money in an import-export business and she's loaded," Patrick said.

Lester chuckled. "She's loaded, all right, but not with money. She's a con artist—you know, the kind of crook who fleeces you for everything you're worth. She's very high-class, though—only goes after the cream of the crop. Too high-class for you, so you couldn't have been her mark. How did you end up with her?''

Patrick couldn't breathe. ''What?''

''What part didn't you understand? Want me to talk slower? You've been duped. She lied. She doesn't come from money. She comes from a family of thieves,'' Lester said, and laughed again, obviously finding humor in the fact.

''The stocks and bonds she gave me—''

''Fakes,'' Lester said. ''I couldn't find any money anywhere—at least, not in the name of Grant. Because her name's LaGrand.'' Lester laughed harder. ''Oh, I'm sure she has money, but believe me, you'll never get your greedy hands on it. This woman is a professional. You've been swindled, chump, and by one of the best.'' Lester hung up, still snickering.

Patrick lowered the phone into the cradle, afraid to make any quick movements for fear he would come apart, fly into a million pieces. It amazed him how calm he was. He felt weightless, numb, almost like he was having an out-of-body experience. He feared he wasn't having a stroke because he'd already had it.

Swindled. Conned. Duped. Angie had tried to tell him he was making a mistake, that she wasn't rich. He had thought she was lying. Oh, she was lying, all right. About everything else.

''Too high-class for you, so you couldn't have been her mark.'' Lester's words rang in his ears.

Jack had been her mark! She'd said she was after Jack's money. She had been planning to take Jack for everything and Patrick had bungled into it.

He closed his eyes, his brain nothing but white

static, unable to comprehend just how stupid he'd been. Angie must have had a good laugh over his marrying her for her money—that is, she would have laughed if he hadn't been trying to kill her.

She only laughed until the Jeep hit bottom. So he guessed he had the last laugh, after all. *If* she was in that river, he amended, looking down at the wet footprints on his rug.

He slumped down on the bed. No fortune. No reason to have married her. No reason to have spent all his own money to deceive her. No reason to kill her. How could things get any worse?

He lifted his head slowly, knowing the answer to that. Jack was in Houston with someone who looked enough like Angie to fool Constance. And he was in Palm Springs....

He looked toward the pool, his heart already hammering at the thought of seeing the woman in the bright red swimsuit again.

Instead, he saw what Angie had left him.

Chapter Twelve

Back at Jack's penthouse apartment, he went straight to the bedroom, while she stopped just inside the front door, struck by how much she'd lost. She'd lost Jack. Fallen in love with a mark and ended up being the one taken. She'd almost paid for that mistake with her life. And she had no one to blame but herself.

"I found it," she heard Jack say.

She moved through the living room to the master bedroom. Jack was on the other side of the large entertainment center. He pointed to a camera hidden behind some ornate fretwork.

She stepped closer to inspect the camera. "These don't come cheap." No wonder Patrick was in dire straits right now financially. "It's the latest technology."

"Which means?" Jack asked.

"It's digital and can be accessed by computer much like e-mail." She stepped in front of the lens, then moved back toward the bed until she heard the soft *click*. "It's motion activated, but since you wouldn't want dozens of pictures of you walking past the camera lens, it's been programmed to focus only on the bed—and to shoot only when there is significant movement."

"I get the picture," he growled. "And you're telling me that Patrick was able to download the photographs without ever coming back here."

"Exactly."

"Did he have a computer at his apartment?"

She nodded. "He must have packed it up when he cleaned out everything else."

Jack raked a hand through his hair. "Too bad. I'd love to take a sledgehammer to it." He reached into the cabinet, ripped the camera out and smashed it under his boot.

"Feel better?" she asked.

He smiled. "Much. Hungry?"

The change of subject threw her for a moment. The same way Jack's grin and the warm faded-denim color of his eyes did.

"Why…yes."

"Good," he said. "Me, too. You like barbecue?"

"What Texas girl doesn't?"

He smiled, a broad, open smile that squeezed her heart like a fist. She was reminded of the man she'd met that day in the park. A man without a worry in the world. The man she'd fallen so desperately in love with.

"Come on," he said.

"THIS PLACE MAKES THE best barbecue in all of Texas," Jack said as he held the door open for her.

He seemed to be in a better mood after their visit to Patrick's apartment, and she suspected it had something to do with finding out that she—that is, Angie—had never slept with Patrick.

"Jack!" cried the owner, Tiny Durand, from back in the kitchen. "Good to see you! The usual?"

"And some ribs," Jack called back as he and Angie took their usual seat in the booth by the window. The place was empty—it was still early for most people even to be thinking about barbecue.

It had stopped raining. As the waitress slid a couple of sweet teas in front of them, the sun came out, making the late morning sparkle.

An omen? Angie could only hope.

She shifted her gaze from the now sunny day to Jack, and felt her pulse flutter at the look on his face. "What?"

"I was just thinking," he said. "About Angie."

She felt her face flush. Her heart kicked up a beat. "What about her?"

"I'm beginning to understand now why she fell for Patrick's lies," he said.

Her breath caught in her throat. "You no longer think she was in on framing you with Patrick?"

He shook his head. "I think she got taken in the same way I did."

She wanted to laugh and cry and let out a whoop. "What changed your mind?"

"You did."

"Me?" Her voice squeaked.

"You know her better than anyone," he said. "You said all along that she wouldn't have gotten involved in that kind of scheme, it wasn't her style."

"That's true, but why believe me now?" she asked.

He shrugged, his gaze locking on hers. "Like you said, I have to trust you sometime."

She thought her heart would burst. She had to tell

him the truth. That she wasn't Maria, she was Angie.
"Jack, there's something—"

"I hope you're hungry," he said, as the waitress
came over to their table with a large tray filled with
barbecue pork, coleslaw and beans. Jack breathed in
and smiled. "Nothing smells like Texas barbecue. Or
tastes like it, either."

"Jack, I have—"

"Eat," he ordered, smiling as he dished her up a
plate. "I've been thinking what we should do next."

"But there's something I have—"

"Whatever it is, it can wait." He handed her a rib.
"This food can't."

She took it, her hands trembling at the thought that
he already knew.

They ate as if ravenous. Tiny put some country
music on the jukebox. The sun spilled in through the
window, warming her as she watched Jack eat. His
enjoyment of life seemed to show best in food. She
was reminded of the days she'd watched him eat hot
dogs in the park. The man went at life the way he
ate: as if there were no tomorrow. More than ever,
she wanted to prove he'd been framed. She couldn't
bear the thought that she might be wrong about that.

"You like?" he asked, and reached over with his
thumb to wipe a smudge of sauce from the corner of
her mouth.

His touch was pure electricity shooting through to
her core. She groaned, closed her eyes and heard him
laugh. When she opened her eyes again, he was smiling at her as if he'd never seen anyone like her before.

ANGIE HAD BEEN ABOUT to tell him the truth. Jack
was sure of it. Just as she had last night when he'd

pretended to be asleep. Now as he looked at her, the sunlight making her hair shine like burnished mahogany, he wondered why he'd stopped her.

Because it would change things between them and he wasn't ready for that yet. He was having enough trouble with his feelings for her. It was so much easier this way. Mostly, it kept him from kissing her, something he was dying to do right now.

"Did you get enough to eat?" he asked, loving the way she looked sitting there.

She laughed. "Are you kidding?"

He smiled, feeling better than he had in weeks. Learning about his father had come as a blow. Now, though, he knew why he'd become the LaGrand twins mark. Somehow it helped. Having Angie here with him didn't hurt either.

All he needed was proof that Patrick had set him up. He couldn't let himself think past that.

"So can you find out what I need?" Jack asked after their table was cleared and Angie had had him bring in her laptop from the rental car. He might be a genius when it came to business, but he didn't known squat about women—or digging into other people's private lives.

It seemed there wasn't anything this woman couldn't find out through that computer and her remarkable number of contacts across the country—both legit and not. Con artists, it seemed, had a network of friends in both high *and* low places. The true information highway.

"We look at the players," she said, and booted up the computer. "Starting with the obvious. Who had to have known about the substandard materials going into the houses?"

"The construction workers."

She nodded. "Who did they take orders from?"

"The foreman, Leonard Parsons."

She typed. "And who did he answer to?"

"Del Sanders, the general contractor. Patrick was overseeing the housing project."

She nodded and typed. "What did Leonard and Del have to say about the charges?"

"According to Montie, they both thought the orders were coming from me and loyally just did as they were told."

Her gaze flicked up to his. "You didn't talk to them?"

"Montie didn't think it was a good idea," he said.

She arched a brow. "How much do they make?"

He told her and she typed furiously for a few moments.

She smiled over the top of the screen. "Del has to be getting something, but he was too smart to leave a trail. Leonard, on the other hand, seems to have been depositing his share of the kickbacks every week."

Jack shook his head. "Leonard has always been good with the men and seeing that the work gets done, but he's no rocket scientist."

"Obviously. So there is a good chance he'll tell us what we want to know."

He realized that Angie had been right. He was totally out of his league, but he was now in the hands of the master, he thought looking at her. "Nice work."

She smiled ruefully. "Sometimes it takes a thief to catch a thief."

He wondered how long he could keep pretending

this woman wasn't Angie as she smiled one of those smiles that warmed him to his toes. He reached across the table for her hand, wanting desperately to touch her.

The sudden touch of his fingers sent a jolt through Angie. She jerked back, knocking over the saltshaker. Hurriedly, she righted it, pinched up some of the spilled salt and tossed it over her left shoulder without thinking.

She looked up to see Jack staring at her.

His gaze moved from her face to the amulet at her throat and so did her hand. She closed her fingers around the good luck charm and tried to breathe. She waited for him to say something. Anything.

"Jack!" Tiny called from the kitchen and motioned for him to come back.

Jack glanced at her. "I'll be just a minute."

She nodded and swallowed the lump in her throat. He went into the kitchen. Did he just think superstition ran in her family? Or had she given herself away? Wasn't she going to confess anyway? Or had she changed her mind?

She needed to talk to Maria. The cell phone rang three times before her sister answered.

"What are you doing?" Angie asked, worried. She'd had a bad feeling all day that Maria wouldn't wait for her. Maria liked to take things into her own hands. It had gotten her in trouble on more than one occasion.

"Lying by the pool, reading a good book," Maria said, sounding a little breathless.

"How is our...friend?"

"Enjoying Palm Springs. I've seen him by the pool. From a distance, of course."

Angie wanted to believe her sister. Another disadvantage of their profession was a standard assumption that everyone lied. And Maria was very good at it.

"How are things in Houston?"

"Rainy." Angie watched Jack talking with Tiny. She thought she might have given herself away. And she'd changed her mind about telling him the truth. At least for the moment.

"Are you all right? You sound funny."

"Fine."

"Uh-huh. And Jack?"

"He's fine, too. He's a lot tougher than I originally thought," she said, and then could have bitten her tongue.

"He's still a mark, Angie. Don't forget that. Unless you've proven he wasn't responsible for the fraud or arson."

"Not yet." She wanted to argue that Jack wasn't like his father, but she still hadn't found evidence to back that up. All she had was what her heart told her—and everyone knew about hearts: they were worse than marks when it came to being easily corrupted. "You are keeping your distance?" she asked.

Maria sighed. "Would I ever not do what you told me to?"

Angie didn't respond.

"Patrick seems a little agitated. I would suspect he's found out by now that you aren't Angelina Grant, import-export heir, and he's out of luck money-wise."

"He's going to be angry and vengeful."

"I know the feeling."

"Remember what Daddy always said about personal vengeance and anger,'' Angie reminded her. It could ruin a good con—or worse, get you arrested or killed.

''You think Daddy would have stood back and let Patrick get away with almost killing you?'' Maria demanded.

''Patrick isn't going to get away. Not if we stick to our plan. Maria, I'm worried about you.''

''Don't worry about me, all right? I'm getting a great tan, keeping my eye on Patrick and waiting for you, little sis. You just clear your boyfriend and get your butt back here so we can take care of this creep.''

Clear your boyfriend. Maria wanted Jack to be innocent, too. ''See you soon.''

Jack watched Angie on the phone. She must have called Maria. He knew her mannerisms so well. The way she cocked her head, brushed her hair back from her face, frowned and tugged at her lower lip with her teeth. He also knew what it meant when she touched the amulet under her blouse. He didn't even think she knew she was doing it.

Her and her superstitions. They made sense now, now that he knew who she was—and what she did for a living. He knew Patrick had found them foolish, childish. But superstition was such a part of Angie, Jack found it charming. Quirky like Angie. Hadn't she told him once that her grandmother had given her the amulet for luck? Her grandmother LaGrand, no doubt. A notorious confidence woman ahead of her time.

But what if she wasn't as good as she thought at pretending? What if she hadn't meant to, but she'd let him see the real her? What if she'd let him get inside? And at the same time, she'd let herself fall for a mark?

Or maybe he just wanted to believe that he wasn't a complete fool.

He could see how anxious she was as he returned to the table and slid into the booth seat across from her. Was she afraid he knew she was Angie? "Everything all right?"

She nodded. "I just had to make a call to an associate of mine."

An associate, huh. Maria. "And what did you find out?"

She ducked behind the screen of the laptop. "I checked on the fire investigator's report—"

The woman was amazing.

"—and there's nothing in Patrick's background that would indicate he knew anything about arson. So I think it is safe to assume whoever wanted the house burned down paid someone to do it."

He realized something. "You investigated Patrick before you came to Houston, didn't you?"

She nodded.

"Your family doesn't leave anything to chance, do they?"

"No, we don't." She took a breath and continued. "The fire investigator's report suggests the arson was set by a professional but made to look like the work of an amateur." He must have been frowning at her. "What?"

"Sorry," he said. "It's just that you talk about professional embezzlers and arsonists as if they were real professions complete with graduate degrees."

"Where I come from, they are," she said matter-of-factly.

"Just like professional thieves, huh?"

"We aren't thieves," she corrected. "In fact, a good confidence man looks down his nose at pickpockets and burglars and small-time hustlers. Daddy always said, 'If you're going to be a crook, be a confidence man and be the best damn one you can.'"

He leaned back and looked at her appraisingly for a moment. "Daddy must have been really something."

"He was." Her voice broke. "He died last spring."

"I'm sorry," Jack said, feeling awful. "I didn't mean to—"

"It's all right. You couldn't possibly understand."

Angie was right about that. He couldn't understand a man who had raised his twin girls to be confidence women. But he did know how it felt to lose a father. He felt as if he'd lost his twice. Once when his dad died. And again last night when he'd learned how the man had found success.

"How did your father die?" he asked, afraid she was going to tell him that he had been shot by a mark.

"A heart attack, in his sleep."

Jack recalled now reading in the dossier about Addison Grant dying in his villa in the south of France. It was estimated that he and his family had made millions of dollars doing "favors" for friends—for a price.

Millions. It seemed the only truth Angelina Grant might have told him was the part about being an heir to a fortune.

"I'm sorry about your father," he said. "You must have been very close."

She nodded. "My mother died when we were two,

so my father raised us with the help of only my grand-mother.''

''The woman who gave you…and your sister the amulets,'' he said, realizing he'd almost blown it.

She met his gaze. ''Yes.'' Then she looked back at the computer screen.

There was so much he wanted to know about her and her family. But even if she did tell him, he wasn't sure he could believe it, let alone understand or for-give. He ached for this woman, wanted her more than he had ever wanted anything in his life. But trust was a whole other issue.

''Did you hire Leonard Parsons?'' she asked after a moment of studying the computer screen.

''No. Del probably did. Or Patrick. Why?''

''Did you know he was a suspect in an arson in-vestigation at a previous job?''

Jack swore under his breath. ''Let's go find Leon-ard and talk to him.''

He took the computer and opened the door, calling over his shoulder to Tiny as they left. He glanced at the cars parked on the street as he and Angie got into the rental car. ''You realize Patrick knows we're in Houston by now.''

She nodded. ''I would imagine Constance called him the moment we left her office.''

He looked over at her. It was warm in the car, the sun shining in the windows. He could smell her per-fume, just a hint of it. ''If there is anything to find on him, Patrick will try to stop us.''

''Yes,'' she agreed, ''but then, we've both known that all along, haven't we?''

He'd never met anyone like her. Amazingly he was more attracted to her than ever—even knowing who she was. Desire shot through him. He wanted nothing more than to take her in his arms and kiss her. Oh yes, he did. He wanted desperately to make love to her—and had for months.

It must have shown in his gaze because she turned away as if afraid he just might. What was she afraid of? Giving her real identity away? Or what would happen if they kissed again?

PATRICK STARED AT THE sliding glass door, the swimming pool and palms beyond it. A small white envelope was taped to the glass. He hadn't seen it when he'd come in. He'd only seen the trail of wet footprints.

But he saw the envelope now and he knew who'd left it even before he saw his name printed neatly in Angie's handwriting.

He thought his heart would beat its way out of his chest, his skin felt on fire, each breath felt like his last as he moved toward the glass door and carefully lifted off the tape and envelope.

He told himself he didn't have to open it. He could just throw it away. He'd never have to know what was inside. He could change hotels. He could change cities. He could run and keep running. But he knew that without money, that wasn't true. He also knew they would follow him, and he wasn't even sure who ''they'' were anymore.

He looked down at the envelope in his fingers.

Patrick. That's all it said on the outside, but the letters had a mocking tilt to them that made anger boil up inside him.

He ripped open the envelope quickly, fingers shaking, nerves raw, and upended it. The contents fluttered to the wet carpet at his feet. He stared down in surprise.

He wasn't sure what he'd expected to find inside. A note berating him for trying to kill her. A death threat. A few words of gloating. But it wasn't a note.

He bent down and picked up the single slip of heavy paper. A ticket? It was gold with small lettering: "Palm Springs Aerial Tramway. Admit One." On it Angie had written: *Take the last car. 8:00 p.m. tonight.*

Angie was finally making her move. He felt a wave of relief. He could end this more quickly than he'd thought. He would be ready. *I'm coming to get you, Angie. Only this time, I'm going to make sure you're dead.*

Chapter Thirteen

The old neighborhood always took Jack back to his childhood. The apartment house where he'd grown up, the empty lot where he'd played ball, the abandoned old building where he and Patrick had built a fort on the roof.

He slowed in front of the tenement where Patrick had lived and looked up at the second-floor window, remembering Patrick's mother. Mary Ryerson had been a small, kind woman and as close to a mother as Jack could remember. She made tuna casseroles and oatmeal cookies for him and Patrick. She did her best to raise Patrick alone, but as far back as Jack could remember, Patrick had been trouble.

"Boys will be boys," Mary Ryerson used to say and smile ruefully.

But Jack remembered how she would turn her back and wipe at her tears with the corner of her apron.

He realized now how much she must have feared for her son. And with good reason, as it turned out.

Memories flooded Jack of the boy Patrick had been—sandy-haired with a mischievous grin and a charm that captivated everyone. Back then, Patrick had been his best friend in the world.

How could Patrick look back on those days with contempt and resentment? Sure, the people were poor and struggling just as many were today, but it had been a neighborhood where everyone knew each other, everyone cared. Jack had thought he could help bring that back by rebuilding here. He still did.

If he got the chance again. He thought of what his father had done and swore under his breath. Both Patrick and Kelly had seen the old neighborhood only as a way out.

"That's where Patrick lived with his mother, isn't it?" Angie asked, bending down to gaze up at the tenement.

Jack shot her a look, realizing the extent of the research the woman had done on him and the people near him. "As if you don't already know that."

Angie leaned back as he drove on past the neighborhood. He seemed upset. She couldn't blame him. He was a private man who didn't want people knowing anything about him. But she knew plenty.

She knew that he'd taken care of Patrick's mom, gotten her into a nice little house in a safer neighborhood. That he had visited her once a week and paid for her funeral when she died. Patrick never went back to see his mother. He didn't even attend her funeral.

"You were good to Patrick's mom," she said.

"She was good to me." He glanced over at her again and smiled. "You really do want to like me, don't you."

She laughed at that and looked out her side of the car at the passing neighborhood. Liking Jack wasn't the problem. "Sometimes I have trouble trusting people."

It was his turn to laugh.

How did she explain the way she was raised? "In the world Angie and I grew up in, there were few honest men. We came to expect the worst. Humans are often weak. We were raised to use that weakness to our advantage."

"So you look for the weakness. Expect it," he said.

"Yes." She was still looking for it in Jack, wasn't she—and he knew it.

Birdie's was a neighborhood bar, dark and narrow with a dingy linoleum floor and black-vinyl-covered stools pulled up to a long, scarred wooden bar.

Birdie was a large doughy-looking woman whose eyes disappeared in her plump face. She slid two bar napkins toward Jack and Angie and asked, "What'a ya'll have?"

A half dozen of the regulars were already pulled up to the bar, most drinking beer.

"A draft," Jack said, and looked at Angie.

"The same," she said, climbing up on the stool.

The regulars were watching them, some turning on their stools, others eyeing them in the bar mirror. The people in the bar looked suspicious, and he wondered if they recognized him. Or had he just changed so much that he stood out from his old neighborhood and the people he'd once been a part of.

He didn't see anyone who looked familiar. He hated to admit it, but he'd forgotten a lot of the faces. But he would never forget the look. Desolation. Hopelessness. Defeat. He found that the hardest to take.

He remembered his father's face in old photos. He had never seen anything but hunger in that face. It was the eyes. A determination. Ambition like a low-grade electrical current that had energized his father.

His father had been driven to get out of the old neighborhood no matter what it took. And now Jack knew what it had taken.

He sipped his beer and looked at Angie in the bar mirror.

She winked at him. "Be right back." She seemed to change the moment she slid from the bar stool. There was a loose swivel of her hips that hadn't been there, an easy set of her shoulders, a slow flip of her long dark hair. Even her expression changed.

Every eye in the place was on her, some more subtle than others. Several turned as she went by, smiling at her.

Suddenly she was one of them. She could have grown up in this neighborhood.

Jack watched her in awe. She was a chameleon, changing with her environment. Or maybe her roots weren't that different from his own. Suddenly he sensed that her life had not always been champagne and caviar, expensive hotels and four-star restaurants.

He remembered their first date. He'd taken her to Tiny's, where they'd gone today. Even now, he wasn't sure why he'd taken a woman who looked and acted like she did to a barbecue place. He never took dates there. But then as today, she seemed to enjoy it as much as he did.

Angie disappeared into the ladies' room, and he turned his attention back to his beer, aware that the regulars were eyeing him with even more interest, wondering about him. Mostly wondering about the woman he'd come in with.

When Angie came out of the ladies' room, the regulars stirred, most trying not to look, some meeting his gaze in the mirror, assuming she was his.

He wished it were true.

Angie stopped beside one of the younger men, asked him something and leaned toward him to listen to his answer. The man was rail thin and looked hungover. He appeared at home on the bar stool, although he was not sitting by the other men. He'd been lost in his beer until Angie had singled him out.

Angie said something to the man that Jack couldn't hear.

The man nodded. His eyes flicked to the mirror and Jack, then jerked away.

What the hell was she doing? She laid a hand on the man's arm. He looked nervous, but clearly was enjoying the attention. Basking in Angie's attention was like being bathed in summer sunlight. Jack ought to know.

He heard Angie's tinkling light laugh, then the sound of her approaching. The regulars were still looking at the man at the end of the bar, obviously hoping he would tell them what she'd wanted.

The man turned back to his beer, curling around the glass, looking down at the amber liquid, smiling a little.

Angie slid onto the stool next to Jack, took a long drink of her beer and licked the foam from her lips, smiling.

"I hate to ask," he said under his breath. He took a sip of his own beer.

"Leonard was in last night, drank too much. Probably still in bed with a bad hangover." She seemed to study her beer. "He lives a couple of blocks from here." She took another drink. "I would imagine someone will try to warn him and if Leonard has anything to hide, he'll run. We'll have to hurry." She drained her beer glass and sighed, leaning into him as she took his arm possessively. Her cheek brushed against his shoulder, and he heard her take a deep breath as if breathing him in.

He put his arm around her, drawing her close for a moment. When he let go he saw the change in her eyes. Just a flicker. She smiled and leaned back, pretending it had been part of her act. He knew better. She was starting to feel comfortable around him. Maybe too comfortable. Just as it had been before all hell broke loose and he ended up in jail.

He threw some money on the bar and rose, calling "Thanks" down the bar. Angie slid off her stool and started toward the door. He was right behind her.

LEONARD PARSONS LIVED in an old apartment house that had once been a hotel. The outside door opened onto a dirty hallway that smelled of boiled cabbage and mold. Up six steps, another hall. Door number two.

Jack could hear the phone already ringing and swore under his breath. He knocked. The phone rang again.

"Hey, baby!" Angie called in a high, loose voice. "Open up, it's me."

Jack could hear cursing. Something crashed to the floor. More swearing. The phone quit ringing just an instant before the door opened. Angie pushed Jack back.

Leonard stood in the doorway, a small man with long dishwater-blond hair pulled back in a ponytail, wearing nothing but boxer shorts and a tank top. A diamond stud glittered in one earlobe. He had the phone tucked between his ear and his shoulder, the cord dragging behind him through a disheveled apartment.

"Do I know you?" he asked Angie in a voice that sounded as if he'd just woken up. "Just a minute," he said into the phone as he leaned past her out into the hall and saw Jack. His eyes widened as Jack took the phone from him, hanging it up as he brushed past Leonard into the apartment.

Leonard stared at him, obviously having trouble keeping up. The side of his face was red and wrinkled and he looked as if he'd definitely had a rough night. "Hey!" he said. "What the—"

"I want to talk to you, Leonard."

"Jack. Right. No problem, but you should have called."

"The line was busy." Jack motioned to a chair.

Leonard looked from him to Angie and back. "The thing is, I was told not to talk to you."

"Who told you that?" Jack asked.

"That lawyer guy."

"Well, Leonard, I know you were getting paid to keep quiet about what was going on at the job site, but what I need to know is who paid you to burn down one of my houses?"

Leonard blinked. "Hey, man, I don't know anything about a fire."

He moved past Jack, then did something Jack never would have anticipated in a million years. He dove out the window in an explosion of glass. It happened so fast that Jack didn't even have a chance to grab for him.

The single-pane window shattered, showering

Leonard with glass. He hit the ground running, all sign of him gone by the time Jack reached the street—except for the trail of blood drops that ended a block away.

When he returned to the rental car, he found Angie standing beside it.

"I did a star sixty-nine on Leonard's phone and got the name and number of the person who called to warn him we were coming," she said. "Del Sanders, the general contractor on the housing project. The bartender must have called Del."

"WE NEED TO TALK," Jack said when Del Sanders answered.

"You know Montie said that's not a good idea," Del stammered, sounding nervous, scared.

Jack figured Del had caller ID and knew Jack was calling from Leonard Parsons's phone. "I don't care what Montie said. Where can we meet?"

Silence.

"How about your office," Jack said, suspecting that was the last place Del wanted to meet. Unlike Leonard, Del Sanders wasn't the kind of man to jump through a window. Del was smart enough to know that running wouldn't help. And the man had much more to lose.

"How about Live Oaks Bayou?" Del said. It was the development he was just starting outside of Houston. "I need to go out there, anyway."

"It should take me about thirty minutes," Jack said, and hung up, feeling sick. He'd already heard what he wanted to know in the older man's voice. Del Sanders was guilty as hell. The question was, who had framed Jack? It was something he knew Del had the answer to.

Chapter Fourteen

Huge old live oaks grew in a thick forest along the edge of the bayous just outside of Houston, except where large earth-moving machinery had plowed a makeshift road through them.

Angie rolled down her window and breathed in the rich scents of earth, trees and water. Nothing smelled quite like this part of Texas.

Jack seemed distracted, frowning as he drove. He hadn't said anything for miles, hadn't said anything since he'd talked to Del Sanders.

Del had worked for Jack's father and had been an old family friend for years. Knowing Jack and how he felt about loyalty and lies, she knew he must be crushed to think that Del might be in on any of this.

The last late afternoon sunlight flickered in the leaves overhead as Jack followed the narrow road deeper and deeper into the darkness of the trees. Ahead she spotted a dirty black pickup parked next to one of the bayous in a small clearing, Sanders Construction painted on the side in block-style lettering.

"I thought Sanders worked for *you*," she said, frowning.

"Used to. He quit to go out on his own about two

months ago,'' Jack said, and glanced over at her as if he was surprised she hadn't known that.

Had she been in on framing him, she would have.

As he parked parallel with the pickup a half dozen yards away, a hot, muggy stillness settled over them.

Del Sanders was sitting in the pickup, but got out now. He waited next to his truck, leaning against it as if he needed the support.

He was a big man, balding with reddish gray hair, his large face florid and head shiny with sweat. He wore slacks and a dress shirt stained with perspiration. A cell phone was clipped to his belt.

He seemed startled to see her as Angie got out of the car after Jack. She noticed that Jack registered Del's reaction to her and frowned.

''You remember Angelina Grant,'' Jack said, surprising her. But then, he couldn't introduce her as Maria LaGrand, could he. ''Del Sanders.''

Del shook his head. ''I don't think we've ever met.''

She took the man's hand. It was moist, and she could feel him trembling. She wondered what was making him so nervous? Jack? Her? The truth?

He obviously knew who she was, just as he'd heard about her marrying Patrick and the accident in Montana.

''Rumors of my death were grossly exaggerated,'' she said.

Del looked confused and didn't seem to know what to say. After a pause he said, ''What's this about, Jack? I really don't think we should be—''

''Del, how long have you known me?'' Jack asked.

The question seemed to catch him off guard. ''How long? I guess twenty-four, twenty-five years.''

The leaves rustled in the huge oaks. Something splashed in the water of the bayou.

Del glanced back over his shoulder.

"Are you expecting someone?" Jack asked.

"No. It's just that Montie said—"

"Right, Montie. Del, I know."

The big man seemed to shrink into himself, his expression grim. "Jack, I don't know what—"

Angie heard the change in Jack's tone. "You remember when I hired you?" He was no longer the Ivy League-educated, wealthy, construction company owner. He was the kid who'd grown up on the rough streets, the kid Del had known as a boy.

"What?"

"I told you what I wanted to do in the old neighborhood, remember?"

"Sure." Sweat was running down into Del's eyes. He wiped his face with his shirtsleeve. "I swear to God, I thought you ordered the changes on the jobs. I thought that's why you hired Patrick to handle things."

"That piss you off, Del?" Jack's voice was low and soft. Angie could hear the pain in it. "Is that why you did this or was it just for the money?"

Del tensed as if expecting a blow.

"You knew damn well I hadn't ordered the changes," Jack said. "You know me better than that."

The silence was dense as cotton batting.

Del swallowed and looked over his shoulder again, his face flushed and sweating. He looked scared.

"Tell me the truth, Del, and I'll fight for the best deal the judge will make you. Lie to me and…"

A sound came out of the older man. A painful groan. He hung his head. "Jack, I never meant—"

"Was it Patrick's idea?" Jack asked.

Del raised his head a fraction. "Patrick?" He mopped his brow with his sleeve, his chest rising and falling as if he couldn't catch his breath. Del began to cry, huge body-shaking sobs that racked his body. "I'm so sorry, Jack—"

THE SHOT CAME FROM out of the oaks. A *pop*, then a grunt. Del's eyes widened, blood blooming across his chest. He stumbled forward, grabbed Angie by the shoulders as he tried to stay on his feet.

The second bullet came only an instant later, followed by two more in quick succession as Jack dove for Angie. Del's legs crumbled under him and he went down hard, taking Angie with him.

Jack heard the next two shots; one pinged off the side of the truck, then kicked up dirt near his feet. By that time he was on the ground next to Angie, trying to shield her body from the gunfire.

In the silence that followed the flurry of shots, he heard an engine start up, off in the trees, then the sound of a vehicle roaring away.

As he lifted Del's dead weight off Angie, all he saw was blood. It was everywhere—all over Del, all over Angie. She lay facedown, deadly still.

"Angie! Oh God, Angie!" He rolled her over and into his arms. "Angie?"

She opened her eyes and took a shaky breath. As if the wind had been knocked out of her.

He looked from her face down to her blood-soaked clothing. "Are you hit?"

She shook her head slowly, appearing dazed,

looked down at her shirt, then up at him again. "You know."

At first he didn't understand her.

"You know I'm Angie," she whispered.

He wiped a smear of blood from her face with his sleeve and nodded. "I've known since that kiss in the alleyway at the Seattle wharf."

She shook her head, smiling ruefully, then glanced over at the man on the ground next to her. "Del?"

He shook his head and reached for the cell phone clicked to Del's hip, to dial 911.

IT WAS DARK BY THE TIME Patrick drove the rental car down Highway 111 to the tramway entrance. The steep road wound up Chino Canyon, leaving behind the hot, dry desert warmth as he ascended to a parking area at the foot of the San Jacinto Mountains.

He glanced toward the tramway, not liking what he saw. The lights of a tiny tram car clung to a cable that seemed to drop straight off the side of the mountain. Behind it loomed the mountain, eerily lit to expose rock and creosote scrub. He had to look away.

He felt physically ill already. It was almost as if Angie knew about his fear of heights and was trying to torment him.

Just the thought of Angie waiting for him up there…made him open his car door and step out. He was surprised at how much cooler it was up here and glad to see there weren't many cars in the lot, glad it was a weekday and not the height of the season. He realized that was probably why Angie had chosen this place to meet.

He glanced up again at the tram car coming down,

instantly nauseated. The bitch. If she really wasn't dead, he was going to kill her for doing this to him.

Inside the Valley Station he didn't see Angie, but then, he hadn't expected to. She would make him go to the top, sure as hell. He checked the time and almost immediately heard the boarding call for the last tram.

He followed a half dozen people through a waiting room and into the tram car, needing to sit down. There were no seats. He grabbed hold of the railing along the side and held on as the door closed, and moments later the car slid out of the boarding dock and began to rock as it climbed slowly up the mountain.

He closed his eyes, trying to ignore the woman near him who was oohing and aahing and telling the man beside her that the first tower was the tallest at two hundred and fourteen feet high.

Suddenly the car paused, then rocked wildly before moving forward as it passed that first tower. Patrick's eyes flew open. Behind the car, the Sonoran Desert spread out in glittering lights far below them. He gripped the railing tighter, trying to hold himself up, sicker than he'd ever been.

"It has a vertical ascent of more than a mile," the woman said. "Would you look at that view. Isn't it thrilling?"

He groaned and moved away from her. He didn't want to hear any more about the tram's three hundred pounds of steel cables or the more than thirty-four hundred feet between towers. It was the longest fourteen minutes of his life.

When the car finally pulled into the Mountain Station dock, he stumbled from the car, just wanting to feel earth beneath his feet. He was dizzy and sick to his stomach and couldn't bear the thought of the trip back down.

The Mountain Station facility was huge—and mostly empty. A few people were having dinner in the dining room. Several others were having cocktails in the lounge. No Angie. He looked in the gift shop and theater, then glanced toward the observation deck, eighty-five hundred feet up the side of the mountain.

Angie wasn't here. *Because she is dead, you idiot.*

Then who had gotten him up here? Who was that woman he'd seen by the pool? The one who'd left the wet footprints and the ticket?

Angie was alive. And on this mountaintop. Only this time, she wasn't going to pull a disappearing act on him. If he could find her.

That's when he spotted the message board and saw his name printed in Angie's handwriting.

He still felt unsteady on his feet and nauseated as he pulled the note off and read it. "Take the Desert View Trail. You'll need a flashlight. They sell them at the gift shop. See you soon."

Desert View Trail. He'd rather poke a sharp stick into his eye. But he went to the gift shop, bought a flashlight—a small one that gave off little light—and picked up a trail map, thinking of only one thing: killing Angie. Again.

The night air was at least thirty degrees cooler up here than down in the desert. He felt chilled and still sick as he headed out the back of the Mountain Station and descended the switchbacked sidewalk for two hundred yards. Pine trees rose up into the dark sky, and ahead he could make out what appeared to be a ranger station. The lights were out. No one around.

He checked his map and saw that a sawhorse with a Closed sign had been propped in front of the Desert View Trail entrance. Angie's doing? No doubt. So she wanted them to be alone. He smiled to himself. Perfect.

The flashlight did little to illuminate the dark night as he walked around the barrier and headed down the trail, but he didn't want to give Angie too much of a heads up. He wondered if she would try to jump him. He hoped so. He was ready for her.

But he doubted her plan was to try to kill him. She could have done that in his sleep when she sneaked into his room and left the jewelry. She wanted something from him. Probably a confession that would clear Jack's name. The thought infuriated him. The bitch was still thinking only of Jack.

He moved through the darkness, the trail skirting the edge of the mountainside. Through the pines, he caught glimpses of twinkling lights far, far below them on the desert floor. At one overlook, he shone his flashlight on a marker: View Coachella Valley. He'd rather view Angie Grant.

Excuse me, Angie LaGrand.

He gritted his teeth until they ached remembering how she'd fooled him.

He continued on up the trail, just wishing she would get this over with. He couldn't imagine how she thought she could get a confession out of him. Beat it out of him? He smiled at the thought of her trying. Trick him? Not likely.

The evergreens grew thicker, the path darker, closing in around him. Through the pine branches he would catch glimpses of stars overhead. He avoided looking down at the valley sprawled below him, so far below him. It reminded him of the canyon where Angie had gone off. Well, where the Jeep had, anyway.

He slowed, still woozy and nauseated, chilled by the night air. He tried not to think how high he was above the desert and suddenly worried this had been a mistake. He'd underestimated Angie at the cabin in Montana, and look how that had turned out. Maybe this had been just a trick to get him away from his hotel room for some reason.

He heard a noise ahead. A soft rustling sound. He pointed the flashlight into the darkness and saw a pine bough move.

Angie.

Cautiously, he moved toward the stand of pines, excited. He couldn't *wait* to see her again.

Suddenly something came out of the darkness and trees at his head; he ducked, throwing up an arm to ward off the blow. At the sound of flapping wings, he slowly straightened and shone his flashlight after it, immediately feeling foolish as a hawk sailed out over the edge of the mountain in the beam of light.

He stood there shaking, trying to still his heart. He'd had too many surprises lately. "Where the hell are you?" he hollered. His words died off. Had he really expected her to answer? She probably wasn't even out here. Might not be on the mountain at all. She could be just jerking his chain.

He thought about turning back, but remembered the trail circled back to the Mountain Station. No reason to backtrack. He had to be getting close to the end.

Was it the altitude up here? He felt even more

light-headed. Maybe it was just knowing that there was an eighty-five-hundred-foot drop just a few yards to his left.

He started up the trail again. All he wanted now was to get off this mountain. There were tram cars going down every thirty minutes. If he hurried…

It happened so quickly he didn't even have a chance to raise his arm this time or duck. A limb the size of a baseball bat struck him in the forehead. He thought he'd walked into the limb—until it struck him again. He pitched forward into the darkness.

THE SHERIFF ARRIVED within minutes after Jack's 911 call. Del was dead. Angie was covered in his blood. Jack had called Montie right after dialing 911.

With Montie's help, he and Angie were allowed to give their statements at the sheriff's department and leave. The sheriff had found tire tracks and spent shell casings out in the woods. They were running the casings for prints.

"It isn't safe for the two of you," Montie said as they were leaving the sheriff's department. "Come stay at my house. I have a good security system and plenty of room."

Jack shook his head. "Thanks, but that would be the first place anyone would look for us."

"Where will you go?" Montie said, sounding worried. "With whoever killed Del still out there…"

"Don't worry. I'll find someplace safe. You've got my cell phone number if you need to reach me," he told him.

Jack couldn't wait to get Angie alone. He wrapped his jacket around her and ushered her out to the rental car.

He found an out-of-the-way motel, paid cash, registered under an assumed name, and ushered Angie straight to their room, where he turned on the shower.

Her bloody shirt was stuck to her skin. She fumbled at the buttons, shaking, her face pale. He suspected violence wasn't often part of the confidence game.

"It's okay, baby," he whispered as he kicked off his shoes and socks, his own clothing bloody, as well, from holding her. Both of them still clothed, he pulled her into the shower.

He wrapped his arms around her, and she leaned against him, burying her face in his chest as the water flowed over them. He had thought nothing could faze this woman but he'd been wrong. Her body began to tremble. He could feel her shuddering sobs. He held her to him and let her cry as the water washed away the blood and her tears.

After a while, she looked up at him, her brown eyes the color of honey. He kissed her under the cascade of water. She wrapped her arms around his neck and pulled him closer, their soaked clothes welding them together.

"Jack?" she whispered, looking up into his eyes. "I'm so glad you're all right. I thought—"

He silenced her with a kiss.

When he released her mouth, she whispered, "Make love to me."

She could have asked him to leap tall buildings at that moment and he would have tried. But there was still so much unresolved between them.

"Angie, I'm not sure we should—"

"I am, Jack," she said, and drew him down for another kiss.

He dropped his mouth to hers. She tasted sweet and

spicy, like something exotic and rare. He could feel her unbuttoning his shirt, slipping it off his shoulders, the warm water drumming his bare skin.

He pulled back. The look in her eyes was his undoing. It fired his blood, making his heart pound. With shaking fingers he unbuttoned her blouse, exposing the tanned, freckled skin above her breasts, then the white satin of her bra as the blouse dropped to the shower floor.

He let out a groan at the sight of her, her dark hair a flowing wave under the water, the pale breasts visible through the wet, white-satin bra, dark nipples hard buds, her soaked jeans hugging her wonderful curves.

She smiled at him, a mixture of tears and desire glittering in her eyes, as he reached for her again.

PATRICK SWAM TOWARD the surface, from a deep blackness to a warm, wet one. He surfaced to sound and movement and pain—lots of pain.

He blinked, one eye full of something warm. Blood. He closed his eyes. Opened them again and saw through his one good eye that it was nighttime and he was moving.

Someone was dragging him by his shoulders backward, his heels scraping across the dirt and pine needles. He could hear the person breathing hard from the exertion. Angie. He found some gratification in the fact that he was making her work hard, but he did wonder where she was taking him.

Suddenly she dropped him. He fell hard on his back, knocking the air out of him. Instinctively, he'd closed his eyes and pretended still to be unconscious. His head ached and blood pooled in his eyes. He wanted to touch his forehead where he'd been hit to see how bad the wound was, but didn't.

His listened to her try to catch her breath. She was strong, but not strong enough to drag a man his size any distance. A breeze blew up on his right, drying the blood on his face, and he realized she didn't plan to drag him much farther, just to the edge of the mountain. She wasn't after a confession. She planned to kill him!

As she leaned down to grab hold of him again, his eyes flew open. He got a glimpse of her surprised expression just an instant before he wrapped his arms around her head and flipped her over onto the ground. She let out a satisfying *ooft!* And he was on her in a heartbeat.

She squirmed under him, but she was no match for him physically. He dug the weapon he'd brought and his flashlight out of her jacket pocket. With one hand, he pressed the gun barrel between her eyes. With the other, he flicked on the flashlight and shone the beam on her face.

She seemed amused by his sudden gasp.

Angie. My God, she really was alive!

She smiled up at him. Smiled!

He pressed the gun between her eyes, his trigger finger itchy with expectation. "You're a dead woman this time."

ANGIE THOUGHT SHE would die if Jack didn't touch her. Her body ached for him. She trembled under the heat of his gaze, the water rippling over her sensitive skin.

But he stood just looking at her, as if needing to memorize her and this moment. Then he reached out and gently rasped his thumb pad across one hard nipple, sending waves of heat through her. She had never wanted a man more than she wanted Jack right now, had never felt such need nor such tenderness.

But she didn't move, didn't touch him. She waited.

His gaze met hers. He groaned again and pulled her to him, his kiss rocking her to her core. He peeled off her jeans and tossed them aside, then removed her satin panties and bra, his lips never leaving hers. He shed the rest of his own clothing, his body more wonderful than she'd imagined.

Finally naked, water flowing over their bare skin, Jack soaped her body slowly, lovingly, intimately. She closed her eyes and reveled in the feel of his wet, slick hands and fingers caressing every inch of her.

His kiss opened her eyes, and she smiled and shyly took the soap from him. She'd never been this intimate with a man. She flattened her palms against him as she lathered his body, and he watched her, his eyes setting her ablaze.

Standing under the spray, they washed away the suds, then he gently kissed her lips, her eyelids, her earlobes. He trailed kisses down the column of her neck to the hollow of her throat over the rise of her breast to her nipple and sucked the hard nub into his mouth.

Her body quivered and she laid back her head and groaned as she pressed her breast against his hot mouth. He moved down her body, leaving a trail of blistering kisses that made her quake against him until she felt him at her center.

He pressed her against the shower wall, this kiss making her bury her fingers in his hair as he took her to the top of a roller-coaster of pleasure, then let her go. She cried out, trembling under his touch.

Turning off the shower, he dried them both, and, skin flushed, they raced into the bedroom to scramble under the covers. The sheets were cool and soft. Her body was alive with sensation as Jack drew her into his arms again.

She could hear rain beating against the window panes and music playing somewhere outside as a car went by. She snuggled against him as his mouth and his fingertips licked across her skin like flames, making her climb again until she thought she couldn't stand it.

He entered her, filling her, completing her. Her heart pounded against his as he made sweet, passionate love to her, lifting her until she was soaring again, higher than she'd ever been.

"Oh, Jack," she cried on a gasp, and felt him shudder, those warm denim-blue eyes gazing down at her, the look in them deep with wonder—and something else. Something that could have been love.

PATRICK HELD THE WOMAN to the ground, the gun barrel pressed between her eyes. "I should pull this trigger right now," he said from between gritted teeth.

He wiped blood from his eyes with the sleeve of his left hand—the one holding the flashlight—and cursed her for the hell she'd put him through. How had she survived the first time he'd tried to kill her, anyway?

"You aren't going to kill me," she said, sounding so confident that he almost pulled the trigger. "You're too smart for that."

"What makes you so sure?" he demanded. "You were about to throw me off this mountain to my death."

"Just like you tried to do to me, you bastard."

He smiled at that. He'd been called much worse. And besides, he had the gun and her now. "This time I'm going to succeed, though. Maybe I'll throw you off this mountain since the last one didn't work." That way he wouldn't have to risk someone hearing the gunshot.

"You kill me and how are you going to explain my death again, here—more than a thousand miles from where the sheriff and the search-and-rescue team are still looking for my body?"

Angie had him there. What *was* he going to do with her? He couldn't just let her go. She could have him arrested for attempted murder. Of course, she'd have to prove it—and the fact that she hadn't gone to the cops right away would be in his favor. That and the fact that she was a professional con man. Woman. Whatever.

But she was right. He couldn't very well kill her here. How would he explain that? He already looked suspicious enough in her first death. He couldn't risk her body being found at the top of the Palm Springs Aerial Tramway in California. Or at the bottom. Not even that hick sheriff would believe her body had washed this far downriver.

"There is only one thing you can do," she said.

He glared down at her. "Oh yeah?"

"Who do you hate more than even me?" she asked.

She had to be kidding.

"Jack," she said.

He felt the breath go out of him. Jack. He'd almost forgotten about him.

"What do you think Jack would pay for my return?" she asked, and smiled. "I'll bet you I'm worth a cool million."

Patrick stared at her. Jack loved Angie. He'd do anything for her. Even if he knew she was a con artist, he would still pay a bundle for her safety. And if he were to find out that she was alive and being held by someone like Patrick...

"Oh, I'd say you're worth a hell of a lot more than a million," he said. "Two, three, even five."

"Then I suggest you get off me before you hurt the merchandise," she snapped. "And put that gun away. You're not going to use it."

He wished she wasn't right about that. He slid off her and stumbled to his feet, keeping the gun and flashlight trained on her just in case she tried to jump him again.

"Don't be a fool," she said. "I need you to pull this off."

"You were just getting ready to push me off this mountain," he cried, still a little shocked by that. He'd never suspected she was such a cold-hearted bitch.

"I was angry and not thinking," she said, dusting herself off. "Now that I've had time to think, I realize you're more valuable to me alive. If the ransom demand comes from you, Jack will know you mean business. He won't jeopardize my life by going to the cops or try to dicker on how much I'm worth." She nodded. "It looks like we need each other."

He found himself nodding along with her. Not that

he didn't still want to kill her. He couldn't believe everything she'd put him through.

But she was right. He couldn't kill her here. And she *was* worth money. Wasn't that how he'd gotten involved with her in the first place?

His head ached where she'd hit him. Again. He felt light-headed from the tram ride up, and was not in the best mood. "Those stocks and bonds were fakes."

She shot him a "duh" look. "I'm a confidence woman, remember?"

He wiped more blood from his eyes.

"Here, let me fix that," she said, and pulled a bandana from her jeans pocket. She wrapped it around his forehead. "That should stop the bleeding. It's just a flesh wound."

It didn't feel like just a flesh wound. He stared at her as she adjusted the bandana. He still had the cut on his temple where she'd hit him with the ice bucket, and his shoulder was black and blue from the champagne bottle she'd cold-cocked him with. It was all he could do not to strangle her as she tied the bandana in place.

"We can clean the wound back at the Mountain Station," she was saying. "If anyone asks, we can tell them you walked into a tree limb."

"Yeah," he said, and made a nasty face at her.

"Stop being such a big baby. It could have been much worse. You could be tumbling off the mountain right now."

He glared at her. "How did you get out of that Jeep?"

"Luck," she said, and pulled that stupid amulet from inside her shirt.

He saw that it was all she was wearing for jewelry.

"Where is the real diamond pendant and wedding ring I gave you?"

"Pawned. How do you think I was able to follow you all over the country?" she asked as she started back through the pines following the beam of her small penlight.

He trailed after her, still holding the gun just in case she tried something. "What about the money you took out of our joint checking account?"

"Don't worry, I haven't spent it all. There's enough to finance our plan."

"Oh yeah? And what is *our* plan?"

She reached the trail and started down it. "Don't worry, I'll come up with one."

He wasn't worried. He had faith that this conniving, devious, scheming woman knew exactly what she was doing. He followed, needing his own plan—a way to get the money and get Angie back into that river. This time her body definitely would get caught in a limb and not float up until next spring.

"The problem is getting Jack to believe I'm still alive," she said as they rounded a bend in the trail. The lights of the Mountain Station shone at the edge of the mountainside a hundred yards ahead.

His stomach roiled at the thought of the tram ride down as he tucked the gun back into his jacket pocket. "Once Jack hears your voice—"

"It won't be that easy. By now Jack knows that my name isn't really Grant and that I'm not really rich."

Patrick nodded. Didn't they all.

"So if I call him from Palm Springs, California, and tell him that I didn't really go off into the canyon..."

He did like the way this woman thought. "We have to get you back to Montana. You have to call from somewhere up there for help. Then I get on the line and tell him I have you and unless he comes up with five million dollars—"

"Five million?" She shook her head. "You're such a greedy bastard, Patrick. Just so you know, we're splitting it seventy-thirty since it's my idea."

He grabbed her arm. "Like hell. I'm doing all the work here."

She mugged a face at him. "Sixty-forty or the deal is off. You need me to make this work, remember?"

Oh yeah, he remembered. But just until he got the money. Killing her a second time had to be easier than the first. Why was he arguing the point, anyway? He planned to take it all once she was dead. "Fine. You'd just better hope this plan of yours works."

"Oh, it will. If you don't foul it up like you did my last one," she snapped, and headed for the Mountain Station.

JACK STIRRED FROM A DEEP, contented sleep to the sound of his cell phone ringing. Reluctantly, he unwrapped himself from Angie's warm naked body. "Hello?"

"Jack?"

He pushed himself up to a sitting position at the sound of Patrick's voice. "Patrick?"

Angie came awake beside him, her brown eyes wide with fear. Why in the hell would Patrick be calling him?

"Did I wake you?" Patrick asked, sounding so casual, as if nothing had happened between them.

"What do you want, Patrick?"

"You sound like you're in a bad mood."

Jack gritted his teeth. "Yeah, being framed and almost killed often puts me in a bad mood."

"Someone tried to kill you?"

"As if you weren't behind it."

"You know, Jack, I'm getting tired of being blamed for everything that goes wrong in your life," Patrick said. "I didn't have anything to do with you being caught for ripping off all those poor people or for burning down one of your own houses or for trying to kill you."

"Right. Is that why you called me, Patrick? To tell me how innocent you are?"

"No, I called about Angie. She's alive."

Jack looked down at Angie. "What are you talking about?"

"Angie—she didn't die in that wreck. How about that?"

Jack held his breath. "How is that possible? I saw it on television."

Patrick laughed, a sound that chilled Jack to the core.

"You believe everything you see on TV but you don't believe me. Really, Jack, you amaze me. Listen to me. I called you because I have something you want."

"I really doubt that you have anyth—"

"I have Angie."

Jack pulled back to look at Angie. "What do you mean, you have Angie?" She moved in so she could hear Patrick's end of the conversation.

"Here's the deal," Patrick said. "A trade, so to speak. You give me five million dollars and I give you Angie."

Angie's nails dug into Jack's arm. He met her gaze. Her eyes were huge, her expression terrified. *He has Maria,* she mouthed.

His heart fell.

"Jack? You still there, old buddy?"

Old buddy. The words grated across his nerve endings like sandpaper. Angie slipped off the bed quickly, dug around in her purse and came out with paper and pen.

"I'm still here," Jack said, reading the scrawled word Angie was writing: *Stall.* "I'm trying to figure out why you'd think I would believe anything you told me."

Angie moved in close to listen again.

Silence. Jack felt his throat constrict. What if Patrick had hung up?

"Okay," Patrick said finally. "I guess I can see your point. Why don't I put her on the phone."

The next sound he heard was Maria's voice.

"Jack, don't do what he—" A cry.

Then Patrick was back on the line. "Well, Jack? You believe me now?"

Jack looked at Angie. She nodded. "Don't hurt her."

Patrick laughed. "Do as I say, Jack. Cross me up, and she really will be dead. You believe me?"

Oh yeah. "Tell me where and when."

"You ever been to Montana, Jack?"

Chapter Fifteen

"You make the arrangements to get the money, I'll take care of everything else," Angie said as she hurriedly got up and started dressing. She knew it wouldn't be easy but Jack could come up with that much quicker than she could. "There is no reason for you to go to Montana. It's too dangerous. I'll take care of it." She stopped when she saw his expression and her heart fell. "You think this is a scam."

"It's crossed my mind." He had pulled on his jeans and now stood bare-chested, his shirt dangling from his fingertips. "Once a mark, always a mark, right?"

She smiled ruefully. She'd just assumed that things had changed between them after making love.

"I'm sorry, but you have to admit it looks suspicious," Jack said. "I'm supposed to pack up five million dollars in two large suitcases and let you go alone to Montana to buy back your sister."

"You won't lose your money, if that's what you're worried about," she said, wishing her heart wasn't hammering so hard in her chest. "You have my word." She saw his expression. "My word. Pretty funny, huh." She fought the tears that stung her eyes.

"I'm sorry, Angie," he said softly, "but I'm going to Montana with you."

"To make sure you don't lose your money."

"No," he said, stepping over to clasp her shoulders in his large palms. "To make sure I don't lose you."

"That's right, you still need me to help clear your name. Del didn't live long enough to finger Patrick."

"It's a little more complicated than that."

She met his gaze. "I don't want you to go to Montana because you think it's too dangerous for me." She and Maria knew how to handle marks who'd gone "hot," the ones who realized they'd been had. "Maria and I have been in situations like this before."

"I'm sure you have," he said, not sounding pleased about that. He studied her for a moment. "Look, if all this—" he motioned toward the crumpled sheets "—was just a plot by you and Maria to get five million dollars out of me, you don't have to go to all this trouble, Angie. Just ask."

She remembered the rough-stubble feel of his beard on her skin, the taste of his mouth, the sound of him catching his breath— She bit down hard on her lower lip, trying not to cry as she quickly busied herself buttoning her blouse so he couldn't see her tears and think they were part of the con. "It's not about money."

Patrick had Maria. Just the thought turned Angie's blood cold. She knew Maria wouldn't be in Patrick's clutches unless she'd planned it that way. And Angie had a pretty good idea what Maria was up to, but she feared Maria didn't know just how dangerous Patrick was—or how unpredictable.

As she bent down to pull on her boots, she surreptitiously wiped her tears before turning to face Jack. "Maria set this whole thing up. She has a plan and it isn't to take your money. It's to get Patrick for you. I would imagine right now she's getting the confession you need out of him."

He stared at her. "How do you know that?"

"She passed me a message on the phone."

He shook his head. "She didn't say ten words."

"She didn't have to. But if you think that I'm not telling you the truth, then we'll wait until Patrick calls back." He would, if Jack didn't show up in Montana. She just prayed Maria would be safe that long. "I can get my own money. I do have money, you know. More than you. It's just not easily accessible."

She started past him, but he grabbed her arm and swung her into him.

"I'll get the money, but I'm going with you. Patrick has already tried to kill you at least once. I don't intend to give him another chance."

She started to argue, but he dropped his mouth to hers, stealing her breath, stealing her words.

The kiss lasted just a few seconds. When he drew back, he seemed to search her gaze. She wondered if he'd found what he was looking for.

"Okay," he said. "Let's hear the plan."

"HAVE YOU LOST YOUR MIND?" Montie demanded when Jack showed up at his office and told him how much money he needed. "You're taking five million dollars to Patrick in Montana?" The lawyer let out a laugh. "This is obviously another of this woman's scams." He shot Angie a look.

"Just help me get the money so it doesn't tip off the court," Jack said.

The older man swore. ''Jack, can't you see? This woman has you under her spell. I told you she'd come up with another scam. Once a mark—''

''—always a mark. I know.'' He was definitely under Angie's spell. ''Do whatever needs to be done.''

Montie shook his head as he picked up the phone. ''You're a damn fool, Jack.''

Jack said nothing as he looked over to where Angie was standing by the window. Her eyes were dark with anger, and he suspected it wasn't all directed at Montie. He wished he could take back what he'd said earlier to her. But he'd be an even bigger fool not to suspect this was another con. If not Angie's, then Maria's and Patrick's.

So why was he going along with it?

He studied Angie. She was beautiful—all that dark curly hair that fell to her shoulders, those wonderful brown eyes, that full, lush mouth of hers. Desire stirred deep within him. Oddly enough, what had attracted him to her originally was the same thing that still did: her innocence.

And he knew he was doing this because he believed her.

''By the way,'' Montie said, covering the mouthpiece on the phone. ''The sheriff found Leonard Parsons. He crashed his pickup on a back road not far from where Del was killed. He committed suicide. Sheriff said looks like the same gun Leonard used to shoot Del.''

Jack shook his head. ''Why would he kill Del to shut him up and then turn the gun on himself? That doesn't make any sense.''

''Sheriff said Leonard's leg was fractured in the car crash. I guess he knew he was caught and suicide was the easiest way out. The sheriff found accelerant in Leonard's apartment, the kind used by arsonists, plus they found a wad of cash.''

Leonard hadn't been smart enough to get rid of the accelerant? The man was more stupid than Jack had thought.

''What's wrong?'' Montie asked.

Jack shrugged. ''It just all ties up so neatly. I can't help but wonder if Patrick didn't pay someone to make sure Leonard never talked.''

''Patrick obviously knew people who would take care of a problem like that for him.'' Patrick had done some time in prison in East Texas. But he'd also tried to kill Angie all by himself. If Jack didn't know for a fact that Patrick was in Palm Springs...

Jack looked over at Angie again. He could hear Montie making arrangements behind him. Angie was staring out the front window. She looked worried. About Maria?

He'd only met Maria that one time in the taxi, but he had a feeling she could take care of herself. With Patrick, though?

''You'll have your money before your plane leaves for Montana,'' Montie said after hanging up. He lowered his voice so Angie couldn't hear. ''Why go to Montana at all? Just give her the money and save yourself a lot of grief.''

''Can you have the money delivered in the two large suitcases I've left for you?''

Montie nodded and wrote down his flight number. ''You must be some woman,'' he said to Angie as he walked Jack to the door.

She lifted her chin, dark eyes snapping.

''She is,'' Jack said before she could answer. He

put his arm around her and ushered her out to the taxi they had waiting at the curb.

"You trust that man?" Angie asked as they drove away.

"I don't know who to trust anymore," he said truthfully. "But what trust I have is all yours."

"I hope I don't let you down."

So did he. He had a lot to lose. Five million dollars, his freedom if the cops found out he was leaving the state, even his life if Patrick had an ambush planned.

But none of that concerned him as much as the realization that Angie might break his heart again. This time, it would kill him.

PATRICK PACED THE CABIN and watched for headlights. What was keeping Jack? In the last call, Jack had insisted on talking to Angie. Like Patrick would be stupid enough to kill her before he got the money? Jeez.

So what was keeping Jack? He didn't think Jack was dumb enough to try to sneak up on the cabin and try to ambush him.

No, Jack wouldn't take any chances with Angie's life.

"Stop pacing, you're driving me crazy," she said from where she was sprawled on the couch in front of the fire. "Get some more logs from the porch."

He turned to glare at her, glad he hadn't even considered staying married to her. "Jack should be here."

She shook her head, not bothering to look up from the magazine she'd been reading. "Jack couldn't possibly reach here for another thirty minutes minimum. I clocked it from the airport."

He stared at her. If she wasn't worth five million dollars... He stomped out to the porch, got an armload of wood and stood listening for a vehicle.

Hurry up, Jack. I'm not sure how much more of this woman I can take.

He regretted that he hadn't let Jack marry Angie. Jack definitely would have gotten what he deserved. A broke con artist with a bad attitude. He smiled at the thought. Too late for that now, though.

He carried the wood back into the cabin and threw it on the fire. He hadn't wanted a fire, afraid it would attract the hick sheriff.

Angie had suggested he tell the sheriff he was back at the cabin, make it sound like he couldn't stay away but wanted to be left alone. He had to hand it to Angie, she was good at this stuff.

"So, come on, tell me how you did it before Jack gets here," she said, putting down the magazine.

He groaned. "I already told you, I never even went to the job sites. I just collected my big salary—"

"Don't insult my intelligence by telling me again that you weren't behind framing Jack."

He wished she would drop this. "Look, if you have to know, Montie's the one who told me about the kickbacks and what Jack was up to."

"Jack's lawyer?"

Patrick nodded. "He told me how Jack's old man had made all of his money—and that Jack was doing it, too." He nodded at her surprise. "That's not all. Montie told me Jack was going to ask you to marry him to get your money." He loved the shock on her face.

"So that's when you came up with your plan to get me," she said. "And turn in Jack."

"Pretty much." He didn't bother to tell her that the plan had jelled when he'd heard her on the phone with her financial advisor.

She laughed. "Montie set you up. He must have known I wasn't who I said I was."

He scowled at her. "What are you talking about?"

"Montie played you." She narrowed her gaze thoughtfully. "But what did he have to gain aside from getting rid of Jack?"

Patrick stared at her. Montie hadn't played him. "You trying to tell me Montie was behind framing Jack?"

"Well, if he is, he's planning to let you take the fall for it," she said, and went back to her magazine as if she'd lost interest.

"What are you trying to pull?" he demanded, leaning over her, angry that she might be right. "You're the only one who's played me. You stole my money, conned me with those fake stocks and bonds, and cheated death. And now you're trying to pull something on me." He grabbed her by the neck. "This time I will make sure you're dead."

She looked up from her magazine at him. "But then you'd lose the five million dollars in ransom money you're demanding from Jack, wouldn't you," she said in a hoarse whisper, since he was cutting off most of her air.

"It almost seems worth it right now." He narrowed his eyes at her and he let up on the pressure. What if she was right about Montie? He was starting to straighten when he spotted the small tape recorder not quite hidden between her and the couch arm, the tiny wheels turning.

He let out an oath and grabbed the recorder, hitting

stop. His gaze went to her. For the first time, she actually looked scared. "You were trying to get me to confess on tape." He swore. "What did you plan to do with this? Give it to Jack?"

She laughed, and he thought he'd only imagined that instant when she'd looked frightened of him. "Get real. I was going to use it to blackmail you out of the rest of the five million."

He stared at her as he pocketed the tape recorder, looking for even a hint that she was lying. If he thought for a minute that she trying to get a confession to save Jack he'd kill her. Money or no money.

Chapter Sixteen

The night was black as Angie drove out Interstate 90 to the Big Pine turn off, then up the narrow dirt road, climbing up the mountain through the dense trees.

Clouds scudded across the dark sky, smothering the starlight. No moon. The air was crisp, the breeze scented with the promise of snow.

The night Patrick brought her up here had also been moonless. She remembered the glitter of stars in the night sky. The silver ribbon of river in the gorge along the edge of the road. The anxiety she'd felt, like a premonition.

Just like tonight. She looked over at Jack.

"There are several ways to 'cool out' a con," she'd told him. "One of the oldest is the crackle-bladder. It involves the element of surprise—and fake blood. But with luck, when this is over, your name will be cleared and Patrick will be behind bars."

"With luck we'll all still be alive," Jack had said.

As the trees opened up and she saw the dark cut of the canyon open off to her left, she touched the amulet at her neck. She didn't look down as she drove along the edge. She needed all the luck she could get tonight.

In a few minutes she would come face-to-face with Patrick. Only this time, it wasn't just her life at stake.

She stopped and extinguished the headlights. She'd already taken the bulbs out of the taillights. All of the interior lights were also turned off.

She waited for her eyes to adjust to the darkness. From here on out, she would be following that cut of lighter colored sky that marked the road through the dark pines. She started up the road.

"I will go in first," she said, reviewing the plan again. "Patrick will hear the car engine, but he won't get a good look at me until I enter the cabin. He'll be expecting you—"

"Angie, I've got it down cold, all right?" Jack interrupted. "I don't like it, but this is your show. Yours and your sister's."

He was right. They'd been over this two dozen times. And he'd hated the plan from the start. He'd put his life in her hands. She felt the weight of it, her heart heavy with worry that she would let him down.

"Maria is expecting this," she said. "If you come busting in—"

"I know," he said, his voice softening. "I'll stick to the plan. I just don't want anything to happen to you. Or your sister."

"I know." She touched his shoulder, and he covered her hand with his, squeezed lightly, then pulled her hand to his mouth and kissed her palm, making her heart leap.

"This is where I get out," he said, and smiled, reminding her that he knew the plan forward and backward.

She stopped the car. "You come in ten seconds after the second shot," she said, unable to help herself. Any change in the plan could change the outcome in the worst possible way.

"Got it." He opened his car door and stepped from the darkness of the car into the darkness of the night. "Do I say 'break a leg' or what?"

Say that you love me. "Say good luck."

"Good luck."

He disappeared among the pines in the direction of the cabin. She waited, remembering when she'd stopped in Missoula to buy the unregistered weapons from a person she'd contacted through "friends" in the business.

Jack had picked up a Smith & Wesson Model 19 combat magnum, hefted it in his hand, then loaded six .357 magnum cartridges into the chamber, spun the cylinder and clicked on the safety before stowing the weapon in his jacket.

Angie had stared at him in shock. It was clear by the way he'd handled the weapon that he'd used one before. The man just kept surprising her. Her research on him had shown that he'd never owned a firearm, let alone knew how to use one—information she always obtained before a con.

It was the unexpected that made the confidence game dangerous. Marks could surprise you. With disastrous consequences.

After a count of fifty, she started up the road again, fearing Patrick had some surprises for them.

As she pulled up in front of the cabin, the lantern lights went out inside. She opened her door and got out. She could smell smoke from the fireplace and see the flicker of the flames through a window. Good, there would be some light.

She didn't see Jack, but she knew he was out there.

She climbed the steps to the porch, knocked softly, waited until Patrick said, "Come on in, Jack," and stepped through the door, knowing Patrick would be armed. She was counting on his not firing immediately.

She was counting on a lot of things. For the plan to work, everything would have to happen quickly—within seconds. Every mark reacted differently. She was banking on Patrick being too surprised to shoot.

She wasn't disappointed.

"What the—" That was all he got out. In those crucial seconds, he looked from Angie to Maria and back.

By then, the con was already in play.

"How dare you pretend to be me!" Angie yelled as she advanced on Maria, who got to her feet from the couch in front of the fire.

They struggled for only an instant. The first shot was loud. Maria cried out and staggered, blood blossoming across the front of her blouse as she struggled for the gun between them.

The second shot came immediately after the first. The gun clattered to the hardwood floor. Maria fell back onto the couch. Angie looked down at her chest, shock on her face. There was blood everywhere.

She looked up at Patrick. He was standing, mouth open, eyes wide, the gun in his hand at his side as if he didn't know what to do.

Angie's eyes rolled back into her head and she slumped to the floor, her body furtively covering the weapon.

"No!" Patrick cried, looking from one Angie to

the other. "Dammit, no!" He jerked up the gun and fired off a shot at the Angie on the floor. "You stupid, stupid bitch!"

Jack was moving, counting down after the second shot. His hand was on the doorknob when he heard the third.

"Angie!" he heard Maria cry.

He burst through the door to find Patrick standing over Angie's prone body. All he saw was blood. Fake blood mixing with real.

"Drop the gun!" he ordered Patrick.

Maria was on the couch, Angie at her feet, lying on her side, curled toward the couch, eyes closed, but he could see the rise and fall of her chest. Still alive.

Patrick glanced up, though he kept his gun trained on Angie. "She's still alive. At least, for the moment. But if you were to shoot me, I'm afraid I'd accidentally pull the trigger." He smiled. "Checkmate, Jack. Now drop your gun and kick it over to me. Now!"

Maria sent Jack a look that made it clear she wanted to rip Patrick's head off—but didn't dare move for fear he would finish off Angie.

Jack put the weapon on the floor and kicked it. Except, not to Patrick. The gun rocketed across the wood floor and under the couch. He heard it hit something at the back of the couch and stop. He shrugged. "Sorry."

Patrick was shaking his head. "I thought you played footfall in college?"

"I was a quarterback, not a punter."

"Where's my money?"

"In the car," Jack said. "But first, I want to make sure that Angie is all right."

"Money first," Patrick snapped, pointing the gun at Angie's head. "You're starting to piss me off, Jack."

"I forgot to mention something," Jack said. "I have the suitcase locks wired to an explosive. If they are opened by anyone but me..."

Anger flashed in Patrick's gaze. The arm holding the gun on Angie trembled, and Jack feared he'd gone too far.

"You would have been disappointed if I'd just handed the money over to you," Jack said quickly.

Patrick stared at him for a moment, obviously keeping an eye on both Maria and Angie in case either made a move. "Take a quick look, but if you try anything, I'll shoot Angie first, then you, then whoever the hell she is—" He indicated Maria.

Jack didn't doubt it as he moved forward cautiously. Patrick stepped back a couple of steps, the gun on Angie.

Angie was curled toward the couch on the floor, her back to Patrick. Jack knelt in front of her, his hands shaking as he felt for a pulse. *Don't let her die. Please don't let her die.*

Her pulse was strong. He felt a surge of joy that made his own heart pound. There was blood all over the front of her, though, some of it real, making it hard to tell where she'd been hit.

He found the bullet hole. It was just below her shoulder. He knelt closer, praying it wasn't life threatening. Angie winked at him.

He stared at her. With a glance she indicated her hip. He followed her gaze, pretending to inspect her injuries, and saw the weapon—her body curled around it, hiding the gun. She closed her eyes again.

"All right, Jack, you've seen her," Patrick said impatiently. "She's not dead, right?"

"Not yet," Jack said, getting to his feet. "But she will be if I don't get her to a hospital."

"Then I suggest you trot out to the car and get those suitcases."

"Try not to shoot anyone while I'm gone."

Patrick laughed. "Then you'd better hurry."

Jack went out to the car, popped the hood and dragged out the two large, heavy suitcases. The story about the explosives inside had been a ruse, the only thing he could come up with on short notice.

But once he opened the suitcases and no bomb went off, he knew Patrick would kill all three of them. Patrick had everything to lose by leaving them alive. And he would have enough money to get him out of the country.

Jack carried the suitcases up the steps, across the porch and through the front door, worrying about the weapon Angie had hidden under her. He feared she wouldn't be able to fire it because of the wound to the shoulder. So what did she have planned? He wished he knew.

All he could do was try to provide a diversion. Angie had given him a code word if anything went wrong. Well, things had gone wrong.

Patrick was practically salivating when he saw the size of the suitcases and assessed their weight. "Put them where I can see you open them."

Jack's thought exactly. He set one down and swung the other one up onto the couch next to Maria. He knelt in front of it so he was beside Angie, and studied the locks.

Out of the corner of his eye, he could see Patrick

watching him closely, but still holding the gun on Angie. As jumpy as Patrick was—

"Come on," Patrick barked. "I want to see that money."

Jack fiddled with the lock, telling himself that Patrick wouldn't kill anyone until the second suitcase was opened. He popped the latch and felt Patrick flinch, thankful the fool hadn't pulled off a shot without even meaning to.

The suitcase lid rose at Jack's touch to expose layers and layers of large bills.

"Open the other suitcase," Patrick cried excitedly.

Jack heard the cabin door open. "Yes, open the second suitcase," Montague Cooke said from the doorway.

Jack turned to see Montie with a gun in his hand, the barrel pointed at Patrick. He got to his feet.

Montie motioned for the figure behind him to get the suitcases.

Jack recognized Montie's investigator, Harvey Ford. Ford picked up the second suitcase and popped it open.

Patrick cowered, obviously expecting a bomb to go off.

Montie laughed. "No explosives. Just a tracking device so I could find you all."

"Put down the gun or I'll kill her!" Patrick cried. "I'll kill them all."

"Be my guest," Montie said. "In fact, I'd appreciate it, since I'm going to need them killed with your gun. That's right, Patrick, you're taking the fall for all of this."

Patrick brought the gun up and pointed it at Montie, but not quickly enough.

Montie fired. Patrick let out a cry and grabbed his side. His weapon clattered to the floor, and Ford quickly retrieved it, being careful not to add his own fingerprints to the stock.

"Jack, here's the man who framed you," Maria said. "He got Patrick to expose the substandard practices at your housing development and accuse you. He also tricked Patrick into going after Angie. It seems your lawyer knew who she was, probably from the first time he met her."

Jack nodded, keeping his eyes on Montie. "I was afraid you wouldn't take the bait. The only way I could prove you were behind the murders of Del Sanders and Leonard Parsons was to get you up here."

Montie laughed. "Nice try, Jack, but I'm not as gullible as Patrick."

Jack saw Patrick push himself up into a sitting position, his back against the hearth. He held his side with both hands. Blood oozed from between his fingers. His face was white. He looked as if he was going into shock.

"Why do you think I asked you to collect the money for me?" Jack asked Montie, all the time worrying about Angie and trying to come up with a diversion. "I left the suitcases so you'd have a way to track us to this cabin."

"Next thing you're going to tell me is that the cabin is surrounded by cops, right?"

Jack shook his head. "No, sheriff's deputies."

Montie laughed. "Come on, Jack. You're out of your league. You could have made another couple of fortunes—instead of building low-income housing."

"You know when I got suspicious," Jack said as if he hadn't been listening. "It was when you got me out of jail in time to *crash* Patrick's wedding—but not quick enough to *stop* the wedding. You wanted me to violate that restraining order. Just like when you told me where I could find Patrick in Seattle. Just like when you forbid me to talk to Del and Leonard. Why?''

"I have your power of attorney, Jack," Montie said. "If anything should happen to you, I have complete control of Donovan, Inc."

Jack nodded. "You knew about Maria, didn't you? That's why you warned me about Angie trying to con me a second time. You set me up from the first. You just didn't know Angie really *was* alive." At least, Jack hoped she was.

Montie shook his head. "You set yourself up, Jack. Building low-income housing instead of making another couple of fortunes building mansions. Anyway, if it wasn't for me, you'd have lost it all to the LaGrand twins here."

"Thanks, Montie," Jack said sarcastically. He glanced at Maria and knew she was ready. All he had to do was say the word. "Just my *luck.*"

It happened in an instant. Maria grabbed the bottle of bourbon next to her on the end table, threw it into the fire and hit the floor next to her sister. The glass bottle exploded, then the alcohol. Flames leapt out of the front of the fireplace in a blinding flash.

Angie came up with the gun in both hands and fired, as Jack shoved the couch back and lunged for the gun he'd kicked under it. The sound of gunfire boomed in the small cabin as his fingers closed over the gun's grip. He rolled over onto his back and pulled off two shots as Montie and Ford lunged out the front door.

Patrick! Jack swung around, expecting to feel the crack of the fire poker.

Patrick was gone. The back door hung open. And over the sound of the last few shots, Jack heard Maria yell, "They're getting away!"

From outside came the sound of a car engine revving, then tires throwing dirt.

Jack crawled over to Angie. "Are you all right?"

She was sitting up, her back against the couch, her face lit by the firelight. She nodded. "Don't let them get away."

Maria grabbed Angie's weapon and went racing out the back door after Patrick. Several more shots were fired, followed by the sound of shattering glass. Then only the roar of vehicle motors dying away in the distance.

Jack didn't give a damn about Patrick right now. All he could think about was getting to a place where his cell phone would work so he could call an ambulance for Angie.

He heard another car engine fire up, then peel out, and he closed his eyes with a groan. Maria was going after Patrick. Damn.

"Go," Angie said.

"Stay here," he ordered her, dragging the throw off the couch to cover her.

She smiled wanly. "No problem."

He stared down at her, knowing what he had to do before he could leave her. "I love you."

Her eyes widened in surprise.

"I should have told you months ago."

She nodded.

"I'm not leaving this cabin until you promise to marry me."

"Jack—"

"Yes or no?"

She smiled up at him. "Yes."

He kissed her quickly. "Good." He got up, grinned down at her. "Good."

Hurriedly, he pulled from his pocket the small flashlight she'd given him earlier for his trek through the trees and took off out the front door at a dead run after them.

PATRICK COULD FEEL the blood soaking his shirt and jeans, but the only pain seemed to be in his head. The anger made his eyes ache as if his blood pressure was too high.

He stared ahead at the red taillights of Montie's vehicle. The lawyer had used him and now had the two suitcases full of his money, money he'd worked hard for, money he more than deserved considering everything he'd been through. And he wasn't letting it—or Montague Cooke—get away.

The beam of his SUV's headlights filled Montie's rental car. The other guy was driving. Patrick crashed into the back of the car with a feeling of déjà vu. Montie's rental car was no match for the larger SUV Patrick had rented. The car lurched forward. The SUV's off-road utility bumper caved in the rental car's trunk.

In his headlights, Patrick saw Montie turn in the passenger seat. A moment later the windshield exploded, showering Patrick with little cubes of safety glass and really making him mad.

He could see where the trees opened up. Beyond it was the ninety-degree turn and the short stretch of road along the gorge.

The rental car's brake lights flashed on. Down the mountain came the blue flash of lights and the *whir* of sirens. Cops. Behind him, he saw headlights.

Why wasn't he surprised? He was wounded and bleeding and broke and on the run from Jack and all the Angies in the world and the law and Jack still couldn't just leave him the hell alone. No, Jack had to have justice.

It wasn't that hard a decision to make. Montie would hire himself a good lawyer and probably get off. Patrick would get blamed for everything and end up on death row while Jack had not one but *two* Angies.

Patrick pushed the gas pedal to the floor. Montie, at least, would not be getting away with what he'd done. Patrick's only regret was the money. He imagined it floating down river for fishermen to find in the spring.

He slammed the SUV into the back of Montie's rental car, just as it started into the turn, with such force it rattled his teeth, driving the car straight for the gorge.

Patrick laid on his brakes, not wanting to make the same mistake he'd almost made with Angie and the Jeep. It took him a couple of seconds to realize he wasn't slowing down—and why.

The SUV's bumper was hung up on the rental car, pulling his vehicle with it to the sound of screaming metal.

He grabbed his door handle, throwing his shoulder against the door, hoping he could get out quickly enough.

The door, jammed from the last crash into the rental car, didn't budge.

Patrick looked up to see his fate as the rental car dropped over the rim of the canyon, dragging the SUV with it. *You win, Jack.*

JACK REACHED THE CANYON in time to see the two vehicles drop over the side of the canyon into the depths. He closed his eyes, leaning back against a tree, filled with horror and regret.

Then he walked down to where Sheriff Truebow was getting out of his patrol car. Maria had already had him call for an ambulance.

Jack barely remembered the ride down the mountain to meet the ambulance, Angie in his arms in the back seat and Maria driving and Sheriff Truebow following behind.

Jack looked up hours later from the hard plastic chair in the hospital waiting room to see the surgeon coming toward him.

"The surgery went well," the doctor said, as Jack stumbled to his feet, heart in his throat. "We removed the bullet. She's resting peacefully. You can see her in the morning. I would expect a full recovery."

Jack felt his eyes sting as he shook the man's hand. "Thank you."

The doctor smiled and patted Jack's shoulder. "You look like you could use some rest yourself." He glanced toward Maria, who'd finally fallen into an exhausted sleep on the floor. "Identical, aren't they?"

Jack shook his head. "No, they just look alike."

Epilogue

"You're really going through with this?" Maria asked as she straightened the train on Angie's wedding dress.

"You mean the marriage?"

"No, giving up the confidence game."

"Daddy used to say that a good con man always knows when to quit the grift," Angie said.

"I wish Daddy could see you." Maria's eyes filled with tears as she met her sister's gaze in the large oval mirror.

"Oh, I suspect Daddy's keeping an eye on us." Angie smiled through her own tears.

Maria nodded. "You look incredible."

"My maid of honor looks pretty amazing, too, don't you think?"

Maria studied herself in the mirror. She wore an emerald-green velvet dress that was stunning on her. Her brown eyes shone brighter than Angie had ever seen them. "Sheriff Truebow's kind of cute, don't you think?"

Angie laughed. Maria had invited the sheriff to the wedding after the two had hit it off in Montana. Only Maria could get a date out of a con gone bad.

"Aren't you going to miss it, though?" Maria asked.

"I'm going to miss working with you," Angie said. "But the confidence game?" She shook her head. "Our house is almost finished and Jack will be busy. He thinks he can save his construction company. He has big plans for the old neighborhood. So I will be in charge of decorating the house and getting it ready."

Jack had insisted they hold off on the wedding until he could carry his wife over the threshold of their "real" home.

"Yes, but once you furnish the house, aren't you afraid of being bored to tears?" Maria persisted.

Angie smiled, her hand going to her stomach. "I think I'll be too busy to get bored." She glanced up to meet her sister's gaze again in the mirror.

"Are you telling me you're—"

"—pregnant. I just found out this morning."

Maria threw her arms around her sister. "Oh, Angie, I'm so happy for you!"

"I want my child to have the mother you and I never had," she said. "And the home. Jack knows how much that means to me. Do you know that he ran out this morning and bought a swing set? This baby is so lucky to be getting such a great father."

"And mother," Maria said. "I'm going to miss you."

"We just won't be working together," Angie said. "It isn't like you're leaving Texas."

Maria grinned mischievously. "Sheriff Truebow—that is, Jeff—wants me to come up to Montana for a while. I guess he owns a small horse ranch."

Angie laughed as she remembered Jack joking with

the sheriff that Maria would steal him blind if he wasn't careful.

Jeff Truebow, a large, handsome man with an honest face and a quiet manner, had grinned. "I don't have much money."

"That's good," Maria had said. "Because your money isn't what I'm interested in."

The first few chords of "The Wedding March" swelled in the nave next to their dressing room.

"There's our cue—" Maria said, her voice cracking with emotion. "Ready?"

Angie touched the amulet at her neck. Jack wouldn't hear of her taking it off, saying he had never believed in luck until he met her.

She squeezed her twin's hand with her other hand. "Oh yes, I've never been more ready."

As Maria opened the door, Angie saw Jack waiting for her, and for the first time she really did believe in happily ever after.

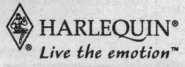

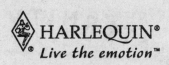 

Harlequin Books and Konica present
The Double Exposure Campaign!

Expose yourself to Intrigue. Collect original
proofs of purchase from the back pages of:

UNDER WRAPS 0-373-83595-7
GUARDED SECRETS 0-373-83593-0
WHISPERS IN THE NIGHT 0-373-83596-5
KEEPING WATCH 0-373-83594-9

and receive free Konica disposable cameras,
each valued at over $5.99 U.S.!

Just complete the order form and send it, along with your proofs of
purchase from two (2), three (3) or four (4) of the featured books above,
to: Harlequin Intrigue National Consumer Promotion, P.O. Box 9047,
Buffalo, NY 14269-9047, or P.O. Box 613, Fort Erie, Ontario L2A 5X3.

---

093 KIL DXHU

Name (PLEASE PRINT)

Address   Apt. #

City   State/Prov.   Zip/Postal Code

Please specify which themed gift package(s) you would like to receive:

❑ I am enclosing two (2) proofs of purchase for one free Konica camera
❑ I am enclosing three (3) proofs of purchase for two free Konica cameras
❑ I am enclosing four (4) proofs of purchase for three free Konica cameras

---

Have you enclosed your proofs of purchase?

Remember—the more you buy, the more you save! You must send two (2) original proofs
of purchase to receive one camera, three (3) original proofs of purchase to receive two
cameras and four (4) original proofs of purchase to receive all three cameras.

Please allow 4-6 weeks for delivery. Shipping and handling included.
Offer good only while quantities last. Offer available in Canada and
the U.S. only. Request should be received no later than **December 31,
2003**. Each proof of purchase should be cut out of the back-page ad
featuring this offer.

© 2003 Harlequin Enterprises Limited

Visit us at www.eHarlequin.com

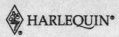

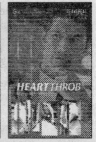

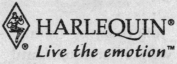

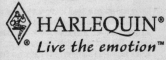